FUN AND GAMES AT THE CIA . . .

"At one time, as part of a complicated operation, the CIA considered using phosphorescent foxes; at another, incendiary bats. During World War II, the agency planned to bombard Hitler with hard-core pornography because their psychiatrist said that this would drive him even crazier. King Farouk's urine was stolen in an attempt to ascertain his state of health. A scheme to cause Castro's beard to fall out was promulgated. The toilets at an international Communist youth festival were to be plugged in order to show that Communism doesn't work.

"This is the kind of fun Aaron Latham pokes at the CIA, the bad fairy of American politics, in *ORCHIDS FOR MOTHER*."
—*The New York Times Book Review*

"A nasty, highly entertaining book."
—*Rolling Stone*

"A delightfully knowledgeable and stirring tale."
—*Chicago Sun-Times*

"One of the best thrillers of the year."
—Richard Growald, UPI

ORCHIDS
for
MOTHER

Aaron Latham

BANTAM BOOKS
TORONTO • NEW YORK • LONDON • SYDNEY • AUCKLAND

ORCHIDS FOR MOTHER
A Bantam Book

PRINTING HISTORY
Little, Brown edition published January 1977
Bantam edition / May 1978
2nd printing . . . November 1985

*Grateful acknowledgment is made to the following publishers
for permission to reprint previously copyrighted materials:*
*Dodd, Mead and Company, for three lines from "The Sol-
dier" by Rupert Brooke, from* The Collected Poems of Rupert
Brooke.
*New Directions Publishing Corporation and Faber & Faber,
Ltd., for three lines from "Hugh Selwyn Mauberley," from*
Personae *by Ezra Pound. Copyright 1926 by Ezra Pound.*
*New Directions Publishing Corporation and The Bodley
Head Limited for excerpts from* The Crack-Up *by F. Scott
Fitzgerald. Copyright 1934 by Esquire, Inc. Copyright 1945 by
New Directions Publishing Corporation.*

ISBN 0-553-25407-3

Published simultaneously in the United States and Canada

Orchids for Mother
is for my mother and father,
Launa and Clyde Latham

Kimball O'Hara . . . said . . . "A red bull and a colonel on a horse will come, but first . . . come the two men making ready the ground for these matters . . ."

—*Kim*, Rudyard Kipling

I

THE RECRUIT

PROLOGUE

After the Fall

MOTHER WORE BLACK shoes, black socks, a black suit, a black tie, a white shirt, and a black homburg. He was not a man who had much affinity for grays. Tall and thin with a stooped, slightly twisted body, he looked like a crooked black snake in a garden of brightly colored orchids.

His tired eyes searched the Miami flower show, not for the paragon of cattleyas, but for the specialist he had come to meet. When he located the man, he slipped through the crowd to join him, slouching toward another conspiracy.

Mother, overdressed for the Florida climate, met a long-haired young man wearing sandals, blue jeans, and a bright orange shirt with flowers on it. But he, too, was overdressed in his way. Although he planned to do no gardening, he wore bulky gardening gloves. He was a man who always wore gloves and always paid in cash. His regular employer was a Miami Mafioso, but he occasionally did some moonlighting for the Central Intelligence Agency.

3

"Welcome to the show," said Francis Xavier Kimball, code-named "Mother," as he grasped the gloved hand. "How do you like it?"

"Never saw so many fuckin' flowers in my life," said Gloves.

"Biggest orchid show in the country," Mother said. "I never had time to come down before. This year I do."

Over the past couple of decades, Mother's duties as the head of the CIA's Counterintelligence Department had kept him quite busy. For it had been his job to protect the agency from penetration by the other side. In carrying out his assignment, he had tried to think like a KGB officer: whom in the CIA would he most like to recruit? He had answered this question by drawing up a list of fifty key "company" people to be kept under surveillance: wiretapped, bugged, and followed. In addition, he had also run spot checks on the agency's other 17,500 employees. All this snooping had left him little free time, but now, suddenly, for the first time in his adult life, he did not have enough to do.

"Come look around," Mother said, escorting the other man down a meandering aisle which wound through the orchid displays in Miami's Bay Front Auditorium. "Have you had a chance to glance at the show's catalogue?"

"Not yet."

"The theme this year is 'Lost Civilizations.' That's Chichén Itzá."

They paused before a miniature styrofoam Mayan city with its Temple of the Warriors, its Court of a Thousand Columns, its Castillo, its sacred Ballpark where losers were beheaded. A two-inch river with rapids and waterfalls gurgled among the monuments. This Yucatán tableau was crowded with orchids, which, in context, looked King Kong large.

"And that's Tenochtitlán," Mother said, indicating another display, "Montezuma's capital."

"Pretty," Gloves said, as they paused before a miniature market and a tiny Pyramid of the Sun, plus a baby lake and infant canals, all dwarfed by monster orchids.

They walked on, excusing themselves as they pushed past people. All the displays covered a regulation fifty square feet. Sand had been hauled into the auditorium and used to build up hills and other topography. Rows of green plants separated the entries. Displays were crowded against the walls and spotted about in islands in the middle of the hall.

"Egypt?" Gloves said.

"I'm afraid not," Mother said, regretting as he often did that the spy business was no longer a gentlemen's preserve. "Greece."

They passed the Hanging Gardens of Babylon, the ruins of ancient Rome, the terraced capital of the Incas at Cuzco, the towers of Angkor Wat . . .

"It's like the Rose Bowl parade," Gloves said, "only here the floats stand still and we move."

"And there aren't any roses."

The crowd bumped the older man and the younger man apart. When they came back together, Mother said, "I've a score you can help me settle."

"What score?"

Mother pulled a sealed envelope from his breast pocket and handed it to the other man.

"Please read this," Mother said.

The gloved fingers tore open the envelope and unfolded a sheet of white bond paper. A single typed sentence named a distinguished man whom Mother wanted assassinated. Gloves found it difficult to read and walk at the same time because the paper kept moving. He went over the sentence from first to last five times. Mother could tell how many times because the young man moved his lips.

"May I have the document back?" Mother asked.

"Yes, of course," said Gloves, handing it over.

"Well, will you do it?" Mother asked. He drew a pack of cigarettes from his right-hand coat pocket, carefully placed one in his mouth, and lit it with a gold lighter. Gloves, who prided himself on his impassive face, showed more surprise at the brand name on the pack than he had at the name on the sheet of paper. Mother smoked Virginia Slims.

Mother did not hurry the assassin. In a lifetime of debriefing defectors, he had learned that the best way to ask a question was simply to pose it once and then to wait in silence for as long as it took to get an answer. He knew that, in time, silence sucked words from people the way he drew smoke from his Slim.

"All right," Gloves said at last.

"Good. I'll have to postpone giving you the finer points of the operation since it's at least remotely possible that even here our conversation's being monitored. If I were in their position, I'd certainly make an effort."

"Can they do that?" Gloves said, looking around.

"Oh yes. So we'll say no more now, but an associate will be in touch with you at an appropriate time. He'll identify himself by this code name."

Mother took another envelope from his pocket. The assassin opened it. Inside was a sheet of paper with one word written on it: Son.

"Good," Gloves said. "I'll wait to hear from you."

"Now, come see my entry in the show."

"One of those lost civilizations is yours?"

"No, no, of course not. You can enter orchids one at a time. That's what I did. Entered one orchid."

They pushed their way through the crowd to a far corner of the auditorium where plants were exhibited individually. Next to the gaudy displays, these flowers, even though they were orchids, looked somehow humbled—poor huddled masses. Mother's heart went out to his own orchid lost in the multitude.

"That one, Number One-thirty-six," Mother said. "It's mine."

"Very pretty."

"It's an original cross. I named it after my wife, I mean my former wife, Livia."

The man in the black suit and the man in the orange-flowered shirt said their farewells. Looking back, the assassin had one last glimpse of Mother standing beneath a hanging pot. A voluptuous white orchid nuzzled Mother's black hat.

Moments later, Mother was in a Bay Front Auditorium men's room. He entered one of the stalls and raised the seat. He fished in his coat pocket and drew out the gold lighter. He touched the flame to two sheets of paper, held them while they burned, dropped them into the toilet at the last second, and flushed.

Staring down at the whirlpool of ashes, Mother had a sudden image of the "Lost Civilization" display he wished he had entered in the show: a Lilliputian Washington with a small, cracked Capitol dome, a tiny, dilapidated Jefferson Memorial, and a crumbling dollhouse White House—a landscape of broken toys entangled in a jungle of giant orchids.

Mother's thoughts began spinning around and around, like the water in the bowl below, regret chasing fury chasing loss. He found himself saying over and over to himself: They should have listened, they should have listened, they should have listened. Overheated in his black clothes, Mother wobbled slightly and thought he might faint.

Mother stumbled unsteadily out of the men's room and once again surveyed the great hall which was so like a giant toy store. This was what his life had come to. This was what a lifetime in the agency had prepared him for. Cultures reduced to playthings and wars reduced to games for small prizes.

Mother took a blank sheet of paper out of his pocket, folded it into an airplane, and sailed it over Babylon.

1

Before the Fall

LANGLEY, APRIL 27, 1973—Mother felt sinful. It was a sweet feeling, as if he were eavesdropping on a confessional. Only better. Mother knew because he had tried both. He was convinced most people would sooner try to lie to God than to a polygraph.

He was standing up, staring through a small window in the hulking headquarters building, nicknamed the Toy Factory. This window did not look out onto the heavily wooded Virginia hills. It looked into another room. Hovering behind a one-way mirror, Mother watched as a lie detector test was administered to a young man named Paul Fitzsimmons who was being considered for a job in the company. Mother already felt an almost paternal affection for Paul. Watching the applicant through the mirror was like looking through a greenhouse window at a prized orchid.

Paul himself felt more like a condemned man strapped into an electric chair. A corrugated rubber tube two inches wide was wrapped around his chest and fastened in back like a bra; it measured his breathing rate. A blood pressure cuff was clamped around his arm. And electrodes were held against his palm by a spring which stretched around the back of his hand; they measured perspiration. With wet hands and throbbing heart, Paul waited for the executioner to throw the switch.

Paul already knew what questions he would be asked. He had reviewed the test with the interrogator before being strapped into the machine. This was done so each question could be tailored to a yes or no response—the only words the polygraph understood. Giving the candidate a preview of the test helped in another way, too, for the longer the test taker had to think about any lies he planned to tell, the more worked up he got.

Paul was worked up, but not because he planned to tell any lies. Quite the contrary. He was nervous because he saw no alternative to telling the truth.

Mother was also concerned, for the man administering the test was Graham Anderson, who bore him considerable ill will. The head of Counterintelligence had once bugged Anderson's home; Anderson had found out about the eavesdropping when he was called before his section head and asked to explain certain domestic practices. After that, Anderson had gone over to the other side, Ernest O'Hara's side. Mother was afraid he might be tempted to revenge himself on Mother's boy.

At first the questions were easy. Some were even trivial, since they were simply intended to get a reading on Paul's vital signs when he was clearly telling the truth.

"Is your name Paul Fitzsimmons?"

"Yes."

"Are you currently a senior at Yale University?"

"Yes."

"Is your major English?"

"Yes."

"Are you writing your honors thesis on Ezra Pound?"

"Yes."

In fact, it was because of Pound that Paul found himself strapped into that chair. While Paul was researching his senior thesis, entitled "Ezra Pound in Italy," his adviser mentioned to him that he should talk to Francis Xavier Kimball, a Yale alumnus who had known Pound in Italy. The professor did not know where to locate Kimball, but the alumni office had a slender file on him which showed that he lived in Arlington, Virginia, and that he was an official in the Post Office. Paul wrote to this Post Office bureaucrat, requesting an interview. He wondered how a friend of Pound's could have ever settled for such a humdrum life. Kimball, who was divorced and lived alone, wrote back, inviting Paul to come to Arlington to spend a weekend as a guest in his home. He was lonely.

Paul accepted. He took the bus down in February. In Arlington, he learned that Pound and Kimball had both been born in Boise but had met one another for the first time in Rapallo. They were both boys from Idaho, the land of the potato, who were glad to find themselves in Italy, the land of the Renaissance. Pound was already an established poet, while Kimball was still a teenager living with expatriate parents. Returning to America, Kimball enrolled in Yale where he started a literary magazine called *The Furies*. Pound wrote for it. So did many other poets—Eliot, Frost, Stevens, cummings. The Post Office functionary proudly showed Paul yellowed issues and played the raconteur.

"You should've seen how mad Frost got at Pound when *A Boy's Will* was published," said Mother that first evening. "Trouble was, Pound seemed to think the book belonged to him because he'd helped Frost get it printed. When the first copy arrived, Pound grabbed it and started going through it before Frost could get his hands on it. Frost was still furious about that the day he died."

Scribbling these memories into a notebook, Paul said how much he admired Frost.

"The problem with Frost," Mother said, "was that he was a grandstander, like reading at Kennedy's inauguration. That's why I liked Wallace Stevens. He wasn't a public man. At his office, most people didn't know he was a poet. And at home you wouldn't have known he was a vice-president at Hartford Fire unless you tried to smoke a cigarette."

Mother paused to inhale a Virginia Slim.

"When I was at Yale," Mother continued, "I was very near Stevens, and I used to visit him. But I was a heavy smoker. I had to walk outside and smoke and then come back in."

"Wasn't Pound something of a grandstander?" asked Paul. "What about all those Italian broadcasts during the war? He sounded like a Fascist Jaycee."

"I don't think anyone ever took Pound's politics seriously," replied Mother. "It was one of his masks. I think it was a part of that kaleidoscopic side of Pound. The fact that he called one book *Personae,* or 'masks,' is reflective of his poetry and the different facades he had."

Discussing poems and poetry with Mother, Paul felt as if he were talking, not to an older man, but to another undergraduate.

Kimball was extremely generous with information about Pound and the other poets he had known, but he was niggardly with talk about himself and his work. Paul really could not blame him. Who would want to discuss the Post Office?

And yet this very reticence exacerbated Paul's curiosity. He did not appear to be a strong person, but his curiosity was incredibly strong. In many ways it had shaped his life, for he *had* to solve every mystery. He had once hoped to be a priest because he wanted to understand God's mystery. Later he turned from God to poetry, because poets possessed a mystery, too. And now he turned his curiosity on the mysterious Post Office bureaucrat. He asked countless unobtrusive questions reinforced by a sympathetic expression.

The mystery was not solved that first weekend. But Paul returned to Washington several times that spring to interview people who had known Pound at Saint Elizabeth's Hospital. Each time, by invitation, he stayed at the Kimball home in Arlington. And he continued to work on the mystery of the mysterious postal official. One day he realized that the main Post Office building was a thirty-minute drive away in downtown Washington whereas CIA headquarters were only five minutes away. Kimball was often home from work at 5:05 P.M. A few questions later he had the mystery solved. The Post Office bureaucrat was a spy.

Paul had learned more than Mother intended to reveal, but Mother had also learned something about Paul. Anyone who could discover that Mother was a spy could be a spy himself.

That same spring, Paul was approached on the Yale campus by a total stranger who offered to buy him a Coke. They went to the corner drugstore, an all-American setting for an all-American proposition. The Central Intelligence Agency favored drugstores because of their wholesome atmosphere and because it liked to recruit boys before they were old enough to spend much time in saloons. While they sipped colas, the stranger plied Paul with veiled talk about national security. Paul maintained that he just wanted to be an English teacher. The stranger said he knew more about Paul and what he wanted than Paul knew himself. There had been a reciprocity of curiosity: Paul had discovered Mother's secret, but recently Mother had been working on some of Paul's.

Fitzsimmons met with the stranger, whose name turned out to be Clay Pearson, several more times. These trysts took place in a suite in a New Haven office building, the existence of this permanent recruiting office a few blocks from the Yale campus betraying the school's status as *the* spy college. After a short courtship, Paul was recruited and was directed to present himself at Langley to be polygraphed.

"Is it your intention," asked Graham Anderson, "to lie to me?"

"No."

"Are you wearing a ring on your little finger?"

"Yes."

Slowly the questions grew more serious.

"Are you an enemy agent?"

"No."

"Has a foreign service ever attempted to recruit you?"

"No."

"Has a foreign service ever made any contact with you whatsoever?"

"No."

Finally the interrogator reached the questions that had Paul's palms sweating in advance.

"Did you masturbate when you were a teenager?"

Paul did not answer immediately. He could not see the polygraph needles, but he could imagine what they were doing. He was sure the emotional seismograph into which he was strapped was registering an internal earthquake while he recalled his days in the seminary, which he had entered at the age of fourteen. The problem was that he had to go to mass every morning at six o'clock. And the problem with that was he had to stand up in front of everyone every morning and file to the rear of the church to confess before he could take communion. And the problem with that was everyone knew there was only one sin which a teenage boy, cooped up in a seminary, was likely to have to confess every morning. The priests had a name for it: self-abuse. And often when he stood up for the long march back to the confessional he would feel an embarrassingly obvious erection pushing out his cassock like the center pole of a circus tent.

"Yes," Paul admitted.

"Do you still masturbate?"

The question was a surprise; they hadn't reviewed that one.

"That's none of your business."

"I'm afraid it is our business."

While Paul thought over his answer, he imagined the needle on the machine acting like the tail of a happy dog.

He finally answered, "Yes."

"Did you ever experience fellatio?"

"Yes."

"Did you ever perform cunnilingus?"

"Yes."

"Have you ever had a homosexual experience?"

Once again, Paul paused. He was remembering the morning when he and a boy from down the hall stood up and marched back to confession together.

"Yes," he said softly.

Anderson came over and looked in the mirror as if he were about to comb his hair. But instead of combing—he winked. Mother was startled. He had not known that Anderson knew he was there. The interrogator returned to his station and took up the questioning once again.

"With more than one partner?"

"No."

"Then with only one partner?"

"Yes."

"Was his name Mickey Flannery?"

Paul, angry all over again at having been forced to reveal the name in the pretest interview, snapped, "Yes."

"Was that more than five years ago?"

"Yes."

Actually, it had been seven years ago, when Paul was fifteen. He left the seminary shortly thereafter. Having joined to discover God's secret, he departed when he decided he was no closer to his goal on the inside than he had been on the outside. Also, the secrets of heterosexual sex had begun to tempt him.

Mother was relieved. A Catholic himself, he had assumed his protégé had flirted with homosexuality in the seminary. What had worried Mother was that Paul might have continued his flirtation at Yale. Now he felt fairly confident his boy was going to make it, unless Anderson just flunked him for spite.

Several questions later, Mother left the small room and headed for his office feeling hopeful. Reaching the

Counterintelligence Department, Mother was inter-
cepted by one of his aides.

"So here you are," said Scott Bannister, a young
man who dressed old. He wore a seersucker suit and
looked the way Harvard men used to look. He had had
trouble finding a store that still carried seersucker, but
it had been worth the effort since his conservative
clothes endeared him to the agency's old guard. He
had the strong ambition an intelligence officer needed
to ascend in the company but only a weak, surface
curiosity. "We've been looking all over for you."

"What's the problem?" Mother asked, drawing on
his Virginia Slim, then holding it straight up so the
long ash would not fall off.

"We've heard from Ladyslipper," Bannister said.

Mother had named his most highly prized agent
after his favorite orchid. The very existence of Ladyslipper was one of his most closely held secrets. Not
even his superiors knew about the spy. Mother had
never felt that his duty to his country included telling
his bosses everything.

"I wonder what's on his mind," Mother said, taking
another puff on his cigarette and this time losing his
long, thin ash.

"He took a chance and used the phone," Bannister
said. "He said, 'I've been smoking too much.'"

"I see," Mother said. The phrase told him that Ladyslipper would leave a message in a dead-letter drop in
the men's room at the Kennedy Center after work.
"Would you arrange for a cutout to service the drop
sometime around six forty-five? Then have the message brought straight to me. I'll be at La Niçoise."

"I'll take care of it," Bannister said.

"I wonder what's up," Mother mused.

"Beats me." Bannister shrugged and went about
his business.

After the lie detector test, Paul Fitzsimmons felt
dirty. He tried not to look at anyone, and he hoped no
one would look at him. He felt sure the agency would

never want to see him again. He had come to Langley
with his self-image burnished brass-soldier bright. After all, he was finally about to do something for God
and country.

But now he was leaving feeling like a pervert.

Interrogator Anderson showed Paul Fitzsimmons
out of the building. Walking down the main hall on the
ground floor, Paul was struck all over again by how attractive the headquarters building was. One corridor
wall was made of glass and looked into an inner court-
yard with a landscaped garden dotted with magnolia
trees. The whole building seemed to radiate cleanliness
and freshness, as if these were agency ideals, which
made Paul feel even dirtier.

Opposite the glass wall was a wall lined with abstract paintings. Paul noticed canvases by Thomas
Downing and Jack Bush among others. Even the doors
looked like paintings since they were purple, fuchsia,
Kelly green, royal blue . . .

"Where did you get the pictures?" asked Paul.

"We have a CIA Fine Arts Commission," Anderson
said. "Somehow we manage to borrow paintings. I'm
afraid we practice the black art in a pretty artsy-craftsy
atmosphere."

Paul turned in his temporary identification badge at
a desk near the main entrance. Above the desk he noticed a biblical verse carved in a marble wall: AND YE
SHALL KNOW THE TRUTH AND THE TRUTH SHALL
MAKE YOU FREE. Sure, Paul thought, but veracity had
its drawbacks. He had told the interrogator the truth,
but all it was likely to make him free of was employment.

Stepping out into the sunlight with Anderson still at
his side, Paul's glance swept the undulating Old Do-
minion hills and Langley's gently rolling parking
lots. Then he experienced a confusing sensation: in-
explicably, he felt as if he were already back at Yale.
It took him a disoriented moment to realize why. At
last he focused on the bronze statue of Nathan Hale
which stood just outside the big doors. Paul had been
too preoccupied upon his arrival to notice the Revo-

lutionary hero, but now he recognized the life-sized metal soldier as an old friend. For the CIA's statue was a copy of the original sculpture standing on the Old Campus. Awaiting execution, his hands bound behind him, Nathan Hale—a member of the Yale class of 1773—watched over spooks and college boys alike.

Paul began to feel more at home until his gaze traveled past Hale to a huge silver dome which stood a few yards beyond. Resembling a tinfoil beehive, it added the appropriate touch of weirdness to the CIA landscape.

"What's that," Paul asked, "or is it a secret?"

"They call it the Dulles Tasty Freeze," Anderson smiled. "It's an auditorium, but sometimes it's used as a church."

Paul, reminded of the seminary, wondered if he might possibly have finally found the religious order for which he had been searching since he was an adolescent. He only hoped he was not too sinful to be acceptable. Perhaps, now that he had confessed, they would forgive him, but he was afraid the agency didn't work that way. He suspected the CIA did not forgive sin—it filed it for future reference.

Anderson showed Paul where to catch the bus that would carry him into Washington. On the bus, riding down Route 123 toward Chain Bridge, Paul wondered how he should pass the four hours before his dinner date with Mother. He considered stopping off at the Smithsonian Air and Space Museum to look at missiles. He considered going up to Capitol Hill to watch the legislators nod off to sleep on the floor of the Congress. He considered going to the National Zoo to see the pandas. He wondered which of these choices would make the best impression on the agent he could feel following him.

Paul left the bus at Fourteenth and K Streets, then turned around and walked east along K, looking behind him to see if anyone had made a similar U-turn. After that he walked in one door of the Ambassador Hotel and out another. He still was not quite sure no

one was following him, but he decided to take a chance
anyway.

Paul Fitzsimmons walked south on Fourteenth Street
and entered a bar named the Thing. He ordered a beer
and looked up at the small elevated stage, where a
young woman was taking off her blouse.

While Paul watched the dancer's bouncing breasts
she stared back at him, partly because he made up half
the crowd at the bar and partly because he was good-
looking. He was tall with blue-green eyes and hair
the color of an Irish setter's. Paul hoped she would
not speak to him, since he had considerably more faith
in his looks than in his conversation. And he had almost no faith at all in his voice. He was a large man
with a small voice. On top of that, he liked strippers'
voices even less than his own. Most of them sounded
like squealing brakes. So long as he and the dancer
looked at one another mutely, they would both be at
their best.

When Noble Jones reported to Ernest O'Hara's office, he was told he would have to wait. O'Hara—the
deputy director of operations, the DDO—was busy
dressing down somebody, according to his secretary.
Jones—the chief of planning, programming and bud-
geting at the agency—wondered who it was. The most
likely candidate, he supposed, was Mother. He hoped
not. O'Hara's and Kimball's fights always upset everyone.

The DDO's door opened and an angry face emerged.
It belonged to François Durand, the Washington liaison
officer of the French service, officially known as the
Service de Documentation Exterieure et de Contre-
Espionage.

Passing into O'Hara's office, Jones said, "He didn't
look happy."

"Good," O'Hara said, still exasperated. "Sometimes
I think the people on our side do us more harm than
the people on the other side. Remember all the money
we gave the French to buy planes to fight the Viet
Minh?"

"You mean twenty years ago?" Jones said. "Sure." He never forgot a budget line.

Jones could see that O'Hara was angry, but his was not the kind of anger which flushed the face. Rather, it seemed to drain his countenance of blood and leave him grayer than ever. Even at his best, O'Hara resembled a Xerox copy of a man. Mad, he looked like a Xerox of a Xerox.

"One plane they bought used to be Queen Elizabeth's," O'Hara said. "A real flying palace. That was bad enough, but the plane never made it to Nam. The French ministers kept it in France to fly their mistresses to the Côte d'Azur. We want our money back."

"I see why he didn't look too pleased," said Jones, handing over several pages filled with columns of numbers that looked, at first glance, like an unbreakable code. It was the budget. Not the whole budget actually. Just the budget for Clandestine Services, which the DDO controlled.

"More cutting?" asked O'Hara.

"How'd you know?"

"How much?"

"Just a hundred and fifty thousand dollars."

Bending over the budget figures, O'Hara appeared very much at home, for he looked like an accountant. But his record indicated that he had balanced his books with bodies: in Vietnam, a few years back, he had headed a program which attempted to dismantle the Vietcong infrastructure through systematic assassinations. The program, according to figures which O'Hara himself had given Congress, was responsible for putting 20,587 people in the dead column. During the years when he was attempting to "pacify" Vietnam, his wife, who stayed behind in Springfield, Maryland, regularly attended peace demonstrations. Many parents in Vietnam lost children to O'Hara's men, but, as if to balance the account, O'Hara had lost a child, too. While his agents were killing in Southeast Asia, his daughter was dying of a mysterious disease back home. Some saw a link between her death and her opposition to her father's role in the war: they said she lost her will to live.

The Clandestine Services budget, which Jones had handed O'Hara, at first seemed as hard to balance as the moral one. But the DDO knew where he wanted to start.

"Where do we put in the knife?" asked Jones.

"Counterintelligence."

"We cut CI two weeks ago," Jones reminded him. "They're still screaming."

"Cut them again and let them scream some more." Jones laughed.

"I'm not joking," O'Hara said. "Cut them deep."

"Well, how much? Seventy-five thousand dollars?"

"One hundred and fifty thousand dollars. That should slow them down."

"But they're on our side, remember?" Jones prodded.

"That's the problem."

Noble Jones did not look forward to breaking the news to Mother.

A black chauffeur-driven Mercedes-Benz dropped a man in a black suit and black homburg at the corner of R Street and Wisconsin Avenue in Georgetown at 7 P.M. He crossed the sidewalk and entered a blue-fronted restaurant called La Niçoise. The maître d' recognized Mother immediately, which was to be expected since it was the CI chief's custom to lunch there daily and often to return in the evening for dinner. Not a flexible man, Mother would no more change his restaurant than he would change the way he combed his hair or the way he felt about communists. He had parted his hair just slightly to the left of center ever since he had been an undergraduate at Yale over thirty years ago, and he had been fighting the Cold War almost as long. Détente had not changed him at all, not a hair.

Paul Fitzsimmons was already waiting at the table. They shook hands and sat down. Paul was on Mother's left, which he immediately regretted because the older man's body twisted in such a way that he seemed to be frozen in a position facing right. Paul spent most of the meal looking at the back of Mother's head.

A waiter glided up to the table on roller skates, for La Niçoise is a hybrid of haute cuisine française and roller rink. When the waiter opened his mouth, Paul half-expected him to say, "Couples only," or "All skate," but instead he said, *"Bon soir, messieurs, qu'est-ce que vous voulez boire?"*

Mother said, *"Donnez moi un Kir, s'il vous plait."* He spoke the individual words correctly, but his rhythm was hopelessly British public school.

Paul said, "Could I have a Scotch and soda, please?"

The waiter skated away, dodging between tables as if they were a slalom course.

"You haven't heard anything about my test, have you?" asked Paul.

"No, but I wouldn't worry," Mother said, deciding to try to reassure the young man without revealing that he had eavesdropped on the session. He continued: "The statistics we get out of that black box are pretty interesting. Turns out ten percent of the single men in the company habitually masturbate. With married men, that goes up to fifteen percent."

"I had no idea," Paul said softly and somewhat stiffly. Mother's intention had been to make Paul feel better by letting him know that he was not alone. But discussion of such a delicate subject just made Paul more nervous.

"Now they give these tests all over the government," Mother said softly. He was another large man with a small voice. "Turns out scientists masturbate even more than we do. They write more poison pen letters, too. You can't trust them. At State, the sin the box turned up most often was a college flirtation with Marxism."

"How good is it?" Paul asked. "If I were a trained KGB man, would it catch me?"

"That's like asking if anyone can beat Bobby Fischer in chess," Mother said. "It's theoretically possible but it's not very likely. Every time the other side figures out a move to beat our box, we think of a move to beat their move. After the Hungarian Revolution, we picked up lots of agents over there. We couldn't run any background checks on them, so we just 'fluttered' them and hired them."

Paul looked puzzled.

"That's our cryptonym for polygraph," Mother explained. "Of course it turned out later lots of them were double agents. The Russians had learned that the flutter doesn't measure lies—it measures the fear of getting caught telling lies. So they taught their agents to hypnotize themselves to believe they couldn't get caught. Once they beat the fear, they beat the flutter."

"So then what did you do?" Paul asked. He leaned closer to Mother, to hear better.

"We found out the machine measures not just fear but mental effort. It takes more mental energy to tell lies. We thought we had them beat then but they thought up another countermove. They learned to do mental arithmetic—like five times five, five times six, five times seven—before answering any questions. So true answers burned up as much mental energy as lies. Pretty cute, huh?"

"How'd you beat that one?" Paul asked.

"With a psychological stress evaluator—a PSE. It measures stress in your voice."

"Do you mean I have to take another test?" asked Paul.

"No . . ."

"Good."

". . . Because you already took it. Your polygraph test was taped. So was your pretest interview. These'll be graphed and the graphs fed into a computer. If you were lying, we'll find out."

The waiter skated up to take their order.

"They pride themselves on their scampi," Mother said.

Paul, who felt a little hungrier than that, ordered the veal scallopini instead. Mother ordered the scampi. The waiter rolled away.

"Was it hard for you to make up your mind about an intelligence career?" Paul asked.

"Not really."

"Didn't you ever consider a literary career?"

"Before the war I sometimes thought about it," Mother conceded.

"Why not after the war?"

"Because I found out the war wasn't over."

"Do you ever think that except for the war you might be writing today's poetry instead of just reading it?"

"I don't read *today's* poetry," Mother said. "I can't seem to find any new poets I like. I go back to the poets I've always read and always liked."

His tastes in poetry were permanently parted, too.

"Are you having second thoughts?" Mother asked.

"No, not really," Paul said a little uncertainly. "Could you tell me a little more about what I'll be doing—that is, *if* I pass your polygraph."

"Sure. Most of your work'll be with defectors. Debriefing them. Babysitting them. They *can* be difficult."

"How?" Paul said apprehensively.

"We once had a KGB man come over, said he'd only talk to one person: the President of the United States. This one was a lot of trouble, but he was smart. He knew he was a valuable commodity, and he was determined not to sell himself cheaply."

"Well, did he talk to the President?"

"The President then was Jack Kennedy. I couldn't deliver him, but I delivered the next best thing: his brother."

"Bobby?"

"The same," Mother said. "The defector's name was Galitziue, but we code-named him 'Martel' because it was easier to say. Bobby Kennedy became his case officer."

Mother realized he was dropping names, but for some reason he enjoyed impressing Paul.

"Was he any good at it?"

"Surprisingly so. Bobby and I persuaded Martel to betray about two hundred KGB agents around the world. A lot of them committed suicide. Bobby even got his brother Jack to write a letter to de Gaulle telling him the French cabinet was full of spies. But the general wouldn't listen. Bobby said he was too proud to admit he was getting gang-banged. I think he picked up that language from his brother, who'd been in the navy."

Mother paused to inhale a Virginia Slim. The ash was a half an inch long and seemed on the verge of dropping off. And then it did. Strewing ashes about him seemed the one element of untidiness which this otherwise fastidious man allowed himself.

"Did you work with Bobby Kennedy often?" Paul asked.

"Oh, sure. He enjoyed company work. I think it was a game to him. He was the younger brother who never really grew up. So he loved playing spy the way he loved playing touch football. That's what made him so good."

A roller derby contestant bearing a tray rolled up to the table, bringing with him two salads. Mother tasted his and pushed it away.

"They keep experimenting with the ingredients," Mother said, "and each time it gets worse."

"It's still better than the food at school," Paul said, digging in.

"Every year, the food here gets worse. The chef even plays guitar in the floor show, which undermines one's confidence in how the food is prepared."

And yet Mother would never have considered changing restaurants.

Mother looked up, which was a strain since he was so stooped. But he did not look at Paul. His eyes followed the progress of a man in a tan suit who entered the restaurant and made his way across the dining room to the men's room. A few minutes later, the man emerged from the rest room and left the restaurant without eating.

Soon Mother discovered that he required a trip to the men's room. He found the sealed envelope in the towel dispenser, as he knew he would. The company was so fond of using toilets as letter drops that one might imagine that the CIA's collective personality was anal. Using his comb as a letter opener, Mother carefully slit the envelope and removed the sheet inside. Then he took a small New Testament out of his pocket and started thumbing through it. The message contained rows of numbers which were actually a book code: the first digit gave the page, the second the line, the third the number of the word on the line. Mother used an old-fashioned pump fountain pen to write down the words as he looked them up. He labored over the encrypted message as patiently and affectionately as if it had been an obscure Pound canto.

As he unscrambled the message, Mother grew more and more excited and more and more alarmed. He shifted his position on the toilet seat, since he was beginning to get sore. And he had a feeling this was just the beginning of his discomfort.

The first word he found in his Testament was "four." The second was "disciples." Then came the verb "to be." These were in Matthew. Leafing ahead, Mother searched through Luke, where he found "cast out." Then "white." Then "house." The next set of numbers contained an extra digit, which indicated not a word but a letter within a word. Mother identified a *d*, then another *d*, then an *o*. Then "to be" again. Then a third *d*, then *c*, then *i*. End of dispatch.

Consulting his notes, Mother wrote out the complete message as follows: "Four disciples to be cast out White House. DDO to be DCI."

Mother always said, "Penetration begins at home," but most people thought he was kidding. He wasn't. His most valued agents were not in Moscow or Peking but in Washington. Now his man at the White House had sent the message he had long dreaded. Ernest O'Hara was about to become the Director of Central Intelligence (DCI). Mother was already trying to think of a way to block O'Hara's appointment.

When he returned to the table, Mother found the chair harder than he remembered it. He picked up his salad fork, turned it over, and started using it to stroke a still recumbent fork, knitting the prongs of the two together like fingers. He sat in silence for five minutes or more, one fork stroking the other, back and forth, back and forth, but it didn't help. He still didn't know what to do.

Paul did not know what to do either. The silence was beginning to make him quite nervous. That afternoon in the Thing, Paul had prayed for silence, but that evening in La Niçoise, he prayed for talk. In moments of stress, some people use humor as a defense. Others fall back on pomposity. Paul asked questions.

"What's the matter?"

"Company trouble."

There was another long silence.

"What sort of trouble?"

"Serious trouble, I'm afraid."

"How serious?"

"I admire you for asking, but I really can't talk about it."

They both sat and stared mutely, Paul at the front door, Mother at the silverware.

"Well, perhaps I could tell you this much," Mother said at last. "I find I suddenly feel like Buck Grangerford in *Huckleberry Finn*. You remember Buck, don't you?"

"No," Paul admitted, thoroughly ashamed of himself.

"No! Well, you *have* read *Huck Finn*?"

"Of course, but I don't remember all the names."

"Read it again. You can't read it too many times. It's the best book ever written about the CIA."

Paul laughed to cover his lack of understanding.

"I'm serious. The key to most of what goes on at Langley is locked up in that book."

"What key?"

"Read the book again," Mother said. "By all means read it again before you come to us permanently."

At the end of dinner, after coffee and brandy, Mother pushed himself away from the table. He carefully folded his red napkin into a compact triangle, as if he were folding the American flag.

2

Transplanting Orchids and Evidence

ORCHIDS DANGLED from the greenhouse ceiling like New Year's Eve decorations, but neither Paul nor Mother felt festive. After their dinner at La Niçoise, they had returned to Mother's Arlington home, where a night's sleep had solved neither of their problems. Morning found Paul still worried about his flutter and Mother still concerned about the message he had received. They both had dirty hands.

"Look," Mother said, holding up a pale plant, "this one's not up to grade. There's no room for it."

"What's wrong with it?" asked Paul, who was not at all sure there would be room for him.

"Too weak."

"Too bad," said Paul, feeling an unexpected empathy.

Mother, dressed in an old pair of black trousers and a white shirt with frayed collar and cuffs, and Paul, in a blue work shirt and jeans, stood side by side in one of the two backyard hothouses. The older man was teaching the younger how to transplant. One community pot, holding some fifty seedlings, had become overcrowded as the young plants grew. The time had come to spread these plants out over several containers, where they would have more room. Mother set out five empty urns in a row.

"We'll put seven plants in each pot," Mother said. "That way we'll only have room for about two-thirds of them."

"What happens to the others?"

"They get culled," Mother said. "In a few weeks we'll have to do the same thing all over again. Eventually we'll get down to one pot, one plant."

Mother knew the agency worked the same way. Intelligence officers either moved up or out. And now, with O'Hara on the verge of the ultimate promotion, Mother knew he himself was almost certain to be one of the culls.

If he did not want to be discarded, he knew he could not afford to be weak. He would have to act to block O'Hara's rise. As his fingers struggled with the complexity of interlocking roots, his mind struggled with complex strategies. He would think of a plan, work over it, nourish it, discover some flaw, and reject it, another cull. The ruined schemes were piling up around him as he transplanted.

"Why do you have two greenhouses?" Paul interrupted Mother's thoughts.

"What?"

"Why two greenhouses?"

"Oh, one's cooler than the other. Some orchids do better in one, some in the other."

The greenhouse in which Paul and Mother stood was a traditional structure, with walls and a peaked roof constructed of glass panes. Visible through the glass was a second, less conventional greenhouse a few feet away. It was a small Quonset hut covered with translucent green plastic. It looked less like a green-

house than like a miniature green army barrack—
seemingly better suited for growing GI Joe dolls than
orchids.

"Which is which?" Paul asked.

"What?"

"Which is cooler?"

"Dark Side."

"Excuse me?"

"Oh, I'm sorry," Mother said, attempting to order
his thoughts. "Of course you don't know that my
greenhouses have names. I call this one Light Side and
the other one Dark Side."

Mother chuckled, but Paul simply looked uncom-
prehending.

"You see," Mother explained, "there are two sides
to the agency, the light side and the dark side. The
light side monitors radio transmissions, studies satellite
photographs, reads scientific journals. The dark runs
agents in target countries."

"Which side are you on?" Paul asked.

"The dark side," said Mother, proudly. "But it's not
that simple. There are two sides to the dark side: the
clean side and the dirty side. The clean side just steals
secrets. The dirty side runs operations—sabotage,
coups, whatever."

"Are you dirty or clean?"

"Clean," Mother chuckled, "at least most of the
time."

"Which side's best?"

"I think you'll prefer the dark side. But I should
warn you that advancement's usually faster on the
light side."

"Oh," Paul said, looking concerned.

"But all the directors who've come up through the
ranks have come up through the dark side. On our side
you move slower at first, but it's the only way to really
get to the top."

Paul smiled.

Then Mother sank back into his musings. His fingers moved through the dirt as his thoughts scratched
here and there for a solution to his problem. Paul could

see that Mother was distracted and made no further attempts to force conversation upon him.

"I'm sorry," Mother said with no warning. "I just remembered something I need to do at the office. We'd better take a break."

Mother held a backyard garden hose while Paul washed his hands, and then Paul held the hose for Mother.

After a quick change of clothes, the Counterintelligence chief drove down Glebe Road to Highway 123. Then all too soon he saw the sign: CIA. The sight of the white initials so boldly emblazoned on a green background almost always startled Mother. For years, the sign had read BPR—Bureau of Public Roads— which Mother considered more in keeping with the spirit of the agency. But two months earlier that sign had come down and a more candid one had gone up. So far as Mother was concerned, it was a bad sign.

Mother turned into the agency approach road. Ahead he saw the flashing red beacons atop the gate. He passed a sign which warned, not against stealing state secrets, but against "short-cutting across parking lots." Pulling to a stop at the guardhouse, he showed his identification badge to a black General Services Administration guard. The badge had red marks marching around its perimeter, each one standing for clearance into a different restricted area. At the agency, where one's peers judged one by the number of secrets one was allowed to know, these marks were status symbols. The guard waved Mother through.

Driving into the compound, Mother's eye was caught by the CIA's red-and-white-checked water tower, which seemed to shine down benevolently on the agency like a huge, wholesome box of Wheat Chex in the sky. Mother was hungry.

Rounding a turn, Mother saw the two bright ribbons of glass which wound around the headquarters building. Sixty years earlier, Joseph Leiter, the son of a Chicago millionaire, had built a mansion on this site which he called the Glass Palace. The Leiter home had burned down in 1945, to be replaced in 1961 by a $46 million glass and concrete palace. A continuous band of floor-to-ceiling windows ran around the second and seventh floors. All that glass had forced the agency to quash a proposal for the construction of a nearby apartment building. Residents of the top floors would have been able to see over the tops of the protective trees and right into the director's office.

Mother parked in his designated slot, clipped his identification badge to his coat, and walked toward the Toy Factory. The guard at the door passed him into the building. He had come in that Saturday morning to do a job which was not unlike cross-pollinating in the greenhouse, taking a little something from one receptacle and transferring it to another. Except Mother would be working not with flowers but with files, moving information from one to another, hoping to germinate a scandal.

Mother made two stops on the way to his office— the first to pick up a file from the flutter department, the second to collect a general personnel file. They both bore the same name: Ernest O'Hara.

Every five years, everyone in the agency was fluttered, and the results were placed in a special file which was segregated from the employee's general file. There had once been a proposal to store polygraph results in a computer, but it had been rejected because of fears about security. For the flutter files were among the agency's most confidential documents. Even within the agency, access to them was severely restricted.

When Mother reached his office, he sat down to study both files. In the flutter folder he found what he was looking for. There was evidence which suggested that O'Hara had had a brush with heroin trafficking when he was Saigon station chief. When he had last been fluttered, he had consistently had trouble answering questions about the drug business.

Mother removed the incriminating material from the flutter file and placed it in the general file. Now, when the President examined O'Hara's file prior to appointing him director, he would discover the narcotics tracks and start looking for someone else to run the Central Intelligence Agency. Or so Mother hoped. After all, he reasoned, the last thing Richard Nixon would want to do was take on another suspected felon. He had enough trouble with the ones he already had.

Mother returned the two files to their places.

Then he drove home to interrupt Paul's attempt to do some homework. They resumed their repotting inside the Light Side greenhouse. Mother appeared to be in a better mood, but he was still slightly distracted. Having set one scheme in motion, he was now at work on a second, this one aimed at blocking the threatened $150,000 cut in his budget.

Paul was reflective, too. He was absorbed by thoughts about his future career. He had already made up his mind to join the agency—*if* he passed his flutter —but he kept second-guessing that decision. It was as though he wanted to frighten himself by imagining he had made a mistake.

"What was your biggest disappointment?" Paul asked.

"Pardon me?"

"Looking back over your career, what was your biggest disappointment?"

"The defection of Kim Philby," said Mother without hesitation. "I should've realized he was KGB years earlier than I did."

Paul felt encouraged. If that was the worst he faced, he supposed the agency might be all right after all.

"Why should you have known?"

"These lady slippers are much harder to grow than cattleyas," said Mother, who did not like to answer questions about his failures.

When they finished transplanting the orchids from the community pot, Mother considered attacking a second overcrowded pot. But he was tired of culling. His heart wasn't in it.

Monday morning, Mother drove Paul to the airport and then headed for the office. By then, he had a plan for protecting his budget.

Arriving at the Toy Factory, he went to work composing a memorandum to O'Hara, the DDO. He wrote in longhand on sheets of foolscap. He was a large man with a small voice and even smaller handwriting. His miniature script marched in absolutely parallel lines across the pages. When he had his memo all written out, he turned to his old-fashioned, heavy Royal. Mother thought he had better type this one up himself.

The memorandum which rolled up out of his typewriter was an attack on the cutting of the CI budget. It said that the agency was the country's shield and that the Counterintelligence Department was the agency's shield. It said the agency could not afford to lower this shield . . . and so on in an unconsciously mock-heroic tone, coming to the conclusion that cutting $150,000 out of the CI budget would seriously endanger the country. The KGB could penetrate us at will, steal our secrets, anticipate our policies.

But the memo was most noteworthy not for its message but for its end matter. There was a list which read:

cc: Director of Central Intelligence
cc: Under Secretary of State for Political Affairs
cc: Deputy Secretary of Defense
cc: Chairman of the Joint Chiefs of Staff
cc: Assistant to the President for National Security
     Affairs

This was the distribution list for carbon copies of Mother's memorandum. Included were all the members of the 40-committee, the interdepartmental panel responsible for overseeing the agency's operations. The name was intentionally misleading—it had five members, not forty.

After hand-delivering the memo to O'Hara's secretary, Mother returned to his own office and went straight to what looked like a filing cabinet but was actually a safe with a dead-bolt combination lock. Every office at Langley had one—at a cost of about

$200 a drawer. Most intelligence officers had two-drawer models. Mother's had six drawers.

He worked the combination, opened the top drawer, and took out the aerial photographs of Moscow. He knew he shouldn't have, but he couldn't help it. He was only getting his hopes up at the very moment when those hopes seemed most likely to be disappointed. He seemed to love this operation more than ever, now that it was very likely doomed. For Mother felt certain that if O'Hara became director, he would do more than cut the CI budget. He would probably veto AESOP altogether. The first two letters of the crypto-nym indicated a project targeted against Russia. All Soviet operations had code names beginning with AE: AELADLE, AEJAMMER, AEBROOM . . .

Mother's finger came to rest on Dzerzhinsky Square, the small park which is overlooked by Moscow Center, the home of the KGB. His finger then traced a path from the square down back streets to a small house which was circled. Inside the circle was a nick-name: "Kim." The paper along the route had been worn thin.

Mother's telephone rang. Scott Bannister wanted to come in. He had some news. Mother was replacing the satellite photographs when his assistant entered.

"What's up?" Mother asked.

"They're playing 'Ten Little Indians' at the White House," Bannister said. "Haldeman, Ehrlichman, and Kleindienst have resigned. And Dean just got fired."

"That's right," Mother said as if he already knew. In an intelligence agency it did not seem right that an assistant should know more than his superior, so Mother did not let on that such was the case.

"Oh, I didn't know you knew," Bannister said, disappointed. "Sorry I disturbed you."

"That's all right," Mother said magnanimously. "By the way, did you hear who's going to replace Klein-dienst?"

"Elliot Richardson," Bannister said. "Is that what you heard?"

"Yes, yes," Mother said. "And did you hear who'll replace Richardson at the Pentagon?"

"No, did you?"

"No," Mother admitted. "Did you hear anything else?"

"The President's going on TV tonight."

"Anything else?"

"No."

"Anything about the agency?"

"No."

"Can you tell me your source?" asked Mother.

Bannister said, "WTOP radio."

Just before Mother left the office that evening, a memorandum was hand-delivered to his office. It was O'Hara's answer to Mother's morning memo. It said the agency needed a shield but not a solid gold one. The CI chief did not care for the metaphor. Worse, the director's memo, like Mother's, was embroidered at the end with a carbon distribution list:

cc: Director of Central Intelligence
cc: Under Secretary of State for Political Affairs
cc: Deputy Secretary of Defense
cc: Chairman of the Joint Chiefs of Staff
cc: Assistant to the President for National Security
     Affairs

Mother had not counted on that. Normally the DDO did not deign to reply to Mother's memos. The CI chief usually found O'Hara's habit of ignoring his messages frustrating, but this time he found the reverse even more unsettling.

Now Mother knew there would be trouble. He supposed he would soon be getting a call. And he was afraid he would have to do some explaining.

Locking O'Hara's memo in his safe, Mother went home to his empty house backed up by two crowded greenhouses.

The call came the next morning at 11:30 A.M. William Schieffer, the Director of Central Intelligence, wanted to see Mother in his seventh-floor office immediately. The DCI's secretary did not ask Mother if it would be convenient.

Moments later, the CI chief was shown into Director Schieffer's office with its fifty feet of windows overlooking the Potomac River. O'Hara, whose office was nearer the director's, was already there. Mother and O'Hara stood side by side before their boss's desk. They looked sheepish, like boys who had been called in to face the principal and explain a fight.

"What's been going on around here?" Director Schieffer wanted to know.

Neither answered. The DCI looked from the one to the other, struck all over again by how different the two men were. Mother wore black; O'Hara wore gray. Mother was tall, with big bones and bold features; O'Hara was short, with delicate features and bones as fragile as a sparrow's. Mother was a rich man's son who had attended British schools and summered in Italy; O'Hara was an army brat who had attended public schools all over America and summered at boy scout camp. Mother's hobby was orchids; O'Hara's was still scouting—he was now a troop leader. They were both Catholics, but one of them had learned his Catholicism from Italian aristocrats while the other was an Irish Catholic, which made them as similar as *fettucine Alfredo* and a boiled potato.

"I said," the DCI repeated, "what's going on here? Somebody's playing games, and I mean to find out who."

"What do you mean 'playing games'?" O'Hara asked.

Mother didn't say anything.

"I mean that crazy memo to the forty-committee," the DCI said. "It had your name on it."

Schieffer took his briar pipe out of his mouth and pointed the stem at O'Hara. He was always stemming people.

"I did write a memo," O'Hara said, "but I wasn't the only one."

Mother didn't say anything.

"Would you care to explain that last remark?" the DCI said.

For the first time O'Hara began to look confused. Mother was apprehensive, and yet he could not help being amused. He wrestled the corners of his mouth to keep from smiling.

"Certainly," O'Hara said. "My memo was an answer to Kimball's."

"So I gathered," the DCI said. "But why did you want to share it with the forty-committee? Don't we have enough trouble with them without involving them in family quarrels?"

"It wasn't my idea to involve them," O'Hara protested.

Mother, who didn't say anything, found it harder than ever to keep from smiling. His eyes sparkled.

"Then whose idea was it?" the DCI asked.

"Kimball's," O'Hara said without looking at his colleague.

"How so?"

"Because he started it," O'Hara said. "He sent his memo to the committee, so I felt I had to, too."

Mother didn't say anything.

"You've been awfully quiet," the DCI said, turning to the CI chief. "What do you have to say for yourself?"

Now that he had finally been called upon for an explanation, Mother found it easier not to smile.

"I'm afraid this got out of hand," Mother said. "I did send O'Hara a memo. And I'm afraid I did append a carbon distribution list. But I didn't actually distribute those carbons. I wasn't *that* presumptuous."

"Goddamn," said O'Hara, who did not normally swear.

"You just wanted to get O'Hara's attention," the DCI said. "Is that it?"

"I'm afraid so," Mother admitted.

"So the forty-committee gets a memo out of the blue attacking a memo they've never heard of," the DCI said, stemming the Counterintelligence chief.

"I suppose," admitted Mother.

"And then my phone starts ringing," the DCI said. "Well, gentlemen, let me just say this. I don't mind a little blood on the walls of our own gymnasium. But I don't want any blood outside those walls. I won't have it! Is that clear?"

The DCI stemmed them both.

After the dressing-down, Mother and O'Hara parted without speaking. As Mother marched at a deliberate pace toward his own office, he allowed his face to relax and the smile to come. The farther he walked, the wider grew his grin. Reaching his office, he closed the door behind him and giggled out loud. Then he sat down at his desk and frowned. The longer he sat, the deeper dipped the frown.

Mother frowned for days. He prided himself upon his patience, which he believed to be one of his most effective weapons. He had often been content to watch a suspected enemy agent for weeks, months, even years, as he assembled his proof. And yet now he was impatient.

Mother had trouble concentrating. Not even AESOP could hold his attention. His mind kept returning to the terrible prediction that O'Hara was soon to be the new Director of Central Intelligence. Yet, as the days passed uneventfully, Mother allowed himself to hope that his intelligence out of the White House had for once been wrong.

Then, a week after the White House purge, the President nominated William Schieffer to replace Elliot Richardson as secretary of defense. And Ernest O'Hara was named to replace Schieffer as the Director of Central Intelligence.

When Mother went to retrieve the heroin trafficking evidence he had planted, he discovered that the O'Hara file was missing. He wondered who had it, the White House or O'Hara himself.

3

Blackmail

ONE MORNING several weeks later, after the change in command at the CIA was announced, Scott Bannister was leafing through the *Washington Post,* looking at the summer clothing ads. He was lost in a Lord & Taylor layout when Kay Johnson, O'Hara's secretary, called. She asked him to come up to the director's suite.

On his way, Bannister stopped in a men's room to check his grooming. Running a comb through his hair, he wondered if he was staring into the eyes of a security officer stationed on the other side of a one-way mirror. He was.

Bannister proceeded to the director's seventh-floor suite, passing, en route, a glass room containing security aides armed with snub-nosed .38 revolvers under their conservative business suits. He always felt a certain pity for these guards, who looked to be men of action trapped in inactive jobs. He had sympathy for their plight but not for their baggy tailoring.

Stopping at Kay Johnson's desk, Bannister realized

that the company was becoming much less colorful at almost every level, including the new director's new secretary. Back when Richard Helms was director, his secretary had been an eccentric old woman who fed the birds on the agency's roof and kept a houseful of parakeets at home. The new secretary and her new boss were, outwardly at least, much drabber sorts. Bannister liked neither but feared both.

Entering the director's office, Mother's assistant sank into the thick carpet. It was supposed to provide a sense of luxury, but to Bannister the pile felt like quicksand.

O'Hara began by asking Bannister to suggest places where the Counterintelligence Department's budget could be cut. Bannister was immediately at a disadvantage, as the director had known he would be, for the aide was not familiar with the budget figures. Bannister was being set up. Now, when the director changed the subject, the aide would welcome the change.

"By the way, how's Mother?" the director asked, his voice betraying none of the animosity he felt.

Bannister said Mother was well.

"I'd appreciate your advice," the director said. His deep blue eyes, the one exception to his grayness, shone with counterfeit openness. "You know Mother better than I do. Some people around here think he could still be of some use on the front lines, but I'm not so sure. I think he's too old. What do you think?"

"He's not too old." Bannister sprang to Mother's defense. He felt intimidated by the director, but he was not ready to defect to his side. "He loves a good fight."

Smothering a smile, the director said, "As you know, some years ago, Mother *was* of some use in Italy, first during the war and later during the forty-eight election. But I'm afraid that may all be behind him now."

"Not at all." Bannister objected right on cue.

"I wish I could believe you, because Italy's in trouble again. It may be in more trouble now than it was in

the forties. She needs the help of her old friends, but
I'm afraid those friends may just be *too* old. What
do you think? Isn't Mother over the hill?"

"No," Bannister protested once again.

"You think he could still handle a job like, say,
chief of station in Rome?"

"Of course."

"I wonder," said O'Hara. "Of course, Italy might
be the worst place for him. We once disagreed over
policy there, he and I. He might sabotage our efforts
there just to get back at me. We need someone who'd
put what's best for Italy above all else."

"Oh, I'm sure he would."

"Well, I don't know," the director said, "but thanks
very much. You've been a great help."

Bannister hurried back to Mother's office to tell him
about his talk with the director, but Mother was not
there. He was in the Miscellaneous Projects office and
could not be disturbed.

Spies are burrowing animals. The CIA once dug a
tunnel under East Berlin to tap the opposition's telephone lines. The agency even dug a quarter-mile tunnel under its own property in Langley to provide a
secret entrance to the complex. At the agency, "going
underground" is more than a metaphor.

That morning, an Israeli agent named Menachem
Ginzburg, who had an appointment with a high
agency official, entered the compound "black," meaning through the tunnel. As he walked along in the dim
light, he held a book of Doonesbury cartoons a few
inches in front of his face. He chuckled every few
steps. When he emerged from the tunnel he was in a
carpeted foyer, facing a mahogany elevator door. A
squad of gray-flannel guards looked the agent over and
thumbed through his curious paperback. Then two of
them escorted him into the elevator, which rose to an
unnumbered floor.

The building led a double life. On the outside it
was just another office building, but once the agent entered the Miscellaneous Projects office, he found him-

self inside a Swiss hunting lodge with exposed-beam rafters and a slanting ceiling, twenty feet high at one end. Flanked by two greyhounds, Mother sat waiting for the agent in a huge leather armchair. Mother was so thin he made the chair look fat.

"What can I get you to drink?" Mother asked, taking advantage of where they were. This room and the director's private dining room were the only places at Langley where hard liquor was allowed.

"Martini with an olive," Ginzburg said, pocketing his book. "And I suppose you'll have a Kir?"

"Right."

"You never change, do you?"

"No."

Mother had first met Menachem Ginzburg shortly after the war. At that time Ginzburg was a member of the Jewish underground and was busy helping European Jews escape to Palestine. In the spy business, making a Jewish connection back when Israel was still Palestine was like buying Xerox when it was still Haloid. For a generation, Mother had owned the "Israeli account" at the agency. Intelligence operations in all other countries were run out of Clandestine Services, but Israeli operations were run out of Mother's Counterintelligence shop. Fearing that others in the agency would try to take the account away from him, Mother had always kept his dealings with the Israelis ultrasecret. For years the Israeli desk had remained hidden under Mother's skirts.

Over the years, many of Mother's greatest successes —many of the CIA's greatest successes—had been accomplished in partnership with the Israeli service. During the coldest years of the American-Soviet distrust, the company had had a great deal of difficulty recruiting agents behind the Iron Curtain. The few they did sign up usually turned out to be double agents. The Israelis had not had that problem. They were able to call upon the remnants of the underground organizations set up to smuggle Jews out of Eastern Europe during and after the war. The Israelis had agents; the Americans had money and plans. They pooled their resources for the benefit of all: Israel, the United States, and Mother.

"I hear Mr. Brezhnev's coming to see Nixon next month," the Israeli baited Mother. "Pretty soon all the disagreements'll be solved. They're even going to make the Arabs and the Israelis love each other. Then you and I'll be out of work. This détente . . ."

"Détente's a trick," Mother interjected.

"No, no, détente's progress," Ginzburg said, knowing from long experience how to provoke Mother. "The only problem is it's like automation—it creates unemployment."

"No, the problem is that the American President and his foreign policy adviser have been taken in."

"What we need is a union to protect our jobs," the Israeli agent said.

"People forget about the days of Lenin and Dzerzhinsky," Mother said, a frown forming as he pronounced without accent the tongue-twisting name of the founding director of Cheka, the forerunner of the KGB. "Remember when Dzerzhinsky had so many agents in Western countries that he asked Lenin, 'What'll I tell them?' "

"And Lenin said, 'Tell the West what it wants to believe,' " interrupted Ginzburg, who had heard Mother's lecture many times before.

"Right, and Dzerzhinsky did just that. Convinced us Russia was falling apart, moving toward capitalism. The Revolution was saved through disinformation."

"And you think it's happening all over again?"

"Exactly," said Mother. "Stalin disbanded the Department of Disinformation but now they've reestablished it. That's how they sold us détente, but they haven't changed. They still want to destroy us."

"No, they want to destroy China," Ginzburg chided.

"No, no," Mother said. "That's more disinformation. Russia and China are close as ever. They're just pretending to quarrel, so we'll let our guard down. You know that."

"Mother, you're like the captain of one of those old luxury liners. You don't know when you're outdated."

"Your metaphors are bad as ever," Mother said. "Now why don't we try to make ourselves useful. I have some pictures to show you."

Mother pressed several buttons on the arm of his chair, and the hunting lodge darkened as a photograph of two men appeared on a wall. They were leaving a building bearing a sign: MAGIRUS DEUTZ FIRE PROTECTION TECHNIQUES LTD.

"Recognize them?" asked Mother.

"The man on the right is Colonel Abd-el-Krim of the Egyptian army engineers. I don't know the one on the left."

"He's Helmut Klein," Mother said, "a Deutz executive and one of their salesmen. He only works on big deals. Deutz is one of the three largest fire equipment companies in Germany."

"It's very like a German to do business with an Arab. They're made for each other."

"The company headquarters are in Ulm, Bavaria. That's the building you see."

"What're they plotting?" asked Ginzburg.

Mother pushed another combination of buttons, and the building was replaced by an interior shot taken in a Bavarian inn which actually resembled the Miscellaneous Projects office. The same two men were in the picture, this time seated at a table.

"They're haggling over price," Mother said. "I'm told it took eight months to reach a satisfactory figure. They finally settled on twelve thousand five hundred per unit."

"I'm sure when you're ready you'll tell me what the Arab came to buy."

Mother pushed another sequence of buttons, and an Egyptian ship named *Kartoum* appeared on the screen. Wooden boxes marked MARGINUS DEUTZ were being lowered into the hold.

"You may recognize Marseilles," Mother said.

"Yes."

Mother played another tune on the tiny keyboard. A close-up of lettering on one of the boxes appeared: TST 40/7.

"The TST forty-slash-seven is a high-powered, turbine-driven, fire fighter's water pump," Mother said. "They're portable."

"I see."

Mother pushed more buttons. A satellite photo of the port of Alexandria appeared on the wall.

"Look closely," Mother said, "and you'll see the *Kartoum* in the upper right-hand corner. This picture was taken just last week."

"All right, what're they up to?"

"We believe the Egyptians bought about one hundred TST forty-slash-seven pumps from Deutz."

"But why? Why do they want pumps? Why a hundred? Why one?"

Mother said, "I don't know."

Prying open the office door of a Director of Central Intelligence generally requires considerable bureaucratic foreplay. The director's aides, who guard the outer office, must be fondled with memos and phone calls. When the aides have been properly wooed, they arrange an appointment.

Only one man in the company dispensed with even perfunctory courtship of the outer office. One morning this man brushed past the director's aides as if they were panhandlers and presented himself, without appointment, at the director's door. Mother had always treated directors in this unceremonious fashion and saw no reason to change just because Ernest O'Hara was now the DCI.

"I got your message," Mother told the director, "and the answer is no."

"What message?" the director asked ingenuously.

"The one you gave Bannister."

The director just smiled.

"So you want to put me out to pasture," Mother said. "What makes you think I'll go? And don't tell me Italy needs me. Is that what they told Cord Meyer? Britain needed him? Are you planning to turn our stations into retirement homes?"

"I want my own team. You understand."

"What if I don't?"

Mother drew his courage from the same well which had so long sustained J. Edgar Hoover: his files. For Mother, like Hoover, enjoyed the considerable leverage which devolves upon a man who is empowered to follow, to peek, and to tap. His files were bloated with other people's secrets. Mother, like Hoover, had too much on agency personnel to be an easy man to "retire."

"If you won't accept a transfer," O'Hara said, "I may have to ask for your resignation."

Since Mother had had so little success with the heroin connection, he decided to switch crimes.

"And what if I won't resign?" Mother asked. "What'll you do then? Maybe what you did to that Vietnamese girl. I hope not, because the tapes make her sound quite uncomfortable. Especially when you, oh, well, you remember."

"Don't put too much faith in your files," O'Hara flared. "I've already made one administrative change around here that'll interest you. I'm afraid you'll find you're now barred from access to the polygraph files."

Walking back to his office, Mother made himself a firm promise: if he was forced out of the agency, he would strike back. When he reached his office, he lit a Virginia Slim and began mentally constructing architectures of revenge. While he thought, he unconsciously folded a blank sheet of bond paper into a sharp-nosed plane. Then he opened his sixth-floor window. Mother's white airship circled twice and crashed at the feet of that bronze evocation of his college days—Nathan Hale.

4

A Talk about OSS

PAUL FITZSIMMONS'S PALMS were already wet. He was not sure why the agency had called him back to Langley, but he was afraid it was to be refluttered. Mother had warned him that might happen. If you failed the first time, they put you through the inquisition all over again.

"Welcome back," said Mother, reaching out to shake Paul's moist hand.

The Counterintelligence chief had come down to sign Paul into the Toy Factory. They walked side by side to the elevator.

"Why do you suppose they want to see me again?" asked Paul.

"Oh, I think your flutterer wanted to clear up a few things."

Paul's palms went even wetter. And he started breathing harder, as if he had been running.

"You mean I failed the test?"

"Not necessarily," Mother said. "I'll walk you over." The closer they came to the flutter offices, the dirtier

Paul felt. Marching past brightly colored doors, the novitiate had a sense that all his inner doors were black. Mother and Paul paused before a Kelly green portal.

"Call me when you're finished and I'll come get you," Mother said. "Good luck."

Entering the flutter chamber, Paul's eyes searched for microphones. He saw none, but he could feel them listening.

"I just wanted to go over a couple of things," said Anderson, the flutter man. "I'll ask you some of the same questions I asked you before. There're a few readings we want to double-check."

The flutterer strapped Paul back into the electric chair.

"Is your name Paul Fitzsimmons?"

"Yes."

"Are you currently a senior at Yale University?"

"Yes."

"Is your major English?"

"Yes."

"Are you writing your honors thesis on Ezra Pound?"

"Yes."

"Is it your intention to lie to me?"

"No."

"Are you wearing a ring on your little finger?"

"Yes."

"Thank you. That'll do."

"What?"

"I said, 'That'll do.' You're excused."

Mystified, Paul got up out of the flutter chair and went to call Mother. Moments later, the CI chief collected him and escorted him to the company cafeteria. Seated across a Formica tabletop from Mother, Paul sized up the company lunchroom.

"It's smaller than I expected," said Paul.

"Well," Mother admitted, "this isn't the whole cafeteria. The rest of it's on the other side of that wall." He nodded in that direction.

Paul looked confused.

"Schizophrenia is the rule around here," Mother said. "Our clandestine boys can eat on the other side of that partition—safe from prying eyes."

"Who eats on this side?"

"Visitors, Congressmen, applicants who haven't passed their flutter test yet."

"I see," Paul said, and then took a sip of his Coke. Looking up, he asked, "Do you have any idea what the problem was with my polygraph?"

"Not really."

"What do you mean?"

"Well, the problem may not be your flutter but your flutterer," Mother said. "He and I belong to different camps. You may have gotten hung up in company politics. I'm sorry."

"I don't understand. What camps?"

"I should warn you. The director and I aren't close. If you join my staff, as I hope you will, it won't endear you to the head man. But then, he won't be on top forever."

"Why aren't you close?" Paul asked, more concerned than ever about his flutter. He wondered what he had gotten himself into.

Mother said nothing.

Paul endured the silence poorly. He pinched his Coke straw, bent it into a Z and then tried to drink through it.

In an attempt to revive the conversation, Paul said, "What I meant was . . ."

"No, no," Mother said. "That's not the way to question anyone. When you ask somebody something, just wait it out 'til you get an answer. Don't ask again or ask something else. Just be patient. Let the silence work for you. Most people can't stand peace and quiet. They'll answer questions just to hear somebody talking." Mother sucked a Virginia Slim. "Want to try again?"

"Okay," Paul said, bending his straw around his finger, "Why aren't you and the director close?"

Once more, Mother was in no hurry to answer. Paul

tortured his straw as he fought back an impulse to try another question.

"Good," Mother said at last, but he still did not answer the question. He just offered more advice. "But you're still not quite on track. You shouldn't come straight out and ask what you want to know. It's too easy for people to sidestep your questions that way. What you should do is get people to tell you a story. Have them tell it from the beginning. That way they don't know what you're after so they don't know what to hide. Try again?"

"Sure," said Paul uncertainly. But he was not sure how to pull a story out of someone, so he asked, "How do I start?"

"There's an easy formula," Mother said. "Try asking a question that begins, 'When did you first . . . ?'"

Since this type of question suited Paul's broad-bored curiosity, he was happy to start at the beginning. He thought a moment and attempted, "When did you first meet O'Hara?"

"Good," Mother said. "That's the idea, but you're still too specific. You've told me you're interested in my relations with O'Hara, so I can guess you're probably really interested in our quarrel. It'd be better to ask how I first got into the business."

"Okay," said Paul. "How did you get into the business?"

"I joined the OSS during the war. I was stationed in Italy. When I arrived on the scene, the bottom of the boot had already been liberated, but the Germans still occupied the top. I was good at the language, so they sent me on missions behind the Nazi lines."

"What kind of missions?"

"Well, I guess the most memorable was when Wild Bill Donovan himself asked me to slip into Rome," Mother said. "As you know, he was the father of the OSS. I was stationed in Naples at the time. I borrowed the official municipal seal from a friend who worked at town hall. Then I tried to forge some identification papers, but I had trouble because my pre-

vious experience with printer's ink had been limited
to my efforts on behalf of *The Furies* at Yale."

Mother paused to light a Virginia Slim to sustain
himself.

Then he took up the story once again. Forgery was
not necessarily harder than publishing a literary magazine, but it proved messier. He botched attempt after
attempt. By the time he finally achieved a forgery on
which he was willing to stake his life, he resembled a
towel in a truck stop. The experience distressed him
because he hated untidiness. He consoled himself by
recalling that if he were not in the OSS then he might
well be in the infantry, in which case he might have
had occasion to get even dirtier.

Next he set out to find himself a proper costume. At
OSS headquarters, a four-story palazzo with ruined
gardens, he dug through a pile of mismatched secondhand Italian clothing. He held his nose with one hand
and sorted through the moldy garments with the other.
He finally selected a blue sharkskin suit which appeared
to be the class of the mongrel litter. After meticulously
cleaning the pockets, he then sprinkled them with a
few pinches of Italian tobacco. "I was always good
at details," Mother told Paul.

Smoking an Italian cigarette to help cover the odor
of his clothes, he was chauffeured to the airfield in an
old Lancia limousine. Climbing aboard an OSS B-25
light bomber, he was flown from Naples to Borgo Field
near Bastia in Corsica. Inside a hangar, he was offered
a look at the best collection of pinup girls in MEDTO.
"But I passed up the opportunity," Mother said. "I
thought it'd be inappropriate, considering my ultimate
destination was the Vatican."

A jeep carried him to the headquarters of Captain
Jacques Antoine, a gray-templed officer in the French
army, who ran espionage operations behind the German lines on the Italian mainland. The problem was
that Captain Antoine considered the OSS competition.
Theoretically he cooperated with the Americans, but
actually he helped them as little as possible. This was
standard operating procedure among the Allied secret

services: the French Central de Renseignements et
d'Action (BCRA), the British Special Operations
Executive (SOE), and the American Office of Strategic Services (OSS) conducted a war against one another within the larger war against the Nazis.

"Captain Antoine informed me that he was going to
put me ashore north of Rome, along with four of his
agents, on a sabotage mission," Mother said. "Then I
told him he was crazy." Somewhat condescendingly,
the young American officer informed the aging French
officer that elementary security demanded that agents
involved in different operations should not be exposed
to one another. What if the saboteurs were picked up
by the Germans? Under torture, they could compromise
his mission. The captain responded that if Kimball did
not want to go with the other agents, he could remain
on Corsica.

The four saboteurs, the French captain, and the
young American intelligence officer all boarded a boat
together and pushed off for Hitler's Italy. The voyage
continued late into the night. The young American
officer decided to pass the time checking his equipment. He hefted his 9-millimeter Beretta automatic,
counted his three hundred gold sovereigns, and un-
wrapped and examined the radio crystals, the reason
for his journey.

Ten miles from the enemy coast the engines were
slowed. The boat lapped along almost soundlessly for
the last several miles. They aimed for a deserted beach
midway between Orbetello and Tarquinia. A few hundred yards offshore they killed the engines altogether.
Kimball, the French captain, and the saboteurs lowered themselves into two yellow rubber rafts and rowed
cautiously toward shore. "It felt as if I were riding a
rubber duck in a giant bathtub," recalled Mother, with
a tight smile.

When they crunched onto the beach, they were met
by a single "bennie," as the Fifth Army called Italian
agents, the name dating from the Salerno landing, when
every Italian who was asked to do something said, *"Va
bene, va bene."*

"Hello, I am Topolino," the bennie said, identifying himself by his code name, which meant "Mickey Mouse." As they shook hands, he said, "I am a great admirer of your father. Please tell him when you see him."

"I was furious," Mother told Paul. "I was mad at the captain because he'd obviously identified me by my real name in his communication with the mainland. And I was mad at my father because he seemed to haunt me everywhere I went. I'd gone to a lonely beach in the middle of the night with Germans on all sides because I wanted to do something on my own. But Dad was waiting there to greet me on the sands, at midnight."

Mother digressed to tell Paul about his father, Mr. J. D. Kimball, soldier, impresario, spy: he had chased Pancho Villa with General Black Jack Pershing. During this campaign, he met a seventeen-year-old Mexican girl whom he married. The couple had settled in Boise, Idaho, where in 1917 they had a son whom they named Francis Xavier. J. D. Kimball was one of those great American entrepreneurs in the tradition of the steel magnates, the railroad barons, the textile moguls, the slave traders, but the product upon which his fortune was based was even more American than theirs. He was an executive with the National Cash Register Company. Unlike a Carnegie, however, J. D. Kimball had had to contend with a new and, he believed, un-American government agency: the Internal Revenue Service. His solution had been to leave the country. He had taken over National Cash Register's European operations and settled with his family in Milan. Later he moved his family to Rome, where they lived in a beautiful villa.

J. D. Kimball became the president of the American Chamber of Commerce in Italy. "That may seem as innocuous as leading a boy scout troop," Mother said, "but in Mussolini's Italy it was more like heading a gang of robbers." Under Il Duce's fascism, the country's economy was so controlled that the key to success was not winning over consumers, but winning over the government. With little competition allowed, Mussolini simply passed out concessions. As president of the American Chamber of Commerce, businessman J. D. Kimball had enjoyed a considerable advantage in dealing with the Italian government. His Chamber of Commerce high hat did his businessman's homburg a lot of good as he collected important licenses for the import of cash registers and got richer and richer. "I guess I did learn that much from my father," Mother said grudgingly. "I mean the importance of the two hats. Two hats that help each other. I suppose the Israeli desk's my chamber of commerce."

While the father was prospering in Italy, the son attended a public school in England named Malvern College, but he returned to Italy for summers. It was during one of these summers that he met Ezra Pound.

J. D. Kimball's son Francis Xavier had entered Yale as a member of the Class of 1941. The literary magazine *The Furies* was born during his sophomore year. He and his roommate edited it, and his roommate's aunt bought most of the subscriptions. Kimball even wrote a little poetry himself; his roommate wrote a lot more. When they were short of money, which was often, they paid their contributors with fine Italian cravats supplied by the Kimball haberdasher in Rome.

With the approach of war in Europe, J. D. Kimball had moved his family to New York. Upon graduation from Yale, his son entered Harvard Law School.

After Pearl Harbor, J. D. Kimball had joined yet another organization of influential Americans working abroad: the OSS. He was commissioned a major and assigned to the Italian campaign.

In 1943, Francis Xavier Kimball had left Harvard Law School to fight in the war. His father brought him into the OSS and had him assigned to Italy.

"My dad was a kind of den mother to the junior officers," Mother told Paul. "I believe you could say he was one of the most beloved men in the OSS. I'm afraid I was another story. The prevailing view was that I was a know-it-all college boy who was always telling people what they were doing wrong. I think I was usually right, but I was generally unpopular. I'm afraid the OSS boys loved the father and hated the son." He paused and then added, "Even O'Hara liked my father, but that was later."

"I promised this Topolino I'd remember him to my father," Mother told Paul, "but, of course, I did no such thing."

He soon learned that the bennie had come to guide the saboteurs on their mission. There was to be no one to guide him. Captain Antoine suggested Kimball try to make his way to a nearby "safe house." If the young OSS officer had not feared the German patrols more than he hated the captain, there would have been violence. Captain Antoine rowed away in one yellow raft, towing the other, while Kimball walked off alone through the woods, swearing.

When he finally located the house, Kimball found helpful agents who put him up for the night. The next morning he bribed the chauffeur of a limousine to drive him to Rome. After the exchange of twenty thousand lire, the driver opened the door of the long black car for Kimball. All during the trip, he kept his hand on the Beretta in his pocket because he did not trust the driver and because he was terrified of meeting a German roadblock. "But at the same time," Mother said, "I was afraid the car would hit a bump and I'd shoot myself in the groin."

They traveled east through Tuscania and Viterbo and then turned south toward Rome. Kimball was beginning to relax ever so slightly when a roadblock suddenly materialized in front of him. The chauffeur got out, handed over his papers, and with incredible sangfroid said, "I'm glad you stopped us. If I don't piss, I'll burst." While the chauffeur limped to the side of the road and began to urinate, Kimball had to use all his concentration to keep from doing the same thing in the back seat.

The door opened and a German helmet was thrust inside. Kimball handed over his forged papers and his bladder let go. He could feel the trousers of his blue sharkskin suit growing wet. He was afraid they would make him get out of the car. And then they would know, because innocent men do not piss in their pants.

The German handed back the forgeries; the chauffeur zipped up his fly and crawled back behind the wheel; and the limousine rolled on toward Rome. Like an incontinent schoolboy, Kimball was going home.

The OSS officer was delivered to a house near St. John Lateran, on the outskirts of the Eternal City. An hour later, a police car pulled up at the house to pick him up. The policeman behind the wheel was a member of the underground. "The safest way to cross German-occupied Rome was in a police car," Mother explained.

They drove beneath the windows of the Germans' Via Tasso prison, where suspected agents were tortured. Kimball had heard terrible stories about a bed of nails where men and women were stretched out naked as a steel bar was drawn across them. The American officer's skin started to itch and he pressed his own nails into his own flesh. He was happy to leave the prison behind.

The police car passed the Colosseum, a monument to a high-water mark of human cruelty, which the Germans had at last surpassed. The car proceeded on past the Victor Emmanuel Monument, the Pantheon, Castel Sant'Angelo, and finally parked near the wall of the Vatican.

Minutes later, Kimball was shown into a small library where rows of volumes were ranked behind glass doors. He took a seat in a gold-encrusted Louis XV chair and let his gaze roam over a tapestry depicting the washing of Jesus' feet, a gilded rococo desk, and a small silver cross bearing a Tom Thumb Christ.

The door to the left of the tapestry opened to admit Monsignor Giovanni Battista Montini. A year earlier, Montini had made an extraordinary proposal to Washington. He offered to provide the Americans with intelligence on bombing targets halfway around the world in Japan. The espionage would be gathered by the

Holy See in Tokyo. The OSS was being given the opportunity to recruit a whole network of long-robed, cross-bearing, Hail Marying spies. The American intelligence service and the pope's army were made for each other: both were secret societies, both had agents all over the world, both were pursuing religious callings.

"We were delighted to accept the offer," Mother told Paul. The Holy See in Tokyo sent information on Japanese bombing targets to Monsignor Montini at the Vatican. He in turn carried the intelligence to the Irish embassy in Rome. The information was then transported by diplomatic pouch to Dublin. In Dublin, the intelligence was picked up from the Irish Foreign Office and carried to London, where it was encoded and transmitted to OSS headquarters in Washington. The operational code name suggested that perhaps the Virgin Mary watched over the efforts of her holy spies. Mother said, "We called it the Vessel Project."

The only problem was the time consumed as the intelligence made its long journey dotted with rest stops. The OSS was convinced that a way had to be found to speed up, if not all messages, at least the emergency communications. They would be much happier if Montini had radio crystals tuned to a secret frequency, so he could broadcast urgent information to the OSS base in Naples.

The young intelligence officer presented the monsignor with the crystals he had brought. Montini thanked him and hoped his journey had not been unpleasant.

Mother told Paul: "I showed the monsignor how to use the crystals to send messages to base. I led him through the ritual of encoding. I taught him about frequencies. I explained how dangerous it was to send long messages because the Germans could use triangulation to trace his signal. I enjoyed the reversal of roles: holding the crystals in my hands, I felt I was teaching a disciple to perform some mysterious, twentieth-century sacrifice."

Pausing, chuckling to himself, lighting another Slim,

Mother added: "Before I left, the monsignor gave me his blessing. I felt as if I were being ordained into some sort of secret-world priesthood. And I really do suppose I thought I was going to save the world. So it seemed appropriate to me that my work should have brought me to such a holy place. My ministry was just beginning, and it seemed right for it to start there." Mother shrugged.

Thereafter, both the young American intelligence officer and the monsignor rose in their respective secretive organizations. When Rome was liberated, Francis X. Kimball was installed as the head of X2, the enigmatically named OSS counterintelligence department, in the Eternal City. In time, Montini did even better. The College of Cardinals installed him as the infallible father of all Catholicism.

"In his new position, his cryptonym became Paul VI," said Mother, with a note of satisfaction.

"Was O'Hara in Italy during the war?" asked Paul.

"No," Mother said, "he was with the Norwegian section. He was in charge of something called Operation Rype, but they should've called it Rotten. Everything went sour."

Mother took out a handkerchief, blew his nose, and refolded the cloth into a geometrically perfect square.

Then he continued: Things started to go wrong while O'Hara was still floating beneath his parachute over Norway's frozen Lake Jaevsjo. As he watched helplessly, his supplies plummeted past him and shattered on the ice below. The air crews had forgotten to hook up the static lines, so the parachutes attached to the provisions never opened. "O'Hara could've checked the lines," Mother told Paul, "but he didn't."

It got worse. Eight planes took off, but only four dropped their para-spies over the target. Three returned to England with their full loads. "One plane dropped its men in Sweden by mistake," Mother said.

"How could they do that?" Paul asked. "Norway's not a dot on a map—it's a whole country."

"Well, O'Hara tried to borrow RAF flight crews who

knew the terrain," Mother explained, "but the British wouldn't give them to him. So at the last minute he patched together pickup American crews. They'd never been over Norway in their lives."

It got worse still. The OSS made another attempt to fly men into Norway. All planes returned unsuccessful but one. It crashed, killing six men. Then a third attempt was made. Again none of the aircraft completed their missions. One plane slammed into a mountain a few kilometers from where O'Hara was waiting. Four men were killed.

Meanwhile O'Hara, known to the Norwegian underground only as Number 95, was playing a deadly game of boy scouts. Number 95's band of ski spies blew up bridges on the Nordland Railroad, tore up miles of tracks, and ambushed German patrols. But without adequate supplies, Operation Rype never really matured into the potent weapon it was designed to be. The scout was not prepared.

"The OSS finally managed to drop reinforcements to O'Hara the day the Germans surrendered," Mother said. "From start to finish, it was one of the most botched-up operations ever run. Of course, it wasn't all O'Hara's fault. He had lots of help. But can you believe the man who ran Rype—or rather Over-Rype—is now running the company?"

"Has he improved with age?" Paul asked.

"No, of course not," Mother said, "he hasn't changed. None of us ever do. He's still the same overgrown boy scout he always was."

"I didn't meet O'Hara until after the war," Mother continued. "We were introduced to each other at an awards ceremony in nineteen forty-five. We were both decorated. As I recall, I won more ribbons than he did, but I dare say he remembers it the other way 'round."

"How long was it before the trouble started?" asked Paul.

"Too explicit," Mother said. "You should ask something neutral like, 'What was the next time you came in contact with O'Hara?' "

"Well?"

"After the war," Mother said, "we both wanted to work for Wild Bill Donovan's Wall Street law firm. It seemed very important at the time. Because the father of the OSS had become a father figure to us all. I didn't get the job, but O'Hara did. In fact, O'Hara became Donovan's protégé. I don't suppose that endeared him to me. Nobody likes favorites."

After lunch, Mother took Paul back to the Counterintelligence Department. A message was waiting for them there. Paul was to call the flutter people. When he did, he was informed that he would have to take the polygraph a third time. He groaned.

Moments later Paul found himself back in a room full of gadgets, talking to his flutterer.

"We're still having the same problem," Anderson said. "Namely, your reaction to my asking if you're wearing a ring on your little finger. The question's trivial, but your answer shows significant stress. Do you have any idea why we're getting such an unusual reading?"

Anderson did not say so, but the stress had shown up not on the polygraph but on the psychological stress evaluator, which graphed the strain in Paul's voice.

Paul silently rehearsed his answer before speaking it aloud.

"A close friend at Yale gave me the ring," he said at last. "Actually, we exchanged rings. My hand's bigger than his so I have to wear his ring on my little finger."

"You say he's a close friend," Anderson said. "How close?"

"There wasn't anything sexual between us, if that's what you mean." Paul knew that was exactly what Anderson meant. He instinctively kept his voice down because he sensed a tape recorder turning. "Nothing like that at all."

"Then why the reaction to the question about his ring?"

"Well, some people at school thought there was

something between us. And I think, well, I know, he wanted there to be something. But there wasn't."

"You mean he made a pass at you?"

"Yes."

"Which you rejected?"

"Yes."

Paul was strapped back into the flutter gear.

"Did you exchange rings with a friend at school?"

"Yes."

"A male friend?"

"Yes."

"Did you ever perform a homosexual act with that friend?"

"No."

When Paul was unstrapped, he returned to the Counterintelligence Department, where he waited in an outer office for two hours.

Then Mother came out and said, "Welcome aboard."

The chief of Counterintelligence took Paul up to the Miscellaneous Projects office for a celebration drink.

5

Intimations of War

MARK HARRINGTON, a furious 47, was shaken by the alarm. It was 1:30 A.M. Time to go to work.

Getting out of bed on this Thursday "morning" early in June, Harrington slouched angrily into his Reston, Virginia, bathroom. He had been angry for a very long time. Part of his anger had to do with his having to get up so early every morning to do his job, but most of it had to do with his having been born too late ever to land one of the top jobs at the agency. Harrington was born in 1926, which meant that he did not turn eighteen until 1944, which meant that he was still in boot camp when first the Germans and then the Japanese surrendered. Harrington had not only missed the war, but more important, he had missed serving in the Office of Strategic Services. The OSS had closed shop after the war, but OSS alumni had dominated the Central Intelligence Agency ever since its founding in 1947. Once having missed service in the OSS, an intelligence officer was almost certainly doomed forever to the second echelon of the business. One could no more appeal this verdict than one could repeal history. The agency's caste system was based, like other caste systems, on birth, but it looked not only to your pedigree, it also looked to your date of birth. And to Mark Harrington, at least, that seemed the cruelest caste system of all.

Harrington honestly believed that if he had been born three years, or two years, or even eighteen months earlier, then he would never have grown disillusioned and would never have gone to work for the other side.

While his wife and children slept, Harrington made himself breakfast. At a quarter to three he left for the office. At least he beat the rush hour.

At exactly 3 A.M., Mark Harrington, product of Yale, twenty-three-year veteran of the Central Intelligence Agency, Communist spy, walked into his Langley office to begin reading the overnight cables. Harrington was a member of a team which reported every morning at that hour to prepare the President's Intelligence Checklist, or PICKLE. It had to be ready by 6 A.M. so it could be on the President's desk at the start of his day.

Morale on the checklist team was not high, largely because its members all suspected that they were coming to work at 3 A.M. day in and day out for almost nothing. In the good old days, Jack Kennedy and later Lyndon Johnson had carefully studied the PICKLE, but Richard Nixon and his foreign policy adviser had lost interest in it and had delegated the job of reading it to the National Security Council staff. Although Harrington was working for the other side, he still hated to see the agency slighted. He regretted his vote for Nixon.

Going over the cables, Harrington came across one which he lingered over longer than he did with most others. It was an update on Britain's latest political/sex scandal. Late one night at a party, a very married MP's girlfriend had suddenly blurted out, "Politicians bore me—I want to make love to a horse." The MP and his date then made their way from stable to stable but found them all closed, so they finally rented a hansom cab. Harrington knew that under the previous administration he would have included this adventure in the President's checklist of world crises, because Johnson appreciated that kind of intelligence. The PICKLE might just as well have been just that if a President paid no attention to it. The agency had learned that by intercutting sex with world crises it could get Johnson's attention, but when it had tried the same technique on Nixon it had offended his puritanical nature. Harrington discarded the cable about the MP and the animal lover.

Working on the PICKLE team was a lot like working for a newspaper. The day began in a leisurely fashion, but as the deadline approached everyone scrambled. Harrington tried to type faster, but his haste simply meant his fingers often fell between rather than on the keys. The pacing of his work—slow, then faster and faster—reminded him of making love, something he rarely did now that he worked this graveyard shift.

When the PICKLE was properly cured, a courier carried it to the White House, entering at the West Gate. And Harrington took a break to relax, but he couldn't really. All morning he had been serving the CIA. Now, as Washington came awake, his thoughts turned to serving the KGB. His Soviet case officer had asked him to deliver the plans for America's new M-60 tank. He wasn't exactly sure where to start looking, but he almost always felt that way with every assignment they gave him, so he wasn't really all that worried.

Harrington picked up a telephone and called a friend at the Pentagon.

Ernest O'Hara still felt a little like an imposter running these meetings, and he suspected that this one was going to be the worst yet. He had not had time to get used to his new title: it still felt more like a cover than something that was really his. .

Since it was Thursday, the U.S. Intelligence Board (USIB) would be assembling soon for their regular weekly session. It had always been his style to blend colorlessly into his paperwork. Sitting at the head of the table with so many important eyes on him, he felt like a bureaucratic guerrilla fighter who had been flushed from the cover of his desk, his reports, his memos, and his closed door.

The first to arrive were the military men: the head of the Pentagon's Defense Intelligence Agency (DIA), followed by the chiefs of the Office of Naval Intelligence (ONI), Air Force Intelligence (A-2), and finally Army Intelligence (G-2), the oldest of the secret services, dating back to World War I.

Then came the head of the National Security Agency (NSA) . . . then the head of the State Department's Bureau of Intelligence Research (INR) . . . then the head of the Atomic Energy Commission (AEC) . . . and lastly a representative of the Federal Bureau of Investigation (FBI).

They all took their places around a long table in a seventh-floor conference room. Most of them had brought with them the classified agenda circulated to them several days earlier by the USIB secretariat.

As the first item of business, Director O'Hara called for the approval of the minutes of the previous Thursday's meeting. The board members voted their assent even though they knew the minutes were incomplete. The record was kept intentionally so in the interest of security.

O'Hara moved the meeting along to the next item on the secret agenda: the Watch Report, prepared earlier in the week by a USIB committee whose job it was to predict the outbreak of war anywhere in the world.

The Watch Report said: War between the U.S. and the U.S.S.R. did not appear to be imminent that week. However, the Russians had moved a new division up to the Chinese border. Moreover, the Russians had just tested a new MIRV missile.

The North Vietnamese continued to infiltrate men and materiel into South Vietnam in defiance of the Paris peace accords. Increased fighting could be expected, but an all-out offensive appeared unlikely that summer.

The most troubling news: The chances of war "coming soon" in the Middle East were "better than even." This assessment was based primarily on the greatly increased flow of arms from the Soviet Union into the Arab countries. Egypt and Syria had recently received a large shipment of Russia's new T-62 tanks. Moscow had also promised to provide Syria with a complete air defense system, including SAM missiles and forty MiG-21 fighters. In all, the Russians had shipped the Syrians $185 million worth of arms in 1973, which compared alarmingly with 1972, when the total for the whole year had been only $150 million. Syria and Egypt did not seem to be preparing themselves for peace.

"Discussion?" Director O'Hara asked.

Normally the USIB spent only about thirty seconds discussing the Watch Report, since the various intelligence chiefs assumed that if a war were really imminent they would hear about it before it showed up in any weekly report. However, since the Middle East was such a sensitive area in so many ways, the USIB spent a full three minutes discussing the possibility of a war there.

O'Hara recognized the head of State's INR, an agency without agents of its own, which confined itself to analyzing the product of other agencies. In that sense, INR was like the Nobel laureates, Watson and Crick, who had worked out the structure of DNA by interpreting other people's data.

The INR chief reminded the board that the previous month his agency had reported "a forty-five percent chance" of a new Arab-Israeli war.

"Contrary to our previous view," he went on to say, "we think the chances are now better than even."

O'Hara agreed.

The other intelligence chiefs waffled.

O'Hara moved the meeting along to the special items placed on the agenda by the various members of the board. The head of Army G-2 requested permission to provide the Bolivian army with American eavesdropping devices. A USIB subcommittee had already turned down the request, but G-2 had a right to appeal that decision to the USIB itself. The board voted not to share U.S. listening machines with the Bolivians. The Air Force A-2 requested permission to retarget one of its satellites. The board voted its approval of the retargeting.

Then the discussion became more sensitive. The USIB went into executive session. All staff left the room. No minutes at all were kept.

The chief of the Office of Naval Intelligence requested permission to have the *Glomar Explorer* manned by a navy crew. Back in the late sixties when Operation Jennifer was in the planning stages, before there even was such a ship, the navy had tried hard to win the project for itself. The navy had argued that it knew more about submarines than anyone else, and if anyone could raise a Russian sub, it could. But the navy had been overruled at the highest level, and Project Jennifer had been given to the Central Intelligence Agency. So the CIA had contracted with Howard Hughes to build the *Glomar,* which was scheduled to begin its shakedown cruises that summer. Having missed out on the construction phase of the operation, the navy still hoped to secure a part of the operational phase. Now that the CIA had built the *Glomar,* the navy wanted to run it.

As the ONI man began his speech, O'Hara's anger rose. He felt his face grow pale, which made him even madder, because he knew he was transparent. He hated knowing everyone could read his emotions.

"I believe," argued the navy man, "that it would be extremely shortsighted to ignore our expertise." He went on and on in praise of his service's qualifications for a role in Jennifer.

O'Hara thought the plan sounded like piracy, but he was not a man to put anger into words. (His wife often accused him of being "passive-aggressive.")

O'Hara said only, "Now isn't the time to reopen a decision made years ago."

The ONI man said, "I disagree. I feel you underestimate the contribution the navy could make. After all, we've had considerable success with the *Seaprobe*. In fact, some people believe the *Seaprobe* would've been a better choice to raise the sub than the *Glomar*."

"We've been all over this before," said O'Hara.

Mention of the *Seaprobe* made O'Hara feel defensive. When a U.S. submarine named the *Thresher* sank in the 1960s, Alcoa Aluminum had decided to build a ship which would have the capacity to raise a sunken sub. The Alcoa *Seaprobe,* constructed entirely of aluminum as a showcase for the company's product, was completed in 1972. The navy was always hinting that if the *Seaprobe* had been assigned the job of raising the Russian submarine, the project would already have been completed: the Soviet sub would already be in American hands.

"I know we've been over it," the ONI man said. "Still, I believe Jennifer could make use of the navy's experience. We know the Pacific better than anyone."

O'Hara said, "The CIA is not without seagoing experience. This won't be our first nautical operation."

"I know," the ONI man said. "The one that comes to mind is the Bay of Pigs."

The chauffeur-driven Mercedes dropped Mother in front of what looked like an elegant jail. All of the windows on all four floors were covered with heavy grating. The windows on the lower floors displayed not only gratings, but also bars which formed six-pointed stars.

The large brown building with its Spanish-tiled roof, decorative balconies, and iron door stood at the corner of R and Twenty-second Streets, N.W. Four Executive Protection Service policemen in black uniforms kept watch over the entrance.

It was a neighborhood of embassies. Across the street stood the Brazilian embassy, with fewer bars, and a few doors beyond stood the embassy of the Dominican Republic, with almost none. Mother looked up at the Israeli embassy and saw the curtains of a window on the top floor open and close, open and close, open and close. He wondered to whom they were signaling.

Mother walked up the steps, opened the iron door, and entered a small entranceway. With the iron door behind him and a locked door in front of him, as if in a submarine airlock, he pressed a button and spoke into a small box. When he heard the terrible buzz of the magnetic lock disengaging, he pushed the door open and walked inside. Mother was shown to the office of an under secretary who was actually a Mossad intelligence officer: Menachem Ginzburg.

Mother handed him the Watch Report. He did so not only because he was a friend of the Israeli intelligence officer and of Israel itself, but also because the United States has an intelligence agreement with the Jewish state. Although this agreement, like many others made by the agency, is in effect a treaty, it has never been submitted to the U.S. Senate for approval.

Ginzburg had some information for Mother, too, some of which the CIA man already knew, some of which he didn't, but all of which he pretended to know.

"Our Arab friends are traveling almost as much as your friend in the White House," Ginzburg said.

"What friend?" Mother said nervously, wondering if somehow the Israeli had learned about Ladyslipper.

"The President's foreign policy adviser," Ginzburg teased.

"Oh, *that* friend."

"Anyway," Ginzburg said, getting serious, "on May ninth we observed Ahmed Ismail in Damascus." He meant the Egyptian war minister.

"That's right."

"Then, on May nineteenth, Sadat showed up in Damascus."

"Yes."

"Then, on June sixth, we monitored a Syrian military delegation traveling to Cairo."

"Uh-huh."

"Then, on June twelfth, Sadat went back to Damascus."

"That's right."

"Well, what does it mean?"

"They're planning something."

"Well, yes, but what?"

"I'm not sure."

"All right, then what're you planning, Mother? I hear you're resigning. I'd hate to have to break in a new man in the middle of . . . well, in the middle of whatever it is Sadat's up to."

There was a long silence, Mother's specialty, as he fished in his suit pocket for his Virginia Slims. O'Hara had obviously been circulating the word that Mother was on the way out. Mother knew that such a rumor could easily take on a momentum of its own because it would tend to undermine him with the people he worked with. The Israelis had always refused to work with anyone else at the agency, but once they were convinced he was leaving, they would certainly begin shopping around for another contact. Although Mother had no intention of resigning, he nonetheless felt a little like a lame duck.

"No," Mother said at last, "I'm not leaving. I'd never leave in the middle of a crisis."

Mother felt strange being so happy about the prospect of continuing trouble in the Middle East. For he suspected that even O'Hara would hesitate to fire him so long as a new Arab-Israeli war seemed likely. The Israelis had been Mother's ally for thirty years, but now, in a curious reversal, the Arabs had become his ally. The Israelis could no longer help him, but so long as the Arabs remained bellicose, he felt his job was relatively secure.

"I plan to be around for some time," Mother said. "I wonder how these rumors get started."

That evening at seven, Mark Harrington was just getting into bed when his telephone rang. It was the duty officer at the Pentagon. He said a problem had come up, something having to do with Vietnam. He wasn't quite sure what it was all about, but he asked Harrington to report to the National Military Command Center.

Wondering if the bombing was about to start again, Harrington dressed hurriedly and rushed out to the car. Once he reached the George Washington Memorial Parkway, he speeded up to ninety miles per hour. His wheels squealed on the exit ramp. He wound his way through a rat's maze of parking lots, pulled into a slot, locked the car, and trotted toward the Pentagon. It was about time they had some action.

When he reached the command center, Harrington was led to an office where two generals were arguing. He entered and introduced himself.

One of the generals asked, "What time is it in Hanoi?"

Harrington paused for a moment to do the arithmetic. "Ten to eight in the morning," Harrington said.

"I told you so," one general said.

"Are you goddamn sure?" the other general asked.

"Of course," Harrington said, "you see, you add thirteen hours to Washington time, then subtract half an hour."

"Subtract half an hour?" asked the second general.

"Right," Harrington said. "The North Vietnamese refuse to recognize the same time as the South Vietnamese, so they set their clocks back half an hour."

"Okay," the second general said, "that's that. Thanks for the help."

"Well, what's up?" Harrington wanted to know.

"Nothing," the first general said. "We just wanted to update the VIP travel board in the situation room. I noticed we were carrying Hanoi and Saigon times as the same. I asked Joe about it and we got into an argument. We thought we'd have you boys settle it. Thanks."

The crisis was over.

Since Harrington was already in the building, he decided to snoop around a little to see what he could find out about those tanks. Moments later he was reading the bids submitted by all the arms manufacturers who had hoped to build the M-60. The bids included specifications. He took notes with a felt-tipped pen. He loved the way it skated so smoothly across the page. If he should ever have to defect, he wondered whether he would be able to get felt-tipped pens in Russia.

6

Company Love

MOTHER STOOD before the class looking professorial.
If one had not known otherwise, one might have imagined that he had acquired his permanently curled backbone from decades of poring over Milton. He felt so at home in his role as a pedagogue that he sometimes wondered what might have happened had he chosen a career in academia. Mother had come to a big blue building in Arlington to deliver a guest lecture to a class of future intelligence officers who were enrolled in a three-month introductory course. The school had a colorful name: Blue U.

"To understand the CIA," Mother told the class, "you must first understand the OSS."

Mother was so sensitive about giving away secrets, even to future intelligence officers, that he preferred to talk about ancient history.

"And to understand the OSS," Mother continued, his eyes meeting the eyes of Paul Fitzsimmons, "you must understand the man who created it, William Joseph 'Wild Bill' Donovan. He was a remarkable man."

A young woman in the front row crossed her legs, momentarily disconcerting Mother. He could never quite get used to the increasing number of women at Blue U—just as he could never quite accept the fact that Yale had gone coed.

"No matter how unorthodox the idea," Mother resumed, "Donovan would listen to it. Someone wanted to try using phosphorescent foxes. Donovan said, 'Try it.' Someone else wanted to try using incendiary bats. Donovan said, 'Try it.' "

Like Mother, Paul Fitzsimmons found the female presence in the classroom distracting. But it was not the abundance of womanhood that bothered him. It was one woman in particular.

Paul had met her two weeks earlier on a tennis court in Georgetown when a friend called and asked if he would be a fourth in doubles. All four players turned out to be apprentice spies. At first Paul was paired with a young woman who played even worse than he did, while across the net were two killers. Paul stroked even more poorly than usual because he was intimidated not only by the forehand but also by the beauty of the woman across the barrier. Her name was Frances Fisher. She was so lovely, crouching there in the distance, that every time he tried to yell "Nice shot," the words caught in his throat. He would end up coughing.

Frances and her partner beat Paul and his partner so badly that they decided to switch partners. Paul was terrified. If Frances's beauty half paralyzed him from across the net, he was sure he would be totally paralyzed with her on his side. He wouldn't even be able to swing his racket.

But as she came closer he felt better. Her strawberry-blond hair turned to muddy-river blond, her nose changed from aristocratic to too long. Paul decided that he was better-looking than Frances—and that he was going to be able to swing his racket.

Paul played better with Frances on his side of the net, but he was still worse than she was. Frances told Paul that she had been the captain of the Princeton tennis team. Paul admitted that he hadn't played any sports at Yale. Frances thought Paul got better-looking the closer he came, but that wasn't why she liked him. She liked him for his ineptness.

In the days that followed, Paul and Frances's relationship traveled on its stomach. They went out to dinner together almost every night. She would drive her mustard-yellow Datsun 240Z—he didn't have a car—over to his apartment across the street from Western High School, the closest Georgetown came to a low-rent district. She would pick him up and they would drive to a restaurant. He liked to think he was liberated and yet it bothered him that she drove. He felt out of control.

They had shared meals at a wide variety of Washington's cheaper restaurants: Paul, the English major, chose places with names like Beowulf and Childe Harold. Frances, the political science major, picked out establishments with names like Tammany Hall and the Hawk and Dove.

Paul soon realized that although he had the edge in looks, he was nonetheless more interested in Frances than she was in him. Sometimes he thought he was infatuated not so much with her as he was with her father, Robert Fisher, a man he would never meet. Paul had learned about Frances's father not from her but from Mother, who explained that Robert Fisher had been head of Clandestine Services until he had a nervous breakdown. One afternoon, his wife found him in a bedroom closet with a revolver in his hand and a bullet in his head.

Paul was fascinated by Frances's father—by his career and by his death. During idle moments, Paul's mind would often wander to that closet, where his thoughts would thrash about among the questions stored there: what had driven Robert Fisher to take his own life? Was it the agency? Was there some flaw in the secret world which propelled people toward self-destruction? Could it happen to him? Try as he might to fight free of this claustrophobic obsession, he could not. Paul was frightened by the way Robert Fisher's career had ended, and yet he was drawn to Fisher's success. The young intelligence officer desperately wanted the rewards without the consequences. He wanted to be like Fisher, up to a point. He hoped to follow in his footsteps, but to stop at the closet door.

Since Paul was young and ambitious, he knew he needed help—needed mentors, needed models. This need had drawn him to Mother, but it had also drawn him to Frances Fisher, the only child of a masterspy whom many in the company regarded as a martyr. In a sense, Paul fell in love with Frances's father before he fell in love with Frances.

Paul and Frances's conversation was always extraordinarily impersonal. They talked about their work, about the intelligence business, about politics. Occasionally Paul would try to coax Frances into talking about her father, but she wouldn't. About the most intimate thing they ever said to each other was: "Do you believe the Cold War is really over?"

After dinner, Frances would drive Paul back to his apartment and drop him off. He would try to persuade her to come in, but she would not even get out of the car. Since she was in the driver's seat, he knew, and she knew, that she could do whatever she wanted. And she wanted to go home. They had never made love.

Alone in his apartment, Paul would get furious and start talking to himself: I'll never see her again. I'll teach her a lesson. But what lesson? So he would change his mind. They would have dinner again and she would drop him off again. Once he stood on the corner in the rain and watched her taillights slowly vanish.

Paul was having a hard time concentrating on Mother's lecture. Not only was he trying to decide where to take Frances for dinner, he was also trying to figure out if he could afford to buy a car. Making an effort, Paul refocused his attention.

"I suppose the bizarrest scheme the OSS ever came up with was one I call Operation Porn," Mother was saying. "A group of our psychoanalysts produced a psychological profile of Adolf Hitler, predicting he'd go insane if exposed to hard-core pornography. The OSS decided to bomb the Führer with dirty pictures. A fine library of the choicest pornography was assembled. But the operation came to a disappointing end because the army air corps didn't have the OSS's breadth of vision. The airmen refused to drop the porn and even went so far as to suggest that no one would ever have to drive the OSS crazy because it already was. I suppose those dirty pictures are still in the file somewhere, marked TOP SECRET or EYES ONLY."

When Mother looked up to see if his story was properly appreciated, he was disappointed. Almost everyone was smiling, but one student was not: Paul. He was staring at another student, a woman.

After the lecture, Paul introduced his girlfriend Frances to Mother Francis. He had long looked forward to bringing his two heroes together.

Mother said, "You resemble your father." His voice did not betray the twinge of jealousy he felt at facing this rival for Paul's affections.

Paul and Frances, whose Blue U life was so sedentary, decided they needed some exercise before dinner. They climbed into Frances's car and she drove to the Arlington Y. After a quick change, they squeezed through a tiny door only 3½ feet high into a squash court. It was like walking into a white closet.

The attractive feature of squash, so far as Paul was concerned, was that it allowed him to play, as it were, on the same side of the net as Frances. Standing side by side, armed with small rackets, they smashed a hard black ball into the far wall. Frances, who was very competitive, quickly took the lead.

"What did you think of Mother?" Paul puffed between points.

"Not much," said Frances, who was in better shape. "He's just a bag of old stories."

"What did your father think of him?"

"He didn't much like him."

"Why?"

"I don't know," Frances said, evasively. "He never said. I don't think your friend is very popular. He's always spying on people."

Frances won the first game largely by playing to Paul's awkward backhand. With mounting frustration, he would bend down time after time to try to dig the ball out of the backhand corner, but the ball rarely made it to the far wall. The final score was 15 to 11.

Paul won the second game by simply overpowering Frances. She might have better strokes, but he was still stronger. The game went to a tiebreaker, but he pulled it out.

During the third game Paul became slightly disoriented. Exhausted, trapped in a white closet, he was going snow-blind. With a blizzard before his eyes, he staggered about in search of the black ball until the ball found him. Frances hit a forehand slam which Paul did not see coming. When the ball crashed into his left eye, he dropped his racket.

"I'm sorry," Frances said.

"Let's sit down a moment," Paul said.

And they both laughed, although Paul's heart did not really seem to be in it. They sank to the floor and leaned back against a wall. Frances said a few more times that she was sorry.

"You owe me one," Paul said.

"I guess I do."

"Then answer me a question."

"Okay."

"Why did you join the company?"

He had asked Frances a number of times before, but she had always changed the subject. This time she didn't.

"For the reason you think," she said. "Because of my father. I always admired him. I always wanted to be like him. If my father'd been a pitcher, I'd probably have wanted to be a baseball player."

"You're right. That is what I thought."

"But it's probably more complicated than that. Maybe I wanted, I don't know, to rehabilitate his memory. Somehow make up for his suicide. Does that make sense?"

"Yes."

"Or maybe I thought that if I joined the agency I might find out why he wanted to kill himself . . . why he died. But I hate to talk about myself. Let's talk about you. Why'd you sign up?"

"Mother," Paul said. "Not *my* mother, but Mother. He recruited me."

"Why? What's so special about you?"

Paul explained about Ezra Pound.

"Once you met Mother," Frances said, "how'd he persuade you to join up?"

"The closer I got to graduation," Paul said, rubbing his injury, "the less I wanted to be an academic. I'd joined the English Department because I believed in literature the same way I joined the seminary because I believed in God. I guess I lost my faith."

"And Mother offered you an alternative."

"He offered me an alternative to teaching, and I suppose I offered him an alternative to his son."

"What's the matter with his son?"

"He went to Vietnam right out of prep school," Paul said. "When he came back, he wasn't just against the war, he was against the whole U.S. government. And he sees his father as a symbol of that government."

"Where is he now?"

"Berkeley."

When they got to their feet, Paul won the third game, but he suspected Frances might have let him, to atone for hitting him.

Over hamburgers at Clyde's a half-hour later, Paul asked if he could watch television at Frances's apartment that evening. He pointed out that NET was doing a same-day rebroadcast of the Watergate hearings every evening. He also pointed out that his own television had recently been stolen.

Frances suspected Paul wanted more than the Watergate hearings, but she said all right, he could come

over. They split the check and they drove to her apartment on N Street in Georgetown. She lived down the
street from the house where her father had died and
where her mother still lived.

Inside Frances's apartment, which occupied the
second floor of a brownstone, they turned on the television and sat down side by side on the sofa. Paul
decided to do what Mother would have done: exercise
patience.

When the color picture came on, John Dean appeared, reading in a monotone from his prepared statement. Fifteen minutes passed, then half an hour. John
Dean did not seem to be saying very much, and Paul
definitely was not doing very much. After forty-five
minutes, however, all that began to change.

Dean: ". . . I told the President about the fact that
there was no money to pay these individuals to meet
their demands. He asked me how much it would cost.
I told him that I could only make an estimate that it
might be as high as one million dollars or more. He
told me that that was no problem . . ."

Paul and Frances were kissing. He still faced the
TV, but she had turned around so that her back was to
it. They had never kissed like this before.

Encouraged, Paul took hold of the zipper on the
back of Frances's dress and started pulling down very
slowly. He kept waiting for her to protest, but her lips
never left his. By the time Paul had the dress completely unzipped he was lightheaded with surprise and de-
light. He thought about saying something about the end
of the cover-up but decided not to press his luck, telling himself silence was sometimes the better part
of wit.

Dean: ". . . The conversation then turned back to
a question from the President regarding the money that
was being paid to the defendants. He asked me how
this was done. I told him I didn't know much about it
other than the fact that the money was laundered so it
could not be traced and then there were secret de-
liveries. I told him I was learning about things I had
never known before, but the next time I would cer-

tainly be more knowledgeable. This comment got a laugh out of Haldeman . . ."

Paul was also pushing forward into new frontiers. He timidly unhooked Frances's bra and then ran his hands up and down her bare back. She shivered. He wondered if she were cold.

Dean: ". . . What I hoped to do in this conversation was to have the President tell me that we had to end the matter—now . . ."

Paul tried to ease Frances's arms out of her dress, but this time she stopped him. She did so by simply spreading her arms, making it impossible to take her dress off without ripping it off. Paul felt a momentary flash of anger as though he had just been dropped off in the rain.

Dean: ". . . Accordingly, I gave considerable thought to how I would present this situation to the President and try to make as dramatic a presentation as I could to tell him how serious I thought the situation was that the cover-up not continue . . ."

Paul tried to force Frances's arms down so that he could pull her dress over them, but she would not relent.

Dean: ". . . I began by telling the President that there was a cancer growing on the presidency and that if the cancer were not removed that the President himself would be killed by it. I also told him that it was important that this cancer be removed immediately because it was growing more deadly every day . . ."

Paul felt a swelling anger. He wanted either to rip Frances's clothes off or to dump her onto the floor and storm out of the apartment. He did neither.

"I can't stand it," Paul said through clenched teeth.

"Yes, you can," Frances said.

Dean: ". . . After I finished, I realized that I had not really made the President understand . . . The meeting . . . was a tremendous disappointment to me because it was quite clear that the cover-up as far as the White House was concerned was going to continue . . ."

Frances drove Paul home.

The next morning Paul's telephone rang. Frances wanted to know if he would like a ride to school. This was the first time she had offered; Paul normally took the bus. When Frances honked, Paul locked his apartment, slipped in beside her, and yawned. He had tossed all night.

"You've got a black eye," said Frances.

"I know. Thanks."

At Blue U they endured another day of classes. During a lecture on agency cryptonyms, Paul was attacked by an especially severe yawning fit. His hand shuttled back and forth between his mouth and his eye. He was sensitive about his shiner. The instructor told the class that all U.S. government agencies had code names beginning with the letters *OD*. Sleepily, Paul made notes in his looseleaf:

    ODYOKE—the entire U.S. government
    ODACID—the Department of State
    ODEARL—the Department of Defense
    ODOATH—the Navy
    ODENVY—the FBI

The lecturer said all components of the Central Intelligence Agency had cryptonyms which began with *KU*.

    KUBARK—the entire CIA
    KUDOVE—the Clandestine Services
    KUTUBE—the Foreign Intelligence Staff
    KUCAGE—the Psychological and Paramilitary Staff
    KUDESK—the Counterintelligence Department

As the day progressed, Paul and Frances attended classes on Russian communism and Chinese communism and the differences between the two. They sat through history courses and an educational movie made by CBS. In a class which could have been called CIA Life, Paul came wide awake when the instructor said KUBARK did not discourage love affairs between company employees. For an intra-agency affair was considered a smaller security risk than an extra-agency affair. It was better to be penetrated by a colleague than an enemy agent.

The day ended with a classroom exercise: the student spooks were instructed to divide up into groups. Once divided, the groups were told to form themselves into Communist cells. They were supposed to try to think like Communists. They were supposed to get inside a Communist's head. It was a sophisticated game. Paul and Frances were in the same group. They both liked that. It gave them both a warm, conspiratorial feeling.

After school they had dinner together at the Peking on Fifteenth Street. Frances invited Paul to watch the Watergate hearings at her apartment. He suddenly wasn't sleepy anymore.

Sam Dash, the committee's majority counsel, was questioning John Dean, which meant that the witness spent most of his time listening. Occasionally, however, Dean got to talk.

Dash: "Are you aware of any other records of the content of these meetings which are the focus of your statement?"

Dean: "I was told by the government prosecutors that the President had taped a conversation between himself and me . . ."

This time Paul didn't try anything. He and Frances sat side by side but as inert to one another as if they were still in class at Blue U. Paul had had another talk with himself the night before and decided to stop torturing himself. He told himself that it was not Frances who interested him, it was her father. And he certainly did not want to go to bed with Mr. Fisher.

Now Fred Thompson, the minority counsel, took over the interrogation. At least his questions, although no smarter, were shorter.

Thompson: "What had been your professional relationship with Mr. Mitchell while you were at the Justice Department?"

Dean: "I had a very—I would have to say it was sort of a father-son relationship in many ways . . ."

Frances said, "Like you and Mother."

Paul said, "Maybe."

The hearings went on and on late into the night. It was almost 2 A.M. when NET finally signed off. Paul and Frances were both red-eyed and exhausted.

"I don't want to drive you home," said Frances. "Do you want to stay over?"

"Sure." He couldn't believe it. He was finally going to make love to the legendary Fisher's daughter. And, at last, she was seducing him.

Frances headed in the direction of her bedroom and Paul followed, imagining, as he did so, what it would be like to undress a hero's little girl. He never got a chance to find out. Before he could touch her, she slipped out of her dress and pantyhose and crawled into bed. She was still wearing her panties and bra.

Paul took off his suit and hung it on a chair. He took off his socks and laid them over his shoes. Then he stopped. He was undecided as to what to do next. He could emulate Frances and keep his underwear on. Or he could come to bed naked. He made up his mind and then felt himself blush as he headed for cover.

"Do you always sleep dressed like this?" Paul asked.

"Yes," Frances lied, turning her back toward him.

Paul reached over and unhooked her bra. The anticipated protest never came. He slipped the bra off and tossed it on the floor. Then he reached down and removed her panties. He had not been this excited in a long, long time.

"You can only stay if you don't wiggle," Frances announced.

Paul reached around Frances and took hold of her left breast.

"I told you not to wiggle," Frances said, removing his hand.

Paul tried to insert a hand between her legs.

"I'm warning you," Frances said, blocking the hand, "don't *wiggle*."

"Why not?"

"I want to sleep. *I* have to work tomorrow."

Paul lay quietly for a while, his confidence wilting, and then tried for the breast again.

"That's more wiggling," Frances said. "I warned you. Get dressed. I'll take you home."

"No, no," Paul said. "I'll stop. Let's go to sleep."

Paul did not sleep very well. Every two hours or so he would attempt advances, but each time he was rebuffed and labeled a wiggler. At four o'clock in the morning, Frances demanded:

"Who do you think you are, anyway? Uncle Wiggily?"

"That's right, 'Uncle Wiggily in Connecticut.'"

"What are you talking about?"

"That's a short story by J. D. Salinger."

(Reading over bugging transcripts a few days later, Mother was pleased to see that Paul had managed to turn defeat into a literary allusion.)

7

The Blue Book

"THE WISE MEN have sent us a blue book today," O'Hara announced.

It was Thursday again and the new director was once again presiding over a meeting of the U.S. Intelligence Board (USIB). The expurgated minutes were approved. The usual thirty seconds were spent discussing the Watch Report. Then O'Hara turned the meeting to a consideration of a National Intelligence Estimate (a blue book) prepared by eight senior analysts known as the National Intelligence Officers (Wise Men).

The blue book had been requested by the President's foreign policy advisor, who had been responsible for a major change in the way blue books were produced. O'Hara preferred the old way. Under previous administrations, the books were the work of a dozen-man Board of National Estimates. The BNE turned out long, detailed, carefully researched reports on such subjects as "The Outlook on Latin America over the Next Decade" or "Soviet Strategic Strike Capabilities over the Next Five Years." At Langley, where reports of all types and sizes were produced, the BNE blue books had long been considered the Cadillacs of the line. They were the pride of the agency. But President Richard Nixon and his foreign policy adviser were unimpressed. They replaced the Board of National Estimates with the National Intelligence Officers. And they changed the product. The old, thick blue books, which took months to produce and looked far into the future, were phased out. They were replaced by new, ten-to-twelve-page blue books, which were produced on short notice and made short-term forecasts. These new estimates generally covered whatever subjects happened to be the current preoccupation of the President's foreign policy adviser. The Cadillac had been replaced by the scooter. O'Hara had once prepared a memo in defense of the old way but at the last moment had fed it into the shredder.

The members of the USIB leafed through the latest National Intelligence Estimate. Its subject: the Middle East. The blue book echoed the warnings in the Watch Report, but at greater length. Once again, the message was that a war in the Middle East was very likely "coming soon."

There was not much to say. An interagency subcommittee had already reviewed the estimate. Arguments had already been voiced. Compromises had already been reached. Continuing disagreements had already been placed in footnotes. After a short but perfunctory discussion, the USIB approved the blue book.

O'Hara moved the meeting ahead to the special items on the agenda. The NSA chief requested permission to provide the Israelis with its latest encoding machine, which was regarded as a cryptographical breakthrough. The Israelis already had less sophisticated American coding devices.

The FBI's man on the board objected, surprising no one. The Bureau was always coming up with nitpicking objections reflecting a larger, long-standing objection. For appropriately named ODENVY objected to the very existence of all the other agencies represented around the table.

Before World War II, the FBI had owned the clandestine world, and it did not appreciate the new outfits which had taken over much of its territory. During the war, the FBI had gone so far as to fight a secret war against the OSS. One night in 1942, OSS officers broke into the Spanish embassy. While they were peacefully photographing documents, they heard sirens and saw flashing red lights outside. J. Edgar Hoover had sent over a few FBI cars to scare the OSS men half to death. In recent years, the Bureau's relations with its neighbors in the secret world had mellowed into a distrustful détente.

The other intelligence chiefs considered the FBI's presence at the USIB table a joke, but they listened anyway. The Bureau's man said that they should not overlook the possibility that the Israeli government had been penetrated by the Russians.

O'Hara asked if the FBI had any direct evidence of such a penetration. Underlying his question was a suspicion that the FBI might have overstepped its authority and done some extraterritorial spying.

The Bureau's man said he was extrapolating from the FBI's experience in this country. The Bureau had reason to believe that the Soviet Union was sending out some spies mixed in with the Jews it allowed to emigrate to the United States. So it seemed reasonable to suspect that some agents might also be mixed in with the Jews allowed to emigrate to Israel. And if the Russians were shipping spies into Israel, how could the Israelis guarantee the integrity of the American code machines?

The FBI's objection was noted but not heeded. The USIB approved furnishing Israel with the latest cryptographic device.

O'Hara left the meeting depressed. When he returned to his private office, he dispatched the National Intelligence Estimate on the Middle East to the White House. Now the CIA was officially committed to the proposition that a crisis was building in that part of the world. O'Hara's mood was traceable, in part, to his realization that now was no time to fire the head of the Israeli desk.

A crowd loitered in the foyer. It looked like a fancy unemployment line or perhaps a splashy bread line. And, in a sense, the crowd was hungry, ready to eat out of someone's hand. They were reporters waiting for the President's foreign policy adviser.

Behind the white louvered doors, the Senate Foreign Relations Committee was meeting in executive session in its Capitol hearing room. The senators wanted to be briefed on U.S.–U.S.S.R. relations, for Brezhnev was coming to Washington in a few days. Actually, what they wanted was reassurance that the Watergate-weakened American President was not going to be hugged to death by the Russian bear. Those assurances were made.

When the President's foreign policy adviser emerged from the hearing room, he faced microphones, television cameras, and a few notebooks. A reporter asked him if the Watergate scandal had caused the President to reconsider his invitation to Brezhnev.

"As I said yesterday," the foreign policy adviser said, "the President sees no reason to reevaluate Chairman Brezhnev's projected visit."

Another reporter asked if the foreign policy adviser thought the President *should* reconsider.

"As I've said many times before," the foreign policy expert said, "I don't discuss the recommendations I make to the President."

A third reporter asked a third question.

The foreign policy adviser began his answer: "As I said last week . . ."

A fourth reporter asked something else.

The answer began: "As I said yesterday . . ."

A moment later, the foreign policy adviser stepped back from the microphones and started toward the exit. Lesley Stahl, a CBS correspondent, hurried after him, catching up with him in front of a bank of elevators.

"Sir, this is the first time I've covered you," she said. "Couldn't you have said just one thing you hadn't said before?"

"I've found," the foreign policy adviser said, "that the best way to stay off the Cronkite show is to begin every answer with, 'As I said yesterday.'"

When the presidential adviser returned to his office, he found the CIA's blue book on the Middle East waiting for him. He opened it immediately and studied it with growing annoyance. As he read, he turned a pencil over and over, faster and faster, like a majorette twirling a small yellow baton.

When he finished reading, he used the pencil to scrawl something on the blue cover. Then he rerouted it back to the agency.

He had written: "Piece of crap."

"I'll take Dante's Coquette."

"When are you going to learn to stop betting on a horse just because it's got a literary name?"

Mother and Menachem Ginzburg, the Mossad agent, had driven out to the Shenandoah track for an evening of horse racing. Mother had also brought along Paul Fitzsimmons, because he thought a few connections might help the boy's career. There was another less unselfish reason for Paul's presence: the senior spooks found it convenient to have an apprentice spook around to stand in the pari-mutuel line and place the bets.

"I don't know," Mother said. "I won money on that horse a while back so I thought I'd try him again."

"How much?"

"Oh, about four dollars."

"And how many times have you bet on him since?"

"Oh, a couple of times. I'm not sure."

"And did he win?"

"No, but I think he's about due."

The three men were seated at a table with a white

tablecloth overlooking the track. When a waiter appeared, they ordered dinner and a bottle of wine. Then Paul left the table to place the bets. Five dollars for Mother on Dante's Coquette. Five dollars for Ginzburg on Dawn Clipper. And two dollars for himself on Uncle Wiggily.

While Paul was at the pari-mutuel window, Mother and the Mossad officer did business. Mother gave Ginzburg the Wise Men's blue book on the Middle Eastern situation.

The Israeli told Mother about more trips taken by the peripatetic Arab leaders: on June 18, Jordanian Prime Minister Zeid Rifai sent his uncle, Abdel Moueim Rifai, to Cairo to meet with Egyptian ministers. On June 30, the prime minister's uncle flew to Damascus. On July 19, the avuncular traveler flew back to Cairo. On July 28, Prime Minister Zeid Rifai himself flew to Saudi Arabia, where he met with King Faisal for twelve hours.

"What do you make of our busy boys?" asked Ginzburg.

"I wonder if Faisal isn't the key," Mother speculated. "Maybe Jordan got into another spat with Egypt and Syria—and then called on Saudi Arabia to patch it up."

"Could be, but what do you suppose they're fighting about this time?"

"Well," said Mother, "what if Egypt and Syria were trying to get Jordan to join in an attack on Israel. Perhaps they think Israel couldn't afford to fight a war on three fronts."

"Is this off the top of your head?"

"No."

"It makes sense," Ginzburg said, looking more serious than was normal for him. "Especially when you link it to another piece of information that's come into our hands. The Syrians just welcomed five hundred exceptional visitors."

Abruptly, the Mossad man stopped talking. He was determined to force Mother to admit he did not know about Syria's new guests. He waited.

"All right," Mother said. "Who?"

"Cuban soldiers. We think they're mostly tank commanders and crews."

"The Russians are behind this," Mother said. "They must be. They're the only link."

When Paul returned to the table, the conversation veered from worries about the future to recollections of the past.

"Did Mother ever tell you about the time we stole King Farouk's piss?" Ginzburg asked.

"No," said Paul. "Why in the world . . . ?"

Mother said, "The company wanted to check up on the fat king's health, so they asked me to obtain a specimen of his, er, well . . . I gave the assignment to Menachem."

"I took a team to Monte Carlo where we tapped into the plumbing of the men's room in the king's favorite casino," recalled the Israeli. "Then I stationed myself on a toilet seat where I could see the urinals. By the time Farouk came in, my ass was pretty sore. I coughed three times. That was our code, so my man on the other side of the wall knew the king was pissing in the third urinal. Old Farouk flushed his pee all the way to Langley."

When the announcer called "Post time," the crowd in the bleachers below jumped to their feet. At their table, Mother and his guests remained seated, but Mother did lean back in his chair so he could see the starting gate instead of just the tablecloth.

Shortly after the announcer called "And they're off," Mother relaxed his muscles and his body reassumed its curl. While the thousands all around him watched the horses gallop down the backstretch, he watched the silverware: his gaze was so steady that one would have thought he had bet on the fork to beat the spoon.

Mother, who could tell from the decibel level of the cheering when to look up, raised his head just as the horses were coming out of the far turn and into the homestretch. Dante's Coquette was in the lead. Dawn Clipper was third. Mother was afraid his horse had made its move too soon, but Ginzburg's horse seemed to be in perfect position. It occurred to Mother that he might have picked a horse with a smart name but a dumb jockey.

Mother, who hated to lose to a friend, watched helplessly as Dawn Clipper pulled up into second place and challenged Dante's Coquette for the lead. Straining to keep his head up and straining for his horse, Mother began to wonder if this kind of excitement was good for a man of his age. After all, he was not an OSS wonderboy any longer. Only seconds from the finish line, Dawn Clipper swept past Dante's Coquette and Mother let his head bow down again. He took these losses harder than he should have, and he was glad no one could see his face.

Then the announcer's voice blared: "And it's Uncle Wiggily by a neck!"

"Uncle Wiggily?" asked Mother.

"Came out of nowhere," Ginzburg said, disappointed and disgusted.

"I won," announced Paul a little sheepishly.

"You bet on Uncle Wiggily?" asked Mother.

"That's right," Paul admitted.

Mother started laughing, and try as he might, he could not stop.

The President's foreign policy adviser had an office on the ground floor of the West Wing of the White House, down the hall from the Oval Office. There was a certain sense of clutter created by the kind of bric-a-brac most people display only because it was given to them by aunts who might drop in unexpectedly. Only his "aunts" were heads of state.

The nicest gifts were paintings. One wall supported a bouquet of flowers painted by the Russian artist P. Kongolovsky, a gift from Leonid Brezhnev. Another wall was armed with a picture of a horse painted on a scroll by Hsu Pei-hung, a gift from the Chinese. The foreign policy adviser's favorite painting, a canvas by Jules Olitski, hung over the couch. This was not a gift but a loan from a Cambridge friend who had warned the presidential adviser not to tell the antiwar artist where his picture now hung. The abstract painting was purple at the edges, shading to a red center—the red-hot center where the foreign policy expert had always longed to be, the red-hot center where he now found himself, at last.

The President's foreign policy adviser sat behind his desk, dividing his time between reading cables and glancing out the tall French windows at reporters on their way to the press room. Occasionally, when he saw a reporter he knew, he would wave. He was in a fairly relaxed, convivial mood, until he reached the cable from the embassy in Tel Aviv. The Israelis were once again putting pressure on the United States to provide them with more arms. What interested the presidential adviser was not the request but the justification. The Israelis had buttressed their own arguments by quoting from a CIA National Intelligence Estimate.

With one sweep of his arm, the President's foreign policy adviser knocked everything off his desk—cables, memos, reports, paperweights, souvenirs, bric-a-brac, pens, and telephones, one a direct line to the President of the United States. During a recent physical examination, a doctor had told the adviser that he did not have a single muscle in his body, but the violence of his attack on the desk suggested otherwise. The sound of multiple crashes brought aides scurrying to peek in the door. They supposed the boss was just having another temper tantrum, but there was always a chance that he had fallen and cracked his erudite head.

The cursing began when the faces appeared in the doorway. It began with "goddamn fucking cocksucker" and escalated. When he grew tired of obscenities, the President's foreign policy adviser yelled:

"Get O'Hara's ass over here!"

The aide who placed the call to O'Hara's office put the request more diplomatically. The KUBARK director said he could be at the White House at 12:30 P.M.

When O'Hara entered the West Wing office, he found

the foreign policy adviser's desk in perfect order. In fact, he was impressed by the meticulousness reflected there. O'Hara was an orderly man who admired orderliness in others. He kept his own desk as neat as a priest keeps his altar.

The director took a chair in front of the desk. The foreign policy adviser handed him the cable from Tel Aviv.

"I'd like to hear your explanation," the presidential adviser said, his eyes on their way to turning the color of the center of his favorite painting.

"I'm as surprised as you are," said O'Hara. "I had no idea the Israelis had access to that blue book. But, as you know, we do have an agreement with their service."

"I don't care if we have an agreement written on stone tablets. I won't stand for this. They're squeezing us with our own intelligence. It's intolerable—it's dangerous."

"Well, agreement or no, the book shouldn't have been passed without my approval," O'Hara said. "Someone's acted out of line."

"Do you know who?"

"Probably, probably."

"Well, *who?*"

"Probably the head of our Israeli desk," O'Hara said. Force of habit prevented his mentioning the man by name to an outsider, even this outsider.

"Well, fix him," the foreign policy adviser said. "Because we can't have this. He's playing a dangerous game. It isn't just that the Israelis'll want more arms. No, it's that if we keep telling them they're about to be attacked, then they may attack first. And I won't have that."

"I'll take care of it."

"If this administration weren't in such trouble already, I'd say fire him. But I don't think we can afford another casualty right now. So just shut him off."

"I will," O'Hara promised.

"This mustn't happen again, or measures will have to be taken."

When O'Hara returned to his office, he instructed one of his aides to send for Mother. But the aide reported back shortly that the KUDESK chief had already left Langley for the day. O'Hara glanced at his watch. It was only 4 P.M.

"Well, get him back!" O'Hara ordered.

It was not an easy assignment. Before Mother could be hauled in, he had to be found. A call was placed to his home, but no one answered. Another call went to the maître d' at La Niçoise, but he could be of no help. O'Hara's aides were getting nervous.

At last, one of Mother's own aides found him serving his country at a cocktail party.

When Mother returned to Langley, he walked a slightly crooked path down the corridors, wobbling toward trouble. He was not really drunk, but he had had a few Kirs. He wondered if O'Hara would notice. He wished he were wrapped in a little more dignity.

As he walked along, Mother kept meeting people who he knew hated him. They hated him no more now than they had in years past, but they were less afraid to show it since the word had spread that O'Hara wanted to get rid of him. Fortunately, Mother was so stooped he did not have to look at their faces. He passed pair after pair of angry shoes.

When he entered the director's office, he only caught a brief glimpse of his antagonist's face before ducking back down again.

"We've been looking all over for you," said O'Hara.

Mother knew the director was really asking where he had been. The KUDESK chief decided to make his boss wait for an answer. He reached into his coat pocket and pulled out his gold lighter and Virginia Slims. The tall, thin man put a long, skinny emblem of himself in his mouth and set it on fire.

"I was at the Israeli embassy."

"I might've known," O'Hara said. Then he tried to make a joke: "What were you doing? Selling secrets for drinks?"

Mother took a reflex step backward. He hadn't realized he was broadcasting Kir.

"No," Mother said, and just left it there.

"Then may I ask what you were doing there?"

"If you must know, I was attending a surprise birthday party for a friend of mine. Menachem Ginzburg's fifty-five years old today."

"Did you by chance take him a present? Perhaps something wrapped in blue?"

"Excuse me. I'm afraid I don't follow you."

"I was referring to one of our blue books."

"No, I gave him nothing at all, I'm sorry to say."

"Well, perhaps you gave him his present early. Say ten days ago? I understand one of our blue books fell into Israeli hands about that time. I thought perhaps you were responsible."

"I believe I was," Mother said. "After all . . ."

"You know you shouldn't have done something like that without my approval," the director interrupted.

"But we have . . ."

"I know all about our agreement with the Israelis," O'Hara said, staring involuntarily at the ash on the end of Mother's Virginia Slim, which grew longer and longer. "But I'll decide how to implement that agreement. You've made a decision that should've been made by the Director of Central Intelligence. From now on, I'll sign off on any information to be passed to Israel. Is that understood?"

"Yes, but . . ."

"The White House was very upset," O'Hara continued, the ash making him squirm. "There was even a discussion of firing whoever was responsible. I protected you as I'd protect any subordinate, but I won't be able to protect you forever. It must never happen again. Do I have your word?"

"I . . ."

"Do I have your word?"

Mother said nothing.

"Do I have your word?" O'Hara asked again, his voice sharpened by frustration and by his anticipation of the ash's fall. As much as he dreaded the smudge, he felt that if the gray inch did not break loose soon he might do something desperate. He was the prisoner waiting for the next drop of water to strike his forehead, the drop that never came. "Do I have to get out a Bible! I've got one, you know."

"No, that won't be necessary. You win. After all, you're the director, and I've always obeyed orders."

The ash fell and left a nasty mark on the carpet.

"This incident has helped me make a decision I've been putting off. I've made up my mind to cut your budget not a hundred fifty but a hundred seventy-five thousand dollars."

"Jesus," said Mother, who only rarely broke the first commandment. "You want to shut down the whole department."

"I don't think that'll be necessary. But we will have to shut some of your safe houses."

"You mean all my safe houses."

"Have it your way."

When Mother stood up to go, he stepped on the fallen ash and ground it into the carpet.

Returning to his office, Mother was so mad his mind seemed to shake like an angry fist. He couldn't focus on anything. He couldn't concentrate. He felt helpless. And then he found a thought he could hang onto. He began once again to brood about revenge.

The rough geometry of a plan slowly took shape in his imagination. Then he turned to details. The first question to which he addressed himself was what type of transportation to use. He considered a police car but, upon reflection, felt it presented too many problems. It would be too hard to steal and too conspicuous once stolen.

While he pondered his choice of vehicle, his hands were busy folding a sheet of blank paper. He opened his sixth-floor window. The white plane headed toward Washington, then turned toward Richmond, then crashed.

Mother considered using a Volkswagen, but it presented drawbacks, too. For it would not be able to double-park with impunity. An official or quasi-official car would be better.

Another paper plane sailed out of a sixth-floor window, circled, and nose-dived.

Perhaps a limousine. That sounded about right. A long black car would do very nicely.

Another tiny aircraft took flight.

When Mother rose to go home, he looked out his office window and saw three paper planes lying at the feet of that other son of Eli, Nathan Hale.

8

The Party

WHEN MOTHER RETURNED home that evening he tried to look more cheerful than he felt, for he had more than flowers and books waiting for him. His fourteen-year-old daughter, Carol, and his twenty-one-year-old son, Matt, were spending two weeks with him, as they did every summer. At the end of the fortnight Carol would leave Mother and return to the custody of her mother in Tucson. And Matt would return to Berkeley. Mother, who missed his role as family man, greeted his daughter warmly.

Then he asked, "Where's your brother?"

"I think he's in his room, Daddy," said Carol.

Moving faster than was his custom, Mother climbed the stairs leading to the bedrooms. He had something he wanted to ask his son.

Mother knocked respectfully at his son's door. There was no answer. Mother knocked again. Still no answer. Mother wondered if he was being snubbed by his own son. His patience failing him, Mother opened his boy's room. He wasn't there.

Mother looked inside, then walked in. His son was not there but his books were. The father frowned at Goddard's *Buddhist Bible,* at Morgan's *Path of Buddha,* at Snellgrove's *Buddhist Himalaya,* at Vasubandhu's *Treatise in Twenty Stanzas on Representation-Only* . . .

Mother looked all over the second floor, but his son was nowhere to be found. Raising his voice, always a last resort, he called out, but there was no answer. He hurried back downstairs. His son had escaped.

"He's gone," Mother called to his daughter.

"Maybe he's out back," Carol said.

Mother grabbed his homburg off the hall rack and shuffled out the back door. Matt was nowhere to be seen. Mother was on his way back inside when he thought of one place he had not looked.

Opening the door of Light Side, his warmer greenhouse, Mother peeked inside. Dressed in army fatigue trousers and a black pajama top, his son was sitting in the full lotus position among the orchids. The young man had chosen the greenhouse for his meditation because it approximated Buddha's own jungle.

"So there you are," said Mother.

"Hi," replied Matt.

Mother had fathered Matthew Mark Kimball in 1952, at the height of the Cold War. Since Francis Xavier Kimball was not especially fond of his own name, he had not bequeathed it to his son. But he had not been able to resist giving his son a name which, like his, had a religious resonance. That had been an act of faith, of hope. It suggested a desire for some sort of generational continuity. Mother's son, however, had grown up as determined not to become his father as Mother himself had been determined not to become his.

"Am I disturbing you?" asked Mother.

"That's okay. I'll meditate longer tomorrow."

Mother's son's hair was only about an inch long. A year ago it had been a foot long. This sort of hirsute inconstancy disturbed Mother.

"Do you have any plans Friday evening?" asked Mother.

"No."

"Would you like to go to a party?"

"What kind of party?"

"A cocktail party," said Mother defensively.

"A *Georgetown* cocktail party?" Matt asked derisively.

"Ah, yes," Mother admitted.

Nervous, the father felt a need to do something with his hands, so he began searching his orchids for enemies—rot, fungus, bugs. Discovering a small green worm, he removed it and carefully decapitated it with a thumbnail.

"Are you deliberately trying to upset me?" asked his son.

"What?"

"You know I'm opposed to killing. Buddha teaches us that all life is sacred. Even the life of a worm. It upsets me to see life murdered."

"I don't like killing either," Mother said, "but sometimes it's necessary. If I let the worms live, they'll kill the flowers."

"That's just Western sophistry. You actually like killing. It fascinates you. You even like war. You're in love with World War Two."

"Couldn't you stand up?" asked Mother. "It's hard to talk like this."

"Tell the truth," Matt said, not budging out of his lotus. "Didn't you enjoy the war? Weren't those the best years of your life?"

"We were attacked. They were barbarians. They wanted to wipe out civilization. We didn't have any choice but to fight."

"Ooohhhmmm . . ."

"Oh, don't start that."

"Ooooohhhhhmmmm . . ."

"For God's sake, that's no answer."

"Oooooooohhhhhhhmmmmmm . . ."

"I think even Buddha would've fought for his life."

"Oooooooooohhhhhhhhhhmmmmmmmmmm . . ."

"Please stop chanting. Can't we talk? How's Berkeley? Do you like it?"

"OOOOOOOOOOOOOHHHHHHHHHHHHMMM-MMMMMMMMM . . ."

Mother turned his back and headed for the door, brushing orchids out of the way as he went.

"How many people have you killed?" his son called after him.

At the Hawk and Dove that evening, a Monday evening, Paul drifted uncertainly toward a proposition. He and Frances would be finishing up their course at Blue U on Friday and then they had a week's vacation coming before they were scheduled to start the next phase of their training. Paul wanted to make plans for that week. So far Frances's skirt had proved an iron curtain, but he still hoped someday to infiltrate it.

"Do you like Cape Cod?" he asked, and then took a bite of his Reuben sandwich.

"Yeah, sure, it's beautiful," Frances said between bites of Maryland crab cakes.

"A friend of mine has offered me a house up there for a week," said Paul.

"I'll miss you."

"I hope not."

"No, I really will."

"I mean, I thought we might spend the week up there together," Paul said. "You know we get a week off."

"Well, I suppose that'd be all right."

Stunned, Paul said simply, "Thank you."

"Don't thank me, but there's a problem we really should consider."

"What?"

"Well, if we spend that much time together, we'll probably end up making love."

Paul had been thinking exactly the same thing, but he said, "Not necessarily."

"No, we would. But what if we're sexually incompatible?"

"Don't worry about that."

"If we are, we'll be miserable for days. It'll be terrible."

"We won't be incompatible," Paul promised.

"Well, I think we'd better have a trial run. It could save a lot of trouble later on. How about Friday night after my mother's party?"

"Why not sooner?"

"Because all the other nights are school nights," Frances laughed.

At Frances's mother's party, Matt Kimball was embarrassed.

Shaking hands with a man who looked familiar, Mother's son struggled to join a name to the face. He couldn't. This always happened when he got stoned: his memory went up in smoke. Matt now regretted having finally agreed to accompany his father to this affair marking the retirement of a right-wing columnist. Mother's son had prepared himself for the evening by slipping into a pair of black Levi's, donning a corduroy jacket, and smoking two joints of marijuana.

"I'm sorry," Matt said, sure he was addressing an old friend. "I know that I know you, but I can't remember your name."

"Hubert Humphrey," said the man.

"Oh," said Matt, flustered, "I thought you were a friend of my dad's."

"Maybe I am," bubbled the Minnesota senator. "Who's your father?"

"I'm sorry, I didn't introduce myself," the young man said. "I'm Matt Kimball. My father's Francis Xavier Kimball."

Humphrey looked blank.

"I didn't think you'd know him," Matt said. "He's got an anonymous job."

A man whom Matt didn't recognize rushed up and shook Humphrey's hand. Then another man did the same. Matt detached himself from the group and drifted into a corner of the room.

Matt stared blankly at the faces that drifted before him. He knew they were famous faces, important faces, powerful faces, but try as he might, he could not link them to their equally famous, important, powerful names and titles. There were a few exceptions, for his memory was not entirely a tabula rasa. After great mental exertion, Matt did at last manage to recognize Katharine Graham, the publisher of the *Washington Post*. And, after staring rather rudely for several minutes, he succeeded in identifying a familiar countenance as Elliot Richardson, the new attorney general. But in general he found marijuana was a great leveler. In his eyes most of the celebrated guests were bereft of their names, their titles, their positions, their offices.

Matt liked that. No one knew him and very few knew his father, but Matt didn't know them either. Allen Dulles used to say intelligence officers were people with a passion for anonymity, which Matt knew was true enough. But he also knew, or at least he thought he did, that it was easier to be Mr. Anonymous than a member of Mr. Anonymous's family. He thought that was why his mother had left his father. At least that had been a part of it. She couldn't stand being Mrs. Anonymous. The husband-spy had his work for consolation, but what did his wife have? Matt's mother, Mother's wife, had been brought up to believe a woman should be ambitious not for herself but for her husband. She had been ambitious for him, and he *had* been successful, but it was, by its very nature, an invisible success. So she had left three years ago to pursue her career as an as yet unpublished author. In a sense, Mrs. Anonymous's son was revenging her on this crowd of Washington celebrities by not recognizing them.

The hostess, Mrs. Faith Fisher, found Matt staring up at a chandelier, which, to his stoned eyes, gave off rainbows. Mrs. Fisher was one of the few people in the room who knew Matt's father, knew he was an important man, and therefore knew Matt. She knew about the secret world. And she knew about anonymity, although she herself had broken out of it because her husband had become rather well known, as spies go, first by becoming head of KUDOVE, and last by committing suicide. The ultimate extinction of personality had made the late Robert Fisher something of a personality in Washington. Faith Fisher had fallen heir to an identity. She was recognized as a leading Georgetown hostess—and Matt did recognize her, after some effort, as she led him away.

Mrs. Fisher towed Matt Kimball over to the fireplace, interrupting a tête-à-tête between Frances and Paul. Mother's favorite and Mother's son were introduced to one another for the first time.

"Oh, *you're* Paul," Matt said, "the English professor."

"Yes and no."

"You went to Dad's alma mater, didn't you?"

"That's right," Frances answered for Paul. "He's a Yale man. I'm a Princeton man."

"I'm a Berkeley man," Matt said. "Want a joint?"

Paul and Frances, seeing their security clearance going up in smoke, bumped into each other saying no.

"Whatsa matter, pa'dnah," Matt said, slipping into his John Wayne imitation. He always imitated the cowboy star whenever he got stoned. When he was sober he was a peace-loving Bodhisattua, but marijuana transformed him into a counterfeit of the ultimate gunslinger. "Are you ascared of a lil ol' joint?"

The no's stumbled over each other once again.

"I just wanna tell ya, pa'dnah," Matt drawled, "if you're not outa town by sunup, I'm gonna . . . I'm gonna . . . I'm gonna . . . I'm gonna . . ."

He had forgotten what he wanted to say.

"Oh yeah," Matt finally remembered, "if you're not outa town by sunup, I'm gonna get outa town . . . 'cause this town ain't big enough for two sons."

Frances's mother suddenly appeared to fetch her daughter away to introduce her to a young attorney who worked for the Edward Bennett Williams law firm. Frances suspected that the real reason her mother was giving the party was not to honor the columnist but to force her daughter to meet some up-and-coming young Washington men who did not work for the company. Frances soon broke away from the young attorney and rejoined Paul. Her mother's maneuvering was pushing her closer to him.

Paul and Frances joined a group where Art Buchwald was telling funny stories. Joseph Kraft wandered up and someone asked him about a column he had written about the CIA's role in Watergate. Kraft, a longtime friend of KUBARK, said he thought Nixon was trying to hide behind the agency.

On the fringe of the group, a Supreme Court justice said in a meek voice, "I was once in intelligence."

No one paid any attention.

The justice tried again: "I used to be in intelligence."

Only Mother's son gave the man his full attention. He was trying to remember who he was. When Matt finally did recognize the justice, he was still puzzled. For Matt was his mother's son and had always associated social invisibility with the absence of an impressive title. And yet, the Supreme Court justice had one of the top titles and people were ignoring him anyway. It was as though the whole party were stoned and all titles had been forgotten. Matt's sympathy went out to the justice.

The Supreme Court justice tried once more: "I used to be in intelligence."

Still no one paid any attention. If he had had his gavel, he might have reached for it, but since he did not, he reached for the next best thing: Frances's mother.

Leaning across three people, he took her by the elbow and said, "Would you please ask everyone to be quiet? I have something to say."

Mrs. Fisher immediately silenced every voice except one: that belonging to the justice's wife.

When she was finally hushed, the justice made a little speech which turned out to be somewhat anticlimactic: he said he had been in air force intelligence during World War II and his experience in that outfit had persuaded him of the importance of an intelligence-gathering apparatus.

Everyone said, oh, well, yes, and the justice never got another word in.

Mother leaned over to Paul and whispered, "He helped break the Axis's enigma-machine code."

Matt Kimball made his way over to the justice and introduced himself. He normally felt nothing but hostility toward people who worked for the government, but he felt a great stoned warmth for this highest of federal officials. Talking to Justice Anonymous, Matt felt as if he had met a totally unexpected secret sharer.

Mother took another sip of his fourth drink. Like his son, he was beginning to acquire a buzz. He was fortifying himself not against the party, as his son had, but against something that had happened at Langley that afternoon: Mother had been upset by a memorandum from the director. Mother had requested permission to share with the Israelis information he had received concerning Egypt's finances. Sadat had made a secret flight to Riyadh, the capital of Saudi Arabia, in early August to meet with King Faisal. The trip had proved worthwhile: Faisal had given Sadat $500 million for military spending and had promised another $650 million in long-term, low-interest loans. Since Sadat was not planning to build another big dam, Mother suspected he might well be planning a big war. Mother felt it extremely important to convey this intelligence to the Israelis, but the director's memo denied him permission to do so. In the face of this order Mother felt impotent, so he drank.

Mother sat down on a flowered couch. He felt as if he were sitting in a dark audience watching a stage play. He liked the feeling. That was where a classic spy belonged, in the audience, not on stage. His life's work was observing and so he observed.

He watched Shirley Wade, a society reporter, and her escort and boss, Wallace Burns, the editor of an important Washington daily. Burns, who looked like a casting director's idea of a gentleman cat burglar, stood in a corner talking to the editor of a weekly magazine. Mother imagined they were discussing Watergate or détente or the tension in the Middle East. Actually, they were talking about what journalists often talk about once they have reached the top: the price of paper.

In the center of the room Shirley Wade, with bright Harlow hair and a skinny Hepburn body, stood talking to Eugene McCarthy. Mother imagined they were fascinated by one another. Actually, they were beginning to get on one another's nerves. Shirley Wade spent half an hour telling McCarthy about Burns's strengths and weaknesses in bed.

McCarthy, embarrassed, eventually succeeded in changing the subject to the approaching 1976 presidential campaign. Wade asked if he thought Humphrey would run. McCarthy said he probably would if anyone could get him to the starting post.

Wade said, "I don't understand your sports references."

McCarthy said, "Well, you have to change the metaphor *sometimes*."

Watching Burns and Wade, Mother felt deliciously colorless, deliciously inconspicuous, deliciously anonymous. He was beginning to cheer up, thanks primarily to the buzz, when he noticed someone who sent his mood plummeting.

Director O'Hara had just come in. The two men noticed one another right away, but they did not acknowledge one another. They stayed as far from each other as possible, moving about the living room like the north and south poles of a compass.

And then suddenly Mother was horrified. For his son was approaching the director. Mother was enough of a spy to know that Matt was stoned. And he knew his boy well enough to know his favorite imitation. Mother couldn't believe it: John Wayne was bearing down on his boss in a Chippendale Dodge City.

"Howdy, pa'dnah," Matt Kimball said to the Director of Central Intelligence.

"How do you do?"

"Could I ask a question?" said Matt, snapping out of it.

"Go right ahead."

"Why'd you kill Ché?"

"We didn't," the director said tersely, hardly moving his lips.

Watching and listening from afar, Mother grew increasingly nervous. He kept trying to catch his son's eye without catching his boss's. When he could stand it no longer, he walked over to break up the confrontation. He touched his son's arm.

"Are you about ready?" Mother asked.

He led his son away without saying a word to the DCI. At the front door, they said good-night to their hostess.

Matt said, "Thank you, Mrs., uh, Mrs., uh . . ."

"Fisher," she said.

When Mother and his son pulled into the Arlington driveway, they gave two people in the living room a terrible scare. Cat burglars would have been happier to hear the crunch of wheels on gravel than were Mother's fourteen-year-old daughter and her fifteen-year-old visitor. They scrambled into their clothes as fast as fear-stiff fingers could fasten buttons and zippers. When the front door opened, they were disheveled but covered. As Carol hurried forward to greet her father, her crotch felt unusually cool and airy, for she was wearing no panties. She couldn't find them.

After the hellos, all four sat down in the living room for some light conversation before bedtime. How did the boy like his summer job? He did. Was he looking forward to the start of school? Well, not exactly, but he would be glad to see football season get started. Why had they come home so early? Mother said the party had been a disappointment.

Over this light talk a heavy burden hung. Everyone in the room pretended not to notice, but actually everyone noticed little else. Everyone tried to meet everyone else's gaze, but inadvertently everyone kept

glancing up. What everyone saw but no one acknowledged seeing was a pair of red bikini panties hanging
from the living room's small chandelier. The young man
now regretted having tossed them there in an impish
moment.

When the father and son finally went upstairs to bed,
the teenagers were seized by a fit of giggles, which
continued intermittently for another hour and a half.
In that time Matt dissolved into a deep, drugged sleep.
But down the hall Mother lay awake, listening to his
daughter downstairs, hearing the sounds of another
revolution he was helpless to put down. To him, mo-
nogamy was individual sexual ownership, whereas
promiscuity was multiple ownership, a spreading of
wealth, sexual communism.

The giggles rising from the floor below told Mother
that his side was losing the sexual cold war.

Paul yawned.

"I'm getting sleepy," he said.

"No, you're not," Frances corrected him. "You're
getting horny."

"No, I'm really sleepy."

"I'm not ready to go."

Paul looked around at the handful of guests who
seemed to be refusing to go home. He assumed they
were husbands and wives who had known each other
too long. He remembered a time many years earlier
when he had driven guests out of his parents' house by
carrying a big clock into the living room, but unfortunately he had outgrown such ploys.

"I need another drink," Paul said.

"Don't pout," said Frances, who was irritated. Paul
had been fairly well behaved the past few weeks, not
trying to wrestle her into bed, but now that she had
finally agreed to make love with him he was as bad as
ever, pushing too hard.

It was after 1 A.M. when Frances agreed to leave
the party. Her apartment was only a couple of blocks
away. They walked along the silent sidewalk side by

side but not touching. They planned to make love that night, but holding hands would take longer.

When they reached Frances's apartment, she handed him her key. He tried to open the door but had trouble with the lock.

"Don't be in such a hurry," Frances said. "It'll work better."

In the bedroom, Paul kissed Frances and simultaneously reached for her zipper. She pulled away from him.

"I'll do my own undressing," she snapped.

Frances jumped on her bed and marched up and down as if it were a stage. Paul stared up at what appeared to be a Brobdingnagian stripper. Frances unzipped her dress and threw it across the room. She danced in her underwear to music which was not playing. Her half-slip flew through the air. Her bra fluttered to the floor like the tail of a broken kite. Then Frances threw her white panties at Paul's head. He ducked as if the undergarment were a rock.

"Aren't you going to take your clothes off, too?" Frances asked coldly.

Paul, who suddenly seemed to remember why he was there, began hurriedly undressing. When he was as nude as Frances, they both crawled into bed. Paul could hardly believe it. After months of being in love with Frances, he was finally about to make love to her. After months of humiliation, he was about to resurrect his pride. After an eternity of torment, he was going to fuck his tormentor. He desired her body and he desired his revenge. He would love her, he would move her, and he would stab her with his body.

And he had a stomach-ache.

Paul hugged Frances and felt a slight stirring in his penis. He fondled her breasts and felt himself stiffening. He reached down and felt his penis to be sure. And, sure enough, it was hard. He rolled on top of her.

"Don't be in such a hurry," Frances said. "I'm not ready yet."

Paul rolled off Frances and his hands moved to her pubic gorge. Slowly he coaxed forth a moistness and a softness.

The problem was that as she softened so did he. The first fine rush of excitement which had overcome his fear had faded. His stomach ached and he could feel chills.

"Now," she said. "Please, now. Do it now."

Paul rolled on top of Frances, but he knew it was no use. His stomach only hurt worse, his chills came faster, and his penis went softer. He desperately wished he were somewhere else.

"What's the matter?" Frances asked.

Paul did not answer.

"What's the *matter?*"

Paul, still mute, rolled off her. He tried with all his willpower to raise his penis, but trying did not help at all. Several miserable days later, he would think of the Iwo Jima Monument with its bronze soldiers permanently frozen in the act of straining to raise a flag which, despite all the best efforts of bulging metal muscles, remained forever only half erect. He would chuckle as he imagined little marines trying to raise his penis and having no luck. But that was later. At the time he saw no hint of humor. He just felt sick. "Yes" had turned out to be more humiliating than "no."

"What's the matter?" Frances asked again, this time more softly.

"I'm afraid of you," Paul said.

At that moment, or shortly thereafter, Frances fell in love with Paul.

9

What the Secretary Wanted

"THE DIRECTOR's in the library," Scott Bannister said.

"Good," said Mother. "If he develops an affection for books, he may even fill up those empty shelves in his office."

Mother was so perpetually short of bookshelves for his many volumes that he could never forgive other men their bare or sparsely filled bookcases.

"Thank you," Mother said, as his aide withdrew.

Mother was pleased to learn of O'Hara's presence in the library because recently the director's door had been barred to him. When he tried to make frontal, unannounced assaults on the boss's office, as had been his habit for a decade, he was told bluntly, if falsely, that O'Hara wasn't in. Now that the director had surfaced in a public place, Mother planned to confront him.

Mother wanted an answer to his latest memorandum requesting permission to share certain new information with the Israelis. For recent satellite pictures clearly showed that the Egyptians had installed exten-

sive field communications all along the west bank of
the Suez Canal. Mother considered this field network
the most alarming evidence yet that Egypt planned
to launch a new war *soon*. But his request to warn the
Israelis had gone unanswered.

Before leaving his office, Mother locked up the papers he had been working with. Then he headed for
the library, or, as it was officially known, the Historical
Intelligence Collection.

As Mother entered the library his eye was caught,
as always, by the relief map of Italy. This had been an
OSS project during the war and was the first map of
its kind ever constructed. Mother's gaze hiked up and
down the three-inch Alps in the north near his boyhood home, Milan. Then his eyes traveled south to
Rome, the centerpiece of a secret war he had fought
first against the Fascists, later against the Communists,
and later still against Ernest O'Hara. It seemed appropriate that Mother should once again confront
O'Hara before this miniature Italy, for this was just the
latest battle in a long war which had started in Italy
twenty years earlier.

Moving up behind O'Hara, Mother noticed that the
director was reading not a book but a back issue of
the agency's trade journal, *Studies in Intelligence*. The
founding of this periodical had been a preventative
measure necessitated by the makeup of the light side
of the agency, which employed many academicians.
Since the agency realized that in academe the urge
to publish is often stronger than the sex urge, it
decided to provide some outlet. The agency feared that
if the urge were completely frustrated, its professors
might be driven to such perversions as publishing in
public. So this secret publication was conceived. KU-
BARK wrote about KUBARK for KUBARK, a
slightly masturbatory endeavor.

O'Hara did not see Mother until they were sitting
opposite one another. The director simply nodded at
the head of KUDESK and went on reading.

"I wondered," Mother whispered, "if you'd decided whether I can tell the Israelis about the Arabs' field communications networks."

"I've taken it under advisement," whispered O'Hara.

"Does that mean you still haven't made up your mind?" Mother said, amplifying his whisper slightly.

"It means you'll be informed through proper channels," O'Hara whispered brusquely.

"Wars aren't fought through proper channels." Mother's whisper took on pedagogical tones. "And if we're going to prevent a war, we may have to go outside channels, too. I want a decision, yes or no."

"Shhh, you're disturbing the other readers."

"But I don't suppose"—Mother was no longer whispering—"that a war would disturb anyone."

"Shhh, this isn't doing anyone any good. And there are people trying to work."

"If you think I'm noisy, wait 'til you hear how loud a war can be," Mother said, his low voice rising higher in the library than it normally did even at, say, the racetrack.

"Please lower your voice," the director whispered.

"I won't," Mother said, his voice even louder. "We've got to warn the Israelis!"

Mother punctuated his sentence by slamming his fist down on top of the table. In the silent library it sounded like a mortar.

Everyone was staring.

O'Hara stood up and walked out of the room. Mother got up, too, but he was determined not to appear rattled. So, in a show of conspicuous composure, he stopped on his way out to study the display of bugs, invisible inks, miniature cameras, and other espionage bric-a-brac in a large glass case.

Another meeting, in another quiet setting, took place a few minutes later. Mark Harrington, of the PICKLE team, finished his regular eight-hour workday at 11 A.M. Then he strolled out into the company parking lot where he crawled behind the wheel of his Volvo. He took a perverse pride in not buying American automobiles. If you were going to sell out your country, you might as well sell it out all the way.

Driving into Washington, Harrington took a slightly circuitous route, winding through several residential areas. His path was not so eccentric as to be obvious evasion. In case anyone was following him, he did not want to arouse their suspicions. But it was unusual enough to allow him to see if he was being tailed. He wasn't.

Harrington drove through Georgetown on Reservoir Road. Then he turned left on Wisconsin Avenue.

Suddenly an alarm went off. Harrington slammed on his brakes and ducked behind the dashboard for cover. Three other cars slammed on their brakes in chain reaction behind him.

Then Harrington felt silly.

For he realized what had happened. He had hit a bump and the Bible on the seat beside him had set off the seat belt buzzer. The belt monitor had mistaken the holy book for a person who had forgotten to buckle up.

Harrington told himself he would have to calm down. He was so jumpy about driving around with state secrets in the car that he had almost caused a four-car collision in the middle of the busiest street in Georgetown just a block from the precinct station.

Taking a firm grip on the steering wheel—and, he hoped, on himself—Harrington accelerated once again. He drove on through the intersection of Wisconsin and Massachusetts Avenues and made a right-hand turn. He parked in the lot beside the Washington Cathedral.

Harrington picked up his troublesome Bible and walked into the lofty hall of worship. He loved the cathedral, and yet it always reminded him of a great Gothic gymnasium—just as at Yale the Gothic gymnasium always reminded him of a cathedral. In college he had wanted to grow up to play on God's team, but he had long since lost track of which team that was. Harrington stared up wide-eyed at the glowing stained-glass windows. He never quite got used to their being there.

Selecting a seat near the altar, he sat down. He lay his Bible on the chair to his right. Then he pretended to pray. After a while, he was not sure he was pretending.

Harrington glanced up involuntarily when a man sat down in the chair next to the chair occupied by the CIA man's Bible. The American intelligence officer recognized the Russian intelligence officer as Boris Zukov, supposedly a press attaché at the Soviet embassy. Zukov, too, had a Bible. And he, too, laid his holy book on the seat next to him. Now Harrington and Zukov sat on either side of a chair which held two Bibles—both bound in black leather, both with gold lettering on their covers, both King James versions, both identical.

Harrington was the first to leave. As he rose from his chair he picked up Zukov's Bible. A few minutes later the KGB man left, taking with him Harrington's Bible.

When Harrington reached his home, he took the black book into the bathroom. Seated on the toilet, he carefully removed hundred-dollar bills from between the thin pages of the Gospel. When Zukov reached his office, he removed from God's book the specifications for the M-60 tank.

"Go ahead," President Richard M. Nixon said the next day.

Ernest O'Hara launched into a briefing on a problem which required watching in South Africa, the short lecture illustrated by poster-sized charts carried by an aide. As graph gave way to diagram, gave way to table, gave way to map in rapid order, the show began to resemble an elaborate card trick performed by a giant.

O'Hara was addressing a meeting of the National Security Council (NSC) in the Cabinet Room at the White House. Before him sat not only the President, but also the vice-president, the secretary of state, the secretary of defense, under secretaries of state and commerce, a man from the National Aeronautics and Space Agency (NASA), and the chairman of the Joint Chiefs of Staff.

When O'Hara finished his discourse on the problem in South Africa, a short discussion ensued. The most vociferous champion of South Africa turned out to be Vice-President Spiro T. Agnew, who had problems of his own since it had recently been revealed that he was the target of a bribery investigation being conducted by the U.S. Attorney's office in Baltimore.

"I support the South Africans," Agnew said. "Now that they've declared their independence, they're not going to let anybody push them around. Their country is like our country was at the beginning. Ian Smith is their George Washington."

President Nixon leaned over to Agnew, touched him on the elbow, and said, "You mean Rhodesia, don't you, Ted?"

A few minutes later, the President moved the meeting on to the second item on its agenda: the situation in the Middle East. O'Hara briefed the members of the NSC on the latest developments. He said the Egyptian army regularly held maneuvers near the canal, but he pointed out that, for the first time, they were maneuvering in formations as big as a full division. He also told the NSC about the unprecedented installation of a sophisticated field communications network.

O'Hara knew he was taking something of a chance. He wanted a decision on whether or not the American intelligence community should share with the Israeli intelligence community the satellite photographs revealing the installation of the field communications system. Of course, the safest course would have been to go directly to the President's foreign policy adviser—who had recently been given another title, secretary of state —for a decision. But O'Hara thought he knew what that decision would be and he was not sure it was the right one. So he had decided to risk bringing the matter up before the full NSC. He put the question to them and leaned back to listen to the discussion.

When O'Hara saw the secretary of state begin turning his pencil over and over, he suddenly felt his shirt go wet under his arms. He knew by how fast the pencil revolved how mad the ODACID boss was. O'Hara hated Mother for getting him into this.

The secretary said, "We shouldn't encourage the Israelis to make another preemptive strike. And if we put it in their minds that the Egyptians are up to something, that's precisely what we'll be encouraging them to do. Make no mistake."

"Let me play devil's advocate," O'Hara said, his drab voice camouflaging his nervousness. "Suppose only a first strike could save the Israelis from a defeat. If that were the case, shouldn't we warn them?"

"No," rumbled the secretary of ODACID, "that's precisely the case in which we shouldn't warn them. Because, so long as Israel continues to believe she's invincible, she'll never give up any of the territory she captured in sixty-seven, and there can never be peace."

"Do you mean you want the Israelis to lose?" asked O'Hara.

"Only to suffer a military setback," said the secretary of state.

Director O'Hara was running in circles. The harder he ran, the sooner he doubled back on himself. The small track in the basement of the Toy Factory was an emblem for the bureaucracy itself. The gray director was dressed in a gray sweat suit. He tried to run three times a week, but since he had moved up to the top job he had difficulty finding time to run even once a week.

So his half-hour on the track would not be entirely lost, he had prevailed upon an aide named Andrew Wilson to run with him. The aide, who wore blue sweat clothes, was an awkward runner. His sport in college and ever since had been playing with compu-

ters. He now found himself installed in an office next
to the director, thanks to a computer operation he had
run in the mid-1960s. It had been designed to answer the question "Who's in charge of Moscow?"
Khrushchev had just been fired and no one knew who
was minding the Kremlin. Wilson did a statistical analy-
sis of the Soviet party congress which followed Khrushchev's fall and had found one statistical anomaly:
an extraordinary number of new members had spent
World War II in Dnepropetrovsk. After some checking, he discovered that Brezhnev had also served there
during the war. At last, KUBARK was able to tell the
President who was running Russia.

And now Wilson was running beside the DCI who
was running KUBARK. He wished he had the dexterity to write in a notebook and run at the same time.
As it was, he had to rely on his memory.

"Call Kimball," the director said. "He won't like
dealing with you instead of me, but that's just too
bad."

"Yes"—huff—"sir."

"Tell him," the director continued, "that his request
to communicate certain new information to the Israelis
has been turned down at the highest level."

"Yes"—puff—"sir."

"He'll put up an argument, but point out that there's
nothing he can do. You don't even know what the issues are. You're only delivering a message. Play dumb."

O'Hara ran through several other items he wanted
Wilson to take care of that afternoon. Each time the
director raised a new subject, the assistant raised a
finger. He hoped that if he kept track of how many
chores he was supposed to do, then perhaps, if he
racked his brain, he would be able to remember
to do them all.

The last subject the director wanted to discuss with
Wilson was the stock market. The agency had for
years played the market with money from its pension
fund, from its credit union, and from certain agent es-
crow accounts. In the beginning the CIA had turned
over its funds to a Boston brokerage house, which

made the final decision on which stocks to buy. But
this arrangement eventually proved unsatisfactory, for
the brokerage house was less daring and also had less
adequate research facilities than the CIA. Now an
agency investment group, made up primarily of econ-
omists, picked the company's stocks.

"Tell Jones," O'Hara said, "to buy Anaconda Copper."

The director did not go on to explain that, in a few
days, Salvador Allende, the Chilean president who
planned to nationalize Anaconda's assets in his country, would be the target of a coup.

After a shower, Wilson returned to his office and
called Mother.

"The director asked me to telephone you," Wilson said. "To give you a message . . ."

Mother was insulted, as O'Hara had known he
would be, for Wilson was by no means the KUDESK
chief's equal.

"Excuse me," Mother said. "I'll put my assistant
on."

He did. The next voice Wilson heard belonged to
Scott Bannister. Aide talked to aide.

Mother might have been less interested in games-
manship and more interested in the message had he not
already known what the message would be.

For Mother had already seen the minutes of the National Security Council meeting. His White House spy,
Ladyslipper, had left them for him in the men's
room at the Library of Congress.

10

The Farm

"LET'S STOP AND ASK," Frances said with an edge to her voice.

"You can't just stop and ask somebody how to get to Camp Peary," Paul protested. "It's a secret installation. Nobody knows where it is but us spooks, and we can't find it."

"Don't be naïve," Frances said. "Of course people know where it is. You've got a lot more faith in the agency's ability to keep secrets than I do. Let's stop at that gas station."

"No."

"Goddamn you, I'm sorry I ever let you drive my car."

They had rehearsed this scene several times before, which is to say that when they had gone on their short vacation up to Cape Cod they had gotten lost even there, and had had a series of arguments as a result. If all of humanity is divided into two categories, those who stop and ask directions and those who don't, then Paul and Frances represented the opposing sides of that great divide. The only arguments they had ever had were over stopping to ask.

They had somehow managed to escape the Cape with their love affair still intact, but now the dense woods of Virginia were threatening it. They were supposedly on their way to Camp Peary—code-named ISOLATION but better known as "The Farm"—where they were to undergo their next phase of training and indoctrination. It was the end of August, and all over the country students were going back to school, including, in their own way, Paul and Frances. But first they would have to find the school. They were the bright hope of an organization whose motto was: "And ye shall know the truth and the truth shall make you free." And it *was* their ambition to fight for freedom. But at the moment they did not even know the truth about where they were.

"If you don't ask, I'll never speak to you again."

"Starting now, I hope."

"Yes, starting now."

Frances remained silent for a few seconds only.

"Stop the car, I want to get out."

"Don't be silly."

"If you don't let me out, I'm going to jump out."

"Look, be reasonable. We can't just stop and ask someone how to find a classified base. Just mentioning the name would be a breach of security. Didn't you learn anything from your father?"

"My father never got lost."

They drove for another twenty minutes hopelessly and humorlessly. When the gas gauge reached "Empty," they finally stopped at a filling station.

Frances asked the attendant, "Could you direct us to Camp Peary?"

"Oh, you mean the Farm," the attendant said. "Why, sure, lady, you go right down here, take your first left, then take your second right; you can't miss it. Of course, if you do get lost again, just stop and ask anybody."

When they reached the Farm, they parked and made their way on foot to the large main building known as the Club. Entering the bar, Paul and Frances were confronted with what at first appeared to be the ultimate liberal nightmare: a Georgetown cocktail party invaded by Green Berets. Closer examination, however, revealed that the two factions were coexisting remarkably amicably. Men in houndstooth jackets with leather patches on the elbows stood chatting fraternally with men in camouflage fatigues with blacking on their faces. Frances asked one of the blackened faces what was going on.

"Maneuvers," the mask explained. "We're just taking a break. In a few minutes another group'll take its turn at the bar and we'll take our turn at the 'battle.'"

Paul and Frances were the last of the new trainees to arrive, but no one made anything of it. They were treated as though they had simply chosen to arrive fashionably late at the party.

They were assigned to separate barracks. The Farm had been described to them as a combination college campus and boot camp—the quarters they checked into were more the former than the latter. Each room had two beds. Two people shared one room and two rooms shared one bathroom. Paul found himself rooming with a young man with pimples who had also gone to Yale. Frances found herself rooming with a young female graduate of Texas A&M who smoked smelly cigars. Paul did not like his roommate and Frances liked hers no better: it was just like college.

The next morning, the first day of classes, they learned how to steam open envelopes. Paul was pretty good at it, but Frances burned herself. Frances said that was because Paul was handier with kitchen utensils. When they progressed to lock picking—which they called E. Howard Hunt 101—she turned out to be better than he was.

Their favorite class dealt with agent handling. It was conducted by a short, gray-haired man with gold-rimmed glasses who looked like a high school math teacher. A stern disciplinarian, he wasted no time in stamping out talking in his classroom. He divided his subject into categories, which he carefully wrote on the blackboard.

> Spotting
> Evaluation
> Recruiting
> Testing
> Training
> Handling
> Termination

While he was writing with his squeaky chalk, Paul wrote surreptitiously with a felt-tipped pen. When he had finished, he passed a note to Frances. Their courtship was in its high school phase. Reading the note, Frances strove to smother a blush.

"The term 'spotting' should be self-explanatory," the lecturer said, adding to himself that he had already spotted two troublemakers in his class. "The most sought after recruits should be officials of the target government who find themselves in opposition to their own government's policy. However, if you can't identify such a prospect, then look for officials with weaknesses: alcoholics, drug addicts, philanderers, homosexuals."

Frances pretended to be taking notes, but she was really composing a reply to Paul's epistle. She knew that he blushed more easily than she, and she looked forward to seeing his ears turn red. She covered her note with a sheet of paper as she wrote.

"Once a prospective agent has been 'spotted,' " the teacher droned on, "the next step is 'evaluation.' A name check is run through the agency's computerized files developed exclusively for us by IBM. Once the potential recruit's background has been thoroughly researched, a decision is made as to the best way to approach him. Should one rely on ideology, money, or blackmail?"

Finishing her note, Frances passed it to Paul and waited for his face to turn the color of a police car's flashing light.

"The 'recruiting' is done by a 'pitchman,' " the

teacher continued, pretending not to see the note. "He's given a false identity complete with a counterfeit passport. That way, if anything goes wrong, the resident agent in the country isn't blown."

As Paul read the note, he felt as if a powerful infrared lamp had been turned on his face.

"For 'testing,'" the teacher said, "we have come more and more to rely upon the lie detector test, the black box. For training, agents are often sent right here to the Farm, where we teach them the same tradecraft we're teaching you . . ."

Paul went to work on his reply.

". . . When it comes to 'handling,' there are two prevailing views. Some favor the 'buddy' approach, while others prefer the 'cynical' technique. The case officers handling Penkovsky found that flattery worked best. They awarded him a secret agency medal and even made him a full colonel in the American army—which caused some problems. When Penkovsky visited London on Soviet business, he slipped away to one of our safe houses for a debriefing. Before sitting down to talk, he asked to try on his American uniform. In a panic, his case officers rushed all over town until they found an American colonel Penkovsky's size. They stripped him . . ."

Paul passed his note to Frances. As she read, she pretended to sneeze to cover a giggle.

". . . The decision to terminate an agent can only be made by the chief of station with the approval of Langley. This can usually be done by money or threat. If anything more drastic is required, it must be approved by the Director of Central Intelligence himself. In the past, agents have been known to have heart attacks, traffic accidents, or commit suicide. We call this dying of the measles . . ."

As he spoke, the diminutive lecturer strolled down a classroom aisle. When he was directly beside Frances, towering over her—from her perspective at least—he demanded in a voice six feet six inches tall:

"Now, young lady, hand me those notes you've been passing! Where do you think you are, junior high?"

Frances reluctantly handed over the correspondence.

"I propose," the teacher said, "to read these to the class so that we can all share your amusement."

He made a great show of unfolding one of the white sheets. He had the air of a soloist readying his music. Then he opened his mouth but said nothing.

The message on the page read as follows:

"92116 21342 1192 14 291362 47 23114841 7447538 22 18 9655676 986 4600 321142896 . . ."

The teacher scrutinized the page for a few seconds and then said simply: "Well done."

Soon the classes were going on "field trips." In order to practice their tradecraft in a realistic setting, they would be turned loose on bucolic Virginia towns like, say, Harper's Ferry, which they would pretend was, say, Prague, where they would participate in spy maneuvers.

On one trip, Frances was assigned to set up a "meet" with an agent she had never seen before. She reconnoitered a small community named Middleburg, selected a small cafe, and went inside to case the interior. She did not realize that she had no money with her until she was already seated in a booth. Since she had been instructed to carry no identification, she had left her pocketbook back at the barracks, but that same pocketbook contained all her cash.

"Just a glass of water, please," she told a waitress who stood wilting beside the booth.

Frances then realized she didn't have a pencil either, so when the waitress returned with the water, she asked to borrow hers. The waitress handed over a sharp Venus #3, and Frances did a quick sketch of the interior of the restaurant on a napkin.

As a part of the drill, she had been instructed to map the meeting site, noting all exits. The only one she could see was the front door, but she suspected there might be a back way out through the kitchen. She signaled to the waitress, who returned to the booth.

"Another glass of water, please," Frances said. "and, well, I was wondering if you'd mind if I took a look at your kitchen. I'm remodeling mine and I'm, well, looking for ideas."

"Go right ahead, honey," the waitress said. "Lookin' don't cost nothin' either."

"Thank you," Frances said.

She went back, looked the kitchen over, found the back door, and returned to her booth to draw the exit on her napkin.

The sheriff's deputies arrived before she could finish her second glass of water. The manager of the cafe was convinced she was mapping his place for a robbery. The deputies marched her out and sat her down in one of their radio cars. Her heart was pounding the way it had been the time she was caught shoplifting in the supermarket. The police back then had called her mother, which had meant humiliation was added to all her other troubles. And now it was the humiliation that worried her once again. What if KUBARK ever found out?

When Frances admitted she had no identification papers, the deputies started growing suspicious. When she came up with a name and address which a call to Washington Information knocked down, they were pretty sure their suspicions were confirmed.

One of the deputies radioed headquarters and said: "Call up the Farm and tell them we've picked up another one of their spies. See where they want this one delivered."

Paul felt like a greyhound chasing a wooden spy around the track. He was part of a four-man team which had been sent out to Lynchburg to follow one of the instructors, a man who taught advanced students and so would know none of the neophytes by sight. If the instructor spotted you, you were out of the game. If you lost the instructor, you were out of the game. Paul walked down Lynchburg's main street, keeping the "rabbit" in view up ahead of him, feeling conspicuously nonagricultural in this farming community.

The instructor entered a department store and took the escalator up to the second floor, where he plunged into the lingerie section. While the teacher caressed polyester panties, Paul fondled a pile of padded bras. Then they moved on to shop for maternity dresses. Paul felt as if he were marked by a scarlet A: his blush.

Then the rabbit headed for the escalator again, followed by the student spooks. Communicating by hand signals, they set the order they would follow in taking the mechanical stairs. Paul would be last. Just as he was about to step aboard, he backed up and retreated to the bra department. For the rabbit had stepped off the down escalator and directly onto the up. As he ascended, the rabbit tipped his hat to the three descending junior spies, trapped on the human conveyor belt.

Paul took the elevator down and picked up the "spy" as he was leaving the store. The instructor walked to a shoeshine stand and stopped for a polish. While Paul was loitering across the street, a little boy came up to him and asked:

"Hey, mister, are you a Bible salesman?"

Paul said the only thing he could think of:

"Yes."

Bible salesman was as good a cover as any, he thought.

Soon the rabbit was running again. Paul followed him up one street and down another, in and out of dime stores, even across an occasional vacant lot. The junior spook kept the instructor in sight for another half-hour and then lost him in a supermarket. He scurried up and down the aisles, like someone driven crazy because he couldn't find the cornflakes, but the rabbit had disappeared down a hole. At first Paul was disappointed, but before long he realized he was relieved. He was a tired greyhound.

Paul was, however, premature in his belief that it was all over. When he left the supermarket, he had no idea where he was. He had been so intent on following the instructor he had forgotten to drop mental bread crumbs. Now he had no idea how to get back to the rendezvous.

An hour later he was still lost. Humiliated, he asked directions of a farmer in a pickup truck. A few blocks later he had to ask directions again, this time of an old woman pulling weeds in her flower bed.

Paul was glad Frances was not there to see.

They felt as if they were getting ready for a costume party. From the neck down, they were going as marines. From the neck up, they were going as the cast of a minstrel show. Frances blacked Paul's face and then Paul blacked Frances's. They were having such a good time it was hard for them to take the exercise seriously. It seemed to have nothing to do with them. When they were dressed, they would go to a party out in the woods where everyone else would be wearing costumes and playing roles ranging from agent on the run to torture-chamber sadist.

When Paul looked at his black face in the mirror he said, "Who says the company isn't an equal-opportunity employer?"

An hour later Paul and Frances were fugitives inside a very small Communist country set up deep in the Virginia woods. This small Soviet satellite had a well-protected border complete with barbed wire, a high fence, a plowed strip, watchtowers, searchlights, roving Commie guards—as if the Reds were afraid of their redneck neighbors beyond the frontier.

"I can't see you," Paul whispered.

"That's the idea," Frances whispered back.

It was a cloudy, moonless, starless night. With the camouflage uniforms and dark faces, they became almost invisible, especially in the shadow of the trees. Frances took Paul's hand so they wouldn't lose each other. In spite of Paul's occasional impotence, he and Frances had become lovers. For the past ten days they had been making love, or at least trying to, almost every day. And yet they still had never held hands.

Even in bed Frances was businesslike. They would make love, roll over, and Frances would say, "Do you think the Sino-Soviet split's a charade?" They enjoyed one another in bed and out, but they were not affectionate. Frances had an aversion to physical displays, but it went deeper than that. She would tell Paul, "When people touch you, they hurt you." So, with the exception of their copulation, they didn't touch.

Until now. Paul and Frances walked toward the heavily guarded border hand in hand, like high school students walking home together.

Their army boots crashed through the brush like wounded animals. The enemy guards would have had to be deaf not to have heard them. It was so dark that they often could not even see their own feet, so they had no chance of avoiding brittle twigs. Every step crackled. Paul, who liked to amuse himself constructing metaphors, thought the forest floor sounded as if it were covered with a mat of Rice Krispies.

When they came to a small clearing, they sat down on a log and Frances produced her compass.

"Which way do we go from here?" she asked.

"I don't know. You've got your compass out."

Staring at the bobbing needle, Frances said, "I think the border's north by northeast." Looking up and pointing, she said, "That way."

Their assignment was to escape from the Communist country by crossing the border under cover of darkness. The whole class had been sent out that night at different intervals to attempt a crossing. Working in teams of two, they were all supposed to scale the fence and slip quietly back into the free world. Paul and Frances, in spite of certain reservations they both felt, had chosen one another as partners. Earlier in the day they had gone out to reconnoiter the frontier. Now they were on their way to cross it, or, more likely, they were on their way to capture, interrogation, and the discomforts of make-believe torture.

Paul and Frances crackled their way through the woods for another two hundred yards and then stopped again. This time they both got out their compasses, as if one instrument might show the way more clearly than the other.

They continued to walk north by northeast to the best of their ability in spite of fallen trees, intervening streams and occasional impenetrable brush. They walked wordlessly for several minutes. They climbed a small hill, looked around, recognized nothing, and pushed on.

"Let's stop and ask directions," said Paul.

"Shut up!"

She always seemed to get angry when she did not know exactly where she was. It was no longer a costume party. She was tense.

They thrashed about in the forest for another half-hour before Frances announced disgustedly:

"We're lost."

"I know."

"I knew I should've picked another partner," Frances said, pulling her hand out of Paul's.

"It's as much your fault as it is mine," Paul said angrily.

It was the same old story. Getting lost made Frances mad, and Frances's getting mad made Paul mad.

"Climb a tree and see if you can see anything," Frances ordered.

"I don't want to climb a tree," Paul fumed. "Besides, it's too dark to see anything."

"Goddammit, climb a tree," Frances ordered. "Do you want to stay lost all night?"

Paul decided not to ask Frances why she thought she was strong enough to issue commands but not strong enough to climb her own tree. Instead, he said wearily, "All right," and started up the nearest oak.

When he was halfway up, he could see even less than he could on the ground because the leaves blocked his view. Against his better judgment and natural inclination, he climbed higher. As he neared the top, the limbs began to sway, and he felt the way he always felt when an airplane hit an air pocket. But he still could not see, so he moved cautiously higher, wondering, as he climbed, if he was going to throw up, and, if he did throw up, would any of it land on Frances.

When at last he was high enough to see over the

other trees, he still could not see anything. The dark hills which were dimly visible all around him gave him no clue as to where he was.

"I can't see anything," he said in a loud stage whisper.

"Shhh!"

"It's no use," he stage-whispered. "I'm coming down."

"Damn, damn, damn, damn," Frances said, each "damn" louder than the last.

It occurred to Paul that perhaps she would rather be caught than lost.

Climbing down was even worse than climbing up, not only because he could not see where he was going, but also because he was in no hurry to reach the sullen, angry woman he knew awaited him on the ground. If he had liked heights better, he might have given some passing thought to staying up the tree.

Paul reached the bottom tier of limbs and was about to wrap his legs around the trunk and slide down when a small dead branch broke in his hand. He lost his balance and reeled backward. While he was in midair, a similar incident in his childhood flashed into his mind. An oak tree had been at fault then, too. He should have remembered how brittle their dead branches could be. In that boyhood fall he landed on his back and lay there for what seemed half an hour because he was afraid to try to use his legs. He had been afraid he might be paralyzed, and if he was, he didn't want to know about it.

These reveries stopped when Paul hit the ground. The impact made him momentarily groggy. When his consciousness cleared he could hear someone laughing. It was Frances. She was kneeling over him and laughing so hard that she too appeared to be in pain. She no longer seemed to care if anyone heard her or even that they were lost. At last Paul knew how to entertain her.

"Let's make love," Frances said.

Paul thought she was joking until he felt her loosening his belt. Then she unzipped his pants and reached inside. When her hand crept into his underwear, Paul was pleased to discover he was not paralyzed.

In the past when he had been impotent with Frances, Paul had diagnosed the problem as fear. But now he was learning that there were different kinds of fear, that sometimes a little danger could be incredibly exciting, that the fear of somehow being caught in the act made his penis feel like an oak tree.

Making love in uniform turned out to be something of an engineering problem. Paul stood up to lower his pants to the top of his high-laced army boots. He also unbuttoned his shirt. Frances lowered her trousers to her boottops, too, and opened her shirt, but when they tried to make love she could not spread her legs.

"Wait, wait," Frances said. "Don't be in such a hurry."

She sat up, unlaced one boot, took it off, slipped off one trouser leg, and lay back down on the dead leaves.

Paul climbed on top of her. He knew she was ready because he could smell her excitement even above the smells of the forest. When he entered her, she gave a little gasp and then complimented him upon his size. He had never felt so big inside her. And yet he was terrified. The forest seemed to be crackling all about them. He was sure the Commie guards were going to arrest them in the middle of coitus.

It seemed to Paul that he had never enjoyed making love so much. He loved the primitiveness. He loved the wind blowing on his balls.

"Let's do it from the back," Frances said.

When she was on her hands and knees, Paul entered her from behind.

"This is how God meant people to make love," Paul said, a little out of breath.

"No it isn't."

"Sure it is. This is the way chimpanzees do it. But civilized man wanted a kinky thrill, so he started doing it from the front."

"Shut up and fuck me," Frances said.

When Paul came, he thrust forward so hard he

knocked Frances flat on her stomach. While she was still lying face down in the leaves and he was still lying on top of her, she said "I love you" for the first time since they had met. Paul rolled off Frances and they hugged. No one spoke of politics.

When they were dressed, with dry leaves trapped inside their trousers, they set off hand in hand in search of the border once again. They were still lost but they were more easygoing about it. They gave up on the compasses and just walked. They wandered about in the wilderness for another half-hour or so and then sat down on a rock to neck.

Suddenly a spotlight seemed to focus on them. Paul took his hand out of Frances's army shirt and they scrambled behind the rock. It was only then that they realized they had not been singled out by the light. Rather, the whole countryside was lit by a flare which was slowly floating to earth three-quarters of a mile away.

"Must be the border," Frances whispered.

"That's right," Paul whispered, "somebody must've hit a trip wire. I'm afraid the Commies are about to pick up another defender of the free world."

"Too bad," Frances said, pulling out her compass. "That's south-southwest of us. Shall we go?"

"Let's."

They walked hand in hand for another forty-five minutes, the rough ground and their own caution slowing their progress. At last they reached a slime-filled ditch which protected the border. They had never been so happy to see anything so disgusting.

They huddled in the brush until they saw a patrol pass in a jeep. Then they scurried to the ditch. Slipping down into the muck was easy enough, but climbing up the other side was almost impossible. Every time they tried to crawl out, they slid back into the mire. They felt like bugs trying to crawl out of a toilet bowl.

"This is never going to work," Paul whispered. "Let me boost you up and then you pull me up."

Frances nodded.

Paul cupped his hands. Frances stepped into this improvised stirrup and Paul hoisted her up. Getting out still was not easy, but she managed to scramble onto the bank.

Then Frances reached down and took Paul by the hand. She strained as he started scrambling up the bank, but to her horror she realized she was slipping.

"Watch out," she whispered.

But it was no use. Frances landed on top of Paul in the bottom of the ditch. Their bodies were so entangled they looked as if they were making love again, this time in a bed of slime. When they got to their feet they were black with muck from head to foot, and Paul's nose was bleeding.

"I'll boost you up again," Paul said.

"Okay."

Paul hoisted Frances up out of the ditch. This time she dug two holes with her boots before reaching down to take Paul's greasy hand. She pulled and he fought his way up over the lip of the ditch. Then they caught their breath for a few seconds as they stared up at the ten-foot wall they still had to scale.

Frances tried to climb on Paul's shoulder, which was like climbing a greasy pole. After repeated failures, she made it to the top of the wall and then started pulling Paul up. For a moment Frances and Paul both perched on top of the wall like black ravens. Then they dropped down on the other side and started rolling across the plowed ground toward cover.

When they finally reached the brush, they crouched and scurried on into the protection of the trees and the shadows. Once they had left the border fifty yards behind, they stopped to hug each other in spite of the slime.

"Ugh," Frances said, "you feel just awful."

Frances and Paul were the only members of their class to cross the border successfully. All the others were captured by Commie border guards, whisked away to small cells, and interrogated by East German security officers. Frances and Paul had succeeded where the others had failed largely because they had reached the border so late that the guards, thinking the exercise was over, were taking it easy.

The instructors commended Frances and Paul on their strategy. The other members of the class were advised to emulate them.

II

THE WAR

11

The Call

AT 5 A.M., MOTHER GOT UP to care for his children. He had been awake since four and had finally given up trying to go back to sleep. Putting on his gardening clothes, he went out to his orchids. Since the late September morning was unusually cool, Mother chose the warmer of his two hothouses. It did not seem the right hour to pollinate, so Mother went to work transplanting. He had been neglecting his flowers. A lady slipper had died.

Mother worked peacefully for almost an hour before he began to imagine he heard a telephone ringing. He hurried toward the house, the bell growing louder with every step. As he was crossing the kitchen the phone stopped.

Hoping the caller would try again, Mother sat down in a child's miniature Empire chair which he kept beside the telephone. It had originally been made for a little boy or girl who had grown up and died of old age in the Loire River Valley over two hundred years ago. Sitting in the juvenile chair, Mother leaned forward and rested his elbow on a juvenile table. He had bought both in Europe after the war. Hunched over by the phone, he looked like a waiting giant.

Mother was restless because he hated to waste time. He kept remembering the dead lady slipper and wanted to get back to his orchids. Deciding the call probably wasn't very important anyway, he gave up his vigil. He was halfway out to Light Side when he heard the phone ring. Mother reached it in time.

The caller was Tom Baker, the duty officer on the Israeli desk. Mother's telephone was continually swept for taps and was considered secure, but still the conversation was guarded.

"I thought I should alert you," the duty officer said. "The Egyptians've called up A, B, and C."

"I'll be right in," said Mother.

Mother had been warned by one of his last remaining agents in Egypt that when the Egyptians activated all three classes of their reserves it meant war. Over the past year, the Egyptians had called up one class or another some twenty times, on a regular rotation, as a diversionary tactic. The idea had been to lull the Israelis into accepting call-ups as an ordinary occurrence, but this triple-class call-up was extraordinary.

A part of Mother wanted to rush to the office in gardening clothes, but another, stronger part could not leave the house without showering, shaving, methodically dressing, and retying the bows on his black wingtip shoes several times until he got them perfect.

When Mother reached his office he called the duty officer. Moments later, the cable from the Middle East was on his desk. It simply confirmed what he had already assumed from the cryptic telephone call. Now he was certain Egypt was about to attack Israel.

It was 6:40 A.M. when Mother reached for the telephone and called the director at home. His heart was beating so loudly it nearly drowned out the sound of the phone ringing. Mother hated to admit it to himself, but the director frightened him. Alice O'Hara answered the phone. She said her husband had already left for the office.

Mother stood up, carefully folded the cable, inserted it in the breast pocket of his suit, and left his office. As he walked down the corridor, it was so quiet that Mother half expected to meet monks on their way to their morning prayers. One assumed that quiet was the partner of peace—peace and quiet. In the deserted halls, it was difficult to focus one's mind on war.

Mother took the elevator up to the seventh floor. He followed the corridor to the director's office, which was locked at that hour. Mother stationed himself outside, like a sentry, to wait for the director's arrival.

At precisely 7 A.M., Director O'Hara stepped out of the elevator. When he saw Mother, he reacted as if his enemy greeted him at his door every morning. The two men nodded wordlessly to each other and Mother followed the director into his office uninvited.

"This morning we received proof," Mother said before either man had time to sit down, "that Egypt is planning an immediate attack on Israel."

Mother went ahead to outline the triple call-up and its significance. O'Hara did not interrupt him to say that he, too, had received a call that morning from the duty officer and that he had already been on the telephone to a sleepy secretary of state to ask guidance.

While Mother talked, the director sought the cover of his desk. He sat down behind it, but his visitor continued to stand.

When Mother finished his short discourse, the director said, "And now you want to pass along these alarmist rumors to the Israelis?"

"This isn't a rumor, it's reliable intelligence. And it isn't alarmist, it's alarming."

"We aren't here to debate. If we pass along scare stories, we're likely to provoke a war. The matter's closed."

"Is the secretary of state behind this?"

"This isn't a cross-examination."

"Aren't we any better than our enemies?" Mother asked in a low, angry voice. "In sixty-seven, while you were in Vietnam, the Soviets found out the Israelis

planned a preemptive strike. But they didn't tell their
Arab allies because they were afraid they'd sue for
peace. Now *we* know the Arabs plan to strike, but we
won't tell our allies for fear they'll go to war. We're as
bad as the other side, maybe worse."

"Spare me the history lecture. I'm sorry, but I'm
afraid I have work to do, if you'll excuse me."

When the director realized Mother was not going to
move, he himself got up and walked into the conference room adjoining his office. He closed the door
behind him, and sat down all alone at the big table,
and waited.

Mother mounted the steps of the Israeli ambassador's residence on Chesapeake Road. He did not like
the large, modern ranch house, which seemed out of
keeping with the antiquity of the Jewish people. Mother thought the residence should have been as traditional as Jerusalem, but instead it was as modern and
ugly as Tel Aviv.

A butler opened the door. As Mother entered, his
shoulders were stooped even lower than usual, as if
in deference to the low ceiling. The butler ushered
him into the living room, where he recognized several
Pentagon and State Department officials standing over
by the sliding glass doors. The Israeli ambassador was
having one of his frequent cocktail parties. Mother, as
usual, had been invited. The room was loud with raised
voices.

Mother accepted a Kir from a waiter and slipped
into a corridor as he usually did at these affairs. He felt
out of place in the big room with its big voices. In
the hallway, Mother huddled with an Israeli military
attaché named Chaim Gur. They both spoke in voices
just above a whisper. The Israeli knew Mother only as
"Fran."

Mother could not talk about what he wanted to talk
about, the threat of war, so he talked Jewish history
and Jewish philosophy. The man to whom he spoke
was short, dark, and a little fat. At a distance they
looked as if they must be exchanging state secrets, but

actually they were discussing the works of an Israeli philosopher-diplomat named Jacob Herzog.

Mother said he had known Herzog when he was stationed in Washington. At parties like this one they had often huddled together in hallways, whispering philosophy as if it were top secret. They had become close friends.

"You know, Fran, I was attached to the embassy in Ottawa when Herzog was ambassador there," said Chaim Gur.

"Then you were there when he debated Arnold Toynbee."

"In the front row. Herzog went white when Toynbee called the Jews a 'fossil of Syriac civilization.'"

Mother subdued an impulse to tell Gur that within days the "fossil" would be threatened with another extinction. As they reminisced about the Herzog-Toynbee debate, another debate took place in Mother's mind: one side argued that orders must be obeyed at all costs; the other side argued that friends must be warned at all costs.

"Toynbee's problem," Mother said, "was that he thought nations were people. He believed a country coming back to life was as unnatural as a man coming back. He, of course, ignored the examples of Lazarus and Jesus."

"Herzog actually started to shake," said Gur, "when Toynbee said the Jews' treatment of the Arabs was as bad as the Germans' treatment of the Jews."

Mother wanted to warn that the more pressing issue would soon be the Arabs' treatment of the Jews, but he could not bring himself to do so. Instead, he showed off his memory, of which he was proud.

"Herzog said," Mother recalled, "'How can the two be mentioned in the same breath?'"

"What upset Herzog most," Gur said, "what upset us all, was Toynbee's challenge to our very right to existence. He seemed to be saying history was working against us."

"Exactly."

"Of course, that was before the Six-Day War. We showed them something about whose side history was on in sixty-seven, didn't we, Fran? It'll take them a generation to get over that war."

"No nation can afford to be overconfident," Mother cautioned, his private debate reaching the shouting stage. "After all, you struck first last time, but what if they strike first this time? You surprised them, but what if *they* surprise *you?*"

"Don't worry," replied the military attaché. "They'll never strike 'til they've built up an air force. And if they're foolish enough to attempt an attack, it'd take them over twenty-four hours to bridge the canal. We'd have plenty of time to call up our reserves and crush them again. There's no chance for surprise."

"That's what we thought before Pearl Harbor," Mother warned, trying to drop hints without disobeying orders. "It's a very dangerous attitude."

"Well, there's one difference: the Japanese had a pretty fair force."

Mother knew that if he did not break off this conversation, he would end up revealing more than he was supposed to. Orders had won the debate.

"I've got to be going," he said.

Before leaving the party, Mother went out through the glass doors onto the patio to say hello to the ambassador. While they were chatting, they were dive-bombed by mosquitoes.

On the morning of October 4, Mother received another message from the agent in Egypt: the Arabs planned to launch a coordinated attack against Israel in two days, on Yom Kippur.

Once again, Mother made the trip to the director's office. As always, the two men seemed to be shouting at each other through a wall. This time O'Hara was sufficiently concerned not to dismiss Mother's request to inform the Israelis out of hand.

"I'll get back to you," the director said. "Right now I'm a little busy."

Since Mother felt there might be some hope, he took the hint and left the director's office.

The director picked up the telephone. He called the secretary of state in New York City, but once again the secretary said no. He was still convinced that, if the Israelis knew they were about to be attacked, they would strike first, rout the Arabs, and be more intractable than ever at the negotiating table.

Later that day, the secretary of state met with the foreign minister of Israel. The two men gave only five minutes to a discussion of the possibility of an early war. The Israeli foreign minister said his intelligence people were not predicting war. The American secretary of state said his weren't either.

The American secretary closed out the discussion by predicting: "Nothing dramatic can happen in October."

All day long the director kept planning to call Mother back just a little later. At the end of the day he still had not gotten back to the man who ran the Israeli desk. O'Hara, who tended to put off difficult tasks, decided to call Mother tomorrow.

That night Mother could not sleep. At 3 A.M., he decided to get up. He went to his study, took down *The Oxford Book of English Verse,* and started leafing through the fat black volume from the back, knowing what he would find there.

The first poem he read was Julian Grenfell's "Into Battle," which ended:

> *The fighting man shall from the sun*
> *Take warmth, and life from the glowing earth . . .*
> *And find, when fighting shall be done*
> *Great rest, and fullness after death.*

Mother wondered if the poet had felt any less benign about restful death as he lay dying of his battle wounds in 1915.

Mother moved backward through his book to Rupert Brooke's "The Soldier":

If I should die, think only this of me:
That there's some corner of a foreign field
That is for ever England.

Mother found himself asking if literary courage had anything to do with real courage. Was bravery just a literary tradition, or did those young poets actually believe what they wrote when they wrote it? And did they believe it still when they were tested? As Rupert Brooke lay dying in 1915, was England really a consolation? And as young Jews lay dying in 1973, would the existence of Israel console them? Mother really did not know.

Mother fixed himself a tall Scotch on the rocks, drank it too fast, and wobbled back to bed.

Mother slept.

The next morning, he went to Langley early to wait for the phone to ring. In his office he turned the page on his desk calendar and found that he had an engagement that evening. Under the date, October 5, was written: "Hickory Hill dinner for Robert Lowell, 8 P.M., black tie."

When he had received the invitation weeks earlier he had been surprised and pleased. He had had no contact with the mistress of Hickory Hill, Ethel Kennedy, since her husband's assassination. But after all these years she evidently still remembered that the chief of Counterintelligence, who once worked closely with her husband, had a literary side. Perhaps she recalled his stories about Pound and Eliot and Frost. So she had invited him to dine with Robert Lowell. And Mother wanted to go, for he considered Lowell to be—if not the equal of those giants who had once written for his little magazine at Yale—at least the foremost poet of this minor age. Preoccupied by the mounting Middle East crisis, Mother had forgotten the date of the dinner. Now that he saw it on today's page, he felt better about the day.

Still, an invitation to a special dinner could not cure Mother of his special worries. His gaze traveled from the calendar to the latest Central Intelligence Bulletin. He thumbed through it disgustedly. It was twenty pages long, filled with pictures and maps, and looked like a news magazine without advertisements. It was circulated daily to the White House, Cabinet members, and to some lower officials. It was also cabled to American embassies abroad. It looked impressive, but on that day, Friday, October 5, it was worse than useless.

Mother paused to underline a sentence: *"Egypt— the exercise and alert activities in Egypt may be on a somewhat larger scale and more realistic than previous exercises, but they do not appear to be preparing for a military offensive against Israel."*

In the margin Mother wrote, "NO!"

Then he put down the Bulletin and stood up to go see the director, but he sat down again.

Mother had lunch with Scott Bannister, who was wearing a new pin-striped suit, at La Niçoise. He was glad he did not have to sit across the table from an Israeli.

Returning to Langley, Mother went up to the director's office, but someone was with him. Mother would wait. Fifteen minutes later Mother walked into the director's long, airy office.

O'Hara repeated the same old excuses about not provoking a first strike.

"It's too late to be cautious," Mother said. "The war's going to start tomorrow."

"Let me put it this way," the director said. "If we tell the Israelis nothing, there may be a war tomorrow. But if we frighten them, there'll definitely be a war. It'll be a self-fulfilling prophecy because the Israelis will attack at dawn."

As O'Hara spoke, he perched on the forward edge of his chair. He rested his elbows on the desktop and with his hands played with two paper clips, pressing them into a Kama sutra of ingenious interlocking positions. Mother, angry as he was, could not help noticing, and even admiring, the director's dexterity with the clips. For he played without damaging them.

"This is too cold-blooded," Mother said.

"It doesn't become you to call others cold-blooded. This isn't something you want to get into."

"I suggest we let the secretary of state make this decision."

"I suggest you obey orders, as you've sworn to do."

"I've always obeyed orders."

"Good. Now, if you'll excuse me."

Mother left the director's office and returned to his own floor. Sitting at his desk, he tried to decide what he could possibly do. He reached into a desk drawer and fished out a paper clip. A short while later he reached into the drawer again. And then again and again and again. His desktop looked like a miniature battlefield littered with the bodies of an army of dead paper clips, all horribly mangled.

Mother left his office at six-thirty and was home a few minutes later. He went into the bedroom and removed his tuxedo from the back of the closet. The wrinkles weren't too bad. A part of Mother always dreaded parties, but a larger part of him very much wanted to attend this literary evening.

And yet he felt guilty. He would be out indulging his literary ego while the Arabs were making their final preparations for a surprise attack on Israel. He felt like a sentry about to desert his post, just before the assault, to go to a whorehouse. He dressed slowly. He had more trouble than usual with the studs. The cummerbund fought him. Then he retied his black tie seven times. But when he was dressed he didn't leave home.

He sat down in his tiny antique chair and stared. He was paralyzed. Feeling helpless as a child, he rocked back and forth.

If he was not going to the dinner party, he knew he should call and make some excuse. "Something's come up . . ." But he could not bring himself to do so. He worried about them waiting dinner. He imagined Ethel Kennedy looking at her watch. He pictured Robert Lowell staring at an empty chair.

Mother was a patient man but not one who could endure total idleness. Patience implied a conviction that eventually one would prevail. Idleness meant that one made no effort to prevail. Mother admired the one and hated the other. And yet he was completely idle and felt he could not help himself.

Mother was troubled by two visions: he saw an empty chair at a table. Then this image gave way to another: he saw a surprise attack. These pictures alternated: empty chair . . . attack . . . empty chair . . . attack . . . He sat that way until 9 P.M.

Then he made up his mind.

Picking up the nearby receiver, Mother telephoned Moshe Dayan in Tel Aviv, disturbing the fighting man's dreams. In Israel it was already tomorrow, already 4 A.M., already Yom Kippur.

"*Shalom*," said a sleepy voice.

"*Shalom*," answered a tense voice.

And then the head of the Israeli desk disobeyed orders.

When he hung up, Mother went out to pollinate orchids in his tuxedo.

12

The Palestine Connection

WHILE THE ISRAELIS were fighting for their existence
along the banks of the Suez Canal, Mother was fishing
with two friends on the banks of a Virginia stream.
The war in the Middle East was two weeks old. After
spending eighteen hours a day fussing over the Israeli
desk, Mother had at last taken a brief respite. He was
an old man and had to get away, or break down. Leaving a map with the duty officer, showing where he
would be, Mother had driven off into the woods.
While Mother fished, he had no idea that an important
ally was putting out lines, trying to find him. Menachem Ginzburg searched all over Washington, but
Mother was hidden in a pocket of the Joseph's coat
worn by the bright autumnal hills.

"Take it easy," Mother said to one of his compan-
ions.

But his advice did no good. A line snagged. Now
this was a mess. There were knots inside of knots. The
line seemed hopelessly snarled beyond untangling.

"Oh, not again," said Osvald Lapusnyik, a Czech defector. Three months earlier he had been a member of the Statni Tajna Bezpecnost (STB), the Czechoslovakia service. He was slightly overweight because he had gotten little exercise since changing sides, spending most of his time puttering about a small house in McLean, afraid to go out. He was fortyish and had prematurely gray hair which he kept dyed black. Lapusnyik tried to unravel his tangled fishing line, but he was unable to help himself.

"Paul, see if you can give him a hand," Mother called.

Paul, wearing rubber hip boots, sloshed over to Lapusnyik, also in hip boots, and applied himself to the fouled line.

Mother often took defectors fishing so he could combine two of his favorite activities: angling for trout and information. He had invited Paul—who had a free weekend before reporting to the Canal Zone for war games—to come along and learn the technique. Mother told his protégé that some of his greatest debriefing successes had been accomplished beside a trout stream.

Paul began his assault on Lapusnyik's knot patiently enough, but after some initial success his fingers began to try too hard. In the end, his efforts accomplished only the further tightening of the knot.

"I'm just making it worse," confessed Paul.

Mother, his hip boots making him awkward, waded over to take charge of the tangle.

"You can do it," Lapusnyik said. "You're the expert on complexity."

It took Mother ten unhurried minutes to unscramble the knots. Then he splashed back to his part of the stream and soon caught a fish with a fly he had tied himself. Fly-tying was another of his hobbies. He was good at creating as well as dissolving knots. He loved to fish because it was slow, because it was intricate, because it required skill, and because he loved to catch things. Catching was his vocation and his avocation.

"Whoops!" yelled Lapusnyik, stumbling backward

and sitting down hard on a sharp rock. He had tried a mighty cast which tipped him over. Before getting up, he reached inside his rubber boots, fished around, and with a smile on his face pulled out a bottle of bourbon, a drink he was trying to learn to love.

"I was afraid I broke it," he bellowed. He unscrewed the cap and took a jolt. "Want some?"

Mother and Paul both declined. Getting up, Lapusnyik rubbed his sore behind.

"That reminds me of Schwirkmann," the Czech defector said. "The West Germans sent him to Moscow in sixty-four to look for bugs in their embassy. Only Schwirkmann didn't just yank out the bugs. He shot a big charge of electricity into them. The people listening got a big shock. Ha! Ha! Very funny. But the KGB got him back. They shot him in the ass with nitrogen mustard gas."

"Sounds pretty childish," Mother said.

"Okay, okay," said Lapusnyik, "except it hurt him very much and he almost died. And then the Germans told Nikita that their big trade deal was off. That was the beginning of the end for Nikita. The party congress called him home from vacation and told him he wasn't running the country anymore."

Mother was surprised by the denouement of what had at first seemed a trivial story—and yet he knew he should not have been. For he had learned long ago that spies were much more likely to destabilize regimes in their own countries than in foreign countries. Governments embraced intelligence organizations at their own risk.

Mother took Paul fifty yards upstream to instruct him in angling, but soon Paul was asking about matters unrelated to fishing. At first he tried questioning Mother about the Middle East war but with no success. The head of the Israeli desk did not enjoy discussing his failures. And now he believed he had failed: he should have disobeyed orders sooner.

So Paul began casting in less troubled waters. Mother

realized Paul was attempting to debrief him, just as he had debriefed Lapusnyik. But Mother didn't mind. He admired Paul's curiosity. And Paul knew it.

"I heard you and O'Hara were both stationed in Italy after the war," said Paul. "That so?"

"Yes, but not at the same time. He showed up in Rome right after I returned to Washington."

"How'd your Italian politics compare?"

"You're still being too direct."

"All right," said Paul, recalling his previous lesson. "When did you first, uh, return to Italy after the war?"

"That's more like it. It was in forty-seven. My orders were to make sure the Reds lost the forty-eight election."

Mother explained: He had been briefly out of the secret world right after the war, when Harry Truman disbanded the OSS because he was a little afraid of it. But by 1947, Truman was more concerned by external threats, so he asked Congress to create the Central Intelligence Agency. The leaders of this new spy cartel remembered the young man who had done such a good job as head of the OSS X2 in Rome. They decided to send him back. Returning to the Italian capital under diplomatic cover, the new CIA recruit was given an office on the second floor of what had once been Queen Margarette's palace. Remodeled, it was now the American embassy.

"How do you fix an election?" asked Paul.

"We didn't exactly fix it. We would've if we could've, but it wasn't that easy."

Soon Mother found himself behaving like one of his defectors, telling a story. One of his duties in Rome had been to attend meetings of the embassy's "political action committee," which convened often in the ambassador's lavish conference room. The other members included the heads of the political and economic sections, the naval attaché, the air force attaché, the military attaché, the treasury attaché, and of course the ambassador himself. Beneath the gilded ceiling, they plotted to win the Italian election for the Christian Democrats.

One afternoon, as the ambassador was going around the table asking for ideas, the young CIA officer raised his hand.

"I thought," he said, "we might take advantage of one of America's great natural resources. Greta Garbo. I realize she once belonged to another country, but I believe by now we're justified in claiming her as our own. So I suggest we import one of her best pictures. I'd like to expose the Italians to *Ninotchka*."

"I'm afraid I'm unfamiliar with that picture," said the ambassador.

"It's an excellent movie, sir," Kimball said. "Garbo plays a Russian commissar who comes to Paris, falls in love, and defects. It's a wonderfully funny movie. We'll have all Italy laughing at the Soviets."

"This is a novel approach to propaganda," the ambassador said. "What do the rest of you think?"

"I like the idea," said the head of the economic section. "It'd not only be good propaganda, it'd be cheap propaganda. It'll pay for itself."

Kimball had fed these lines to the economic adviser the day before. He could not bear not to scheme.

"All right," the ambassador said, "if it's not going to cost us anything to speak of, let's do it."

"Good," said Kimball. "I believe Miss Garbo will prove a most lethal secret weapon."

"That's when I first met Ginzburg," Mother told Paul. "In Italy in forty-eight. He was in the Jewish underground. While I was working on the election, he was smuggling Jews out of Europe into Palestine. I helped him as much as I could. You see, right after the war I went to Buchenwald, and, well . . . I did what I could."

"So that's when you made that connection."

"Right. It's been a good connection for twenty-five years. We've helped them and they've helped us, but this time I'm afraid we've let them down."

"You must've been busy in forty-eight."

"I'll say. It was like having two full-time jobs. Hurting the Communists and helping the Jews. It's hard to believe I ever had that kind of energy. But then, I haven't always been a bent old man, rumors to the contrary notwithstanding."

"What was the team of Kimball and Ginzburg like in the good old days?"

"We used to meet in the Piazza Navona. At the Bernini fountain. Right in front of the lion. I loved that old cat. Always reminded me of Bert Lahr."

Paul wanted to know what the CIA had done for the Jewish underground, and Mother wanted to tell him. The debriefing continued to go smoothly. Mother recalled a ship.

In front of the lion one afternoon, the young American intelligence officer announced proudly, "I've located a captain who's willing to put his ship at your disposal."

"Really," said Ginzburg. "How're the captain's nerves? Would a blockade scare him?"

"Quite the contrary. Blockades are his business. He's a smuggler."

"What does he smuggle?"

"Does it matter, so long as he wants to smuggle Jews now?"

"I'm grateful, but I'm also cautious. Couldn't you tell me a little more about your captain?"

"He works for one of my Sicilian friends," Kimball said. "Runs poppy extract from Turkey to Marseilles."

The Sicilian friend was a don in a powerful Mafia family. The don had fought against Mussolini because the Italian dictator wanted to break up the crime syndicate. After the fall of Il Duce, the don had joined the struggle against the Communists because he feared they would try to do the same. The don and Kimball had become allies in the war against communism. The don had offered Kimball the services of one of his ships, and Kimball in turn was offering the ship to the Jewish underground.

With the English attempting to restrict the number of Jews immigrating to Palestine, then a troublesome British protectorate, a brisk human smuggling business had grown up. And Italy had become to Zionism what Turkey was to the poppy trade.

"I'm not sure I like working with a criminal," Ginzburg said. "You're not going to get me in trouble, are you?"

"What are you talking about?" said Kimball. "*You* are a criminal."

"But I don't feel like a criminal."

"Believe me, you are. But don't worry. Some of my best friends are criminals."

Paul asked, "Were there any policy disagreements?"

Mother, who knew Paul was really asking if he had quarreled with O'Hara over the election, decided to string the young man along.

"Yes, a serious one."

"What happened?" Paul asked with growing excitement.

"Well, you know George Kennan. These days he's got everybody convinced he's always been the voice of sanity in an insane world."

"Kennan?"

"He may be sanity itself today, but he wasn't ever so."

"Was Kennan in Italy?"

"You ask too many questions," Mother said. "What I mean is: you should start a person talking and then just let him run on and on 'til he runs down. People'll tell you the most extraordinary things that way."

"All right, but *was* he in Italy?"

"No, the argument was carried on by transoceanic cable."

Mother described for Paul the Kennan plan: the voice of reason recommended that the Communist party be outlawed in Italy. He predicted the Communists would reply with civil war. Which in turn would give the United States an excuse to send in the marines, occupy Italy, and partition the country.

Kimball knew about these recommendations because he received copies of all cables to and from the embassy—without the ambassador's knowledge. The embassy's communications clerk was also a CIA officer. Kennan's proposal alarmed Kimball. Afraid the United States might be about to overreact, he sent a secret cable to CIA headquarters in Washington imploring his superiors to use their influence to block or at least to delay implementation of the Kennan plan. "I wanted to give Garbo a chance before resorting to the marines," Mother told Paul.

But he did not put all his faith in Greta. He also relied on a man named Aldo Tozzini, who was not only his best agent, but who had once been one of the best agents in Ovra, Mussolini's secret service.

"Mussolini's service?" Paul asked.

"Of course. During the war, Ovra compiled a very complete list of the Communists in Italy. I'd already decided the Reds were the real enemy. So I hired Ovra alumni and used their list."

"But wasn't it hard to work with people you'd fought against?"

"No," Mother said. "I didn't like them and I let them know it, but I used them. I've never believed an intelligence organization had to be a mutual admiration society."

One day he called in Tozzini, swore at him, threw a cigarette at him, and gave him an assignment. He wanted some people in Sicily to disappear for a while. They were all leaders in the Confederation General of Italian Labor (CGIL), a Communist-dominated union.

"I don't want to hear them making any more speeches," Kimball instructed his agent, " 'til after the election."

Tozzini went away to arrange an audience with the don who had offered the CIA his ship. Now the agency had another favor to ask.

A few days later, at a tryst in the Piazza Navona, Ginzburg asked Kimball if his ship could pick up a group of refugees in Naples in ten days. The CIA man thought that would be possible. Then he asked if the Jewish underground leader would like to take in a movie.

"What's playing?" asked Ginzburg.

"Well, *Ninotchka* opened today," Kimball said.

"That's an old movie, isn't it? Don't tell me your taste in pictures is reactionary, too?"

"You're quite right about the age of the movie. It was originally released back home in thirty-nine, but I believe you'll find *Ninotchka*'s aged gracefully. The theme remains quite contemporary.

"You've sold me."

They twisted through narrow streets until they reached the Via del Corso, where they turned north. They passed a poster depicting soldiers beating, bayoneting, and shooting protestors. The caption read: ANGLO-AMERICAN IMPERIALISM. A few feet farther along they passed another poster, this one showing a map of Italy with Libya annexed as a territory. Superimposed on the map was a handshake. Caption: THE HAND OF SOVIET FRIENDSHIP.

A block later a handbill was pressed upon each of them. Kimball studied the sheet as he walked along. It was a chart showing the number of hours the average Russian, Italian, and American had to work to earn a kilo of bread, a kilo of meat, a kilo of sugar, or a man's wool suit.

"What do you think?" asked Kimball.

"What do I think about what?"

"The handbill."

"Oh, that. I threw it away."

Then prayer cards were handed to them. These bore the picture of Saint Frances Cabrini, known as Mother Cabrini, the first American citizen to be canonized. Born in Italy, she took herself to the New World where she worked among the Italian immigrants. The prayer on the cards asked that American aid be continued. All the CIA's wars were religious wars.

"Not my flavor," said the Jewish underground leader, letting the card slip through his fingers.

Mother noticed that the sidewalk was littered with prayer cards. Well, if Mother Cabrini could not save the election, perhaps Greta could.

When they arrived at the movie theater, they had no trouble finding seats because the house was more than half empty. All those unoccupied chairs were depressing. Mother told Paul, "My spirits sank so low, not even that scene in the workingman's cafe could cheer me up."

Mother did not tell Paul that one reason he wanted to go to the movies with Ginzburg was because he needed an alibi. But he did describe several of the memorable events which took place that evening, leaving vague his relation to those events.

In a small restaurant in Messina, Sicily, Antonio Gambino was having dinner with his large family, including his wife, mother-in-law, five daughters, and three sons. He ate tripe, washed down by mineral water and the house red wine.

All that liquid eventually took its toll. Descending to the basement toilet, he slammed the door behind him a little too hard since he was a little drunk.

Thinking nothing of the broken lock, Gambino unzipped his fly and a moment later heard the soothing sounds of running water. His concentration was so focused on the joy of his easing bladder that he did not hear the approaching footsteps. Suddenly the door was thrown open, once again too hard. Good manners prevented Gambino from turning to defend himself: he did not want to piss on the floor. One man held a knife to his throat while another handcuffed him and then stuffed a rag in his mouth. Gambino continued to drain his bladder, but, without his hands to improve his aim, he missed his target. The floor was getting wet.

When Gambino finished urinating, the two men spun him around. One of them reached inside his open fly, fished out his testicles, and slipped a noose around

them. Now they had Gambino on a leash. Pulling
on this leash, they led him out of the toilet, up the
stairs, out the back door, and to a waiting car.

All over Sicily that evening similar scenes were
acted out. One particularly outspoken Communist
union leader was found the next morning, hanging by
his belt in his bedroom. A note was found in his typewriter. It said he was depressed about the upcoming
election. He had neglected to sign it.

Mother told Paul how afraid he had been. Not of the
Communists, but of the American ambassador. He
was worried the ambassador would find out about his
union operation. His anxiety increased when the
Communist press began loudly denouncing the "Amer-
ican-engineered" kidnappings. When the ambassador
asked to see him, he was weak with worry.

"I've just had some news about one of your operations," the ambassador said.

"Yes?" The young intelligence officer cringed.

"The Soviet ambassador has sent me a note. He pro-
tests most fervently against our plot to have *Ninotchka*
shown in Italy at this time. He warns of grave consequences if the movie isn't withdrawn immediately. Isn't
it wonderful?"

"Yes, of course," said a relieved Kimball.

"Now I've got a job for you," the ambassador said. "I
want you to leak this note to the press. I've a feeling
the Soviet ambassador's just created a hit."

In the days that followed, the American ambassador
in Rome had occasion to send several cables to the
secretary of state in Washington. One read: NINOTCH-
KA ENJOYING EVEN MORE SUCCESS FOLLOWING
PROTEST OF SOVIET AMBASSADOR.

Other cables contained more good news. There was
a general consensus in the embassy that the Christian Democrats were gaining and the leftist Popular
Front was slipping. The most serious danger seemed
no longer to be the Communists but overconfidence.

Then came a welcome cable from State. The ambassador was relieved. So, too, was Kimball when he read

his bootlegged copy. The Kennan plan to send in the marines had been vetoed.

"Were there disagreements with anyone besides Kennan?" Paul asked Mother.

"Well, there was my dad, of course."

In those days Kimball often lunched with his father, who had returned to Rome after the war. These rendezvous always followed the same pattern. They always met at a sidewalk cafe on the Via Veneto. The tables always had pink cloths, and the father always had advice for his son.

"I think you're making a big mistake," J. D. Kimball said one noonday.

"How's that?" the son asked patiently.

The waiter appeared. The father greeted him like an old and dear friend. How was the family? The business? The senior Kimball sounded as if *he* were up for election.

When the waiter departed, the son said, "What was that about a mistake?"

"Oh, yes," the father said. "Well, if what I hear's true, then I think you're being too ruthless. Your tactics may be effective in the short run, but they'll defeat you in the long run."

"If we don't win in the short run, there'll never be a long run for us here in Italy. We haven't done anything to the Communists that's worse than what the Communists've done to us."

"No, that's not what I mean," the father said. "I don't care what the hell you do to those damn Reds. I was talking about the way you handle your own agents. I've always believed an officer's greatest asset is the affection of his men."

"I know, you've told me a hundred times. But I'm not you. Your heart's a showroom. Any customer's welcome."

"See, you can't even be civil to your own dad."

"You're a man everybody likes, but you don't have any friends. I'm a man most people don't like, but I have friends."

"Like who?"

"Like Ginzburg."

The waiter appeared bearing pasta.

"How's the wife?" the father asked the man with the tray.

The son said, "The spaghetti's overcooked. Take it back."

"Of course, both our ships came in," Mother told Paul. "The captain smuggled the refugees safely into Palestine, and the Christian Democrats won the election. I remember one headline just said: NO TO STALIN!"

"Did you write Kennan an I-told-you-so letter?"

"No, but I did write someone else. It was the only fan letter I ever wrote in my life. It began, 'Dear Miss Garbo . . .'"

A man came walking out of the forest toward the fishermen. At first Mother did not recognize the intruder because he was so surprised to see a man in a pinstriped suit emerge from the trees.

"What's wrong?" Mother asked when Ginzburg was close enough.

"How'd you like to take a trip to Jerusalem?" the Israeli intelligence officer asked.

Ginzburg had called Mother's home, then his office, then La Niçoise, then the track, then the Langley duty officer, who did not know the Israeli and so gave him the runaround. At last he tried Paul, who did not answer, so he telephoned Frances. She knew that Mother had taken Paul fishing but had no idea where. Ginzburg, however, knew that Mother had been returning to the same stream for a decade. Every year the fishing got worse, but Mother remained faithful. Ginzburg had been in such a hurry to find Mother that he had not even taken time to change clothes before plunging into the wilderness.

"Sure, I'll go," Mother said. "But why?"

"We've rolled up a KGB man," said Ginzburg. "We'd like you to talk to him."

Paul immediately started packing up his gear, but

Lapusnyik took one last cast. He tried too hard. The line snagged on a bush on the far side of the stream.

Mother waded across and went to work. It would have been much faster to cut the line and go, but that was not Mother's way.

13

A Trip to Israel

MOTHER HATED HIMSELF for having no willpower. He despised all airplane food, but especially El Al food, and yet plane trips were so boring he could not bear to pass up the meals. He ate the awful food just to have something to do. With so little willpower, Mother wondered how he would stand up under interrogation should he fall into enemy hands.

He was flying to Israel to test the will of a spy whom the Israelis had arrested. They had broken him down, and he had admitted passing Israeli secrets to the Russians, who, in turn, had passed them to the Arabs. Then a complication had developed. The uncovered agent claimed to have information about a KGB penetration inside Langley. The problem was, the man could not supply a name. Just a description. The Israelis wanted Mother to question him to see if he could come up with a name. They had been unusually insistent.

At first the director had turned down Mother's request to go, but the Israeli ambassador had intervened

168

personally. The director asked the secretary of state for guidance. The secretary instructed: let him go, but watch him.

After many hours and four El Al meals, Tel Aviv finally appeared beneath the wing. Mother found it difficult to believe that the same race of people who had once built Jerusalem had also built Tel Aviv. The whole city seemed to be constructed of Nabisco cracker boxes.

The plane landed at Lod Airport at 4:30 Sunday afternoon, October 21. Mother was met by a limousine, a driver, a Mossad man, a man from the prime minister's office, and a bodyguard with a machine gun. They all drove toward Jerusalem, just under an hour away.

"Well, now we know why they wanted the fire fighter's pumps," the Mossad man said. "I hate to admit it, but they were pretty smart."

"That's right," Mother said, "and even frugal. Those TST forty-slash-sevens were pretty cheap as secret weapons go."

The Israelis had based much of their defensive thinking on the premise that they would have twenty-four hours' notice of any Egyptian assault because it would take at least that long for Sadat's army to carve out passes in the huge dikes on the banks of the Suez Canal. Unfortunately for the Israelis, the Egyptians had spent years studying the problem of how to cut those barriers quickly and had at last struck on an ingenious plan. First they had tried guns of all caliber. Then they tried explosives. Finally, in the middle of 1971, a young officer in the Egyptian corps of army engineers suggested fire hoses. Tests soon proved that by using water under high pressure, in three to five hours holes could be punched in the dikes—holes big enough to drive a tank through.

The limousine pulled up in front of Jerusalem's Intercontinental Hotel, which has the best possible hilltop view of the city. Mother washed up in his top-floor room and then returned to the lobby, where he rejoined the driver, the officials and the gunman. They all walked out on the terrace as the sun was setting. Far beneath them, Old Jerusalem stretched like some miniature mock-up of a city in a museum. Herod's wall, the Alasqa Mosque, the Dome of the Rock—they all looked too perfect to be real. It was difficult to believe that such a city could be the capital of a nation at war. Jerusalem seemed so small way down there that its battles would almost have to be fought by toy soldiers.

They all climbed into the limousine and wound back down the mountain, honking to clear the road of goats and Arab children. They drove across the city to a complex of rectangular office buildings which would not have been out of place in downtown Cincinnati. These edifices were the bureaucratic ant colonies of the Israeli government.

Mother and his entourage made their way past one checkpoint after another until they finally gained admittance to one of the buildings. They walked down an undistinguished hall and into the office of the prime minister of Israel. Mother shook hands with the world's most famous Jewish mother. They traded compliments and then the prime minister got down to business.

"Your secretary of state is going to arrive here tomorrow," said the prime minister. "I've never met him. I wondered if you could tell me what sort of man he is."

"I've never met him either," Mother said, "but my intelligence is that he can be charming if he thinks you're bigger than he is—and the opposite if he thinks you're smaller. Trouble is, there're fewer and fewer people he thinks are bigger."

"I suspect he wants us to stop fighting—now that we're winning."

"Yes," agreed Mother.

The Israelis had lost the first three days of the war, suffering heavy losses, mainly because they had not had sufficient advance warning of the Arabs' attack plans. But then Israel had mobilized her citizen army and counterattacked. Five days earlier, on October 16, Israeli Major General Ariel Sharon had led a crossing of the Suez Canal. In the past few hours, Sharon's beachhead had been expanded into a major Israeli counteroffensive on Egyptian territory. The war had been turned around.

"I'd like your advice," said the prime minister. "Should I agree to his cease-fire or not? Help me out."

Mother began by making a speech about not presuming to tell the Israelis how to run their affairs. Then he presumed: "I think you should stand up to him."

"Why?"

"Because strength is the only thing he respects. If he perceives you as weak, that perception could be very costly to you."

"We didn't start the war, so why should we be the ones to stop it?" the prime minister said. "What does he want from us?"

"I think he wants you to give up land. The price of peace will be much of the territory you won in sixty-seven."

"What do you suggest?"

"Win more land. That way, later on, you'll be in a position to bargain away new land instead of old land."

At the end of the interview the prime minister asked Mother:

"If you had to sum up the secretary of state in one word, what would you say?"

"Metternich."

While Mother and the prime minister talked, a motion picture camera hummed in a nearby government office building. The telescopic lens was aimed at the lighted window of the Israeli prime minister's office. The film moved on tiny wheels the way the tracks move on the wheels of a tank. The camera, too, was a weapon of war.

The prime minister thanked Mother for coming and the crooked man left her office. The black car retraced its path past the Knesset, past the Dead Sea Scrolls, past the Monastery of the Cross. Mother was exhausted. He had gotten up before dawn and flown all day. In the middle of a war, on the way to uncover a spy, Mother yawned.

Mother walked through the dimly lit catacombs, his stooped shoulders fitting the tunnels perfectly, as if he had spent his whole life snaking through subterranean passageways, and in a sense he had. The catacombs under Jerusalem seemed a metaphor for his whole dark, underground, twisted life's work. He carried a small suitcase in one hand and a briefcase in the other. At one point his black hat struck the ceiling a glancing blow and collected some three-thousand-year-old dust on its crown.

The tunnel emptied into a small cave of a room furnished with a metal table, four metal chairs, and a bare bulb suspended overhead. Something about this austere place reminded Mother of a hospital room. It took him a moment to realize what it was. Then he focused on the intravenous bottle suspended beside the table.

"Before our guest joins us," one of the Mossad men said, "we'd like to show you some photographs."

The man dealt the pictures as if they were cards in some subterranean card game, the cards oversized to fit the oversized stakes. The photographs were all of disabled tanks. Upon closer inspection, Mother realized they were all the same kind of tank. He was not familiar enough with armor to know just which tank.

"As I'm sure you have noticed," the Mossad man said, "these are all M-60s."

"Of course," Mother said.

"And as you may have also noticed," the Mossad man said, "they've all been destroyed the same way. Shells hit the one chink in their armor: their hydraulic systems."

"I see."

"As you know," the Mossad man said, "the British Centurion uses an electric motor to raise and lower its gun. But the M-60 uses a hydraulic system. *Now* we discover the fluid's flammable."

"Oh, no."

"The Arabs seem to know considerably more about the M-60 than even we do. That's why we began to suspect some sort of security failure—possibly American."

The Mossad man went on to explain how they had captured the man whom Mother had come to interrogate. It all began with the misnamed Battle of the Chinese Farm.

In one of the bloodiest clashes of the war, Israel's Major General Avraham Adan had defeated Egypt's Lieutenant General Saad el Shazli at the "Chinese Farm." The Israelis captured stacks of documents written in Oriental characters, so they assumed the farm was being worked by Red Chinese, but it turned out the writing was Japanese and the farm was a Japanese agricultural experiment station. The Israelis were good at fighting their battles but bad at naming them.

Besides farm records kept in Oriental characters, the Israelis also captured several Egyptian army documents. Among these the Israelis discovered, to their horror, copies of their own code maps, revealing all the cryptonyms given to all cities, towns, mountains, passes, and other geographical configurations in the Sinai. They also found a number of Israeli radios. The Israeli army realized immediately that the Egyptians had been able not only to intercept Israeli radio transmissions but to decode them. In all probability, this Egyptian advantage had cost the Israelis many, many lives.

When this code map had been completed earlier in the year, the Israelis had made only nine copies. It was one of their most closely held secrets.

Even before they found their cryptomap in enemy hands, the Israelis had known they were not impermeable to spies. Nine months before Yom Kippur, a spy ring had been broken up by the Shabak, the Israeli internal security service. The ring's headquarters were in Majdal Shams, a Druze village at the foot of Mount Herman, atop which perched a crucial fortress. This ring interlocked with another in Haifa run by a bookseller. The discovery of these rings traumatized the Israelis because among those arrested were several *sabras,* Jews born in Israel whose name was taken from the Hebrew word for prickly pears.

After the discovery of the Haifa–Majdal Shams rings, the Israelis had changed all their code maps. The existence of an up-to-date map in Arab hands seemed to prove that the enemy still had a high-level spy or spies operating in Israel.

They had been able to identify and arrest the spy whom Mother had come to interview precisely because the code map was such a closely held secret. They were able to trace everyone who could have copied it. Once they drew up a list, they reviewed it in a way which would not have pleased civil libertarians but which was effective. They began with some educated prejudices. First of all, they looked for Jews who had come from Arab countries. There were none on the list. Then they looked for Jews who had come from Russia. There were two. They picked both up and gave them polygraph tests. And they found their man.

They had given him truth serum and questioned him exhaustively. He had given them the names of several other members of the ring, but when they had gone to pick them up they discovered that all the suspects had fled.

In questioning the spy about his past, they learned he had once been assigned to the Soviet embassy in Washington—under another name of course. Since the Israelis had reason to suspect they had suffered many tank casualties because of an intelligence leak in Washington, they questioned the spy closely about his activities there. And he had revealed his contact with a man who spied for Russia inside the Central Intelligence Agency.

Mother leaned back and turned his head to the side so that, in spite of his bent back, he could see the prisoner being walked into the room. The captured spy was dressed in baggy gray. He had not shaved for several days. Two intelligence officers, one on each side, guided him. He stumbled several times during his short walk to the table. He was obviously drugged.

They sat the prisoner down in one of the chairs at the table, rolled up his sleeves, and taped his arms to the arms of the chair, palms up. An IV needle was jabbed into one of his exposed veins and taped there. Mother never asked what drugs had been given to the prisoner before or what was in the IV bottle. Throughout the questioning, the spy appeared sleepy but coherent.

The prisoner's will to resist seemed to have been drained out of him many hours earlier. Mother wondered if the man had been tortured, but the etiquette of the business prevented his asking. He assumed the prisoner would tell him the truth, but he naturally took precautions.

"That suitcase contains a polygraph," Mother told the man, nodding at the luggage he had brought in with him. "We'll get around to that later, but I'd like us to get to know one another first."

Mother took a small tape recorder out of his briefcase, set it on the table, and pushed the record button. He would run the tape through a psychological stress evaluator when he returned to his room. And he intended to take one additional measure to insure the prisoner's truthfulness.

"Excuse me," said Mother, placing his fingers on the confessed spy's throat, searching out the pounding jugular. "I've found," he went on, "that I can tell almost as much feeling a man's pulse as a polygraph can tell me with all its needles. So, while we talk, I'll just rest my fingers against your artery."

Mother had picked up the trick from a flutterman who claimed all lie detection was based on intimidation. The polygraph frightened people into telling the truth, but, properly used, the fingers on the throat would scare people into candor, too. The pulse-taking trick was not entirely a bluff—just mostly.

"Are you comfortable?" asked Mother.

"Yes," the prisoner lied.

Mother questioned the agent according to the rules he had evolved over the years, the first and most important of which was: start at the beginning. He had found that if you asked your questions in chronologi-

cal order, the answers took on a momentum of their
own, carrying people far past what they had intended
to tell you. That is what he had been trying to teach
Paul.

"Where were you born?" asked Mother.

"Kiev."

"What year?"

"Nineteen twenty-two."

Soon Mother had the man telling a story. He talked
about his parents, about his schooling, about his military service, about his marriage. At last they reached
the man's posting to the United States under diplomatic
cover.

The man described the job he was pretending to do
in the United States; then he described the job he
was really doing. He had worked mainly as a cutout,
picking up and delivering information, so he never
knew names. Since many of his pickups were from
dead-letter drops, he often did not even know faces.
However, he had occasionally made brush contacts—
bumping against someone to receive a packet of information—with a man he assumed worked for the Central Intelligence Agency.

"Why did you assume he worked for the agency?"
asked Mother.

The man did not say anything. Mother waited. He
was vain about his toleration for silence. He increased
the pressure on the man's throat.

"Once," the man said at last, "I followed him after
the contact. It was strictly forbidden, but I did. I didn't
normally disobey orders, you know. Really. He went to
Langley."

"Did you ever follow him home?"

"No."

Mother asked for a description of the man. The prisoner gave a description which could have fit anyone.

Opening his briefcase, Mother removed a manila
envelope containing a stack of photographs.

"Excuse me, gentlemen," Mother said to the Israeli

intelligence officers. "I'm afraid I'm going to have to ask you to face the other way while I show your prisoner these pictures. Otherwise I might give away the identity of some of our people."

The Mossad men politely complied.

Mother held up a picture with one hand while placing his other on the man's throat. It was a little awkward, like trying to read a book with an arm around one's girlfriend.

"Please limit yourself to yes and no answers," Mother said. "Now, have you ever seen this man?"

"No."

"Have you ever seen *this* man?" Mother asked, holding up another picture.

"No."

"Him?"

"No."

There were eighty-three pictures in the stack. With each succeeding photo, the man's pulse beat faster. Halfway through he started perspiring. By the time number eighty-two came up he was wet. Mother held up number eighty-three.

"No," the man said, starting to shake all over.

"Good," Mother said and then fell silent, waiting for the prisoner to fill that silence.

"Good?" asked the prisoner tentatively.

"Yes, good. You've passed your first test. Those were all Washington policemen."

Mother reached into his briefcase again and withdrew a second manila envelope. There were only sixty-seven pictures in this one.

"Did you ever see this man before?" asked Mother.

"No."

"How about this man?"

"No."

When they reached picture fifty-one, the prisoner smiled.

"Yes," he said with a note of relief.

"Are you sure?"

"No."

"But he looks familiar?"

"Yes."

Mother laid number fifty-one aside. He thought the man's pulse seemed normal.

"I think you should look at the rest," Mother said. They resumed the drill. "No, no, no, no, no." When they finished the last picture, Mother said, "Thank you." He returned all but the one picture to his briefcase.

"You may take him away, please," Mother told the Israeli intelligence officers. "We'll hook him up to the polygraph later on."

As Mother and his coterie of Mossad men made their way back through the catacombs, winding their way toward the surface, one of the Israelis asked him how he had narrowed down the suspects.

"Well, first of all, I made a list of everyone in the agency who could've gotten his hands on the tank specifications," Mother said. "It was a long list. Too long. So I threw out everyone who wasn't at Langley when your man was at the Soviet embassy in Washington. But that still left too many, so I took a step of faith."

"Yes?" the Israeli asked.

"Yes," Mother said. "I eliminated anyone who had served in the OSS."

The man the Russian agent had identified was Mark Harrington, who had been born too late to join the Office of Strategic Services.

"You'll take care of this man?" the Israeli asked.

"Of course."

"Good; now, do you speak Spanish?" the Mossad man asked to the surprise of the CIA man.

"Only French, Italian, and a little German," Mother said, simultaneously defensive and vain.

"Too bad," said the Israeli.

"Why do you ask?"

"We've got some Cuban prisoners we thought you might take a crack at."

"From the Syrian front?"

"Yes."

"Are the Cubans good soldiers?"

"Better than the Syrians."

"Sorry."

Mother held tightly to his black homburg to keep it from blowing off. The jeep—bearing Mother, an army driver, and a military intelligence man—wound through the thirsty mountains of the upper Negev Desert. The beautiful but cruel landscape was dotted with the camps of the Bedouin—squat tents, camels, goats, women in black.

"Very picturesque, no?" said the driver, whose name was Moshe Stern.

"Yes, yes," Mother said. "I wonder how many of them are spies."

Mother was feeling good because he was on his way to see the front lines. Coming to Israel in wartime without seeing the front seemed like coming to Israel in peacetime without seeing the Wailing Wall. So Mother had contrived an excuse. He had told his Israeli intelligence friends that he needed to see with his own eyes the M-60 tanks which had been destroyed.

The Israelis might not have agreed so readily had not a cease-fire just been declared, one arranged by the American secretary of state. Arriving in Jerusalem on Monday, October 22, he had extracted from the Israelis a promise they would stop shooting that evening at 6:52 local time. Then, two hours before the cease-fire was to go into effect, the secretary left Israel. Once he was gone, the press asked Golda Meir for her impression of him. She said: "Metternich."

It was now Tuesday morning, October 23, which meant the guns should already have been idle for half a day. So the Israelis had allowed not only Mother but a wave of reporters to set off for the front. But actually the war went on. The Israelis and the Arabs were now fighting what would be called the Battle of the Cease-fire.

The jeep bearing Mother pushed on through Beer-sheba, where the camel market is held every Thursday

morning. The next city of consequence was Gaza, in
the Gaza Strip. They passed along the outskirts of the
Shati Refugee Camp, the home of twenty-nine thousand displaced Palestinians.

"Have there been any incidents in the refugee camps
during the war?" Mother asked.

"No," said the military intelligence man, whose name
was Abraham Horowitz. "They seem to have adopted
a wait-and-see attitude. Besides, we have the camps so
penetrated no one can shit without our knowing about
it."

They drove on through Rafah, the last town in the
Gaza Strip; then they moved on into the Sinai. The
farther they drove, the drier the landscape became.
At first they passed an occasional almond orchard,
but eventually all vegetation evaporated in the glar-
ing sunshine. Along the road they passed wrecked,
rusted-out Egyptian trucks, relics of the 1967 war. Occasionally they passed a ruined tank which had been
disintegrating in the desert for the past half-dozen
years. When they stopped in Al-Arish, they were ambushed by a band of Arabs—all under eight years old,
all asking for money. Mother insisted they flee back to
the jeep and get out of there at once.

A few miles from the Suez Canal, Stern, the army
driver, and Horowitz, the military intelligence man,
donned steel helmets. They offered Mother a helmet,
too, but he declined, preferring his homburg. Riding
toward the fighting, Mother was thinking of Pierre, the
awkward hero of *War and Peace*, who had gone to see
the Battle of Borodino wearing civilian clothes and a
white stovepipe hat. When Mother was frightened or
confused, he often sought comfort in literature. For
literature told him that everything had happened before. Everything had been endured before. And so
everything could be endured again. Pierre had survived
his battle wearing a white hat, and Mother would survive his wearing a black one.

On the road they passed long military convoys moving toward the canal. And planes occasionally shrieked

overhead. A few miles from the Suez, they began to hear explosions.

When the jeep reached the site of General Sharon's crossing, Mother saw that the pontoon bridge across the canal had been severely damaged by recent shellings. Israeli engineers were busy with blowtorches patching it up. The jeep had to wait in line to cross the canal.

Rolling ashore on the far side, Mother felt an unexpected thrill at being with the Israeli soldiers on the continent of Africa. He thought of Joseph with his coat of many colors, who had originally led the Jews into the land of Egypt so many thousands of years before. Mother felt like a modern Joseph. A Joseph in a black coat.

The ground seemed to have been plowed by shells, hundreds of them, digging furrows as they crashed to earth. The landscape was sprinkled with dead Israeli tanks which had taken part in the battle for the beachhead five days earlier. The jeep, shifting into four-wheel drive, left the road and pulled up in front of a burned-out M-60. Mother, wearing his black hat and coat in spite of the heat, got out of the jeep.

"Aren't you too hot?" asked driver Stern.

"No, no," Mother said, "the Bedouin are right. It's better to wear too much in the heat than too little. If heavy clothing'll keep you warm when it's cold, it'll also keep you cool when it's hot. Ask any camel driver."

The army driver, who worked every summer in the fields of his kibbutz naked to the waist, thought Mother was even crazier than he had originally imagined.

Mother took out a Minox camera and photographed the M-60 tank. Then he climbed up on the blackened half-track and took a picture of the hydraulic system, which happened to be intact. Then he photographed the holes in the side of the tank, punched by APFSDS shells. These letters stood for "armor piercing Fin Stabilized discarding sabot." These shells acted somewhat like multiple-stage rockets in that they shed part of their weight in midflight. They could only be fired by Soviet T-62 tanks with 115-millimeter guns.

The jeep moved on to other tanks. Mother was like a bee moving from one ugly metal flower to another. Over half of the M-60s did appear to have been disabled by shells which knocked out their hydraulic systems. After ninety minutes at the site of the first Israeli-Arab tank battle in Africa, Mother and his team moved on.

As they drove along the road toward the city of Suez, Mother began to smell the dead. Knowing the odor could have been much worse, Mother was thankful the Israelis were so fastidious about burying the enemies they killed. The jeep passed rows of neat graves with individual markers: Egyptians buried by Jews. As they moved on, the length of time the dead had been dead shortened. The meat grew fresher. They came upon dead Egyptians piled like trash in open pits awaiting proper interment. The stench grew stronger.

Suddenly Mother winced as the smell became overwhelming. Then the jeep crested a hill and he saw up ahead a truck loaded with bodies. He had smelled this truckload of death before he had seen it.

They passed the truck and the smell abated for a while. Then the wind striking Mother in the face became unbearably foul again. He knew that over the next rise they would find another truckload of bodies. And they did.

Soon they were passing bodies which still lay where they had fallen beside their still-smouldering trucks and tanks. Some had been killed the night before. Others had been killed that morning. Mother found himself thinking of Hemingway's awful essay, "The Natural History of the Dead," which describes the way bodies on a battlefield swell, how they eventually turn black, and what the ants do.

They began passing live men loitering in front of tanks parked on both sides of the road. The dead and the living shared the ditches. The jeep stopped occasionally so that Mother could photograph a dead tank or interview a live crew.

"Did the Egyptians seem to be aiming at any one particular place on your M-60?"

There was disagreement. Some said yes. Some said no. Of those who said yes, some said the tracks were the target. Others said the hydraulic system. However, the crews could agree upon one thing. They were unanimous in their opinion that the crooked man in the black homburg and black overcoat in the middle of the war was a queer duck.

In the late afternoon, the hitherto idle tank crews along the road suddenly became animated. The engines were started and the tanks roared off in packs. Mother had no way of knowing it, but the last major battle of the war was about to begin.

14

War

UP AHEAD, MOTHER NOTICED a pack of tanks behaving strangely. They suddenly divided, the way a river does when it flows around a boulder; then the two forks rejoined one another a few meters farther on. When the jeep pulled even with the spot where the tanks had separated, Mother saw a body with its knees pulled up to its chest.

In the distance the sound of firing grew louder and louder. Over the jeep's radio, Mother heard excited voices speaking in Hebrew. He had dabbled in the language but the crackling radio words came too fast for him to translate. And yet he understood their urgency.

Driving through Egypt, Mother thought back to his clandestine journey through Italy during World War II. Once again he found himself out of uniform, although this time he was in his own rather than borrowed clothes. The smell of bodies was bad enough without a smelly secondhand suit making it worse.

Three-quarters of a mile off to the left, a mortar shell landed and exploded.

"Maybe we should take cover," Abraham Horowitz, the army intelligence man, said.

"Where?" asked Moshe Stern, the driver, looking around him at the flat terrain.

Stern got on his radio and asked instructions in Hebrew. Again the words came too fast for Mother to understand. When the driver put down the microphone, he said in English:

"We've been ordered to turn back."

The jeep made a U-turn and headed back toward the pontoon bridge across the canal. They drove without saying anything, listening to the sound of the guns. Another mortar shell fell a half-mile away. And then another. And another. The shells kicked dirt into the air. It was as if some invisible but enormous bull stood over them, pawing the earth.

Mother had no perspective. He would have loved to have examined satellite photographs of the battle so that he could see what was going on. For the past quarter-century he had viewed battles from on high. In the early years he had studied photos taken by reconnaissance airplanes. Later on he had had the pictures from orbiting spies-in-the-sky. From this perspective, all wars looked like a child's game played with child's toys. The equipment and especially the men who fought the wars were scaled down in size and importance. It had been as if Mother were a boy standing among his Christmas toy soldiers.

But now he had forfeited his child's view. Now he could see that wars were fought by blind adults.

If Mother had had satellite eyes, he would have seen the Israelis attempting to close a trap around the Egyptian Third Army—a fighting force made up of two hundred tanks and twenty-two thousand men. The Third Army was on the east side of the canal, in the Sinai. The Israeli plan was to cut off the Egyptians' line of retreat so that they would wish they had never crossed the canal in the first place. In order to encircle the Third Army, the Israelis needed to fight their way south along the west side of the canal all the way to the Gulf of Suez. Then, to lock the door, they needed to take the city of Suez.

Mother had inadvertently wandered into the Battle for Suez City, but to him the sound and fury of the guns signified no shape, no plan, no grand design. He was unable to appreciate the way an army was being circumscribed. He had no perception of the plight of the soon-to-be trapped men who would be cut off from all supplies, including medicines and water. He had no mental picture of the waterless island of Egyptian soldiers who were being surrounded by a sea of Israeli warriors. He was even denied any enjoyment of the irony of all those Egyptians, who had so desperately wanted to return to the Sinai, now wanting even more desperately to leave it. But they couldn't get out because the Jews wouldn't let them. Now the Egyptians needed a Moses.

Mother had exchanged the big picture for the smells, the sounds, the tastes, the fear. A mortar shell exploded off to the left. The jeep suddenly swerved to the right, crashed into a ditch, and came to a halt, bleeding water from its punctured radiator. Moshe Stern, the driver, was slumped against the steering wheel. Mother, sitting directly behind him, leaned forward to see what the matter was. Half-rising from his seat, Mother saw a gaping hole in the driver's steel helmet. A piece of shrapnel had crashed through the metal hat and destroyed the driver's brain. Mother's hand went up instinctively to adjust his black felt hat.

A few minutes later, Mother and Horowitz were hiking along the road in the direction of Sharon's beachhead. The jeep was useless. Mother had stuffed the driver's pistol into the pocket of his black overcoat, he wasn't sure why. Except for checking the body's pulse and then disarming it, they had left it undisturbed. The driver was still in the driver's seat.

Mother and Horowitz, the military intelligence man, were afoot in the desert with no water. They passed tanks and half-track personnel carriers, all moving in the opposite direction. Mother saw an Egyptian body lying on the shoulder of the road up ahead of them. He moved over to the right to avoid it. The mortar shells started pawing the earth again. One fell about two blocks away. Mother and Horowitz hit the earth. When they got up, the front of Mother's black coat was brown. If this continued, his clothes would soon be as dirty as they had been on his way to Rome.

Mother sat, more hunched than ever, in the bowels of a tank. He and Horowitz had hitched a ride. The tank was an M-60 with its hydraulic system shot out. Unable to raise or lower its 105-millimeter gun, the tank was on its way to the rear for repairs. It was manned by a crew of two, rather than the usual four, since it was out of action. Mother sat in the absent gunner's seat, Horowitz in the absent loader's seat. The tank left the road—which was clogged with armor on its way into the battle—to travel cross-country. Two other damaged tanks followed behind, nose to tail like a line of injured circus elephants.

In his black civilian clothes Mother felt embarrassed. Ever since the driver had been killed, Mother had felt out of place, like a man who shows up in a tuxedo at a gathering of sport jackets. When he hailed the tank he had felt silly standing there in black, especially when he climbed up on the big iron machine and began descending through the hatch on top. He just didn't belong.

As he bounced along, Mother had time to wonder if clothes were a moral force in our lives. Dressed as he was, he felt more than a little ridiculous playing soldier. Clad in his business clothes, he felt sure he would be too embarrassed to start shooting at anyone. But an army uniform gave you permission to kill—or to be killed. Blood looked all right on olive drab.

Feeling his black homburg bump the steel roof of the tank, Mother thought again of white-hatted Pierre in *War and Peace*. At the Battle of Borodino, Pierre had watched amazed as the Russian General Kutuzov had fought a bloody draw with Napoleon, but for Kutuzov, the underdog, a draw was a victory. Mother feared something similar might be happening now. This war, too, was likely to end as a draw, which would really mean a defeat for Israel.

Mother remembered the way Pierre had wandered into what was later called the "great redoubt," where the soldiers shook their heads at "the man in the white hat." He recalled Pierre sitting passively beside the cannon, a spectator, while tens of thousands of men perished while attempting to take or to defend the redoubt. And he rehearsed the progression of Pierre's emotions: at first Tolstoy's awkward hero had been fascinated by the fighting, but the fascination had been abstract. The soldiers in their bright uniforms had been as unreal to him as he in his white hat had been to them. Then the dying had come closer. Pierre saw men bayoneted a few feet away. He saw men—men to whom he had actually talked—die. The actors in colorful costumes turned into real dead men in tattered, dirty clothes. As death came closer, it became more personal. Pierre had felt it at Borodino—Mother had felt it on the west bank of the Suez when he saw the hole punched in his driver's head.

And Mother remembered what Pierre had thought as he followed the stretchers: "Oh, now they will stop it, now they will be horrified at what they have done!"

Mother heard the shooting break out, but he had no idea what was happening. Inside the tank, he was now entirely blind. He was in the middle of his first firefight, but he had the worst seat in the house. He could not know that the three crippled tanks had suddenly and unexpectedly stumbled onto a pocket of Egyptian troops stranded behind Israeli lines. The Israelis had not wanted to run into the Egyptians, and the Egyptians had not wanted to meet any Israelis. But they had met and now they were trying to kill each other.

The commander of the M-60 in which Mother rode

quickly became the gunner since there was no one else to do the job. Mother huddled and listened. All his adult life, his profession had been finding out what was going on, and now that his own life was in danger, he had no idea what was going on. He remained externally composed, but mentally he was frantic. Mother had a vision of himself dead in a tin can, like canned meat.

Not only could Mother not see, he could not even understand what the Israeli soldiers were shouting to each other, so he did not even know to be terrified when the Israeli tank commander yelled in Hebrew:

"Missile at two o'clock!"

It was a Soviet-built Sagger missile, one of the weapons that had contributed most to the Arabs' surprising success in the early days of the war. The Sagger turned the oldest weapon, the infantryman, into one of the most modern weapons, a missile launcher. The spear carrier had become the missile carrier. For the Sagger missile could be packed in a suitcase and carried by one man.

In a sense, the Sagger's father had been a rocket and its mother had been a model airplane. When the Sagger is fired, it trails fine electrical wires behind it like a model plane. These wires are connected to a joystick with a simple control system which is used to guide the missile to its target: a tank. This hand-luggage weapon has a range of almost two miles. The Israelis had assumed that the Arabs would not dare start another war until they had an air force to give them cover. But the Arabs had discovered that their new antitank and antiaircraft missiles were as good as an air force. The missiles had been the foundation of their whole plan of attack.

The Central Intelligence Agency should have known more about these missiles than it did. Mother should have known more about them. He wanted to learn more. But now that a Sagger had actually been aimed at him, he could not see it and did not even know it was coming.

All Mother knew was that the tank suddenly started

to zigzag. He had no idea that the tank commander had approximately thirty seconds to dodge the missile, but every time the M-60 zigged to the east, so did the Sagger, and every time the tank zagged to the west, the missile did too. It was as if they were dancing. Besides giving directions to the driver, the tank commander manned a machine gun perched on top of the M-60 and blazed away at the Egyptian who worked the joystick. During the Six-Day War, the Arab would probably have turned and run, but in this war, the October War, the Arab, like the army to which he belonged, displayed a new steadfastness. While machine-gun bullets bounced all around him, the Egyptian infantryman remained at his post, guiding home his deadly toy. The tank moved so fast and so erratically that Mother bumped his head on the steel roof repeatedly. Bumps began to rise on his head, making his hat fit poorly.

The driver screamed. Mother had never in his life heard such a horrible sound. It was worse than the cry of a man being tortured. Much worse. Mother scrambled on hands and knees to the driver's seat in the front of the tank.

"Get out!" Horowitz screamed in English.

But Mother was paralyzed by what he saw. On impact, the Sagger's head had exploded, melting its copper core and firing this liquid metal through the wall of the tank. The tank driver was being scalded to death in molten copper.

"Let's go!" Horowitz screamed, grabbing the tail of Mother's long black coat. "Get out! Get out! Fire!"

Mother began clawing his way toward the open hatch overhead like a drowning man trying to fight his way to the surface. He held his breath as if he were underwater, because the inside of the tank was now filled with smoke and the stench of burning human flesh.

"Help!" Mother screamed, to whom he did not know. "Help! Help!"

A hand grabbed Mother's outstretched hand and pulled him up out of the stove. Mother's eyes were full of smoke tears and fear tears, but he was able to recognize the tank commander as his savior. Then the commander pushed him off the tank. Mother hit the ground, collapsed, and rolled.

"This way!" yelled Horowitz. Running, Mother felt something heavy bumping down the right leg of his pants. When he had seen the tank driver die, his sphincter had let go.

Mother huddled behind a boulder, thinking of the tank driver who one moment had been a living man and another moment a copper statue. Like a bronze soldier in a park. Like a fixture on a war memorial. *Oh, now they will stop it . . .*

The firefight continued as the two surviving tanks blazed away with their machine guns. And the tank commander, who had lost his tank, occasionally raised himself up and popped away with his pistol. Horowitz also had his handgun out and was using it. But Mother simply lay flat on the ground with his head down.

So Mother did not witness the firing of the second Sagger missile. He did not see the tank and the rocket perform their death dance—the tank leading, the missile following. But he did hear the explosion and look up. The tank immediately burst into flames. No one got out. The cries of the doomed could be heard as they burned to death. *Now they will be horrified at what they have done . . .*

Mother looked away.

He could hear machine-gun bullets bouncing off his rocks. He was being shot at by people who had no idea who he was and who could not even see him.

When Mother heard a moan he turned his head. He saw that Horowitz had been shot in the right calf. The man sat up behind a rock and went to work dressing the wound himself. Mother could have tried to reach him to help, but he would have exposed himself to the Egyptian machine-gunners. Besides, he was embarrassed, the way he had been in 1943 when he wet his pants on his way to Rome. Only worse. His

black business-suit trousers had been stained an ugly
brown by his accident.

Mother wondered what vanity had brought him to
this terrible place. He had wanted to be known in the
agency as the man who had been to the front during
the October War. He had wanted to know more about
that war than anyone else in the company. He had
wanted to wear his expertise proudly, like a medal.
And now his vanity had laid him face down in the dirt,
with shit in his pants, afraid to face anyone, friend or
foe, again because of his vanity.

The Egyptians were apparently out of Sagger missiles. They lobbed hand grenades at the third tank, but
these were only an annoyance. The tank's machine gun
kept firing at the Egyptian position on top of a small
hill. When Horowitz finished bandaging his leg, he
turned back over, picked up his pistol, and started
shooting again. Mother reached into his overcoat pocket, touching the cold metal of the gun there. But he left
the weapon in its nest.

There was a hiatus in the shooting. Still, Mother
did not peek from his hiding place.

"You okay?" yelled Horowitz.

"Yes," Mother called. "How about you?"

This attention flustered Mother. It made him even
more aware of his soiled trousers. In his embarrass-
ment, Mother was suddenly aware of parts of his body
about which he had not really thought for weeks or
months, or maybe even years. Oh, there's my hand.
Doesn't it look bit and awkward? Oh, there's my leg!
What's it doing there calling attention to itself? Oh,
look at those shoulders! They are even more stooped
than I remembered. Oh, look at the pores on the back
of my hand! They're craters. Will everybody notice?

The tank rolled forward, drawing more machine-gun
fire from the Egyptians on the hill. As the tank moved
slowly toward the Arab position, the Egyptians must
have realized that they would have to stop the machine
or the machine would stop them.

The Egyptians attacked. If they could drop a grenade into the tin can they would save themselves, at least for the time being. The tank's machine gun raked the charging Arabs, spinning some of them around, tossing some in the air, making some stumble. Mother heard the fighting intensify, but he did not look.

When half the attackers were sprawled on the ground, the others turned and ran. Most of them were machine-gunned in the back before they could regain their hill.

Once the shooting died down, Mother's curiosity at last got the better of his survival instinct. He peeked from behind his rock at a landscape of bodies. One Arab was spread-eagled, another was curled up, another seemed to be running even in death, another was sucking his thumb.

Mother ducked back behind his rock, but a few moments later he peeked out again, drawn to the mayhem. That was when he saw it. That was when the terror hit him. That was when he reached instinctively but clumsily into his pocket. A body ten yards away wasn't dead. It was moving. It was pulling the pin out of a hand grenade. Mother's instinct was to yell for someone else to shoot the Egyptian, but there wasn't time.

Mother was surprised to see himself aiming the pistol. Oh, there's my hand! Oh, there are my pores! Oh, there are the freckles on the back of my hand! Oh, there's a pistol in it! How big it looks and how awkward! Mother stared down the barrel past the site at the wounded man drawing back his arm to hurl the hand grenade.

A part of Mother's mind sought an emotional justification for what he was about to do. He searched for some comprehensible feeling: like hate. He needed an understandable motive to kill: like revenge. But all he felt was fear.

Mother squeezed the trigger, the Arab collapsed, and his killer ducked down behind his stone. Mother heard the percussion of the grenade. He did not want to look back over the rock, but at the same time he could not resist. He raised himself slowly. *Now they will be horrified* . . .

The Egyptian's head was missing. The hand which once held the grenade was gone too. Mother felt sick. He had never before seen one of his victims. He had never before pulled the trigger himself. He felt a hot geyser rising inside him. Mother threw up all over his black suit.

15

War Games

"IT'S NOT A PENIS, YOU KNOW," Frances said.

"Nobody said it was," Paul said.

"Well, you act like you thought it was."

"That's unfair."

"So there's no reason why a woman couldn't do just as well with one as a man could. Right?"

Exasperated, Paul looked away from Frances, fixing his gaze on the jungle.

"Look, I'm in charge of this exercise," he said.

"You know," she said, "I'm beginning to believe in cultural osmosis: I think you've absorbed Latin American machismo right out of the air."

Paul and Frances's CIA class had been shipped to an agency base in the Panama Canal Zone to participate in war games against the army's green-bereted Special Forces.

"Listen," Paul said, "for the duration of this exercise I'm your commanding officer."

"Listen yourself. This isn't the army. We're here to

fight the army. You're not my commanding officer any more than you're my father."

"No?"

"No. If I can't shoot a bazooka, I'm not going at all."

The exercise concerned an unwanted ruler of an imaginary Latin American country. The CIA trainees had been assigned the role of assassins. The Green Berets were assigned the role of bodyguards. While the CIA trainees tried to kill the chief of state, the army's Special Forces would try to protect him.

Paul had come up with a plan: his team would use bazookas to ambush the ruler's car as it drove through the jungle. Actually, the plot was not original. He had plagiarized its primary elements from a group of Cuban CIA agents, code-named AMBLOOD, who had attempted to assassinate Fidel Castro near the Havana sports complex with bazookas in September 1961. The entire Cuban team, along with its leader, Luis Toroella, cryptonym Amblood-I, had been arrested, lined up in front of a wall known as the *paredon,* and executed by firing squad.

Paul, who had chosen as his model a tragic failure, had located a stretch of jungle road which was almost completely straight for a quarter of a mile. His idea was to station two men with bazookas in the middle of the road so they could shoot at the car as it approached. He reasoned that it would be much easier to hit the car head-on as it bore down on the guns than to try to hit it in the side as it roared by.

Paul's assassination squad consisted of a leader (himself), two gunners, and two loaders. That was the problem: who would stuff shells up the ass of the bazooka tube and who would pull the trigger? Paul had assigned Frances to be one of the loaders. He had done so quite innocently, having no idea what he was getting himself into.

The rest of the team had been sent off to procure the necessary weapons, but Frances had stayed behind to fight. After delivering her threat not to take part in the exercise at all unless she got her way, she sat down in the grass, as if to underscore her point. Paul turned around furiously and walked over to a banana tree, where he stood with his back to Frances.

"Your ears are turning red," Frances chided. "Please turn around. You're so cute when you blush."

Paul decided to retreat. Without ever turning to face Frances, he started walking and did not stop until he reached the barracks. He sat down on the side of his bunk and started running his hand through his hair. He realized his anger was out of all proportion to the cause, but he was still madder than hell. Paul even wondered if he and Frances might break up over this. He had wondered the same thing before about other fights, and each time he had tried to imagine how it would sound if he had to explain to someone why they had broken up. "Oh, well, you see, we decided not to see each other anymore because I didn't want to stop and ask directions." That would have been bad enough, but this new fight would be even more inexplicable. "Oh, well, yes, we decided to break it off because she wanted to shoot the bazooka."

Paul tried to analyze why he was so angry. Part of it, he decided, was what he regarded as Frances's unfair tactics. She knew he would not be able to endure a fight with his girlfriend in front of his peers, much less the instructors. Paul told himself that before "the movement" women had gotten their way by using their sex and that after "the movement" they got their way by accusing men of sexual bias. But it was still the same old manipulation.

And yet another possible explanation occurred to Paul. Perhaps he was angry because he felt guilty. Perhaps his fury was exacerbated by his doubts. Perhaps he had automatically assigned Frances a passive role out of some unadmitted reservoir of prejudice. Paul was convinced Frances had not been fair to him, but he was not convinced he had been fair to her.

Paul got up. He had to keep a rendezvous with his team at the edge of the camp. When he arrived, John,

Tom, Richard, and Frances were already assembled. They had the bazookas, the shells, the two submachine guns, bedrolls and packs. Paul produced a notebook which he used the way a football coach uses a blackboard. As he went over the plan one more time, he never let his eyes meet Frances's. When he finished his lecture, he added a final postscript.

"There's been one refinement of the plan," Paul said, looking at no one. "Richard and Frances are going to switch places. Richard, you'll be a loader. And Frances, you'll be a gunner."

Frances wanted to take him in her arms and kiss him. She always felt that way whenever he backed down. She loved him most when he was least like her father.

The team made camp deep in the jungle. The four men and one woman would sleep on the ground that night. They would have all the next day to rehearse the "kill." The despot's car was expected in the evening after dark.

Paul and Frances sat on the ground, leaning back on the same tree, eating a dinner of K rations. They were friends again. The conversation eventually turned to the Arab-Israeli war. Frances had been to Israel, Paul had not. Paul wanted to know what had impressed her.

"The role of the Israeli women," said Frances.

"You mean they shoot bazookas?"

"No, quite the contrary. The women in the Israeli army don't shoot—they serve the male officers tea. They also type and file. At least, that's all I saw them do."

"You wouldn't put up with that, would you?"

"I don't know. I mean, I don't know what I'd be like if I were an Israeli woman, if I'd grown up in Israel, in that atmosphere. The women there seem not only indifferent to sexual equality, they seem hostile to it. Golda's the exception."

"Why's that?"

"While I was there, I gave that question a lot of thought," Frances said. "Part of the answer may be the battle of the babies. If the Jews don't increase their birthrate, Arabs'll outnumber Jews in Israel by nineteen ninety. So there's a lot of pressure to stay home and have kids. The government gives prizes to Jewish mothers who have more than ten."

"They also serve, who get pregnant."

"Right." Frances laughed.

"Maybe the Israelis are right," Paul teased.

"Maybe."

"Then maybe we should reconsider the bazooka assignments. I could still change my mind."

"No you couldn't," Frances said. "You know, I really loved you when you caved in."

"Caved in—is that what you said?"

"Yes."

"And you loved me for it?"

"Yes."

"This relationship is upside down," Paul said. "In *Othello,* Desdemona tells the Moor she loves him for the dangers he has faced. That's how it's supposed to be. But I think you love me for my weaknesses."

The next morning Frances rerolled her bedroll and repacked her rucksack. As a final touch, she tied on what looked like a two-and-a-half-foot length of stovepipe with a three-and-a-half-inch bore. Her loader, Richard, carried the other half of the bazooka.

The team hiked for three hours. Paul carried a machette to hack through jungle obstructions. When they finally reached the road, they were not sure whether they were above or below the designated assassination site. Paul, as leader, suggested they march north. Frances, as gunner, suggested they march south.

They walked south. Forty-five minutes later they turned around and walked north. They finally located the sought-after stretch of road five minutes from where they had originally come out on the blacktop.

"Let's run through it a couple of times," Paul said.

They hid their packs in the brush beside the road and then assembled the two guns. Frances joined her piece of aluminum stovepipe to Richard's, while the other gunner-and-loader team did the same. Then they took cover in the bushes.

"All right, I'll give the signal," Paul said. "On your mark, get set, *go*."

Three men and one woman burst from the leaves like a covey of startled quail and raced to the center of the road. Frances and John appeared to genuflect, going down on one knee on the asphalt, in position to receive the bazookas from Richard and Tom. The big guns were empty now, but when they did this for "real," the tubes would be loaded with 23 ½-inch, 8 ½-pound rockets. The plan was for each gunner to fire, for the loader to reload, and for the gunner to fire again. If they had time, which was unlikely, they would each fire a third rocket. Out of deference to the army Special Forces team, they planned to use not antitank but smoke rockets.

Using the reflecting sights, Frances aimed the tube at the point where the despot's car would first appear. She felt a disquieting thrill. A part of her wished it were not an exercise. A part of her wished her tube were charged with high explosives. A part of her wanted to see what would happen when an antitank rocket hit an onrushing limousine. She had always paid lip service to the proposition that beneath their sexual gear men and women were the same. And yet she had secretly believed men were more violent than women, that the world would be more peaceful if women had more power. The problem was that at the moment she did not feel at all pacific. She wanted to blow up a car full of human beings.

Frances had learned to fire a bazooka at the agency's demolitions training camp in South Carolina. She had also learned to use silencer-equipped machine guns, bullets that explode, and homemade napalm for deadlier Molotov cocktails. She had helped blow up new cars, railroad tracks, and gas storage tanks. She had even learned to blow up a room by saturating the air with flour and then igniting it.

Once she had incinerated a school bus with a homemade minicannon. An instructor showed her how to fill a number 10 can with plastic explosive. A concave piece of steel was fitted onto the top of this bomb. When the explosive was detonated, the cannon would fire a white-hot metal projectile. Frances was given the honor of attaching this cannon to the gas tank of a school bus. When the cannon went off, the white-hot steel shot ripped through the gas tank and then tore the length of the interior of the bus, trailing flaming gasoline behind it. When Frances had seen the bus turned into a vision of hell—in which she imagined schoolchildren dancing—she had been horrified. She wondered what a busload of burning kids had to do with defending democracy. She had felt like she thought a woman was supposed to feel: horrified by the violence.

But the bazooka was different. For some reason it did not horrify her. Why? She was not sure. Perhaps it was because the bazooka was a standard military weapon. Perhaps it was because skill was required to aim the rocket. Hitting the target would provide a certain satisfaction even though the bull's-eye in this case was men. The plastic explosives had made her feel like a monster. The bazooka made her feel like a craftsman. When Frances squeezed the electric trigger, she felt a shiver of joy.

They ran through the drill three more times and then went swimming. The road followed a small creek, and they hiked over to it. Paul broke the slender stalk of a dead weed into four pieces, and they drew straws to see who would stand guard while the others splashed. Richard lost. The rest took off their clothes. As Frances ran into the water, her breasts bounced up and down like headlights on a bumpy road.

Paul was a mixture of jealousy and self-consciousness. He was surprised by how possessive he felt. He did not want the other men looking at his girl's tits and pussy. At the same time, he was not so sure that he liked the idea of *her* looking at *them*. He could not help wondering how he measured up in her eyes.

From his perspective, Paul thought he had John beat, but Tom had a bazooka between his legs. Like

Mother, Paul often sought solace in literature. He recalled that episode in *A Moveable Feast* where Ernest Hemingway, who was the embodiment of manhood, took Scott Fitzgerald, whose own manhood was intimidated by Ernest's, to the Louvre to look at the Greek statues. Scott had come away convinced he had a penis of classic proportions.

Deep in his heart, Paul had never really liked getting wet. He did not much care for showers, baths, or swimming. Paul splashed around for a few minutes, swam underwater between Frances's spread legs once, and then relieved Richard. He held a submachine gun across his knees and kept watch over the others as they played. Studying Frances's breasts floating in the water, Paul recalled the childhood game of bobbing for apples at Halloween.

Hours later, Paul sat on a rock on top of a small hill with binoculars pressed to his eyes. It was dark. Paul had assigned himself the job of lookout. When he saw the target approaching, he would signal with his flashlight to the rest of his team waiting below. Then they would scramble onto the road in order to be ready to fire when the car came into view.

Waiting was boring.

Paul had no idea when the car would pass that way except that it would be sometime after dark. He wished it would hurry. He knew the theory about the test of a well-educated man being an ability to sit in a closet for hours entertaining himself by just thinking. Paul had never believed in that theory. He thought a well-educated man should be too curious about the world around him to want to spend much time in a closet. Sitting on that rock, he occupied himself with such thoughts. Or, rather, he bored himself with such thoughts.

Frances, hiding in the bushes beside the road, wished the car would hurry too, but she was not so much bored as anxious. She ran her hands through her wet hair and shook her head.

Paul felt the way he felt during long, boring movies. His ass even hurt where it met the stone. He squirmed the way he did at a Bergman picture.

When he saw the car, Paul reached down for the flashlight. *It wasn't there!* His right hand groped all over the top of the rock. *No, it wasn't there!* The adrenaline pouring into his blood was mixed with self-hatred. Why were things like this always happening to him? Why was he always mislaying things? When was he going to grow up? He loathed himself for being so disorganized.

As Paul got down on his hands and knees, groping around the base of the rock, the car raced closer and closer to the site of the ambush. This car had been ambushed many times before and looked it. It was a 1968 Cadillac limousine with so many dents in its skin it looked as if it had had a serious case of adolescent acne. The windows contained no glass but were covered with wire screens so no one would get cut up.

Paul felt as if he were going crazy. He sometimes felt the same way when he bumped his head hard. Blind fury.

His hand bumped metal. He fumbled as he tried to grasp the flashlight, which had fallen off the rock and rolled several feet. He managed to get his hand around the handle.

Flash, flash, flash.

The four assassins below reached the edge of the pavement as the target's headlights suddenly appeared. The killers stumbled forward in the dark to the center of the road. Frances and Tom knelt to receive their bazookas, but when they looked into their sights the headlights were as big as rising full moons.

Frances was terrified. She wanted to dive for the ditch, but she felt she had somehow been caught up in an involuntary game of chicken. She did not want to be the first one to crack, especially not after she had put up such a fuss to be allowed to be a gunner. She didn't want to "act like a girl."

Then, out of the corner of her eye, Frances saw

John drop his unfired bazooka and run. She squeezed the trigger, heard the whoosh, smelled the rocket burning the air—and dove. The missile sailed over the roof of the Cadillac. She had aimed high. A second later, the limousine's wheels crushed two bazookas, narrowly missing two bodies.

God seemed to watch over despots.

Paul wandered down to the road, his head hanging. He still hated himself. He still wondered when he would stop losing things. He still wondered when he would grow up.

Frances ran up to him, threw her arms around him, and kissed him. She didn't care if it embarrassed him. He needed her now and she loved him for it. To cheer him up she said:

"It's too bad John Kennedy didn't draw us."

16

The Nuclear Alert

THE SECRETARY OF STATE sat in his office staring at the bouquet of flowers painted by Kongolovsky—wondering if he might not soon be giving it back to Brezhnev. On his desk lay a cable containing the final wording of the U.N.'s Resolution 339, passed with both American and Soviet support. It called for an end to Israeli-Egyptian hostilities and a return to the original cease-fire lines.

Next to this cable lay another. It detailed the fate of seven United Nations teams dispatched into the Sinai to oversee the cease-fire. The patrols had left Cairo shortly after 10 A.M. Egyptian time. Two patrols had taken up positions, one to the east of Port Said, the other east of Kantara. Two other patrols encamped on the west bank of the canal, one at Abu Suweir, another south of the Abu Suttan road. The last three set off for the city of Suez.

These patrols never achieved their destination. When they reached Bastat El Hemira, they heard the guns. They were surprised to discover the war was still going on. An artillery and tank battle was in progress. The Egyptian Third Army was attempting to fight its way out of the Israeli trap. The U.N. patrols turned back.

Another cable concerned a convoy of Red Cross trucks. It carried blood plasma and medical supplies for Egypt's Third Army. Outside of Suez the Israelis stopped the trucks, turned them around, and sent them back the way they had come.

Still another cable was a transcript of an interview with General Chaim Herzog on Israeli radio. Herzog said the Third Army had only one choice: SURRENDER WITH HONOR.

The final cable contained an accusation issued by Sadat's information adviser, Ashraf Ghorbal: ISRAEL IS CHEATING ON THE CEASE-FIRE, AND THE UNITED STATES IS HELPING IT TO CHEAT.

Next to the cables lay a pile of broken pencils.

An aide entered the ODACID secretary's office carrying yet another cable. The secretary frowned as he accepted it. He had come to feel about cables the way his President felt about newspapers: he dreaded opening them.

It *was* bad news. Sadat was calling upon both the United States and the Union of Soviet Socialist Republics: TO SEND FORCES IMMEDIATELY FROM THE FORCES STATIONED NEAR THE AREA TO SUPERVISE THE IMPLEMENTATION OF THE CEASE-FIRE.

The secretary suspected that Sadat had started the war to precipitate a superpower confrontation: Sadat had supposed that if the U.S. and U.S.S.R. could be drawn into the crisis, then they would be forced to resolve the Middle East dilemma once and for all. Sadat had not been sure he could win a war against Israel, but he had been confident he could win a superpower crisis. The Egyptian leader was sanguine that the major powers would force Israel to give back much of the land conquered in 1967.

With his Third Army in jeopardy, Sadat was acting to intensify the crisis. He wanted a literal eyeball-to-eyeball confrontation between the Americans and the Russians in the Middle East. If the U.S. and the

U.S.S.R. could not solve the problem when they faced one another at ICBM range, perhaps they would work harder at solving it if they faced one another at bayonet range.

The American secretary of state sent a strongly worded message to the Israelis, demanding that they cease firing at once and allow Red Cross trucks through their lines. But the Israelis, who had decided to stand up to him, simply went about their war.

Furious at his impotence, the secretary raked his arm across the top of his desk, sending the cables, the broken pencils, and everything else flying. His vociferous tantrum sucked aides into his office. The more they tried to quiet him, the louder he swore. He seemed completely out of control until an assistant announced that Nelson Rockefeller was calling.

When the secretary lifted the receiver, he was as composed and circumspect as Solomon.

At 8 P.M., Anatoly Dobrynin, the Soviet ambassador to Washington, arrived at ODACID to deliver a note from Brezhnev. The Russians wanted to comply with Sadat's request: they wanted to send a joint Soviet-American force to the Middle East to enforce the cease-fire.

In a face-to-face meeting, the American secretary told the Soviet ambassador that the United States opposed the proposal. The Russian left ODACID.

At 10:45 P.M., Dobrynin was back with another note from Brezhnev. This one said:

> I shall state plainly that if the United States rejects the opportunity of joining with us in this matter, the Soviet Union will be obliged to examine as a matter of urgency the question of the unilateral institution of appropriate measures to stop Israeli aggression.

At 10:50 P.M., the secretary of state telephoned the President, who was locked in what had virtually become his hideout, the upper-floor living quarters of the White House. The secretary suggested some sort of military response would be appropriate. The President agreed, but left it to his secretary to work out a plan.

The President was busy.

At 11 P.M., the secretary of state convened a rather unusual meeting of the Washington Special Action Group in the Situation Room in the basement of the White House. This committee, known as WASHAC, is normally chaired by the President and composed of representatives of the State Department, the National Security Council, the Defense Department, and the Central Intelligence Agency. This particular gathering, however, consisted only of the secretary of state, in his capacity as secretary of state; the secretary of state, in his capacity as chairman of the National Security Council; the secretary of defense; the director of the Central Intelligence Agency; and the chairman of the Joint Chiefs of Staff. The Commander in Chief remained upstairs.

He was busy.

The secretary of state/National Security Council chairman called the meeting to order and presided over the discussion.

He turned to Ernest O'Hara and asked, "What evidence do we have that the Russians aren't bluffing?"

The director said, "We have quite a bit, I'm afraid." He gave them the rundown: passing around satellite photographs, he pointed out the Soviet naval buildup in the Mediterranean southeast of Cyprus. There were seventy vessels, including a helicopter carrier and seven amphibious assault crafts.

"Sounds bad," the secretary of defense volunteered.

"Not necessarily," the director said, pleased at the chance to demonstrate he knew more about such matters than the ODEARL boss. "There have been larger Soviet buildups in that area before. So the evidence is inconclusive."

The KUBARK director continued. The U.S.S.R. had placed six divisions in East Germany and Poland on alert a few hours earlier. These troops included paratroopers and mechanized infantry.

"That sounds bad, too," the ODEARL secretary said.

"Well, that's inconclusive, too," the director said, enjoying his work. "There have been other alerts during this war and they all came to nothing."

The director went on: a seventh Soviet airborne division had been flown the week before from its base south of Moscow to a base near Belgrade, Yugoslavia. Its alert status: ready to move. Worse yet, the division's staff had already been sent to the Syrian military headquarters at Katana near Damascus.

"Is that inconclusive, too?" the ODEARL boss asked.

"No," the director said. "We believe this is serious. We believe that at the very least the Russians are trying to tell us they would not tolerate an Israeli attempt to capture the Syrian capital."

The director had another disquieting development to report: a particularly infamous Soviet air transport unit equipped with some thirty Antonov freighters had been shifted from Prague to Belgrade. It was this unit which had led the Soviet invasion of Czechoslovakia in 1968. One of the unit's Antonovs had landed at Prague Airport and taxied to the end of the runway. It had served as a control tower talking-in the rest of the Russian fleet. The men in the White House Situation Room had a vision of this same plane landing in Cairo, taxiing to the end of the runway, and talking in another fleet of Russian planes crowded with Russian soldiers.

"That's old news," said the ODEARL secretary, glad to get back some of his own. "We've known for several days about the arrival of the Antonovs in Belgrade."

"We've known for a week," the director said. "We tracked the flight of the big planes from Prague to Belgrade on Wednesday, October seventeenth. I mentioned this 'old news' because there's another fleet of Antonov transports in the air at this very moment."

"That *is* news," the secretary of state/National Security Council chairman said.

"Yes," the director said. "I received the report just before I left my office to come over here. There're several Antonov-22s—we're not sure just how many—on their way from Russia to Cairo at this very moment. They may simply be loaded with supplies, but they could be loaded with personnel."

"Very ominous," said the secretary of ODACID/NSC chairman.

"Yes," the director said, "and then there's that matter I mentioned to you earlier."

He loved secrets. Since knowledge is power, his secrets made him feel potent. He hoped the secretary of state would not ask him to tell the others.

"What matter?" the secretary of ODEARL asked.

"Go ahead," the ODACID secretary said.

"Well, as you know," the director said, "the Israelis have a nuclear capability. And now we have reason to believe that the Russians may be arming the Arabs with nuclear weapons."

"What?" asked the ODEARL secretary. As soon as he said it, he wished he had not. Now it would be impossible for him to pretend he had known all along.

"That's right," the director said. "We have satellite photographs of a battery of Soviet Scud missiles a few miles east of Cairo. These pictures contain an alarming detail: a neat row of warheads alongside the missiles. Our analysts tell us that these warheads have a characteristic shape—the shape of nuclear warheads."

He produced the pictures and passed them around.

"Why would they line these warheads up in plain sight?" asked the secretary of ODEARL. "Why didn't they at least throw a tarp over them?"

"We're not sure," the ODACID secretary said. "Perhaps they wanted us to see them. Perhaps they wanted to send us a message."

The men in the Situation Room discussed the possibility of a nuclear exchange. The secretary of ODACID pointed out that the danger was greatest when one side or the other faced a devastating defeat. The Egyptians, whose Third Army remained trapped without food, medical supplies, or even water, faced just such a prospect. The ODACID secretary said the American response should be strong enough to persuade the Russians to persuade their Egyptian allies not to flirt with doomsday.

At 11:30 P.M., the WASHAC group decided to put the worldwide armed forces of the United States of America on defense condition alert 3. There are five such conditions: 5, no readiness, troops untrained; 4, normal peacetime state; 3, troops standing by awaiting orders with all leaves canceled; 2, troops ready for combat—as during the Cuban missile crisis; 1, war.

The President did not participate in the decision. He was busy.

At 11:35 P.M., Admiral Moorer, chairman of the Joint Chiefs of Staff, transmitted the following order to the chiefs of all the services: "All Commands: Assume Def Con 3." Around the world, SAC bombers rolled out onto the tarmac and waited for the Third World War.

At 1 A.M., the first friendly diplomat was informed of the alert: Lord Cromer, the British ambassador.

At 1:30 A.M., the secretary of ODEARL arrived back at the Pentagon, where he issued orders which caused the aircraft carrier *John F. Kennedy,* then cruising in the eastern Atlantic, to head for the Mediterranean.

At 2 A.M., the U.S. informed the North Atlantic Council at NATO headquarters in Brussels of the American alert.

At 2:30 A.M., the secretary of ODACID finished his note to the Russians. He said the United States would not tolerate unilateral Soviet intervention in the Middle East, but he did not mention the alert. Perhaps he thought they already knew about it. They did not have the KGB for nothing.

At 3 A.M., the ODACID secretary called the President of the United States to tell him what many thou-

sands of GIs already knew: that America was pulling
back the hammer on the gun it held to the world's
head.

To answer the telephone, the President had to remove the earphones from his head. The last few days
had not been easy for him. Three days earlier, on
Saturday, October 20, he had fired Archibald Cox,
the Watergate special prosecutor, setting off what was
later called a "firestorm." The most dangerous fire had
raged in the House of Representatives, where twenty-
two bills had been introduced calling for his impeach-
ment. Only yesterday the President's lawyer, Charles
Allan Wright, had appeared in Judge John Sirica's court-
room to announce that "because of the events of the
weekend" the Chief Executive would shortly surrender
six White House tapes.

Just over twenty-four hours after promising to give
them up, the President of the United States was listening to his tapes. While his secretary of state sat downstairs trading notes with the Russians and plotting a
worldwide military alert, the President of the United
States sat upstairs editing the past.

The tapes were hard to understand, so he would
often hit the Stop button, rewind, and listen to a passage again. Occasionally he would hit the Stop button,
rewind, and then hit the Record and Play buttons
simultaneously. That wiped out what was on the tape.

The President was in his study with a blazing fire
going. It was a little early in the year for such a fire, so
he had the air conditioner on to offset the heat.

Sometime around midnight, as members of the SAC
battle staff in Bellevue, Nebraska, were being awakened, the President removed his earphones, got up
from his chair, and walked over to the fireplace. He
carried with him two tapes, one of a Nixon-Mitchell
phone call which took place on June 20, 1972, another
of a Nixon-Dean meeting on April 15, 1973.

They burned like kindling, but they left a bad odor.

17

The Transfer

DRINKING IN A BEAUTIFUL tableau of marble monuments and light shimmering on water, the director was about to throw up. He stood at the rail of the *Sequoia* with his feet slightly spread, trying to listen to what the secretary of state was saying. But he was actually paying closer attention to his stomach.

The President was holding a Cabinet meeting aboard his yacht that evening. The director had been invited to sit in on the meeting to provide a situation report on the Middle East. He would tell the Cabinet officers that the cease-fire appeared to be holding, but that should the delicate negotiations at Kilometer 101 break down, the fighting could swiftly flare up again. War and peace could not have been more precariously balanced.

The director's mind was preoccupied with balance because he was having a difficult time maintaining his. He had been looking forward to his evening on the *Sequoia*, but that was before the wind came up and the President's yacht started to pitch on the Potomac.

The director was not a good seaman. At the end of his OSS days, he had been sick all the way across the Atlantic. He had come home on a slow carrier, dividing his time between throwing up and putting together jigsaw puzzles upside down—the faceless puzzles a reflection of the man himself.

The director and the secretary huddled together before the Cabinet meeting began. While an upside-down Jefferson Memorial floated by them in the water, the secretary warned O'Hara not to be too frank with the Cabinet.

While the secretary talked, the director worried. For he knew that maintaining his balance in what he was about to propose would be even more difficult than keeping his footing on the rocking deck. He had to persuade the secretary that Mother was dangerous enough to transfer but not dangerous enough to fire. The director feared what Mother might do to the peace negotiations if he remained at the head of the Israeli desk. But he also feared what Mother might do to *him* if he were fired. O'Hara had not forgotten about the tapes of the Vietnamese woman screaming. He did not want anyone to hear those recordings, least of all his wife, who had always opposed the war and could never be made to understand.

Bracing himself against the roll of the boat, O'Hara said, "I've been wondering what to do about the head of our Israeli desk."

"I understand he was a big hero in the war," the secretary chided. "You must be very proud."

"Not really," O'Hara said.

The story of Mother's adventure in the war had spread all over KUBARK and beyond. Everyone knew about the firefight in the desert, about the Israeli jets which had been called in to wipe out the Egyptian pocket, about the ride out of Africa in an Israeli ambulance, about the three hours in a field hospital. Mother had emerged bruised but otherwise unhurt and a bigger legend than ever within the company—if no better liked. The director feared that Mother's new "celebrity" status might complicate his plans.

"What do you recommend we do with him?" the secretary asked.

"I'd like to take the Israeli account away from him, transfer him to something else."

"Why?"

"The peace negotiations are too sensitive right now to let anyone jeopardize them," the director said. "And who knows what he might do?"

"You really think he might try to stiffen the Israelis' will?"

"I'm not sure, but my intuition says yes."

"Then perhaps we shouldn't satisfy ourselves with half-measures," the secretary said. "Perhaps we should just fire his ass."

The yacht tilted and the director's stomach tried to turn inside out.

"I'm not so sure," the director said.

"But you're the one who says he's dangerous."

"I know, but I think he would be even more dangerous if we fired him. Because he wouldn't go quietly. I'm convinced of that."

"What do you think he might do?"

"Oh, hold a press conference at the gates of Langley and accuse us of betraying Israel," the director said —naturally leaving out other measures Mother might take.

"Perhaps you're right," the secretary said. "This administration's still teetering. We don't want to rock the boat."

O'Hara, his stomach lurching, said, "But you do think we should do something, don't you?"

"Yes, yes."

"Does that mean I have your permission to transfer him? To get him off the Israeli desk?"

"Do it," said the secretary.

The director's stomach felt better.

"I wish you'd known Allen Dulles," Mother said to Paul when the young intelligence officer reported for his first day of work on the staff of the Counterintelligence Department. "He used to welcome each new class to Langley by telling them his 'Geneva Nineteen seventeen' story."

"Sorry I missed it."

"In seventeen, Dulles was a young foreign service officer posted to the American embassy in Geneva," Mother said. "One Saturday he got stuck with the job of duty officer. Around noon he got a call from the railroad station. The caller wanted to talk to an American official. Well, Dulles was the only official available, and he had a tennis date that afternoon with a comely young lady. The duty officer had to decide between duty and romance. He chose the latter."

Mother paused for dramatic effect, taking out a cigarette and lighting it.

"Twenty-two years later," he continued, "Dulles learned that the man who wanted to talk to an American official was Nikolai Lenin."

Paul laughed. The unexpected often made him laugh.

"Now I *am* sorry I never knew him," said Paul. "Anyone who'd tell that story about himself must've been an interesting man."

"Oh, he was. I think every person has his or her story. It's the one story they tell most often, the story that seems to fit them best. And in that sense, 'Geneva Nineteen seventeen' was Dulles's story. Mine's 'Rome Nineteen forty-five,' I suppose, when I met Montini. What's yours?"

"I'm not sure," Paul said. "I'd have to think about it. Maybe 'The Farm Nineteen seventy-three,' especially the border crossing I told you about."

Paul did not say the reason was that he had stumbled all the way but still reached his goal. That seemed to him to be his style. It was his image of himself.

"I'm sure Dulles told his nineteen seventeen story because he liked it," Mother said, "not because there was a moral. But there was a moral. Anyway, he always tacked one on. He said the story showed that even the most trivial assignment can be important. I mention that because I'm about to give you what may seem like a trivial job."

Mother turned to his safe, worked the combination, and withdrew his favorite file. He was leafing through it when the telephone rang.

Putting aside the file, the KUDESK chief took a call from the director's office. Kay Johnson, the DCI's secretary, said the director would like to see Mother at 3 P.M.

Hanging up the phone, Mother returned his attention to his project and his protégé.

"I'm assigning you to AESOP," he said.

"What's that?" Paul asked.

"I can't tell you," Mother said. "Now here's what I want you to do. Go down to the Smithsonian museum. As you walk in the front door, you'll see the Apollo capsule on your right—the one that took Scott Carpenter to the moon and back."

"Yes?"

"I want you to photograph every inch of it, inside and out. Your cover is that you're a tourist. Don't try to hide the camera. Wear it like a badge. And if you could borrow a couple of kids, that'd make the cover even better."

Paul left Mother's office and went to his own brand-new office to examine all the empty drawers. Seated behind his desk, he picked up the receiver of his scrambler phone and dialed Frances's number. He could have used the regular phone, but he wanted to use his new toy. Paul asked Frances, who had been assigned to the West German desk, if she was free for lunch.

At 12:30 P.M., Paul and Frances showed their new badges to the armed guards who kept watch over the entrance to the company cafeteria. Now they were official members of the dark side of KUBARK and could eat on the dark side of the company lunchroom. The new covert operators found covert seats.

"I need a kid," Paul said. "Could you help me?"

"Is this a proposal of marriage?"

A reporter named Bob Stanley, who worked for the *Washington Star*, stopped at the gate next to the flashing

red light. He routinely put in requests to interview the
director, requests which were routinely ignored. So
Stanley was naturally surprised that this request had
succeeded where so many others had failed. He wondered why O'Hara had agreed to see him. Oh, well.

Stanley showed his press card to the guard. His name
was on the guard's clipboard, so he was passed
through. He parked his car in a slot reserved for
visitors. Getting out, he stared up at the impressive
facade of the headquarters building: a great rectangle
perforated by hundreds of windows. It reminded him
of a huge IBM computer card dotted with hundreds of
little square holes. He wrote the metaphor in his notebook.

At the main entrance the reporter chatted with a
uniformed guard who raised his arm and pointed.

"You know," he said, "Teddy Kennedy lives right
over that hill."

A public relations man came to the guard's desk to
fetch the reporter. The man clipped a visitor's badge
onto Stanley's lapel and then escorted him to an office
on the first floor where they went over the ground
rules. The director was willing to grant an interview,
but only on a deep background basis. The reporter
could report what he learned, but he could not attribute it to the director. He couldn't attribute it to anyone at all. He would simply have to state what he
learned on his own authority.

The PR man led Stanley to the elevator, which carried them both to the seventh floor. They filed past the
gray-flannel guards, checked in with the secretary,
waited a few minutes, and filed into the long, win-
dowed office. The reporter and the PR man sat down
on the couch. The director sat in an easy chair facing
the Virginia woods. Stanley took a miniature tape recorder out of his briefcase and set it on the coffee
table. The director frowned.

"I should've warned you," the PR man said. "We
don't allow the taping of interviews."

"It prevents mistakes," the reporter said. "That machine takes much more accurate notes than I do."

"It's not allowed," the PR man said, picking up the small machine. "I'll hold it for you."

Stanley wondered if the same rule also applied to them. He was not allowed to tape the interview, but he imagined they were probably recording it.

"Could you suggest what role, if any, the CIA played in the coup in Chile?" the reporter asked.

"I'm sorry. That's a national security matter which I can't talk about. And that doesn't mean we had any role. It simply means what I said: I can't talk about it."

The reporter asked the question several different ways but always got the same answer. So he changed the subject.

"Victor Marchetti says in his forthcoming book that the CIA's annual budget is about seven hundred and fifty million dollars. Could you confirm that figure?"

"Our budget's a classified matter. If we publicized the amount of money we spend, our enemies might be able to deduce what we spend it on."

"How about a ball-park figure?"

"I'm sorry."

"Marchetti says the agency employs about sixteen and a half thousand people. Is that about right?"

"That's a classified matter."

The reporter, wondering why the director had granted the interview in the first place if he was not going to answer any questions, began making notes on what the director's office looked like. He was convinced local color was about all he was going to get out of this interview. He decided to ask a question he knew would not be answered.

"Was Penkovsky the only high-level spy we ever had inside the Kremlin?"

"That's a classified matter," the director said. "However, I'd like to get back to a question you asked earlier. You wanted to know about our personnel. Well, we not only have a certain number of full-time employees, we also pay retainers to a number of outsiders who occasionally do favors for us. They're good people. Some of them are even in your line of work."

"Reporters?"

"That's right. We have about forty reporters and free-lance writers on our payroll."

"Anyone I might have heard of?"

The director reached into the breast pocket of his gray suit and pulled out a folded sheet of paper. He handed the paper to the reporter, who unfolded it. There were some forty names typed neatly in two columns.

Now Stanley knew why the director had granted him the interview. He wanted to trim his payroll.

O'Hara was pleased with himself. He felt he was beginning to master another aspect of his job. Overseas, manipulation of the media had been an important part of his work. And he thought he had been good at it. But it had taken him some time to realize that many of the same skills would serve him well as DCI. What had worked in Saigon would work in Washington, with a few modifications. He was learning that to get along with the American press you did not really have to be open, but you did have to give them something. By carefully selecting what was given out, you could make friends in the press and make the press work for you. And it was the easiest way in the world to do what he normally found so difficult to do: fire people.

The director walked the reporter to the door. On the way out of the Toy Factory, Stanley nodded to the guard.

"Remember," the guard said, "Ted Kennedy lives right over that hill. You should drive by and take a look at the place."

Waiting for Mother, O'Hara wondered if his feud with the KUDESK chief would ever come to that: a war of leaks. He hoped not. But he was convinced something had to be done.

When Mother entered the office, he stood before the director's desk looking like a black knight on a chessboard, his back curving like the horse's neck. O'Hara was supposed to be the king of the board, but he sometimes wondered if he was a match for the lesser piece.

The two men wasted little time on the amenities. The director came to the point:

"I'd like you to take over the Italian desk."

"As well as, or instead of, the Israeli desk?"

"Instead of."

"Sorry."

The black knight turned around and walked off the board.

Back in his own office, Mother started unconsciously folding paper airplanes. During the Yom Kippur War he had had too many other worries to muse about revenge. Now he had time.

At first the thought was distasteful. The war and his part in it seemed to have tamed him. It was harder to translate hatred into a desire to strike back. The vision of a headless man restrained him.

But the longer he sat, the more his feelings changed. For he began to dwell upon O'Hara's role in the war. Mother told himself that much of the destruction had been the director's fault, since he had blocked the flow of intelligence to the Israelis. His mind seemed to revolve completely. What had been a reason *not* to strike back had become a reason *to* strike back: the headless man was O'Hara's fault.

Mother once more went to work on his plan. Again, he searched for the right vehicle. He liked the idea of a limousine, but he struggled for a refinement. And at last it came. He would borrow a senator's limousine. He sat with the idea for a few minutes to be sure. The longer he considered it, the better he liked it. A senator's limousine would do very nicely.

When Mother got up to go home, he noticed five paper planes spread out in a crude circle around Nathan Hale.

18

An Opening to the Left

PAUL TRIED TO FEEL like a working spook, but he felt
much more like a cruising teenager. He thought he
should be excited, but he was actually slightly bored.
For it was his job to drive around a Washington sub-
urb all evening. Signaling, braking, turning, accelerat-
ing again, he wound his car up and down the quiet
streets of McLean. Of course, if he had really been a
high school boy out looking for action, he would not
have had his "Mother" with him.

"I picked up this trick from the Czechs," Mother
said. "They bugged the Czechoslovakian desk in the
State Department, and they monitored it from a moving car. Luckily I had a double agent in the Czech
embassy, so I knew what they were up to. In fact, I
monitored their bug myself, or rather my men did."

"So *you* were spying on the State Department, too?"

"*We* never put it that way."

The company Chevrolet which Paul drove was a
rolling listening post, a copy of the Czech model. The

brand-new intelligence officer was monitoring a bug—actually a minuscule radio transmitter—attached to a headboard in a McLean bedroom. The bed belonged to a CIA intelligence officer, Mark Harrington. Mother had already shown Paul how to tune the receiver and operate the tape recorder. And now he was accompanying his pupil on his first run.

So far the shift had been uneventful for a very good reason. Harrington, who had to be at work at 3 A.M., had been sound asleep ever since Paul's shift had started at 8:30 P.M.

"I had a big fight with Hoover," Mother said. "I wanted to use the bug to feed the Czechs disinformation, but Hoover wanted to expose the bug so he could get in the headlines. Even his own people agreed with me, but he wouldn't listen."

"Who won?"

"Hoover."

Mother didn't add that he got so mad he wanted to bug Hoover and Tolson's bedroom.

It was a long, circular trip to nowhere. Paul and Mother listened to the silence on the receiver and said little. The young man started yawning and could not stop. He thought of turning on a Top 40 station on the car radio to wake himself up, but he suspected Mother would not approve. So instead he decided to make another assault on Mother's secret. He would once again attempt to debrief his mentor about the feud which was legend in the agency. Paul's strong curiosity was better than strong coffee for waking him up.

"When did O'Hara go to Italy?" asked Paul.

"Well, as I told you, right after the war he went to work for Wild Bill Donovan. When the agency was formed, he joined up and was assigned to the embassy in Stockholm. Then, in the mid-fifties, he was transferred to our Rome station. He made something of a name for himself there by running a basketball operation. He coached a team in order to meet and recruit young men. Headquarters used to send him Converse All-Star tennis shoes by diplomatic pouch."

Mother described how one day bad news had tumbled out of the pouch along with the sneakers. A memorandum from the head of the Italian desk said that an alumnus of the Rome station had been criticizing O'Hara's work. At first this person had contented himself with voicing his complaints to desk officers, but lately he had started complaining to the boss, the DCI, Mr. Allen Dulles himself. The complainer was Francis X. Kimball, also known as Mother.

The next day Mother had received a terse cable from O'Hara asking that future complaints be addressed to him rather than to his superiors.

Several weeks later, Mother paid a surprise visit to the Rome station. He found O'Hara sitting in his office attempting to write a Field Project Outline. Mother explained that he was en route home from Israel and had decided to stop over in Rome for a couple of days. The two intelligence officers chatted about restaurants for a while—which ones had closed since Mother lived in Rome, which ones had gone downhill. Then there was a pause in the conversation because they both knew the small talk was over.

"You asked me to express my reservations to you personally," Mother said. "Fair enough. I object to the change you propose in your RMD."

(Paul recalled from a Blue U lecture that every station has a Related Missions Directive, RMD, a charter setting forth its priorities and objectives.)

"You mean Priority C?" O'Hara said.

"Right," Mother said.

The Rome station's A priority was penetrating the Soviet mission in Italy, Mother explained to Paul. The B priority was weakening the Italian Communist party, which continued to pose a threat to the Christian Democratic party. The C priority was weakening the Italian Socialist party, which, for many years, had been allied with the Communist party. C was the point of contention. O'Hara wanted an opening to the left. Mother didn't.

"It's the only way out," O'Hara said. "The Christian

Democrats are in trouble. Their only hope, in the long run, is to form a coalition with the Socialists. But first we have to pry the Socialists away from the Communists. And to do that we'll have to give them some support. Spend some money. But we can't do that 'til we change that damn Priority C."

"I know the theory, all right," Mother said, "but I disagree. They want you to think there's a chance of splitting the Communists and the Socialists, but there isn't. It's just a trick. They just want your money and whatever else they can get."

"I don't believe that. Pietro Nenni's not that kind of man. So long as he's running the Socialist party it's worth courting."

"The hell it is!"

They had gone on repeating the same arguments like two records debating one another. O'Hara stuck to his belief that the only way to beat the Communists in Italy was to drive a wedge between the Reds and their allies, the Socialists. Divide and conquer. And Mother was as faithful to his belief that O'Hara was proposing an alliance with cancer.

"The whole political spectrum's black and white to you," O'Hara said. "I still believe the way to defeat the Communists is to recognize and enlarge the gray area."

"But I know Italy," Mother said. "I grew up here and I worked here. I have a *feel* for Italian politics."

"I've been waiting for that one," O'Hara said. "You don't have a feel for Italian politics. You have a feel for Fascist politics."

"Are you calling me a Fascist?" Mother asked angrily.

"I'm just saying I've heard you worked closely with the Fascist element when you were here."

"I didn't come here to be called names," Mother sputtered. "I don't appreciate your accusations."

"And I don't appreciate your going to teacher," O'Hara said.

Before the meeting was over, Mother had damned

O'Hara and his Commie friends, and O'Hara had damned Mother and his Fascist friends.

Paul asked, "Is that what caused the, uh . . . ?"

"Feud?" Mother filled in the blank.

"Yes."

"That's what I'd call a sensitive question. It's generally best to save something like that 'til the end of an interview. No use spooking somebody 'til you have to. Then ask the question as though it were an afterthought."

"Fine."

Mother continued his story. Returning from Rome by commercial flight, he had landed at Washington's National Airport and taken a taxi directly to headquarters, then located in Washington proper. He had decided to go straight to the office rather than going home because he wanted to be the first to get his version of the argument before the director.

He told the cab driver, "Take me to the Government Printing Office, Twenty-four thirty E Street, North West."

The hack made its way to Foggy Bottom. Returning to headquarters after a two-week absence, Mother found a surprise waiting for him. The old, familiar U.S. GOVERNMENT PRINTING OFFICE sign was missing. It had been replaced by a sign which proclaimed boldly, shamelessly: CENTRAL INTELLIGENCE AGENCY.

Mother asked the guard inside, "Where'd you get the new sign?"

The guard explained that, a few days earlier, President Dwight D. Eisenhower and his brother Milton had set out to keep an appointment with Director Dulles, but they ran into a problem. They were unable to find CIA headquarters. The incident had prompted Dulles to make a few inquiries. He made up his mind when he learned that the guides on the tour buses were pointing out the agency's headquarters as if it were another capital monument. Dulles concluded that if any tourist could find CIA headquarters but the President of the United States couldn't, it was time to change the sign.

Mother made his way down the central corridor of the drab building which had originally been a navy hospital. During the war, it had served as OSS headquarters. Then, in 1947, it had become the first home of the CIA.

Mother walked directly to his office, carrying his suitcase. Reaching his desk, he sat down and wrote a memorandum to the DCI about his debate with O'Hara—maximizing his own arguments and minimizing his adversary's.

A few days later, Allen Dulles ordered O'Hara to Washington: he was to face Mother in a bureaucratic shoot-out. The duel took place in Dulles's conference room at 3 P.M. one autumn afternoon. Also in attendance were the chief of the Western Europe (WE) Division and the head of the Italian desk.

And presiding was Allen Dulles himself, who knew Italy intimately. He should have. He had liberated the northern half of the country. During World War II, Dulles had rented an office at Herrengasse 23 in Berne, Switzerland. The sign on his door read: ALLEN W. DULLES, SPECIAL ASSISTANT TO THE AMERICAN MINISTER. It was a shingle in the "Government Printing Office" tradition. Had the sign been more candid, it would have read: ALLEN W. DULLES, OSS MASTERSPY.

From this unpretentious office, Dulles had directed an espionage network which stretched all across Europe, from Rome to Berlin and beyond. In March of 1945, Dulles received a message from General Karl Wolff, the SS commander in northern Italy: the general wanted to surrender all the troops under his command. In an operation code-named SUNRISE, Dulles sent a Jew named Paul Blum to talk to the SS officer. On April 22, 1945, Wolff had surrendered unconditionally—the only terms the Americans would accept.

Allen Dulles opened the meeting. They all knew why they were there, but he told them anyway. They were all to state their positions vis-à-vis the proposed change in Priority C of the Rome station's Related Missions Directive. Dulles asked O'Hara to speak first.

The deputy chief of the Rome station presented his argument: the way to beat the far left was with the near left.

Director Dulles called on the other men around the table. The chief of the Italian desk backed O'Hara. The head of WE did, too.

Then Mother, speaking in a low voice, presented his objectives. Put simply: a Socialist is a Communist in democrat's clothing.

When Dulles called for discussion, O'Hara and Mother did most of the talking.

"How long are we going to be bound by past mistakes?" O'Hara asked rhetorically. "After the war, our people in Rome chose to ally themselves with our former enemy: the Fascists. All in the name of fighting communism. The time has now come to reverse that untenable policy. The time has now come . . ."

"Excuse me," Mother said in a low but insistent voice. O'Hara immediately gave way. "By the 'people in Rome' I assume my colleague means me. However, I would like to remind him that the people in Rome were not unique. There were others, too, who chose to enlist our old enemies to fight our new enemies. For example, our people in postwar Germany did the same thing. I refer, of course, to our employment of General Gehlen."

(Never having heard of Gehlen, Paul did not appreciate the ingenuity of the remark, so Mother explained: in April of 1945, General Reinhard Gehlen, the head of a Wehrmacht intelligence unit, had passed word to the Americans that he wanted to make a deal. He and all his men were willing, even anxious, to surrender to the Americans. But they did not want to go to prison. They wanted to go to work. They wanted to do for the Americans what they had been doing for the Third Reich. Namely, spying on the Russians. They had more to offer than just their services. They also had their files on Soviet intelligence targets, for they had been sending agents into Russia since 1942. A deal was cut. General Gehlen led his men into the Alps and surrendered to the American forces. After the war, while the OSS was helping to prosecute many Nazi leaders, it put General Gehlen and his men on the payroll. General Gehlen's new commanding officer: Allen W. Dulles.)

Unable to think of a rejoinder to Mother's introduction of the Gehlen-Dulles axis into the argument, O'Hara decided to try to ignore it. But as he pressed ahead he found it more difficult to look at Dulles.

Allen Dulles—who resembled Lewis Stone in his role as Mickey Rooney's father in the Andy Hardy movies—hardly seemed a man to provoke fear. And yet he did. O'Hara especially appeared nervous in his presence.

"We're not here to discuss Germany," O'Hara said. "We're here to discuss Italy. And not Italy a decade ago but Italy now. And I promise you the Christian Democrats can't make it alone today; there has to be an opening to the left."

"I still say," Mother said, flicking a long ash into the ashtray before him, "that you're asking us to play directly into the hands of Togliatti."

He was referring to Palmiro Togliatti, the leader of the Communist party in Italy.

"What would you suggest?" O'Hara asked. "Taking another shot at him? That might've worked in forty-eight, but it won't work now. I say the way to deal with Togliatti is to isolate him."

(Mother told Paul: on July 14, 1948, months after the crucial election, an attempt had been made on Togliatti's life. The result had been a forty-eight-hour strike called by the Confederation General of Italian Labor, CGIL.)

"My only regret," Mother told O'Hara, flicking another ash, "is that whoever attempted to assassinate him failed. I feel the same way about the attempts on Hitler's life. Sometimes drastic remedies are called for."

(Paul needed another history lesson to understand

why this remark was so ingenious and why it made O'Hara so furious. For Mother had done it to O'Hara again—he had interjected another Allen Dulles operation into the argument. Working with German agents, Dulles had plotted time and again to kill Adolf Hitler. One assassination attempt, code-named VALKYRIE, involved Admiral Wilhelm Canaris, former chief of the Abwehr—German military intelligence—one-time U-boat commander, veteran German espionage operative, former employer and lover of Mata Hari. When the plot against Hitler failed, Canaris was among those executed. Allen Dulles was the father of the assassination attempts carried out by American secret services.)

"Togliatti's not Hitler," O'Hara said, stammering slightly, "but more to the point, Nenni isn't Togliatti. I'm proposing an opening to the Socialists, not to the Communists."

"It amounts to the same thing," Mother said. "It also amounts to a counterintelligence nightmare. You'll actually be paying the other side to steal our secrets. I couldn't remain as the head of CI if this proposal were implemented. I'd have to resign."

"And if Priority C isn't changed," O'Hara said, "I'll resign. I couldn't go on implementing a policy I no longer believe in."

Mother had not expected that. He had assumed his beliefs were more deeply held than other men's. For the first time he found himself wishing he could kill his CIA brother. Sitting at the table in his black suit, black tie, and white shirt, Mother felt like a primitive, skin-clad Cain.

"Who won?" Paul asked.

"He did," Mother said sullenly. "I was bluffing about quitting."

They rode in silence. Paul let the quiet work for him as Mother had taught him to do.

"I think this fight was doubly bitter," Mother said after a ten-block pause, "because O'Hara and I both looked up to Dulles as a kind of father."

Paul took his eyes off the road long enough to glance over at his own father figure, Mother.

"You might think we should've been too old for that sort of thing," Mother continued. "But you must remember that neither of us really had a chance to grow up before we entered the secret world. And once inside we were insulated. We never changed."

"Why not?" asked Paul, who wondered if he should be concerned about his own future growth.

"Going from Yale to the OSS to the agency was like never leaving school," Mother said. "But Allen Dulles was a different matter. He had a career before there was an OSS or CIA. As you know, he was a distinguished diplomat for twenty years before the war. He was 'finished' in a way very few others in the agency ever were. I think that's why we looked up to him. And that's probably why we got so mad at each other. We were both showing off for Father."

Once again they sank into silence for blocks. Paul wondered if the quiet would work for him once more. It didn't. Guessing the interview was over, he decided the time had come to try his sensitive question.

Paul asked, "So that's what caused the, uh . . . ?"

"Well, not quite. Actually, it was just the beginning."

The old man did not elaborate. The silence made Paul sleepy. Soon he was yawning again.

"Let's stop and get some coffee," Mother suggested.

They patronized a Hot Shoppes Jr. so they would not have to leave the car. Pulling into a slot in the parking lot, they gave their orders to a microphone. A carhop carried their coffees out to them. Sitting in the drive-in, Paul felt more than ever like a teenager. A teenager out on a date. A date with Mother.

When Paul first heard the static-charged voice, he thought it was coming from the box that had taken their order. But he finally realized that it was what they had been waiting for. The bug in Mark Harrington's bedroom had picked up a telephone conversation. The voice-activated tape recorder attached to the car's receiver was turning.

"Hello," said a sleepy voice crackling with electricity.

"Hello, Mark Harrington?" asked another voice.

"Yes, who's this?"

"Sorry to disturb you. This is General Cook at the Pentagon."

"Hanoi's a half-hour earlier," Harrington said irritably.

"Excuse me?" the puzzled general said.

19

Miscellaneous Projects

MOTHER TURNED to his safe. He twirled the dial—
38–12–96—and opened the top drawer. He removed
a file and headed for the Miscellaneous Projects office.

Arriving before his guest, Mother fixed himself a Kir.
It was unlike him. He normally preferred to stay a
drink behind. And yet he drank as he waited. He had
been more nervous lately, ever since the end of the
Arab-Israeli war. For Mother knew that it would be
easier to fire the head of the Israeli desk during
peacetime than wartime.

When Menachem Ginzburg arrived, Mother gave
him a martini. As they drank, seated opposite one another beneath the exposed beams, Mother stroked one
of the greyhounds at his feet. When the small Israeli
tried to pet the other dog, he got snapped at.

"Would you like to see some pictures?" Mother
asked.

"Of course."

Mother punched the buttons on the arm of his chair as the lights dimmed.

"Do you recognize the man with the briefcase?"

"No," said Ginzburg, "but I recognize the location. That's Foggy Bottom, isn't it?"

"That's right."

Mother punched up three more pictures. Ginzburg did not recognize any of the men, but he guessed from the backgrounds that they were all associated with ODACID.

"Who are they?" Ginzburg asked.

"The secretary of state's four closest aides," Mother said matter-of-factly.

"Don't tell me one of them's a KGB penetration," Ginzburg said.

"No," Mother said. "I've no evidence that the Russians have placed agents inside the secretary of state's office, but they really don't need to, do they? The secretary does what they want him to anyway."

"All right," Ginzburg said, "why are you showing me pictures of the secretary's men? It can't be because they're such handsome fellows because they're not."

"The secretary will visit Prague next month," Mother said. "Those aides I showed you will be with him. He'll be wrapped up in a security blanket, but they'll be more accessible. Do you think your people could keep them under the microscope?"

In a time of personal crisis, Mother was turning once again to the connection which had served him so well during that national crisis, the Cold War against Stalin. He was turning to the CIA–Mossad–old Jewish underground connection. He felt confident that through this connection Ginzburg would be able to put together a network in Prague to watch the secretary of state.

"I think we probably could," Ginzburg said. "Do you happen to have his itinerary?"

Mother opened the file which lay in his lap. It contained photostats of letters the secretary of state had written to various girlfriends. From these epistles, Mother had been able to piece together the secretary's schedule—which hotels, which parties, which concerts . . .

"That'll be no problem," Mother said. "This time I want to know what my government's giving away."

That evening, Paul stood at the Avis counter at 1722 M Street, N.W. He signed the rental agreement and initialed the two squares indicating he did not want the extra insurance. Someone had once told him the extra dollars from the insurance was a rip-off, that it was where rental agencies made most of their money. Paul had no idea whether it was true. He couldn't even remember who told him. But he never took the extra insurance.

A Pinto pulled up outside. Paul slipped behind the wheel, stuffed the rental agreement in the glove compartment, and drove off toward the suburbs. Reaching McLean, he parked the rented car in front of a modest red brick home which the company rented for Osvald Lapusnyik, the Czech defector.

Paul was one of a group of young intelligence officers who took turns baby-sitting Lapusnyik. When he fled Czechoslovakia he left his family behind, so he was lonely. Young KUBARK men rotated keeping him company.

They usually took him out to dinner and to a play or a concert or the ballet. The defector's tastes were, in general, slightly more elevated than his sitters'. He was always prevailing upon them to drive him out to theaters like the Olney, way out in the sticks, to see a revival of some American classic. Paul, who enjoyed irony, told himself that the baby was giving his baby-sitters an education.

Osvald got into the Pinto beside Paul. Driving a rented car was part of the drill. The defector was never supposed to be exposed to traceable license tags just in case it later turned out that he was not what he appeared to be. Just in case the other side had deliberately sent him to KUBARK as part of some elaborate Soviet plot. Osvald Lapusnyik was never supposed to know for sure that Paul worked for the CIA. And he was never even supposed to learn Paul's last name.

"Paul," the defector said, "where are we going tonight?"

"I don't know. Where would you like to go?"

They went through this catechism every time they met. Paul knew Lapusnyik already had their evening minutely planned. When he wasn't being debriefed, the defector had little else to do except to plan elaborate programs.

"Well, I thought we would have dinner at the Jockey Club," Osvald said in his lightly accented but otherwise perfect English.

"All right, and then where'll we go?"

"Oh, I don't know," Osvald said, being considerably more tentative than was normal for him. "I thought we might, well, 'check out' a new singles bar I heard about. I would like to study all aspects of contemporary American culture."

Paul found a parking place on Massachusetts Avenue, just half a block from the Jockey Club. Osvald had made a reservation under a phony name. They were given a table near the kitchen since the maître d' had never heard of "Thomas Jefferson"—the name Osvald had selected.

"Would you like anything to drink, Mr. Jefferson?" a waiter asked.

"Vell," said Osvald, "have you got any Russian vodka?"

A few minutes later, over oysters Rockefeller, "Jefferson" brought up a matter that had been disturbing him.

"You know, Paul, I'm worried."

"What's the matter?"

"It's something I read in the newspaper. The *Washington Post.*"

"What was it?"

"It said in the *Post*—you know, I read the *Post* all the way through every day, the *Times* too, and the *Star* in the afternoon—I have lots of time and I want to learn about America."

"Of course, but what was it in the *Post* that upset you?" Paul asked. Why was it that every conversation with Osvald was like a debriefing session? Why was it that he made you draw everything out of him? Was he just a child demanding attention? Or was it his way of attempting to exert some control? The only clout he had left in this world depended upon the secrets he had locked in his head. Perhaps he did not want to squander his information too rapidly. Perhaps this habit of using his memory like a miser extended over even into trivial areas. You had to beg him to tell you what the *Washington Post* had already told everybody.

"Perhaps I should not have brought it up," Osvald said. "After all, I don't know your feelings on the matter. I may be picking a fight, and I don't want to pick a fight with you, my friend."

"Osvald, if you don't tell me, I'm going to stick this toothpick under one of your neatly manicured fingernails."

"Well, if you're really interested."

"I am *really* interested," Paul said. "You have my full attention."

"Well, it was about the war in Vietnam."

"What about it?"

"The *Post* said your President was threatening to start the bombing again," Osvald confessed.

"Well, what about it?"

"This is my adopted country," Osvald said. "I gave up everything to come to America, so I feel I have a big stake in everything America does."

"So?"

"So I hate to see America do something dumb, like dropping more bombs on Vietnam," Osvald said. "I never could understand how such a supposedly smart people ever got themselves into such a dumb war. America's all I have going for me now—I don't want to see her . . . do you say 'fuck down'?"

Two hours later, Paul and Osvald left the restaurant—"Goodnight, Mr. Jefferson"—and made their way to the Cave, located in an alley behind the 1100 block of Eighteenth Street, N.W. But there was a problem. The line in front of the bar stretched for half a block.

Paul and Osvald made their way to the back of the line. Osvald took the wait gracefully for a few minutes, but he grew rapidly more impatient. The former STB officer read all the papers every day, but he still had a good deal to learn about America. He naturally assumed a CIA officer would enjoy the same privileges in his home country that an STB officer enjoyed in his country. So he could not understand what they were doing hanging around at the end of the line.

"Paul," Osvald said, "tell them who you are."

"Your man Lapusnyik had quite a night last night, didn't he?" Mother asked.

"Oh, nothing special," Paul said. "We went to the Jockey Club for dinner and then had a few drinks at a bar. That's all."

"I meant later on. Somewhere along the line, our defector picked up a woman."

"That's right. At about 1 A.M. I put them in a cab. Didn't Lapusnyik get home all right?"

"Oh, yes, he got home all right. So did she. I mean she got to his home all right."

"Good for him. I hope he had a good time."

"As a matter of fact," Mother said, "they got off to a rather uncertain beginning. Our defector was impotent until he tied her up. Then he was fine."

"Oh, really," Paul said, suddenly feeling a special kinship to his charge.

"He used neckties. Here, would you like to read the transcripts?"

"No, thanks," Paul said, embarrassed. Deciding to try to change the subject, he asked, "How many guards do we have assigned to protect Lapusnyik?"

"None. When he first came over, we had a bodyguard live with him for a few weeks. We always do. But we do it for psychological rather than protective reasons."

"Psychological reasons?"

"Of course. There's really little danger, but the defector believes there is. We don't protect the defector from the other side, we protect him from his own imagination."

"You mean the other side wouldn't want to punish a defector as an example to others?"

"We have sort of a gentlemen's agreement with the other side," Mother said. "It's based on reciprocity. We won't kill our people who defect to them if they won't kill their people who defect to us. It's like a code of ethics."

Paul thought for a moment.

"Well, then, wouldn't our AESOP project violate that code?" asked the young intelligence officer, who was beginning to suspect what the operation involved.

"Maybe a little bit," Mother admitted, "but we don't actually plan to kill anybody. That's not the idea. In fact, it's contrary to the idea."

"Just what is the idea?" Paul asked.

Mother was as silent as a photograph.

20

The Quarrel

BY THE TIME Paul arrived, the face had already turned black. He heard the cameras clicking away. The new kind that advanced themselves automatically. Click. Whrrr. Click. Whrrr. Click. Whrrr. It was the sound of celebrity. When you heard it you knew you were in the presence of a movie star, or a TV star, or a President, or a presidential hopeful. But Mark Harrington was unable to enjoy the limelight. The rope around his neck kept his feet from touching the ground.

The Arlington cops had sent one photographer. ODENVY had sent two photographers. And KUBARK had sent three photographers. They held light meters up to the darkened face to get a reading.

Mother had called Paul at 6 A.M. When the phone started to jangle, Paul clutched Frances as if for protection. When he finally figured out what was causing the racket, he crawled over her inert body and lifted the receiver.

"Did I wake you?" Mother asked.

"No," Paul said groggily.

"Did anyone ever tell you that you're not a convincing liar?"

"No."

"I have an assignment for you. Are you awake enough to understand that?"

"No," Paul said a third time.

"I'm sorry to disturb you," Mother said, "but you've got to wake up enough to understand this. There's been a suicide. A company suicide. I want you to go to the scene to represent CI. Do you understand?"

"No."

Paul woke up Frances and asked her if he could borrow her car. He borrowed it all the time, but he always asked.

He arrived at the scene of the hanging a few minutes after the Arlington police, but a few minutes before the G-men. The man at the end of the rope was only the third corpse he had ever seen. The first had been his grandfather, who was laid out in an open casket at a small-town funeral. The second had been a woman killed in a traffic accident which Paul had the misfortune to pass. And now he stood in the presence of a man who had strangled.

Of course Paul remembered the story his grandmother had told him. She had actually been to a hanging. The man who was executed had committed a heinous crime, murdered a whole family. His grandmother had been sure she would be glad to see the man hanged. After all, she had always experienced a kind of thrill when she killed a poisonous snake. Seeing this killer swing would be the same sort of thing. So she had gotten up early with the rest of her family—with the rest of her town—and gone down to the big tree. She saw more people she knew than she saw even on Sunday. She loved being in the festive crowd, but she did not love the hanging. It horrified her more than she had ever imagined possible. And for months afterward she had nightmares about the dying marionette kicking at the end of his string. As Paul stared

up at the hanged man before him, he wondered if
this corpse might not soon be dancing its way through
his own dreams.

While the photographers clicked away, while the fin-
gerprint men dusted, while the investigators scribbled
in their notebooks, Paul went about the work he had
come to do. He had brought a large briefcase with
him. It was empty. He poked about through the dead
man's papers, the scraps of a bureaucrat's life, looking
for sensitive documents. Any memorandum, any letter,
anything at all that connected Mark Harrington with
KUBARK was slipped surreptitiously into the briefcase. Even as a corpse Mr. Harrington would live his
cover: he would remain a civilian employee of
ODEARL, a GS-18, not a very high grade for a
man with so many years' service.

The police had found an unsigned, typewritten note
on his desk. It said he had been depressed about repeated failures to win promotions. It said, in effect, that
he would rather be dead than be a forty-seven-year-
old GS-18. There was no hint of his involvement with
the agency. Paul preferred to think that this was because the dead man had remained true to his cover to
the very end. Paul preferred to believe that the suicide
victim had written his own note.

Paul was instructed to stay at the house all day, but
he managed to get away long enough to have lunch
with Frances. They met at Mr. Smith's because they
knew the food was so bad it wouldn't be crowded.

"You know," Frances said, "if you weren't such a
favorite of Mother's you might get more sleep."

"I'm sorry I woke you," Paul said. "It was pretty
early."

"What romantic assignment has Mother given you
this time?" Frances asked. "Don't you feel like boast-
ing?"

She knew she sounded envious, but she couldn't
help it.

"It wasn't so romantic this time," Paul said. He had
been dreading telling her.

"Oh, poor baby."

"It was pretty bad."

"Don't tell me you're disillusioned. Don't tell me the looking-glass war is hell."

"Don't be flip," Paul said, growing impatient with her. "I'm not in the mood."

"So what happened? I know you're dying to tell me. Go ahead and spill it."

"I'm not dying to tell you."

"Oh, sure you are. It's written all over your face. Go ahead, impress me with your latest adventure. Of course, you know what they're calling you, don't you? 'Mother's boy.' "

"You don't really want to know."

"I'll decide what I want to know."

"All right. One of our people killed himself last night. He took a . . ."

"I don't want to hear about it," Frances snapped.

The news opened a door she had long avoided. Actually, there was literally a door she had long shunned. It was the door to the closet in which her father had been found with a gun nestled in his hand and a bullet nestled in his brain. She had never gone near that closet since her father's death. And she had tried to keep a corresponding mental compartment sealed also. Now Paul, with no warning whatsoever, had flung open that door, and a jumble of musty emotions had come tumbling out.

"I'd like a drink," Frances said.

A few minutes later, having downed half a Scotch on the rocks in silence, she said, "I'm sorry. I didn't mean to give you a hard time. I had no idea."

"That's all right. I'm sorry I upset you."

"Go ahead and tell me what happened. I'll be hearing about it anyway, and I'd rather hear it from you first. How did he do it?"

Paul hesitated but eventually answered.

"He hanged himself."

"Where'd he do it?" Frances asked, hoping it wouldn't turn out to be the closet.

"In his study."

"Did he get up on a chair?"

"No. He piled up a big stack of government reports. Almost all Government Printing Office stuff. All nice and thick and probably ignored. All with gray covers. He stacked up these reports, climbed up on top of them, and then kicked them over. The room was covered with government paper."

Frances was talking in her sleep. Paul listened intently, but he could not make out any distinct words, much less sentences. Frances was making prelanguage sounds. Then she screamed and opened her eyes.

"What's the matter, darling?" Paul asked, hugging the frightened girl.

"It's just that dream I always have," Frances said sleepily.

It was six o'clock in the morning.

"What dream?"

"The one about my father."

"You never told me you had a recurrent dream about your father," Paul said. His tone suggested he was hurt. Frances was holding out on him. She was keeping secrets.

"Don't pout. I never told anyone. I always thought I'd never tell, but I'll tell you if you want."

"I'd like to hear it."

"It's kind of embarrassing. I always dream I've been bad and my father is mad at me. But I'm not a little girl. I'm grown up. Still, he punishes me."

Frances stopped talking. Paul waited to see if she would start again on her own. When she didn't, he cued her.

"How does he punish you?"

"He, ah, he pulls up my dress—am I blushing?"

"No," Paul lied.

"My father pulls up my dress, pulls down my panties, and turns me over his knee—are you sure I'm not blushing?"

"You don't blush," Paul lied.

"Well, so long as I've gone this far, I might as well go the rest of the way," Frances said. "My father turns me over his knee and breaks an egg over my bare ass. He drops the egg right on my crack as if it were a frying pan. And then he spanks me with his hand. It scrambles the egg."

Paul and Frances rode to work in her Datsun. He drove.

Parking the car, they walked together to a door cut in the face of the IBM card. Inside the building, Frances said good-bye to Paul and headed for the West German desk, where she would spend another day defending the free world with a pocket calculator. As the most junior member on the desk, she got the jobs the other members did not want. And that usually meant the financial reports. She read them. She collated them. She summarized them. She was bored by them.

Frances sat down at her metal desk and began adding column after column of figures, her fingers playing hopscotch on the calculator. As she worked, she could not help wondering what Paul was doing. Nor could she help being jealous of him, for whatever he was doing it was surely more interesting than what she was doing. When they had first met, he had envied her her father, but now she envied him his Mother.

Meanwhile, over at KUDESK, Paul was somewhat discouraged also.

"Did you get anything out of your defector yesterday?" Mother asked.

"Just more gossip about secret service sex. It seems like a waste of time."

Besides baby-sitting Osvald Lapusnyik evenings, Paul also took a regular turn debriefing him during business hours. They would sit at the defector's dining room table while Paul showed him pictures of known or suspected Soviet Bloc intelligence agents. Paul would then take notes on whatever Lapusnyik knew about these people, which rarely went much deeper than who was having an affair with whom.

"No, no, don't be discouraged," Mother said. "It's almost always like that. These debriefings usually turn

out to be about ninety percent sexual. But that doesn't
mean they're useless. We may be able to blackmail
some officers into working for us. Or we may be able
to write letters to their superiors and get them fired."

"I'm sure you're right," Paul said, "but it's not the
way I thought it'd be. When I got there today, Lapusnyik was watching *As the World Turns*. He shut it off,
but when we sat down to talk it was just like he hadn't.
It was one soap opera after another."

"I'm not surprised. After all, the kind of curiosity
that makes a good intelligence officer also makes a
dedicated gossip. We suck up information for the sake
of sucking up information. We're that kind of people.
Beneath all our layers of secrecy, we're gossips at
heart."

"Well, Lapusnyik certainly is."

"It's part of the business. This is a small, sealed, in-
grown profession. Joining the secret world is like moving into a small town."

Mother then proceeded to draw out of Paul all
the gossipy items told him by the defector.

"Actually, I didn't ask to see you to talk about
Lapusnyik," Mother said at last. "I have another
AESOP assignment for you. I want you to get me an
Apollo space suit."

"An Apollo space suit?" Paul said. "How do you
suggest I go about locating one?"

"You're a smart boy," Mother said.

In another wing of the building, Frances was called
in to see her boss. She too was given an assignment,
one both delicate and intricate. The chief of the West
German desk wanted her to tie his black tie.

It was already 6 P.M. He was expected at the White
House in half an hour. Having brought his tuxedo to
work with him, he had dressed in his office. The studs
had given him some trouble, but he had expected no
difficulty in getting to 1600 Pennsylvania Avenue on
time.

Then he got hung up on the bow tie, which proved
as involuted as German politics.

"What's the occasion?" Frances asked as she performed her legerdemain with the strip of black cloth.

"There's a state dinner at the White House for Willy Brandt," her boss said. "It should be fun. I'll be the only unfamous person there. They'll all be scratching their heads wondering who I am."

"Have you ever met Brandt?" Frances asked, her hand at her boss's throat but not checking his pulse for veracity.

"Oh, yes, yes. After the war, I was his case officer."

"Are you telling me that Brandt worked for the company?" Frances asked, botching the knot.

"Sure. He did a lot for us, and we did a lot for him."

"Don't wiggle," Frances said, as though that were the reason for the failure of the first knot. She started over.

"Still, I was surprised to get the White House invitation. I guess Willy has a sentimental spot for his old CO."

"I said don't wiggle."

Paul and Frances sat up side by side in a huge borrowed bed. They were nude, but the bed was dressed, or so it seemed to Paul, for it wore a huge ruffled canopy.

The borrowed bed stood in a borrowed master bedroom in a borrowed house belonging to a Procter & Gamble heiress. The home stood on one of those little feeder streets just off fabulous Foxhall Road, the richest street in town. The heiress had taken off for a couple of months in Tahiti. During the white months, while snow turned the whole town the color of the Capitol dome, while Washington faces turned the color of the marble, the heiress lay on a beach turning brown. And Paul and Frances lay in her bed.

The two young intelligence officers spent their weekends apartment-hunting, but until they found something, they were mansion-sitting. The heiress knew Frances's mother, through whose good offices the arrangement had been worked out.

The Washington home of the perpetually bronzed

heiress was pure white inside and out—it set off her tan. From a distance, the mansion looked like a huge block of Ivory soap. It appeared to be the embodiment of cleanliness. It was the kind of house where the heiress to a fortune amassed by a company dedicated to keeping America clean should have lived.

Pale Paul and pale Frances sat beneath the white canopy, working on reports. They both wrote on yellow legal pads. Paul was preparing a report on his latest debriefing of his defector. Frances was struggling with a report—really a collation of several field reports —on the amount of money Arab countries were investing in German munitions.

"Let's go to a movie," Frances said, putting down her work. "We could still make a ten o'clock show."

"I should finish this report," Paul said. "I promised Mother I'd get on it right away."

Frances was suddenly furious. She was jealous of how well Paul was doing in the company. Jealous of the time and attention he gave to his job rather than to her. She had loved him for his failures; now she was beginning to hate him for his success.

"Don't pull that one on me," Frances flared. "I've got a report to write, too. We'll work after the movie. Stay up late."

"I'd better not. I've got a lot to do."

"And I suppose I don't."

"I didn't say that."

"That's what you meant. You're teacher's pet, and you're turning into a grind. I knew people in college like you, but I didn't like them."

"I'm *not* going to any damn movie," Paul said, getting angry now. "Please be quiet."

Frances jumped out of bed and ran from the room. Paul was upset, but at the same time he was not sorry to see her go. Now he would get some work done.

Paul had no idea how long Frances was missing because he was lost in the permutations of faraway STB incest. He looked up when he heard footsteps, but his mind was slow in returning from Czechoslovakia. The missile was already on the way before he realized what it was. Then it hit him in the shoulder and he knew.

Frances stood naked in the doorway, cradling a carton of eggs in the crook of her elbow like a baby. His eye seemed to record her movements in slow motion. She carefully reached into the carton for more ammunition, cocked her arm, and then let fire. She did not throw "like a girl." The egg crashed into one of the bedposts and exploded all over the white bed, the white wall, the white carpet, and the ashen Paul.

Paul was actually frightened. He felt so helpless. It had never before occurred to him how helpless a nude man in bed really was. With the eggs came the questions: what if she were throwing bullets instead of eggs? What if she had gone after a revolver instead of an egg carton? What if she had really been mad enough to kill him? He remembered all those statistics about how most murder victims were knocked off by their loved ones.

When the eggs landed, they went off like bazooka shells, and this time the gunner had plenty of time to take aim. An egg hit the wall next to Paul's head, splattering yolk on his right ear. An egg hit his knee. Paul wondered if Frances was throwing at his crotch. A wild pitch hit a lamp beside the bed.

An egg hit Paul in the forehead. When he opened his eyes, all he could see was yellow. And he kept saying to himself: what if it had been a bullet? What if it had been a bullet? What if it had been a bullet?

Paul was the unhappy victim of the ultimate female weapon: eggs. But eggs were supposed to be passive. Eggs were supposed to sit there like props in a shooting gallery while the male fired away at them. The problem was, Paul had been transformed into a passive target. And Frances was an egg machine gun.

Blinking through yolk, Paul saw that Frances was out of ammunition. Looking about the badly splattered room, he was suddenly furious. His whole body grew hot as if he were about to ejaculate. Bursting out of bed, he dove at Frances. He crashed into her, knocking her down.

Then Paul pulled Frances to her feet and twisted

her arm behind her in a hammerlock. By the time she realized how mad he was, she was already helpless. She never had a chance to use all those fancy self-defense tricks she had learned at the Farm. Her right arm felt as if it were going to break.

Using his leverage, Paul marched Frances ahead of him down the hall, down the stairs, and across the living room. A trail of yellow tracks stretched out behind them.

When they reached the back door Paul unlocked it, opened it, and marched Frances out into the backyard. They both stood there, nude and shivering in the snow. Paul gave Frances a hard shove, and she staggered a half-dozen steps before stumbling and falling on the snow, breasts first.

Paul raced to an outdoor spigot and turned on the water, which came gushing out a garden hose. He picked up the hose and adjusted the nozzle so the stream approximated that of a firehose. Then he trained his water gun on the woman, who had risen to her hands and knees in the snow. He knew how cold the water would be and how much it would hurt. Frances screamed at him to stop, but he didn't. Paul held tightly to the long rubber phallus and sprayed Frances unmercifully.

A few hours later Paul and Frances made up, without quite forgiving each other. They sealed the peace by making love in the sticky bed.

III

VENGEANCE

21

Fired

"HE'S OVER in the Tasty Freeze," said Kay Johnson, the director's secretary.

"When do they expect him back?" the director asked.

"They don't," Mrs. Johnson said. "He told his secretary he was going home right after his talk."

"What talk? Who's he talking to?"

"A group of congressmen."

"I've got to talk to him before he leaves for the weekend. Send Andy over to get him."

On his way to fetch Mother, Andy Wilson passed the bronze statue of Nathan Hale, bound hand and boot with bronze ropes. Wilson often identified with the statue, for he too felt bound by red tape and other bureaucratic restrictions.

Andy Wilson entered the ice cream cone and sat down at a desk which had been especially constructed for the director. Atop it sat a red telephone and a desk plate which read: DCI.

Mother did not notice the director's assistant sitting in the director's chair right away. When he did, the circular room seemed to begin to spin. The auditorium changed from an ice cream cone into a merry-go-round. Mother was dizzy.

The KUDESK chief tried to concentrate on what he was telling the twenty-five congressmen scattered over the bright orange seats, but it was hard to keep his mind on his speech. The rising menace of communism around the world—the subject of his talk—seemed less menacing than the director's assistant perched on the "throne" at the back of the auditorium.

Mother droned on, his small voice picked up by the microphone and amplified so the congressmen could hear. He was torn between cutting his speech short so that he could find out what the director's assistant wanted and stretching it out so he would not have to find out.

". . . Edward Landsdale was an expert at what he called psywar," he told his audience. "In the Philippines, we backed Ramón Magsaysay in his struggle against the communist Huks. Landsdale discovered that in the countryside the people had a lively belief in a mythical vampire called the *asuang* . . ."

When congressmen came to visit, it was standard procedure to show them gadgets or tell them war stories. The idea was to entertain them so they would never get around to asking about how KUBARK really worked.

". . . Landsdale sent a psywar squad into Communist territory to spread the word that the *asuang* had been seen near a Huk base. They gave the rumor a couple of days to circulate. Then Landsdale's men set up an ambush. They waited for a patrol to pass, then grabbed the last man in line. They punched two holes in his neck, hung his body up by the heels until all the blood drained out, then left the body on the trail. When the Huks found the vampire's victim, they cleared out . . ."

Regretfully, Mother wound up his talk. The congressmen clustered around the podium for a moment to shake hands, then filed out of the auditorium to continue their tour. As they passed out of the dome one by one, Mother felt more and more like the last Huk in the jungle line.

When the round room was empty except for Mother and Wilson, the two men approached one another like a sperm and gamete meeting at the center of a giant egg.

"What can I do for you?" Mother asked apprehensively.

"The director would like to see you," Wilson said.

Walking from the auditorium back to headquarters, Mother identified with the bronze Nathan Hale. He felt he was being led away to be executed.

All the way to the director's office, Mother half wished another Arab-Israeli war would break out. He knew that in such international instability lay his security.

When Mother entered the director's office, O'Hara did not get up.

"I'll come right to the point," the director said. "I'm afraid I must ask you for your resignation."

Mother waited for an explanation but received none. "I don't understand," he said.

"As I'm sure you know, there's a provision in the nineteen forty-seven law which allows the DCI to dismiss any employee without explanation, so long as it's in the national interest. I'm availing myself of that provision."

"So I'm not to know why I'm being fired."

"I think you know why. I'll expect your letter of resignation Monday morning."

For once Mother wanted to go home to an empty house, but he could not. Matt was visiting his father during Berkeley's spring vacation.

During dinner, Mother lost his appetite but kept his secret. The father knew his son hated his position at the agency, but he still could not bring himself to tell his boy that he was losing that position. For Mother was afraid his son would think less of him somehow. And Mother was probably right.

Over coffee, Matt asked his father, "Would you like to go to an Allen Ginsberg reading tomorrow?"

"Love to," Mother said, although he did not want to do anything of the sort. Father and son had been making a special effort to get along with one another.

Before going to bed, Mother went into his study to be alone with his secret. He had two nightcaps, both brandy and sodas. He drank not only because he was losing his job, but also because he was afraid he would not be able to sleep. Yet when he lay down in his bed, he began to grow surprisingly drowsy. There was a moment, just before he was completely gone, when he actually said to himself: this is going to be easier than I thought. It was as though, rather than keeping him awake, his troubles chased him down the hole.

He slept soundly for two hours, from 11 P.M. to 1 A.M.

Then Mother woke up feeling as if he had been running a race, heart thumping, arteries jumping, lungs sucking. He knew immediately that he would not fall asleep again for many hours; this knowledge acted as a self-fulfilling prophecy. He was already thinking of getting up. And he began to wonder how he would pass his time if he did leave his bed. In his mind, he rehearsed the scene: he imagined himself walking into his study, examining his library shelf by shelf, volume by volume, looking for a book to read, until, at last, he came to F. Scott Fitzgerald's lyrically bleak *Crack-Up*. Yes, that would do. Mother swung his feet over the edge of the bed and stood up.

When Mother reached his library, swaddled in robe and slippers, he took down *The Crack-Up* from the exact place on the exact shelf where he had known he would find it. He leafed hurriedly through the book until he found the essay he was after. Fitzgerald called it "Sleeping and Waking." Mother thought it was the best dozen pages ever written on insomnia.

Scott Fitzgerald—an expert on all kinds of failure including the failure to sleep—wrote that going to sleep was easy. The hard part was keeping the night from breaking in two. He woke up in the middle of the night, tossed, twisted, or just lay with misery wrapped around him like a tangled sheet. And in the dark he heard a voice hammering:

> *I need not have hurt her like that.*
> *Nor said this to him.*
> *Nor broken myself trying to break what was*
>   *unbreakable.*

Fitzgerald listed all the mistakes insomniacs make. Getting up. Trying to work. Doing some reading.

As the sleepless hours passed, Fitzgerald wrote, the regrets were muffled by sheer exhaustion. At last his worries would be dissolved by "real sleep, the dear, the cherished one, the lullaby." And then his dreams would carry him back to a time when he could sleep:

> *In the fall of '16 in the cool of the afternoon*
> *I met Caroline under a white moon*
> *There was an orchestra—Bingo-Bango*
> *Playing for us to dance the tango*
> *And the people all clapped as we arose*
> *For her sweet face and my new clothes.*

Once again Mother was turning to literature for reassurance. Tolstoy comforted him during times of war. Fitzgerald comforted him at 3 A.M. Pierre had survived Borodino. Scott had survived the night. And Mother would survive.

At 4 A.M., Mother returned to bed, hoping to dream of the fall of '45 when he danced the tango in Rome in a new black suit. But Fitzgerald had been right. Getting up was a mistake. Reading was a mistake. Mother was nowhere near "the lullaby" of sleep.

Soon Mother realized that the night had a face. It was the face of the clock-radio. He looked into that face every five minutes or so to keep track of how badly his night was going. The last time Mother remembered seeing the face, it was 6:10.

Two hours later he woke up suddenly.

When Mother got up, he discovered that his son was still asleep. The father was glad. He did not feel like talking to anyone. He retreated to his study to read, but he was haunted by his desk. It seemed to summon him to a dreaded chore: the composition of his letter of resignation.

The desk drove Mother from the house. He went out to his orchids. A rock-throwing vandal had broken three glass panes.

That afternoon, Saturday afternoon, a sleepy Mother and his well-rested son set off for the reading. The father started to slide behind the wheel of the family car but thought better of it and handed the keys to his boy.

They arrived at the auditorium on the urban campus of George Washington University at 3:30 P.M. They had come early to get a good seat up front, but they need not have bothered. It was too late to worry about being early—that is, the man they had come to see was beginning to outlive his popularity. During the sixties, he packed the largest auditoriums and started riots. But his reading at George Washington attracted only about a hundred listeners.

Those who did show up looked like refugees from the sixties who had accidentally been stranded in the seventies. They wore beards, long hair, blue jeans, fringed leather jackets, red bandannas, cowboy boots, and no bras. And then there was one truly weird outfit. A man in the front row wore a black suit, a white shirt, and a black tie. He balanced a black homburg on black knees.

"When I heard Allen read in Berkeley," Matt said, "I met a funny girl. Not funny ha-ha. Funny strange."

"Yes," Mother said, wondering if his son was going to tell another story chosen for its shock value.

"After the reading," Mother's son said, "we went to a party for Allen. We did a lot of dope and had a pretty good time. As the party was breaking up, I asked her if she wanted to come home with me. She said she'd promise to fuck her girlfriend that night, but she'd fuck me the next night if I was still interested."

Allen Ginsberg, who walked on stage at that moment, saved Mother from having to think of a response. The poet's few loyal fans were loyal indeed.

They jumped to their feet and clapped and cheered loudly. When the applause at last subsided, Ginsberg laid a stack of paper on the podium and adjusted his glasses.

"I was," Mother's son said.

"You were what?" Mother asked.

"I was still interested. I wasn't too proud to take seconds. She went home with her girlfriend that night but she went home with me the next."

"Shhhh," a girl with long, dirty hair said. Ginsberg was introducing the poem he was about to read.

". . . My mother was a Communist," the balding, bearded poet said. "She thought spies were always watching her. Perhaps they were. She went insane."

The big bespectacled eyes seemed to pick out Mother in the front row, like headlights freezing a rabbit in the middle of the road.

"I used to go and visit her in the state hospital when I was a boy," Allen Ginsberg said. "We brought her home occasionally, but she would take off her clothes and run through the halls. We always had to take her back to the asylum. She died there and I wrote this poem to her. It's called 'Kaddish,' a prayer for the dead."

Allen Ginsberg read for an hour without pausing. The audience was completely still. As the poet eulogized his mother, Mother could not help thinking of his father. Ginsberg had been repelled by his mother, but he acknowledged that she had formed him as he was. Mother heard an echo of his own life. He tried to resist "Kaddish," but he could not.

After the reading, Mother's son said, "Let's go up and say hello."

Mother had never wanted to "touch" speakers after a performance. He supposed this was partially out of shyness. But he suspected he might also be trying to deny celebrity. Since Mother had deliberately chosen anonymity, he found it difficult to pay homage to fame. And now, as his secret career was coming to an end, he felt even less like paying tribute to a smiling public man.

And yet he was trying to get along with his son, which meant trying to be a good sport. "All right," Mother said, following his boy onto the stage.

They stood patiently on the edge of the cluster, waiting their turn. When they finally stepped to the center of the circle, the poet's bright eyes grew even brighter.

Allen Ginsberg threw his arms around Mother's son, hugged him tightly, and kissed him on the lips. Mother's stomach twisted painfully. He had had no idea that Matt knew Ginsberg. And the boy had given no hint. But Mother now realized he was not the only one in the family ever to have befriended a poet.

"Allen, I'd like you to meet my father," Mother's son stammered.

"Oh, yes," Ginsberg said gruffly. "The spy." He shook Mother's hand. "How many letters did you open today?"

Mother flinched. Flustered, he turned his back and walked away rather than answer. He could not stand a poet's hostility. He felt as if he had just been bitten by an orchid.

On the way home in the family car, the father and son said nothing to each other for the first few miles. But Mother finally could not resist.

"Where did you meet Ginsberg?"

"Berkeley."

"How well did you get to know him?"

"You mean, did I sleep with him?"

"I didn't say that."

"The answer is no."

Mother wished he could flutter his son.

That night, his sleep broke in two. He woke up in the middle of a dream about a bearded poet making love to his boy.

22

Covert Divorce Work

KUBARK GAVE Osvald Lapusnyik asylum. It fed him. It sheltered him. It entertained him. It paid him lavishly. And it had promised him a new identity. Yet Osvald was not satisfied. He made an additional request. He wanted a divorce.

Sunday at 4 P.M. Paul picked up Osvald in a rented red Camaro. Paul's instructions were to drive the defector down to Farmville, Virginia, that afternoon, to spend Sunday night in a local motel, and to meet with the CIA's divorce lawyer Monday morning. The red Camaro was really the wrong car for the job. Driving it, Paul felt deliciously conspicuous, like a fire chief. He could practically hear the siren.

Then he realized the siren was not imaginary. A Virginia state policeman was flashing his red light at the red car. Paul pulled over. The policeman asked if he was on his way to a fire. Paul handed the uniformed man a counterfeit driver's license. The policeman returned to his black and white car to write out the ticket.

"They always stop red cars," Paul said. "Red cars make them mad."

"Tell them who you are," Osvald said.

When the policeman returned, he handed Paul a ticket. Paul stuffed it in the glove compartment and continued south at 45 miles per hour. At this rate, they would not reach Farmville for another hour and a half.

Paul kidded Osvald, "When do you plan to get engaged?"

"I don't know," Osvald said, squirming beneath his seat belt. "She's what you Americans call a liberated woman. She says she isn't interested in marriage. I don't think I understand her very well."

"If she doesn't want to get married," Paul said, "then why do you want to get a divorce?"

"Well, I told her I was divorced," Osvald said. "I feel guilty lying to her. Besides, I'm never going to see my wife again, so I might as well get it over with while you people still remember who I am and can help me."

They drove on through the Virginia countryside where the spring trees, like the defector, were coming back to life after a long dormancy. Paul decided to use the trip to continue his debriefing of Osvald, but this time he allowed his curiosity rather than the established drill to lead him. So he asked about what he was most curious about: not intelligence officers on the other side but an intelligence officer on his own side. Paul debriefed the STB man about Mother, for who would know more about the head of the Counterintelligence Department than the competition?

"Before you defected, had you ever heard of Mother?" Paul asked.

"Of course."

"How?"

"I used to see Kim Philby from time to time in Moscow. He loved to talk about Mother."

"Did Philby ever mention O'Hara?"

"Oh, sure. Kim used to say he was the best ally O'Hara ever had. Because his escape gave O'Hara a stick to beat Mother with. I hear O'Hara loves to mention Philby in Mother's presence."

"Why's Mother so sensitive about Philby?"

"Because Mother and Philby used to be friends. They used to lunch together at La Niçoise back when Kim was stationed in Washington. He was SIS's liaison with the CIA."

He was referring to the British Secret Intelligence Service. Acronym: SIS. CIA cryptonym: SMOTH. Nickname: MI-6.

"When was that?" Paul asked.

"About nineteen fifty. Philby used to tell Mother, 'You're the thinnest man I ever met in my life.' I think they were drawn to each other because they both had eccentric fathers."

"Philby too?"

"You decide. His father kept baboons as bodyguards. Is that strange?"

"Yes."

"Kim's father's name was St. John Philby. He was a civil servant in India when his son was born. A cobra once got into the baby's bath and almost robbed our side of a great asset. But, thank God, St. John shot the snake and saved our man."

"Thank God."

"Later on, St. John moved his family to Saudi Arabia," Lapusnyik said, "where he underwent a conversion. He became a Moslem, renamed himself 'The Slave of God,' wore Arab clothes, ate camel meat, and took a second wife—an Arabian slave girl. Now you tell me, did Philby and Mother have a lot to talk about?"

"You've convinced me."

"St. John Philby's last words on his deathbed were: 'God, I'm bored.' Naturally his son was a little messed up. He stuttered."

"And Mother whispers," Paul said in a low voice.

"One day Mother told Kim, 'I'm onto you and your KGB friends.' Philby was terrified until he found out Mother said that to everyone he ate with. A dozen years later Mother found out he'd been right, but by then Kim was in Moscow."

Arriving in Farmville, Paul parked his red car in front of the Six Dollar Motel, a string of white-frame cabins which needed painting. Mother had recommended the Six Dollar to Paul as the only hostelry in town. They checked in: Paul registering as Robert Brown, Osvald as Andrew Jackson.

After inspecting their room, Paul and Osvald decided to have dinner at the place Mother had recommended as the best in town: the Rexall Drugstore. Biting into an individually prepared small-town hamburger, Paul decided he preferred a mass-produced Big Mac.

Returning to the motel, the intelligence officer and the defector went to bed early, along with the rest of the town. They lay in twin beds in a tiny ten-dollar room—the cheapest room the Six Dollar offered.

"I can't sleep," Osvald called in the middle of the night.

"What's the matter?"

"I can't stand strange beds."

"Sorry," Paul said sleepily.

"Are there any questions you want to ask me?" the defector wanted to know. In the middle of a sleepless night, Osvald was an easy interrogation. He didn't want to be left all alone.

"I don't know," Paul said in a thick voice.

"How about how Mother finally got onto Philby?"

"You mean he did?"

"Oh, yes. He was about a decade late, but he finally did."

"All right, how?"

"Did you ever hear of a defector named Goleniewski?"

"No."

"He was a Pole," Osvald said. "And crazy. Mother was about the only one who took him seriously. Everyone else made fun of him. And of Mother for listening to him. Especially O'Hara."

"Where'd Mother find this crazyman?"

"In the biggest spy anthill in the world."

"Huh?"

"Berlin. He ran the Polish Second Bureau operations there. Mother persuaded him to defect and then adopted him. You'll never guess who this guy thought he was."

Lapusnyik paused, waiting to be prodded.

"I said, 'You'll never guess who he thought he was.'"

"All right, who?"

"He claimed to be the grandson of Czar Nicholas II and the rightful heir to the Russian throne. He said the czar and his family escaped from Ekaterinburg alive."

"Where to?"

"Poland."

"But what became of the czar?"

"Like any defector, he changed his name. And he supposedly lived to a ripe old age, I should be so lucky."

"And everybody laughed. Why in the world?"

"Not quite everybody," Lapusnyik corrected. "There was one person besides Mother who took the czar's grandson seriously."

"Who?"

"Bobby Kennedy."

"Really?"

"Yes, the czar's grandson turned Bobby Kennedy and Mother into allies. Afterward, they worked a lot together. Mother treated Bobby like a son."

"And the czar's grandson betrayed Philby?"

"He betrayed two spies. Both in the British service."

"'The smooth men of SMOTH,' as Mother says," Paul interjected.

"One was named George Blake. We were sorry to see him go because he had been very valuable to us. He told us about the tunnel you had under East Berlin."

The defector paused for effect.

"The other man was Kim Philby. But Kim knew he'd been betrayed, so he defected before he could be arrested."

The next morning Paul parked the red car in front of a little red schoolhouse. Osvald followed Paul into the building, where they announced themselves to the receptionist. They were then shown into what had once been a first grade classroom. The desk in the room supported a nameplate which said R. CROSBEY HAMMOND and a man in an eggshell suit who was smoking a corncob pipe. He normally smoked a briar but got out the corncob when he was expecting city folk.

Getting up off the desk, the man extended his hand and said, "Hi, I'm Cross Hammond," peeking over his granny glasses.

"Hello, I'm Osvald Lapusnyik," said the defector, extending his hand.

"How do you do, I'm Paul Ffff—Brown," said the young intelligence officer.

"What can I do for you?" Hammond asked, although he already knew.

"I'd like a divorce," Osvald said, speaking right up.

"I see," said Hammond. "Well, that should be no problem. I've been successful with such cases in the past." The lawyer turned to Paul. "I suppose you're prepared to act as Mr. Lapusnyik's witness."

"I don't know," said Paul. The only witnesses he associated with divorce cases were corespondents. "What would I be expected to do?"

"Oh, just swear Mr. Lapusnyik hasn't cohabited with his wife for the past year. Since I assume the wife's still behind the Iron Curtain, that shouldn't be a problem."

"But I've only known Osvald for three months," Paul said.

"Well, could you keep that to yourself?" Hammond said. "There're a couple of corners we're going to have to cut. Like the law says Mr. Lapusnyik has to be a resident of this circuit for six months before a divorce can be granted. You see, we're going to have to telescope several time periods."

"Okay," Paul said. "It's a good cause."

"Now, the proceedings will take place *in camera*," Hammond said. "The records will all be sealed. The whole thing should only take about fifteen minutes. Any questions?"

"Yes. Will the judge know who I am? That I'm a defector?"

"Yes, of course," Hammond said. "He's a friend of mine. We always work together on these cases."

"You mean the judge works for the company?"

"Oh, no," Hammond said, "and neither do I."

"Then who pays you?"

"You do," the lawyer said and smiled. "I'll send you a bill."

Osvald Lapusnyik could not help being a little suspicious. If the judge and the lawyer were not directly tied to the agency, as they would have been in his country, then how could he trust them?

"Could I ask a personal question?" Osvald asked.

"Of course."

"How did you get to be the CIA's divorce lawyer?"

"I'm not quite sure myself," Hammond said. "All I know is that about fifteen years ago I had lunch with a friend of mine in Alexandria. And my friend brought along a friend. I didn't find out 'til later he was CIA. Anyway, a few days after the lunch a stranger in a green Volkswagen showed up here in town asking questions about me. Now this isn't just a small town, it's a very small town. If a strange hounddog wanders into town, there's talk. That green Volkswagen was about the biggest thing to hit Farmville since General Grant. I was the object of an awful lot of gossip, and I got pretty paranoid."

The lawyer paused long enough to relight his corncob pipe. He never smoked it enough to quite get the hang of it.

"A few weeks later," Hammond began again, "I got a call from my friend's friend. He wanted to know if I'd be interested in coming up to Langley for lunch. I went up. He showed me around the plant and introduced me to some people. And, you know, I felt just like I was in another small town, only this time I was the stranger. Everywhere I went, people looked at me in a way that said, 'You don't belong.' I even had a feeling they were gossiping about me."

The lawyer relit the pipe.

"We ate in a private dining room. The CIA general counsel joined us. He asked if I'd be willing to help defectors get divorced from wives they'd left behind. I said I'd think about it. He said, 'Someday when your children ask you what you did in the Cold War, you can say divorce work.' "

When all Osvald's questions were answered, R. Crosbey Hammond led the way to the courthouse, which stood directly across the street from the schoolhouse. The lawyer, the client, and the witness were ushered into the judge's chambers.

"Hello, Cross."

"Hello, Your Honor."

"I understand we've got another national security divorce this morning."

Fifteen minutes later, Osvald Lapusnyik was single again.

"Come back and see me when you need a new identity," Hammond said. "I can change your name even faster than I can divorce you. I know you could just assume a new name, but most people prefer to do it legally. It's better in the long run. Come see me. We'll fill out a form and go see the judge. You'll be a new man."

The lawyer walked Osvald and Paul to their car and then watched it drive away. Hammond was left standing on the curb with a residue of guilt. These cases always disturbed him, for he did not believe in divorce. He hoped he was doing the right thing, but he was never sure. He told himself that as much as he disliked divorce he disliked communism more. He would continue to do what he saw as his duty.

R. Crosbey Hammond watched the red machine all the way to the horizon. The whole town watched. The crimson car sank over a distant hill like a setting sun.

23

Psywar

MONDAY MORNING, shortly after Paul arrived at the lawyer's office in Farmville, Mother arrived at the Toy Factory. He was a little late, but he had been in no hurry to go to work that morning. Waiting for Mother in his office were two messages, one from the director and the other from Ladyslipper. They both wanted to see him. The director wanted him at 5 P.M. Ladyslipper suggested a meeting at noon.

Mother removed several sheets of foolscap from a desk drawer which he always kept locked even though all of the paper in it was blank. Then he took an old-fashioned pump fountain pen from his breast pocket. He could not put off composing his letter of resignation any longer. He wrote a few tiny words in his tiny hand and then scratched them out. He pressed so hard he left a puddle of black ink on the page.

Mother paced. Then he returned to his writing task. He was one of those writers who overworks his page. He revised every sentence a dozen times before going on to the next. If a farmer replowed every furrow that many times, he would scrape off all the top-

269

soil. Mother sat eroding his paper for two hours.

He had hoped to finish the letter before noon, but the sad epistle was only a third done when he saw that it was time to leave for his rendezvous with Ladyslipper. Reviewing what he had already written, he noticed that every sentence had afterthought phrases inked in above and below the line. The phrases were weeds growing out of the neat rows of his sentences. Ever cautious, Mother locked his unfinished letter in his safe before leaving his office.

Mother crossed the Potomac River on Key Bridge and drove on to George Washington University, where he parked in front of the library. Entering the modern building, he took the elevator down to the basement. He approached the microfilm desk and asked to see the *Washington Post* of June 28, 1973—he had chosen the date at random. The desk attendant went to a filing cabinet and located the right spool of microfilm. Mother carried the spool into an adjoining room which was kept dark. He could barely make out the outlines of a couple of dozen microfilm reading machines. He threaded the film into one of the readers and began perusing the newspaper. He discovered that on June 28 the White House enemies list had been published. While he waited, he read through the names with some amusement. He half expected to find his own, although he knew it wasn't there.

In the semidarkness, Mother saw the shiny White House tie clasp before he saw the man. He knew the dim scrawl across its shiny face was Richard M. Nixon's signature. The seemingly disembodied tie clasp sat down at the machine next to Mother's. The new arrival threaded his microfilm into the reader. Then the two men sitting together in the dark began whispering to one another.

By the time Mother got back to Langley after his rendezvous and a solitary lunch at La Niçoise, Paul had returned from his divorce mission. Mother sent for him.

"Did you secure Mr. Lapusnyik's freedom for him?" Mother asked.

"Yes."

"Well done. Now tell me about AESOP. How're you coming with getting us a space suit?"

"I've got it."

"Really," Mother said, mildly surprised. "NASA must not be as tough as I thought. In fact, they sound like a security risk. Maybe we should investigate them again."

"I don't think an investigation of NASA will be necessary. I didn't get it from them."

"Then where?"

"CBS."

"Of course. Cronkite loves the space program so much, CBS probably has more space paraphernalia than NASA."

"Right. With all those simulated maneuvers, I figured they must have some surplus suits around the props department. When I said I was a high school science teacher, they begged me to borrow it."

"Good," Mother said, but he did not linger over praise. "Now I've got another job for you. Go to Pan Am and persuade them to make you a member of the crew they're sending to the Moscow Air Show."

At 5 P.M., Mother entered the director's office. It was crowded. The DCI was flanked by his deputy director operations, Alistaire Adams, and the chief of the Middle East section, Ralph Bennington. Mother supposed O'Hara had called in psychological reinforcements.

After shaking hands they all took seats, Adams and Bennington on the couch, the director and Mother on overstuffed chairs. The KUDESK chief thought he heard his letter of resignation crackle in his breast pocket as he sat down.

"Did you bring the document we discussed?" the director asked.

Mother handed over his composition. The director unfolded it and squinted at it as if it were an eye chart. When he finished reading he leaned back.

"We've been having a little meeting here," the director told Mother. "And we've decided that there might be another way."

"Yes?"

"Perhaps I won't have to accept this letter, after all. Some middle solution may be possible, if you're amenable."

"I don't quite understand," Mother lied.

"We've agreed not to ask for your resignation if you agree to give up the Israeli desk. What do you say? Should I tear this up?"

Mother wondered what his answer would have been if he had not shared ten minutes in the microfilm room with Ladyslipper. Perhaps he would have done just what the director hoped for. Perhaps he would have jumped at the chance to keep his job.

"Do what you wish with the letter," said Mother.

Ladyslipper had warned Mother that the secretary of state was behind a plot to get him off the Israeli desk. The secretary had worked out a strategy and then passed it along to the DCI for implementation. It was based on a negotiating technique which the ODA-CID chief had perfected during his talks with the North Vietnamese.

The drill with the Vietnamese went more or less as follows: in the morning, he would tell the men from Hanoi that he planned to bomb all their population centers to oblivion. Then, in the afternoon, he would tell them that he only planned to mine their harbors. Compared to the destruction of their cities, the mining of their harbors seemed like a bargain, a generous compromise.

On Friday, Mother had been threatened with bombs. Now, having had the weekend to think over the total destruction of his career, he was being offered mines instead. But now he knew the bombs had been a counterfeit threat. The Nixon administration was still too unsure of itself to attempt a purge. (And Mother suspected O'Hara was still worried about being blackmailed.)

"Now *I* don't quite understand," the director said. "Does that mean you're willing to accept this compromise or not?"

"It seems a generous offer," Adams said.

"It's better than losing everything," Bennington said.

"I'm sure it's very generous," Mother said. "But I

don't believe I'd be happy here if I couldn't continue
to run the Israeli operations."

"Does that mean you still want to resign?" the DCI
asked.

"I never wanted to resign. That was your idea, not
mine."

"Let me put it this way: you prefer resignation to the
loss of the Israeli desk?"

"Let *me* put it this way," Mother said. "Either fire
me or let me keep the Israeli account. Period. Now if
this psywar exercise is over, I've got to get back to my
office. I'm expecting a cable from Jerusalem."

"I saw a picture of you and some actress in the *Post*
this morning," the director told the secretary of state.

"They're giving me quite a reputation as a swinger,"
the secretary said. "But I don't mind. Now when I
go to a dinner party and I'm boring, others at the table
think it's their fault."

The line had become one of the secretary's favorites.
He liked it almost as much as he liked his accent.

The secretary of state and the Director of Central
Intelligence were lunching in the secretary's private
dining room in the State Department. The conversation, like the meal, began with light openers but in-
evitably progressed toward the meat of the matter, as
the director had known it would.

"Have you taken care of that personnel problem we
discussed?" the secretary asked.

"He's being difficult."

"You mean it didn't work."

"He won't turn loose of the Israeli desk."

"Sometimes I think he's a bigger barrier to peace in
the Middle East than the terrorists," the secretary
said. "At least the terrorists don't have Golda's ear."

The director had recently shown the secretary a transcript of Mother's discussion with the Israeli prime
minister. O'Hara had obtained the dialogue by resorting to a technique perfected for surveillance of Soviet
embassies around the world. The conversation had not
been bugged but filmed. Then the silent movie had

been shown to a mute lip reader. The transcript was not complete because the lips were not always visible, but the secretary had gotten the drift of the talk. He had also gotten mad. If Mother had been a city, the secretary would have bombed him gladly.

"Perhaps we should just fire him like we threatened to do," the director said. "But he could stir up a lot of dust."

"Ah, yes, I understand he's quite a dustman. A friend of mine who used to work for the agency told me a story about the way Kimball works. Back when Allen Dulles was director, he called my friend into his office and asked: 'Why did you say Bedell Smith doesn't like my brother?' "

O'Hara knew the story. He even knew that the secretary's friend had been right when he said that Bedell Smith, who served as director in 1950–1951, had disliked John Foster Dulles, Allen's brother. But O'Hara did not let on that he was already familiar with the tale the secretary was spinning.

"My friend happened to remember where he had had that conversation," the secretary continued. "It was while he was in bed with his wife. Kimball had bugged his pillow."

"Yes, that's how he works. When you complain, he tells you, 'If you didn't want to give up your right to smoke cigarettes, you shouldn't have taken a job in an explosives factory.' "

"Of course," the secretary smiled. "I understand why Kimball is so greatly feared. But now you must make a decision. Whom do you fear more, him or me? I want him removed."

When the lunch was over, the director went to his car and the secretary went into the ODACID press room to hold a news conference. His eye was caught by Washington's only female television sound technician. She looked like the women with whom the secretary was always having his picture taken.

The secretary walked over to the soundwoman and said, "Tell me, what do you really do with that microphone?"

24

Suicide / Murder

"MAYBE I CAN LOOK UP Philby while I'm there," Paul joked a few days later.

"Maybe," Mother said.

The KUDESK chief, whose resignation had not been accepted, had called in Paul for a progress report on his latest AESOP assignment. And the young intelligence officer had been able to inform his boss that he had been accepted as a member of the team which Pan Am was sending to the Moscow Air Show.

"Can I give him a message for you?" Paul said.

"Maybe."

Mother turned to his safe and withdrew a photograph of a middle-aged man standing in Red Square beneath the Kremlin carrying a London *Times* under his arm.

"Recognize him?" Mother asked.

"No."

"That's Kim."

"And he still reads the *Times?*"

"Yes, follows the cricket scores."

"After all these years?"

"Of course," Mother said. "That's the point about Kim. He hasn't changed since he was an undergraduate at Cambridge forty years ago. That's when he became a Communist."

"He does look kind of boyish," Paul observed, examining the picture.

"Sure, an old Cambridge boy," Mother said. "I've often wondered it he'd've outgrown his Red phase if he hadn't joined the Firm." He meant the Secret Intelligence Service.

"When did you first suspect him?" Paul asked.

"When Guy Burgess and Donald Maclean defected. They were Cambridge Marxists, too. Maclean was stuffy enough, but Burgess was quite a character. Since he was such an obvious security risk, no one guessed he might really be working for the other side. He was a homosexual and proud of it. Used to tell a story about watching two French politicians play Ping-Pong. They were dressed up in white tie and tails, but their net was a young man who wasn't dressed at all."

"Who won?"

"I don't know, but our side lost. When Burgess and Maclean defected two days before MI-5 planned to put on the cuffs, we knew they'd been tipped. I suspected their old Cambridge buddy Philby, but it took me twelve years to prove it."

"Jesus."

Frowning at the expression, Mother said, "The British let Burgess and Maclean get away in nineteen fifty-one—then in nineteen sixty-three they let Philby get away. But perhaps not for good, perhaps not for good . . ."

"What do you mean?"

"I mean I intend to get him back."

"Really?"

"Really," Mother said. "We planned a similar operation several years ago. I've dusted off those old blueprints and added a few innovations."

Mother went on to explain that KUBARK had plotted to kidnap Donald Maclean out of Moscow way back in 1956. The idea had been to turn a devastating liability into an asset. They would snatch Maclean, break him down, make him tell what Western secrets he had given the Russians, and then extract from him Soviet secrets.

The agency had gone so far as to take aerial photographs of Maclean's Moscow neighborhood, locate his house, and measure the ground and the fence. Then the plans for the kidnapping collided head on with the Hungarian Revolution. The uprising frightened the Russians, and a frightened Russia frightened the United States. ODYOKE decided not to make any sudden moves. KUBARK filed away its aerial pictures and left Maclean in peace. Maclean's enemies were unable to touch him, but he was not safe from his friends. When Kim Philby arrived in Moscow, he wasted no time in taking Maclean's wife away from him. Betrayal was a way of life with Philby. He could not stop even when the game was over.

"So that's AESOP," Paul said. "You plan to kidnap Philby during the air show."

"I've been talking too much," Mother said. "Well, you're right. That Apollo capsule you photographed will be on display at the show. I plan to drug Philby, dress him in your CBS space suit, substitute him for the dummy in the space capsule, load the capsule into an air transport, and fly him to America. The West's most famous runaway will reenter our hemisphere in the world's most famous reentry vehicle."

Paul and Frances had a lunch date. They drove to the Astor restaurant in her car. The place was crowded as usual, but they found a table upstairs. They both ordered spinach pie, the *plat du jour*. Frances ate more than Paul did.

"What's the matter?" Frances asked. "It was your idea to come here and now you aren't eating."

"I don't have much appetite today. I have an unpleasant task this afternoon."

"What's that?"

"I've got to go to a coroner's inquest. They're looking into Mark Harrington's death."

"Are you going to testify?" Frances asked, her interest reviving.

"No, no. So far as the official record's concerned, I was never on the scene at all. Harrington never worked for the company and a company man never sanitized his papers."

"So why're you going to the inquest?"

"Just to monitor it. If anything seems to be going wrong, I'll call Mother."

"What could go wrong? Isn't it cut and dried?"

"I hope so," Paul said, "but there could be a few complications. Like the suicide note was written on a typewriter and wasn't signed."

"Are you telling me you suspect it wasn't a suicide?"

"I really don't know if it was or wasn't. I like to think he killed himself. Let's talk about something else."

It still made Paul nervous to talk to Frances about suicide.

"No, let's not," she said. "Paul, when you were going through Harrington's house, did you find anything that made you suspicious?"

Paul did not answer.

"Come on, Paul, you can tell me. We're not going to let the company build walls between us, are we?"

"Well," Paul said, hesitated, and then went on, "I did find an S/W kit."

"Why would Mark Harrington be doing secret writing?"

"That's just it. I don't know. Maybe he was running some covert operation for the company. Or maybe he was writing letters to the other side."

Frances took a drink of water. Then she took a sip of coffee. Then she took another gulp of water. An idea had just occurred to her which made her throat dry.

"You think," she announced at last, "that the company killed him. You think it was murder."

"I didn't say that."

"You think Mother murdered him."

"I didn't . . ."

"I'm getting out of here. You take care of the check."

She got up too quickly, her leg catching the corner of the table. Glasses and coffee cups danced on the table-cloth.

Frances stumbled on the stairs, regained her balance, and kept going right past the cash register and out onto the street. She walked a block, got into her car, turned on the radio, and sat there for a moment. Then she turned on the engine and pulled away from the curb. Paul could take a taxi.

Frances did not go back to work that afternoon. She parked beside a phone booth, called her desk, and said something at lunch had made her sick. She was sorry. The duty officer said he hoped she felt better soon. Frances got back in her car and headed nowhere. Soon she found herself on the beltway driving in a circle around Washington. She was speeding.

Reaching down, she turned the radio up louder. It was blaring. The noise was meant to jam the workings of her brain the way the Russians used to jam Radio Free Europe. It didn't work. The noise just made her more nervous. She reached down and snapped the radio off.

She could not get her own father's suicide out of her mind. She had had her suspicions over the years, but she had always suppressed them. And now Paul had revived the mistrust all over again. Not only had he reopened the case, he had done so with new evidence. Now suspicions were screaming in her head louder than any radio and there was no way to turn them down.

Frances was furious, sick, and relieved—all at the same time. She had always felt guilty for contributing to her father's misery. Nor did it help to tell herself she was being irrational. She could not help feeling that if she had been a better daughter her dad would still be alive. Simultaneously, she could not help blaming her father. If he had been a better parent, he would not have put his child through such an ordeal.

Nor could Frances help fearing for herself. She kept wondering if a tendency toward suicide was inherited. Would she be subject to the same depressions which had destroyed her father?

Suicide meant guilt, blame, and fear. In a sense, murder would be much easier to accept. The guilt and the blame could all be shifted to someone else. And you were not nearly so helpless. There was something you could do: seek revenge.

Frances had joined the Central Intelligence Agency to emulate her father. Perhaps she even felt she wanted to finish the job he had left undone. Perhaps she wanted to rehabilitate his memory.

Now all that would change. If she had joined the company to atone for her father's suicide, she would remain in the company to avenge his death. In her mind, she had already tried and convicted the murderer.

Mother.

25

Revenge

WASHINGTON RESTAURANTS are the greenhouses of scandal.

Mother had invited a reporter named Dick Gross to have lunch with him at La Niçoise. The table was topped with a bouquet of daisies. It was spring and the town was in bloom.

The lunch seemed longer than it was. Time does not fly when people aren't talking. And for great stretches neither Mother nor his guest said anything. All the questions the reporter asked disappeared into the quicksand of Mother's reticence. Eventually he stopped trying. Mother was relieved. He was unfamiliar with reporters and therefore defensive.

Gross found himself wondering why the old spook had asked him to lunch if he wasn't going to say anything. He even got a little angry but tried not to show it. In journalism, as in intelligence, the ability to obscure emotion is a virtue.

After coffee, Mother paid the bill with a personal check over Gross's weak protest. Then the KUDESK chief folded his napkin like a flag and got up from the table. The beaten reporter followed him out of the restaurant.

On the sidewalk Mother asked, "Could you walk me to my car?"

"Certainly."

As they strolled along, Mother withdrew a folded sheet of paper from his pocket.

"You asked earlier about agency wiretaps. I don't have anything on that."

"I see," Gross said, his spirits drooping.

"But I believe that the American people should be aware of certain illegal wiretaps ordered by their secretary of state. Would you agree?"

"Wholeheartedly."

"Then perhaps you'd be interested in this list."

Mother saw no reason to inform the reporter that he had recently reviewed transcripts of a Mossad wiretapping operation carried out in Czechoslovakia. Its target: one of the secretary of state's closest aides. Its message: the secretary had ordered the Director of Central Intelligence to remove Mother from the Israeli desk by whatever means necessary.

Two weeks later, on June 11, 1974, another tense luncheon took place thousands of miles away. The President of the United States and his secretary of state sat glumly across from one another at an ornate table in Salzburg, Austria. They had come to Austria to rest before proceeding to Egypt to meet with President Anwar Sadat, but neither man appeared to be very relaxed. They were both upset about something, although not about the same thing. Out of respect for rank, the secretary of state waited for the President to be the first to unburden himself.

"I'm sorry," the President said. "I'm afraid I'm brooding again. I let my temper go this morning. I know I shouldn't. I should be cool. If I'm cool now, I'll be cool in Cairo. But I really got hot this morning."

The President then went on to describe the incident that had so upset him. That morning he had walked into his wife's bedroom—they never slept together because he was too restless—and received a severe shock. The First Lady was lying in bed reading a biography of Rose Kennedy.

The President had yelled, "What're you doing!"

Then he had gotten so flustered he had turned around and marched out of the room. He had been brooding ever since.

"It's not a very good book," the secretary of state said by way of consolation. He noticed the President's upper lip was wet with perspiration.

"I don't care. She shouldn't have been reading it."

"I've always thought the Kennedys were much too public with their lives. You're much more sensible."

"Nobody'll ever write a book about my mother," the President said.

"Of course not. Your family is much more private."

"That's not what I mean," the President said. "They *should* write books about her but they won't. She was a saint, taking care of all those tubercular boys to support her own boys. And them dying. All that death. But nobody wants a book about a saint. Saints don't interest them. The Kennedys interest them. No, nobody'll ever write a book about my mom, goddamn their souls."

The President attempted to pull himself together as he turned the conversation to foreign relations. What would he say to Sadat? What would Sadat say to him? How should he *act?* How could he prove how tough he was?

"I may not be answering these questions for you much longer, Mr. President," the secretary of state said. He almost never addressed his boss as "Mr. President," but this time he made an exception, feeling the use of the title lent drama and gravity to his announcement.

"What do you mean?"

"I mean that I intend to hold a press conference this afternoon in which I will announce my plans to resign unless my good name is restored."

"Are you talking about the stories about the wire-taps? Is that what's upsetting you?"

"I'm afraid so, Mr. President."

"Come now, Mr. Secretary, don't let what the press says bother you. That's juvenile."

Frances picked the restaurant: the Astor. She liked the food, she liked the price, and she liked the irony. Her betrayal would begin where her suspicions had begun.

Across from her sat Andrew Wilson, one of the director's senior aides. He had been happy to accept Frances's invitation. He would probably have accepted an invitation from any junior intelligence officer out of a sense of duty. But Frances was not any young officer. She was the shadow of a myth. He felt honored.

The Astor did not have spinach pie that day. Frances ordered stuffed grape leaves. Wilson ordered the only dish on the menu with which he was familiar: moussaka.

The two KUBARK officers talked about what everyone else in the restaurant was talking about: the White House scandals.

"After the President's reception in Alexandria," Frances said, "do you think he'll ever come home again? He may defect."

"Then he could read *Al Ahram* in the morning instead of the *Post*. I don't think he'd mind trading."

"He might like to make another trade, too. Like the Egyptian General Intelligence Agency for the CIA."

"We do seem to rank with the press at the White House these days, don't we?" Wilson said.

Frances kept looking over his shoulder. Wilson felt somewhat slighted, but she was simply watching for Paul. She told herself that even if he did walk in he would not suspect. But she was not convinced because she was not sure how good an actress she was. She was afraid she might look guilty and then he might begin deducing. He might think back to all those questions she had suddenly started asking about Mother. She had known how to debrief Paul. She had appealed to his vanity. He was so proud of how much he had learned about Mother that it was easy to persuade him to show off what he had found out. He had even shared certain papers with her.

"Why do you suppose we're so unpopular on Pennsylvania Avenue?" Wilson asked.

"Because the President thinks we're out to get him. In fact, that's why I wanted to have lunch with you. I believe CI's been suppressing a document that might interest you."

Before the two parted, she passed the director's assistant a manila envelope.

The director got into the limousine in front of his home at 5 A.M. The long black car drove him to a small church in Bethesda named Little Flower, where he attended an early mass. Then he drove on out to Andrews Air Force Base. The limousine parked in front of the Base Ops Building. This was the air terminal from which the President and the secretary of state always departed on their travels. It was also the terminal where most foreign heads of state were welcomed when they visited America. And yet it looked like a Greyhound Bus Station in Sioux City.

The director boarded a chartered Air America plane. The agency owned the airline. On board, he sat down next to Andy Wilson. They were on their way to Israel for a routine morale-building tour. The director tried to visit as many of his foreign stations as he could to meet the officers, to listen to their concerns, and to deliver pep talks. He felt that his Jerusalem station had a special need for encouragement in that it had taken so much heat for KUBARK's failure to predict the October War.

"Did you get a chance to read that . . ."

Andy Wilson did not get a chance to finish his question.

"A word of caution," the director interjected. "We do lots of political charters in even-numbered years."

Wilson understood the director's message: If this plane had been chartered by candidates, listening devices might well have been installed to monitor the campaigns. The head of the CIA did not want to be bugged by the CIA.

It was a quiet flight, both in terms of turbulence and talk. The director spent much of his flying time catching up on his reading. He scanned several recent reports from the Jerusalem station and then turned to a folder which Wilson had given him several days earlier. It contained a synopsis of Wilson's lunch with Frances Fisher. Attached were eight Xeroxed pages—the contents of the manila envelope Frances had given Wilson.

These pages turned out to be a transcript of a conversation between Charles Colson, a former White House adviser, and Richard Bast, a veteran Washington private detective. Colson had gone to Bast to ask him to investigate the Central Intelligence Agency. Bast had surreptitiously recorded the meeting. Mother had acquired a copy of the tape, transcribed it and shown it to Paul, who in turn had shown it to Frances.

The director pushed his pink-rimmed glasses—they were the color of some baby pacifiers—higher on his nose and read.

> COLSON: I think Watergate was a setup. In nineteen seventy-one, Hunt left the CIA and went to the Mullen Company. Hunt didn't go to work for the Mullen Company because he happened to find a good job there. He was posted there by Dick Helms. There is a letter in the CIA files written to Mullen asking him to take him on. His salary was calculated on the basis of what his salary had been at CIA. They put him on as a free-lance writer to run the entire operation . . .

The director paused to yawn. He always yawned when he read just as he always ate popcorn when he went to the movies. It had become a reflex.

> . . . Once Hunt came into the White House, he started dealing with the CIA, with Kimball, the director of counterintelligence, with Howard Osborn, the director of security, and with Cushman . . .

The director paused again, but this time it was not to yawn, it was to underline the passage. Colson's lecture continued:

> . . . The President was systematically excluding the CIA and the joint chiefs from a lot of his foreign policy deliberations so they would have two choices: to infiltrate and spy on him, which they did, or they

could see themselves losing their team. You know,
they were in Johnson's knickers six ways to Sunday.
They were in Kennedy's. I imagine they were in Eisenhower's. Along comes Nixon. He's the first guy who
is really independent of the establishment. He says to
the State Department bureaucracy, "You guys handle
the ceremonies and let me do the heavy foreign policy
planning." And he doesn't even invite the CIA to any
of the normal briefings. The question is how they got
back in. I'm convinced that Hunt was the CIA vehicle.
There's got to be a way to crack that—that's the reason I'm talking to you. Obviously if my suspicions are
true, that throws the whole Watergate case into a
cocked hat . . .

The director, who did not smoke, put a pencil in his
mouth, as he often did when he was nervous.

. . . The President is scared as hell, especially when
he's weak and under attack, to alienate the military
and the foreign policy establishment.
   BAST: This is because of a coup?
   COLSON: Yes.
   BAST: This is something I had always suspected.
   COLSON: I also think the secretary of state is in this
up to his eyeballs.
   BAST: With the CIA.
   COLSON: Yes. I'll tell you the thing that scares me
the most. They're all over the place. Almost everywhere you turn, they've got their tentacles. Nixon was
going to remove the head of the CIA, bring his own
people in, investigate internally, and announce everything he had discovered to the American people. General Hess talked him out of it . . .

The director yawned and the pencil fell out of his
mouth. He reached for the recline lever. He leaned
back and closed blue, white, and red bureaucrat's eyes.
After resting for five minutes, he sat up and reread the
part about Mother.

Mother did not hear about the trouble from anyone
in KUBARK. He heard of it from Menachem Ginzburg, who asked for a meeting. Mother rode over to the
R Street embassy.

"I don't want to make too much of this," Mother's old friend said, "but I thought you should know. Those discussions you were kind enough to set up between O'Hara and our people in Jerusalem—they've been canceled."

"Why?"

"I'm told your secretary of state ordered the meetings called off."

"Sounds like him," Mother said. "He doesn't want anybody to have any contact with your government but him. It's the ultimate arrogance. He believes he's the only one who understands foreign policy."

"We realize the meetings would've just been courtesy calls. But canceling them looks like discourtesy."

"I'll see what I can do," Mother said. "Sorry this happened."

Mother was smoking more furiously than usual as he rode back across the river to the agency. He hated the secretary of state for issuing such an order and he hated the director for taking it. He told himself they were both rude men. He told himself they had insulted a valued ally. He told himself they were out to embarrass the Israeli desk. Mother was convinced the secretary and the director were consciously attempting to undermine him.

When Mother reached his office, he immediately dispatched an urgent cable to the director in Jerusalem: IMPERATIVE YOU MEET MOSSAD AS PLANNED. THEY INTERPRET CANCELLATION AS SNUB. MUST REPAIR DAMAGE.

Hours passed before Mother realized that the director not only had no intention of meeting with the Israeli service, he also had no intention of answering the cable. And even when he realized it, he still waited, working up his anger and his nerve before making the call. Transatlantic telephone conversations always represented a security risk, but Mother felt he had no other choice.

Mother put through the call himself. His heart was pounding harder than an old man's heart should pound when the director came on the line.

"I'm calling," Mother said, "about the meetings with the Mossad. I understand you've canceled them."

"You understand correctly. There's been a scheduling conflict."

Mother decided against calling the director a liar over a translatlantic cable.

"If there has been a conflict, then I implore you to resolve it in the Israeli service's favor."

"I'm afraid it's too late to alter my schedule."

"I understand the secretary of state's responsible for the cancellation."

"I don't know where you've been getting your information," the director said, "but I hope most of your sources're not as unreliable as this one."

"I'm disappointed in you. Whatever differences we may've had, I never thought you were weak, never thought you'd kowtow to the secretary like that."

"Be careful."

"Once the agency lets the State Department dictate to it," Mother said, "it's finished. Pretty soon we'll be telling State only what it wants to hear and we'll be no good to anyone."

"This conversation's over."

"I always thought you had the balls to stand up to the secretary."

"Good-bye."

"This used to be a family quarrel, but now you've gone outside the family. You've allied yourself with an outsider. It's unbecoming."

"I said *good-bye*."

26

Breaking Up

SOUNDLESS WHEELS were turning, rolling this way, rolling that way, rolling forward, rolling backward, crossing and recrossing the same ground. The waiters glided, graceful as figure skaters, from kitchen to table, while Frances's thoughts rolled back and forth between her damaged love for Paul and her hatred for Mother. For several days, ever since she decided Mother had killed her father, she had been turning away from Paul, Mother's boy, and then turning back to him.

When Paul had asked her to have dinner with Mother, she had at first said no. But he had worked patiently at turning her around. And she began to tell herself that perhaps she *should* dine with Mother in order to find out more about him. For lately Frances had come to share Paul's curiosity about Mother and his past. Their obsession was the same, but with opposite motives.

Still, Frances had had a hard time making up her mind. She said yes; then she had second thoughts, then second thoughts squared, then second thoughts to the third power. Now that she was actually there at the table, she wished she were anywhere else. The whole room seemed to be spinning around and around and around.

"Another Scotch on the rocks," she told the waiter who rolled up to her.

She was lost in her own whirlpool of thoughts, not paying attention to the conversation. Then suddenly a question was addressed to her directly. Since she had not been focusing, she asked to hear it again.

"When're you and Paul going to get married?" Mother repeated, making an effort to mask his worries about Frances's not being good enough for his boy.

"We're not," Frances said a little too fiercely. Deciding her answer needed softening, she added, "What I mean is we never talk about marriage. I never even think about getting married. Maybe Paul and I belong to a bachelor generation."

"Does that mean you think marriage is old-fashioned?" Mother asked, relieved that Frances had no intention of marrying Paul but disturbed by her point of view.

"Maybe a little. Of course, I may change my mind in a few years."

"You think married couples're living some quaint costume drama?" Mother asked.

"Sort of."

"So marriage is as obsolete as hooped skirts, parasols, bustles . . ."

"And Cold Warriors," she interjected. When the old man frowned, she added, "That's a joke."

"I know it's fashionable to say Cold Warriors belong on the junk heap," Mother said, "but don't believe it."

Frances tried to put out the fire that flared in her stomach by pouring alcohol on it.

"It was a joke," she repeated.

"I'm sorry," Mother said. "I'm afraid the Cold War's no laughing matter to me."

Frances could feel her temper flash, and she could also feel the alcohol. A little drunk and slightly out of control, she sensed that her rationalization for coming to dinner was dissolving. For in her condition she had neither the technique nor the temperament for discovering Mother's secrets.

"That's exactly what the Cold War is and always has been," she said. "A joke. A joke on all of us. Kennedy's threatening to bomb Moscow if the Russians didn't let our trucks past Checkpoint Charlie was one of the funniest jokes I ever heard."

Mother was not laughing.

A waiter rolled up to the table to take their orders. Frances, who was feeling destructive, indulged herself with a fantasy. She imagined a roller derby where all the players carried trays loaded with food. She had a vision of body checks with trays flying, glass breaking, hot coffee spilling. All that pain and chaos.

Mother ordered scampi as usual. Paul and Frances ordered veal.

"You may believe the Cold War's dead as Joe Stalin," Mother said, "but actually, Brezhnev's as dedicated to our destruction as old Joe ever was. Defeating America is still Russia's number one priority."

"I don't believe that," Frances said.

"Then what do you believe *is* Brezhnev's primary goal?"

"Survival. First of all, he wants personal survival as the head of state. Second, he wants the state to survive. He's not so different from our own President. They're both trying to hang on to the power they've already got."

"Paul, what do you think?" Mother asked.

Paul had been dreading getting dragged into the argument between his lover and his mentor. He decided to try to seek a middle ground which he already knew would please neither side.

"You're both right," Paul said. "You're just saying it differently. Brezhnev does want to survive. That is his number one priority. But he probably believes the best way to survive is to weaken America."

"That's no answer and you know it," Frances said. "Your boss didn't say weaken America. He said defeat America. Besides, I'm not sure Russia sees us as her worst enemy. That honor may belong to China."

Paul wondered if anyone would believe him if he said he had to go to the men's room. He decided not to strain his credibility further.

"You're too sophisticated to believe that," Mother told Frances. "Russia and China are best of friends when the blinds are drawn. They only argue in public. It's a trick. You must know that."

"I don't know that at all. They aren't that sophisticated."

"They want us to underrate them. Right up to the day they bury us."

"They donwanna bury us," Frances said, a slight slur beginning to make her words stumble into each other. "You wanna bury them 'cause you're terrified of them. You're dangerous."

"Paul, do you think I'm dangerous?"

Now Paul really did need to go to the men's room. Tightened nerves often affected him that way. He could think of no middle ground. The question called for a yes or no answer.

"No," Paul said, "I don't."

Another gulp of alcohol increased Frances's appetite for an intellectual barroom brawl.

"Sure he's dangerous," she insisted. "It's ideas like his that've gotten us in trouble from the Bay of Pigs to Vietnam. One fiasco after another. Paul, I can't believe you don't see it. Or maybe you do but're afraid to say so. Thass it, isn't it?"

"No."

"Sure it is. He's a menace 'n' you know it, doncha?"

"No," Paul said. "I'm sorry."

"The menace is the Russia-China axis," Mother said. "Their plan's to delude us and then to destroy us. And it appears they're halfway home. Because the delusion phase of their plan's already succeeded beyond their wildest dreams."

Paul had been looking forward to this dinner, but it was turning into the worst possible disaster. He felt he was in the process of losing his job *and* his woman. It was painful enough to imagine losing one or the other, but the prospect of seeing both desert him at the same time was devastating.

"Please, let's talk about something else," Paul said.

"The best way to keep ush from burying them or them from burying ush," Frances said, her slur growing worse, "is to bury the Cold War."

"I never thought I'd see the day when George Fisher's daughter would speak out in favor of accommodation with the Russians," Mother said.

"Leave my father out of it!"

"But your father was one of the greatest Cold Warriors that ever lived," Mother said.

"Goddamn it, shut up about my father! What right have you to ... to ... to ... Just shut up!"

Frances jumped up from the table and ran unsteadily toward the front door of the restaurant. Halfway to her goal she collided with a heavily loaded waiter on skates. He spun around and almost fell.

Paul thought of Scott Fitzgerald's line about a man's life falling apart around him like so many dropped trays.

Frances was just pulling away from the curb when she saw Paul in the rearview mirror. He was running. Her first impulse was to drive off and leave him. Instead, she put her foot on the brake.

Paul swung open the car door and slumped in the passenger seat. He hated sitting there. Not only was Frances mad at him, but she had retaken the wheel. He was losing control and did not know how to get it back.

"Where're we going?" Paul asked.

"For a ride," Frances said, the fresh air having sobered her slur.

The mustard Datsun turned left off Wisconsin Avenue onto P Street, crossed the P Street bridge, made another left-hand turn, and entered Rock Creek Parkway. The car picked up speed.

"You're going pretty fast."

"Don't tell me how to drive." Frances stepped down harder on the accelerator.

"You had quite a bit to drink, you know."

"Shut up."

They entered the tunnel below the National Zoo. Paul was more depressed still.

Suddenly the car swerved toward the near wall. Frances panicked. She slammed on the brakes and gave the wheel a hard turn. The Datsun screeched into a broadside skid in the middle of the tunnel. Paul instinctively reached for the wheel, but Frances knocked his hands away.

"What're you trying to do, kill us!" Paul yelled.

The car came to a stop sitting perpendicular to the center stripe.

"No, that's not my line," Frances snapped. "I think you've got me mixed up with Mother."

"What do you mean by that?"

"I mean Mother's a killer."

A car coming from the other direction slammed on its brakes to avoid a collision.

"Who's he killed?"

"My father."

"Jesus."

Cars were lining up in both directions in the tunnel. Frances backed up, turning the wheel to the left, then pulled forward, turning the wheel to the right. She repeated this maneuver several times until she straightened out the car and cured the tunnel's constipation. Traffic started rolling again.

"Do you really believe that?" Paul asked.

"Sure," said Frances, speeding up. "And so do you."

Paul did not say anything. He just fumbled about for the seat belt.

"Don't you?" Frances asked.

"No. I mean I don't know. But I don't believe it."

"That's right," Frances said, pressing to go faster still, "take his side."

"Be careful."

"I knew you'd defend him."

"I'm not defending him. It's just that . . . watch it!"

"It's just you don't want to believe it," Frances said, pulling hard to make a turn. "You'd rather believe my father committed suicide."

"No," said Paul, distracted by fear. "I know how hard it's been for you to live with your father's suicide, but that's no reason to blame Mother."

"Shut up! Just shut up! You think you understand me but you don't. Just leave me alone. Please!"

"But I do understand . . ."

"I don't want your understanding. I don't want anything from you. Ever."

"Let's stop. We can't talk racing along like this."

The Datsun sped through a deep forest which made it hard to believe they were in a big city. This wedge of tall trees followed Rock Creek to the heart of the metropolis, acting as a wall between poor black Washington and well-to-do white Washington.

"Okay," Frances said, slowing the car.

They parked beside the road on a small hill where the trees shaded out even the light of the moon. Above and below them, other cars were parked. Paul and Frances had driven out to a popular lovers' lane to have their fight.

"Reminds me of the Farm," said Paul, looking through the passenger window.

"We've come a long way since the Farm. We're not the same people we were then."

"What do you mean?"

"I mean we've changed. I've changed, but most of all you've changed."

"How?"

"Mostly for the better. I used to think you were bound to be a failure. Now I think you'll probably be a big success."

"Thanks."

"Only I think I loved you for your failures."

"And now?"

"And now you're different. You used to be my baby. Now you're Mother's boy."

"And you couldn't love Mother's boy?"

"Maybe not. For lots of reasons."

"Because you hate Mother?" Paul asked, looking out the window so he would not have to look at Frances.

"Yes, but that's not all of it. He's changed you." She

laughed and added, "I'll bet you couldn't get lost in the woods again if you tried."

When they reached the big Ivory soap house over an hour later, Frances started packing. She had told Paul in the lovers' lane that she wanted to move out. Soon her huge green suitcase was overfull. She tried to wrestle it shut.

Whenever the two of them had taken trips together in the past, Paul had always helped her force her bag into submission. And so he felt a reflex urge to help her now. But at the same time he felt a stronger compulsion to throw open the bag and scatter its contents around the bedroom.

"Don't help," Frances said, meaning just the opposite.

"Okay, I won't."

He walked over and sat down on the bed where he surveyed Frances's continuing struggles. A pair of panties with tigers on them peeked out of the suitcase at him, making him sad.

"Please wait 'til morning," Paul said.

Frances did not answer, but she began removing clothing from her suitcase. Paul allowed himself a moment's optimism. He soon realized, however, that she was only unpacking in order to repack more compactly.

Wanting desperately to get away from his own unhappiness, Paul searched for some escape. The only place he could think of to hide was in his work. Lifting his briefcase, which huddled beside the bed, he opened it and dived inside. He tried to focus his entire consciousness on reading a report the way people dying in hospitals often focus on the television.

Noticing Mother's boy go to work, Frances's anger flared automatically, but only briefly. She had been jealous of his work for weeks, but now only a memory of that jealousy remained. If she had still loved him as she had once loved him, she would have started a quarrel. But she did not love him enough to fight with him anymore.

Paul was too sad to be able to concentrate on the report. He closed it and put it down on the bed. Frances felt a twinge of fondness, but she went on reorganizing her suitcase.

"Please stay the night."

Frances's only response was to sit on top of her bag and crush it shut. Locking the clasps at last, she sighed.

Paul stretched out on the bed. Now that Frances was not busy any more, she was more vulnerable to a confusion of emotions. She wanted to leave Paul, but she did not want to hurt him. She did not love him enough to hate him enough to want to be cruel. She was simply deeply fond of him and it hurt her to see him look so hurt. Frances went over and lay down on the bed beside Paul.

"Please stay over," Paul said. "You can leave tomorrow."

They rolled together on the bed and hugged tightly. Beneath them the report crackled and ripped.

"Okay," Frances said out of a sense of justice. For her emotions reasoned: she was hurting him, therefore she owed him something, therefore she would grant his request.

They kissed and clutched—and crumpled and tore the report even worse. Paul was sad because Frances was leaving him, happy because she was caressing him, and worried because he had no idea how he would explain the condition of the top-secret report to security.

"Let's go to bed," Frances said.

"Okay."

Frances got up, opened her suitcase, and took out her toothbrush.

While Frances was scrubbing her teeth, Paul entered the large master bathroom wearing a red robe. Slipping it off, he stepped into the shower. Frances caught only a glimpse of his nude body in the mirror before shifting her glance. Now that she was leaving him, she did not think she should look at him, which in turn made her want to look at him. Frances endowed Paul with the magnetism of the forbidden.

In the shower, Paul was trying to wash away a mood. He lathered himself all over and only felt worse.

He was soaping his face with his eyes shut tight when a third hand started soaping his penis.

In chain reaction, Paul shivered, felt the onrush of an erection, reached out for Frances's breasts, opened his eyes, and started crying. Blaming the tears on the soap—which *was* partly responsible—he removed a hand from a nipple to wipe his eyes.

"I'm sorry, baby," Frances said, Paul's tears evoking memories of that old love she had felt in the beginning when he had seemed so fragile.

"I know," Paul said in a thick voice.

Then suddenly they were both crying and hugging in a great rainstorm of tears and shower spray. They felt wet on the outside and wet on the inside. Frances lay her head on Paul's chest and allowed her hair to be soaked. While they clung together, each holding the other up, the salt water from their eyes and the fresh water from the shower flowed together in an inescapable wash of sorrow.

When the sobbing subsided, they lathered each other gently, dried each other, and went to bed red-eyed.

"I don't want to make love," Frances whispered.

"All right."

They lay arm in arm, trying to fall asleep together for the last time, but they couldn't. Paul grew restless as his thoughts returned again and again to the shower. His blind hand explored in the darkness beneath the covers.

"Don't wiggle," Frances said.

The next morning she went home to the house where her mother lived and her father had died.

27

Frances's Report

THE DAY AFTER the thirty-seventh President of the
United States announced his resignation, Frances sat
at her desk, bored. Overnight everything had changed.
The President is dead! Long live the President! But
her job had not changed. The same drab numbers still
marched in military formation across her pages.

Then her telephone rang. It was the director's secretary. Was Frances free that afternoon? She was. Did
she have her car with her? She did. Would it be in-
convenient for her to drive the director somewhere at
2 P.M.? It would not. Very good. Frances bolted from
her office. She wanted to clean the McDonald's bags
and Coke cups out of her car. Since she had broken
up with Paul, she no longer went to many restaurants.
Her Datsun had become her dining room.

Later, as Frances and the director walked through
the parking lot, she launched into an apology for her
car. It was too small, needed a tune-up, could use a
wash, had a broken air conditioner. She did not apolo-
gize to many people, but she had grown up in a home
where the title "director" was spoken with more

reverence than the title "God." She felt shamelessly deferential.

"If I'd wanted a limousine," the director said, "I could've arranged for one. The problem is long black cars tend to come with chauffeurs. Even the cars have ears."

Frances and the director got into her small, mustard-yellow Datsun 240Z. The director wanted her to drive him out to the headquarters of the National Security Agency at Fort Meade in Maryland, where the country's leading code makers and code breakers worked.

"How do you like the West German desk?" the director asked.

"I do. I like it."

"Are you getting good assignments?"

Frances had been disappointed in her assignments, but she could not imagine how the director knew.

"Well, frankly, I haven't gotten anything very exciting yet," Frances said, "but I'm the new kid on the desk."

"How long've you been there?"

"About six months."

"What have they had you doing?"

"Oh, mostly rewriting reports."

"I hear you're very good at it."

"I hope they're pleased," Frances said, warmed by the praise but a little chilled by the inquiries the director had obviously been making about her.

They drove in silence for a while. The director was not a man who worked hard at conversation. And it wasn't even a ploy. When Mother was quiet, it was because he was waiting for an answer. When the director was quiet, it was generally because he did not have anything to say.

Frances pulled onto the beltway and headed north. It was a hot July day, and she had been right about the air conditioner. The ride was not much fun. From time to time the cooler would revive, as would the conversation, but in general neither one worked very well.

"How's Paul Fitzsimmons?" the director asked at last, rather indiscreetly but for a reason.

"I don't know. I haven't seen him in some time."

"Oh, that's too bad."

"Not really."

The director had a job he planned to offer Frances, but he didn't want to if she was still going with Paul. He relapsed into silence.

The car turned off the beltway and plunged through the Maryland woods. The director was as quiet as the trees.

When they arrived at the NSA headquarters, the Datsun stopped in front of a double barbed-wire fence ten feet high. Machine-gun-armed guards in four gatehouses stared down at them. The director presented his credentials and the car was passed through.

Frances was not sure whether she was supposed to follow the director into the building or wait in the car. Her boss gave her no clue. When he opened his door, she opened hers, watching for any signal of disapproval. Since there was none, she followed the director toward a huge, U-shaped, three-story concrete building. The guard at the desk recognized the Director of Central Intelligence and passed them inside.

Frances and the director entered the longest hall in the world. It stretched before them for 960 feet. They passed more guards carrying machine guns.

"I had no idea the place was this big," Frances said.

"It's smaller than the Pentagon, but bigger than Langley. This building has more electronic wiring in it than any other building in the world."

Frances noticed how easily the role of the pedagogue came to the director. She wondered if it came from all those years of leading boy scouts.

They boarded an elevator and rode up to the top floor, where they made their way to the executive suite.

"Would you mind waiting for me?" O'Hara said. "I've got to meet with the deputy director."

NSA, which is actually a part of the Pentagon, is run by the Defense Department's deputy director of defense research and engineering.

"Fine," Frances said.

She took a seat in an outer office while the DCI disappeared into the inner office. While she leafed through a copy of *U.S. News & World Report,* he discussed eavesdropping with the NSA chief. Piggy-back eavesdropping. The Russians were bugging American calls and NSA was monitoring the Russian bugs. So, in a secondhand fashion, NSA was bugging American phones. The question was: was it legal?

After half an hour, the Director of Central Intelligence emerged. Frances and the director walked back down the longest corridor in the world. They were at the heart of the U.S. agency whose business it is to listen in on the whole world, but all they heard was the clatter of their own steps.

They got back in the Datsun and passed out of the double ring of barbed wire. Soon the trees closed in behind them. Out of the corner of her eye Frances noticed a patch of blackberries. They had left behind the world of steel barbs and reentered the world of God's own thorns.

The director took a deep breath. He was slightly nervous, too. The assignment he was about to offer Frances was one which he could not have offered the day before, when the President was still fighting to hold on to the Oval Office. Yesterday the administration could not tolerate any more scandals or any more instability. But the new President began fresh. He could tolerate upheaval.

"I've got a job for you," the director said. "Interested?"

"Yes," said Frances. She almost said "of course" but thought she might sound overeager.

"I'd like you to rewrite a report for me. I'm afraid the assignment would take you away from the German desk for a while. I could arrange a leave if you've no objection."

Frances wanted to look at the director, but she was afraid she would hit a tree. To say she would not object to a leave from her desk was an understatement, but she did not want to be too obvious about her dislike of her present job. She was a little afraid she was being tested.

"Could you tell me more about the report I'd be working on?" Frances asked.

"Not 'til you accept the assignment."

"Then I accept."

"It's on agency wrongdoing."

The report, code-named FAMILY JEWELS, had originally been ordered by William Schieffer when he was the director. When he was brought in to replace Helms in February 1973, he had followed a bureaucratic precedent of long standing: "Cover your ass." Since he was a newcomer at KUBARK, he knew he could not possibly be implicated in the company's past misdeeds, but he could be criticized if those misdeeds continued. Therefore, he ordered an investigation of any and all CIA wrongdoing. He wanted to make sure he did not get hanged for someone else's operations.

When O'Hara took over the agency in May 1973, he inherited Schieffer's report, like it or not. Unlike Schieffer, O'Hara had worked his way up in KUBARK, and so he had more of a vested interest in covering up KUBARK's past mistakes. However, since he had spent most of his career out of the country, he saw to it that the report focused on domestic transgressions. Still, the new director had tended to regard the report with the affection he usually reserved for a head cold. Until now. Now he thought he saw a way to make the FAMILY JEWELS his lever.

"The report needs rewriting for several reasons," the director said. "It's poorly organized, the style's atrocious . . ."

"I'm not the world's greatest stylist."

"You're modest. I've seen your reports and they're quite good. I compliment you."

"Thank you."

"There's another reason I want the report redone," the director said. "I've uncovered some new evidence that suggests Kimball was behind much of the wrongdoing. I realize it's hard to assign blame to one of our own. But in today's political climate I don't think we can afford to jeopardize the agency to protect one man."

Frances and the director rode in silence for a while. She gripped the wheel so tightly her fingers became numb.

"You've agreed to take the assignment," the director broke the silence, "but before I agree to give it to you, I'd like to ask you one question."

"All right."

"Do you agree that the agency can't afford to risk its reputation to save one man's?"

"Yes, I agree."

Frances and the director both realized they were speaking in a kind of code. In their understated way, they were making a pact to get Mother.

The next morning the Director of Central Intelligence stood behind a one-way mirror, feeling like a peeping Tom. He had monitored many other lie detector tests, but this was the first time he had ever watched a woman tested. When the interrogator wrapped the two belts around her chest, one above and one below the breasts, the director felt an unexpected twinge.

On the other side of the mirror, Frances took several deep breaths and felt her chest strain against its bonds. She had been informed that before she could see the report she was supposed to rewrite, she would have to be refluttered. She had not exactly been looking forward to the test, but neither did she dread it as much as she had the first time. She felt she knew what to expect. But she was not entirely correct.

"Your arm's too small for the cuff," Ian Orr, the flutterer, said. "I'll have to put it on your leg."

Frances was on the verge of telling him that her arm had been big enough the first time she was fluttered, but then she decided it would be best not to antagonize the man who would not only ask the questions, but interpret the results. So instead of complaining, she just got silently angry over the agency's refusal to hire a female flutterer.

The interrogator knelt beside her.

"Pull your skirt up a bit," Orr said. "I'll wrap it around your thigh."

As Frances inched up her skirt, the Director of Central Intelligence felt more like a peeping Tom than ever. When the interrogator touched Frances's thigh, the director felt another, deeper twinge.

Since her last flutter, Frances had learned a few

things about these tests. She now knew that the company often recorded these sessions. They did not tell you you were being bugged, but if you asked they would not lie to you.

"Is this test being taped?" she asked.

"Yes," the flutter man replied.

Frances and the interrogator had already gone over the test together, adjusting all the questions so they could be answered with a simple yes or no. Some of the questions were duplicates of the ones she had been asked during her original polygraph. Had she ever had any lesbian contact? Yes. When she was an adolescent? Yes. With more than one person? Yes. With more than two? No. With two people? Yes. With twins? Yes. Were their names Janet and Mary Tyler? Yes. Had she ever had any postadolescent lesbian contact? No. None whatsoever? No.

Other questions were new. Had she, to her knowledge, had any contact with a foreign service since she joined the agency? No. Had she ever lived with a man? Yes. Was she living with a man now? No. Had she ever dated Paul Fitzsimmons? Yes. Was she still dating him? No. Was she loyal to the Director of Central Intelligence? Yes. Excluding immediate family, did she owe anyone else a higher loyalty? No. Did she owe any loyalty to anyone in the Counterintelligence Department? No. Did she owe any loyalty whatsoever to Francis Kimball? No.

"That's it," Orr said at the end of an hour.

"How'd I do?"

"You know I can't say one way or the other."

He reached for Frances's thigh.

"I'll do it," Frances said.

The Director of Central Intelligence noticed a flash of underwear as George Fisher's daughter took off her polygraph garter.

Frances was assigned a small office with an unnumbered door on the seventh floor of the Toy Factory. She was shown the wrongdoing report as well as certain material detrimental to Mother. The simplest way to revise the FAMILY JEWELS would have been to Xerox it, cut up the copy, and do a scissors-and-paste job. Then the report could have been rearranged and reconstructed without every word having to be retyped. But for security reasons the FAMILY JEWELS was not allowed anywhere near a Xerox machine.

Frances worked late in her broom closet of an office night after night. She did not have a secretary and she herself was not a good typist. It was a long, lonely assignment.

Paul was lonely, too. Now he frequented Osvald's pickup saloon without Osvald. He sat at the bar sipping Scotch and soda and not talking to the women he had come to meet. From time to time he would try to console himself by telling himself he had not fallen in love with Frances herself but with her background. It didn't help.

Once Paul did get into a conversation with a woman at the bar, but he ended up quoting W. B. Yeats's "The Folly of Being Comforted," about the poet's inability to ease the pain he felt over the loss of the actress-revolutionary Maud Gonne. That sort of poetry does not abet a pickup. The woman wandered off in search of a married man who hated his wife.

One night, after his seventh Scotch, Paul stumbled to the pay telephone on the wall. He was going to call Frances. He knew her mother's phone number was unlisted, but he thought he had it written on a scrap of paper in his wallet. Paul opened his billfold and went all through it. Then he went through it again. And again. But he could not find the number. Paul staggered away from the telephone, leaving several scraps of paper and two twenties lying where they had fallen on the floor.

After two weeks, the director decided he should have another talk with Frances. O'Hara wanted to be sure the report would be ready for submission to the House and Senate oversight committees by the end of September. Once the committee chairmen read it, they would do their duty and demand retribution from Mother. The director hoped the KUDESK chief would realize that it would be futile to put up a fight and would go gracefully, without holding any tape concerts.

The director's secretary called Frances, but she was not in her office. She took few breaks, but this time she had not been able to resist. She had descended to one of the scientific shops, where a computer had been programmed to replay and analyze the latest Washington Redskins game. Frances was the only woman who regularly attended these sessions, but then, as she always explained, she was "a Princeton man." Almost all of the men at Langley were fanatical Skins' fans, perhaps in part because of their jobs: the spying business was supposed to be a very active, virile profession and yet they were deskbound warriors, so they compensated by playing computer football and spiking their jargon with masculine metaphors like "penetration." The agency had better estimates of Billy Kilmer's potential strike force than it did of the Russians'.

As Frances returned to her office she heard her telephone ringing. She rushed down the hall, through the door, and grabbed it. It was the director's secretary. She said she had been trying for an hour. Frances was sorry. Could Frances come to the director's suite? She could. Right away? Right away. Frances removed a thin folder from her safe and hurried out of her office.

"Well, how's the report coming?" asked the director, seated behind his desk.

"It's coming along. I hope to finish a draft by the end of the week."

"What'll it say about the head of our Counterintelligence Department?"

Frances gave her boss a verbal review of what would be in the draft report: that Mother had conducted extensive domestic operations against the antiwar movement; that Mother had ordered illegal break-ins, wiretappings, and mail covers; that Mother had taken a particular interest in spying on Jane Fonda and Bella Abzug; that Mother had run a mail-intercept program; and that Mother's department had intelligence files on ten thousand Americans.

"Probably more," the director said, "but let's leave it at ten thousand."

"I've also come up with something else," Frances said, a hint of nerves entering her voice. "I'm not sure it belongs in the report at all. I'd like your advice. Could I show you some draft pages?"

"Of course."

Frances handed over the folder she had been clutching all through the interview. The director laid it on the desk in front of him and started reading. He yawned as he always did when he read, but it was not because he wasn't interested. The first paragraph said that Mother had a long record of spying on the White House.

"What's your source on this?"

"Paul told me." Frances saw the director give her a look which seemed to say: I thought you weren't seeing him anymore? "He told me weeks ago," she added.

"And how did he know?"

"Kimball told him."

The director's eyes left Frances's face and returned to her pages. The second paragraph said that Mother had evidently started his White House spying during the Kennedy administration. He had had two operations, one overt and one covert.

The third paragraph concerned the overt side of the venture. It described Mother's special relationship with Bobby Kennedy. It told how they had often worked together debriefing defectors and how Mother would take advantage of these meetings to debrief the President's brother.

The fourth paragraph was about the covert side of the Kennedy operation. It said that one of Mother's agents had been an intelligence officer's wife who also happened to have been the mistress of President John F. Kennedy. She and the Commander in Chief used to smoke marijuana in Lincoln's bedroom. When Kennedy was stoned, he got talkative.

"Christ," the director said, not looking up, "she was murdered, wasn't she?"

"Beside the canal in Georgetown."

"Did Mother kill her?"

"I don't know."

The director read on. The fifth paragraph said Mother had evidently not penetrated the Johnson White House, but had recouped when the next President moved in. It said Mother had two agents in the Nixon White House: Allen Butterworth and General Albert Hess.

The sixth paragraph said they had both been recruited years ago when they were young military officers. Then the company helped them get ahead in their armed services careers. They had worked together in the general counsel's office at the Pentagon. One of their first assignments was to assist in the return of the Bay of Pigs prisoners.

"I wonder if Nixon was ever suspicious," the director said.

"Maybe that's why we were so unpopular with him."

"Actually, I suppose I should've been suspicious myself. After all, Kimball always said, 'Penetration begins at home.' I just didn't take him seriously."

"I wonder what his motive was."

"Fear. After all, it's your own government that can really hurt you. Cut your budget. Even fire you. The KGB can't do that. So I suppose it wasn't any accident Kimball concentrated on Kennedy and Nixon."

"Why's that?"

"Well, after the Bay of Pigs, Kennedy thought the agency had let him down," the director said. "So he ordered a purge. He just flat out and fired a lot of people. When Johnson came along, he was all right. But then Nixon took up where Kennedy had left off. He started firing people again. Axed about a thousand. That's more than the KGB ever got."

"When was that?"

"Under my predecessor. He had put on extra bodyguards."

Getting up from his desk, the DCI collected the draft pages and headed for a corner of his big office. Frances followed after him.

"You asked my advice," the director said.

"Yes."

"I don't think this belongs in a report to Congress," he said, holding up the pages. "Still, it's good to know. You've done a good job."

The director did not tell Frances that it was always a good idea to have a few secrets with which to blackmail a blackmailer. He flipped a switch and then fed her work into a shredder, which turned it into confetti as if for an approaching celebration.

On her way back to her own office, Frances had time to wonder: if some people in the company wanted to get O'Hara's predecessor, wanted to so badly that he had to add bodyguards, then how much more had they wanted to get Nixon. If some faction within the agency thought the President was a threat, not only to the country but to the company, would they have been capable of contemplating the company's first domestic coup? And she asked herself what there might be in a name: was KUDESK the coupdesk? She doubted it.

28

The Purge

THE ALARM AWAKENED THE DIRECTOR in the middle of a dream about his daughter. He was always dreaming she was alive and waking up to find she wasn't. The dreams scratched at the scar tissue.

While he was still upset, he remembered what he had to do that morning. It did not make him feel any better. He shaved more slowly than usual, combed his hair more precisely than usual, tied his shoes more carefully than usual. He realized, of course, that he was procrastinating, that he had been doing so, one way or another, for days, maybe even weeks. As he was slipping on his tie, his dead child caught his eye. She stared at him from her photograph on top of the bureau. His fingers became not only slow, but clumsy. He had to redo the knot several times.

Then he went down to a lonely kitchen. His wife and children were away at her parents' home in Cleveland for the Christmas holidays. He would try to join them there on Christmas Eve if there wasn't a war or too big a scandal. He hovered over his toaster until his English muffins turned a perfect Polynesian tan. This was one morning he did not want to begin with a burned breakfast.

On his way to work, the director made a brief detour by Little Flower Church, where he stopped, as he often did, to attend an early morning mass. He took a seat near the back. Listening to the priest's incantation, he tried to remember when he had last gone to confession. It had been weeks. He promised himself that he would go tomorrow after he had dealt with Mother. He would let God debrief him. When an altar boy rang a bell, O'Hara appeared to pray. But he was not actually doing so. Kneeling beneath a stained-glass window, he was carefully rehearsing a scene in his mind: the man from Little Flower vanquishing the orchid man.

On the continuation of the drive to Langley, the director found himself thinking about the Diem coup. Back then he had been KUBARK's Far East "dirty tricks" chief, but he had been stationed in Washington, so his victim had been halfway around the world. This time, however, he would have to meet the enemy face to face.

The director rode his private elevator up to his suite, sat down behind his desk in the long room, and read through the overnight cable traffic. Later, during his morning staff meeting in the conference room, he lashed out at the deputy director of operations.

Then he retired to his inner office for another long day of putting off. On Monday he had postponed the job to Tuesday, on Tuesday deferred it to Wednesday, and so on down the domino of days. Until Friday. Today. Today he had to act or be overtaken by events. It *had* to be taken care of before the weekend.

Christmas being so near did not help. The director remembered a story he had heard about James "Jungle Jim" Aubrey, who had been brought in to reorganize Metro-Goldwyn-Mayer back in the late sixties. Aubrey planned to fire about half the staff shortly before December 25. One of his aides suggested, "Why don't you wait until after the holidays?" Aubrey said, "What holidays?" The director hated to think of himself as Jungle Jim cruel. It was one thing to wipe out Vietnamese with a Phoenix program. It was quite another not to respect the sentimentality of Christmas. He imagined Mother coming back to haunt him every Christmas in Dickensian fashion.

The director planned to send for Mother before lunch, then after lunch, then . . . On O'Hara's bookshelf stood a small library of books on management, all bought when he moved up to his present job. And they all made one point: the test of a good executive is his ability to fire people. The executive who can "execute" people is an executive who is able to make difficult decisions. And tough decisions are the measure of a good manager. The director had been worried for days that he was failing the test.

He waited until the last possible moment to send for Mother: Friday afternoon at 5 P.M.

In the elevator, Mother was worried. He felt he did not have enough air, which was partially the result of his smoking so fast in a confined area. Mother had not felt so out of control since he had been under fire in that Israeli tank. Then, as now, he knew his fate depended to a frightening extent on the uncontrollable actions of the enemy.

Actually, he had been feeling out of control for twenty-four hours, ever since he had gotten an extremely disturbing telephone call the day before. He had slept poorly.

When the elevator door opened, Mother walked down the hall blowing smoke like a car about to break down. A long ash fell on his black lapel. He brushed at the gray smudge disgustedly.

It was a brief meeting.

"Have you heard what the *Times* is up to?" the director asked. He had his thumb tucked under his chin as if he were feeling his own pulse to make sure he was alive.

"Yes, a *Times* reporter called me yesterday," Mother said, and then sucked deeply at his cigarette.

"What did he ask you?"

"He accused me of all kinds of things, but I denied it all."

"I'm not sure that's good enough."

Matters had not gone exactly as the director had planned. The *New York Times* had somehow gotten hold of some of the information contained in the director's report. He had known that that might happen, since congressmen are not famous for keeping secrets. He had hoped that there would not be any leaks, but he had resolved that if there were any, he would use them.

"What do you mean by that?" Mother asked.

"I mean that I must ask for your resignation."

"But that would be like confirming the story."

"No, we'll keep your resignation secret. I promise you."

"I still have work to do. Important operations are already underway."

"It's for the good of the agency," the director said. "We don't want a prolonged investigation, and this will put an end to it. This is what our former President should have done after the Watergate break-in. We have to learn from the past."

"But . . ."

In this inarticulate moment of agony, as a lifetime of clandestine service was coming to an unhappy end without even a thank-you, all Mother could think of was the unfinished business of AESOP. The loss of AESOP was a small matter compared to the loss of a career, but Mother's mind fastened itself to the lesser disaster, perhaps as a way of protecting himself against a full realization of the greater. Mother knew Philby would be laughing at him the rest of his life.

"There's no telling what a prolonged investigation might uncover," the director was saying. "They might even find out about your penetrations which began at home, the President's home, and we wouldn't want that, would we? Believe me, it's for the good of the agency."

Returning to what had for many years been his office, Mother knew he should begin cleaning out his desk. He should do it now while he was still slightly numb, before the intense pain set in. And he actually did open a couple of drawers, but his hands were soon preoccupied not with packing but with folding sheets of paper.

And his thoughts were preoccupied with revenge. Once again, he began to refine the plot which had been gestating in his mind for months. Watching one of his planes circle, he hit upon the idea of using paper as a weapon. A couple of sheets would probably do. Yes, they would do nicely. They would be the perfect bureaucratic weapon.

Looking out his window, Mother saw nine of his toys scattered about Nathan Hale, as if the Revolutionary hero had been flying paper planes in his war with the pigeons.

Sunday night, Mother could not sleep. The story which had appeared in the *New York Times* that day kept pounding in his head. It had named him as the man responsible for a massive illegal domestic spying operation. Mother, whose successes had all been accomplished in secret, could not bear the thought of his disgrace being acted out in public.

Mother went over and over what he might have said to the reporter to cause the story to come out differently. Should he have cajoled? Should he have threatened? Should he have appealed to the reporter's patriotism? Since Mother had worked all his life hidden from publicity, his dealings with the press had been limited to a very few leaks, which had taught him almost nothing about how to play the media game. Ignorant of how best to deal with the reporter, he had simply thrown up weak denials which were as ineffectual as his aged hands would be against an armed attacker.

Mother had plenty of time that night to think back over his long career. It cheered him some to remember the way he had tracked down KGB masterspy George Blake—it cheered him until he reminded himself that he would never again enjoy such a success. Recalling how he had uncovered other spies also buoyed him up, but then let him down. Then he thought of Kim Philby. He had heard that Philby was despondent in Moscow, that the capital which the spy had served so long had become a drab prison to him now. But Mother wondered which of them, the hunter or the hunted, was unhappier now.

Mother thought a drink might help him sleep. He got up and made himself a brandy and soda. When the sun rose, he was still wide awake—and drunk.

At 7:30 A.M., the television cameras showed up on his front lawn. The wobbly insomniac staggered out to meet them. The TV people gathered around him like coyotes around a dying deer. When the microphones were thrust at him, he was incoherent:

"I've sheen no change in the Shoviets . . . police shtate . . . Shoviet bloc . . . fragmentation . . . I had a son in the infantry in Vietnam . . . went from private to corporal."

A reporter asked if his son had been wounded.

"No, I think he'sh okay," Mother said.

A few days later, the calls from reporters began all over again. And the television people showed up on Mother's lawn again. For the director had broken his promise to keep secret Mother's forced resignation. O'Hara had leaked the story.

Over the next several weeks, Mother sank deeper and deeper into depression. He felt brittle, like a plant that needed water. He tried to read poetry, but his mind kept wandering. For the first time he realized how deeply ran the defeat and hopelessness in all his favorite poems. He kept butting his head against lines like T. S. Eliot's:

> Here I am, an old man in a dry month
> . . . waiting for rain.

For weeks Mother sat, often in his nineteenth-century child's chair, too paralyzed to do anything. He even neglected his flowers. His greenhouses, like his spirits, grew more and more arid. The leaves of his orchids were embroidered with brown. Then a cattleya died, then a lady slipper, then a dozen others. The greenhouses were becoming deathhouses.

Left totally alone for days at a time, Mother began to feel more and more self-destructive—and yet simultaneously the total paralysis passed. He once again started spending time in his two greenhouses. He and his plants began slowly to revive. Water was enough to irrigate his orchids. Hatred irrigated his own vital force.

Over a generation earlier, after progressing from tomatoes to carnations to roses, he had become obsessed by an ambition to grow the perfect flower: an orchid. And now, so many years later, after fathering tens of thousands of orchids, Mother was possessed by another ambition: perfect revenge.

As he moved about his greenhouses, tending his orchids, he also cultivated the plan which grew in his imagination. He pruned and shaped his plot as he made pollen crosses, as he sowed powder-fine seed on agar in an Erlenmeyer flask, as he transplanted tiny plants to a community plot, as he moved larger plants into individual pots, as he examined developing buds. Mother sprayed a row of lady slipper orchids which he had planted the year John Kennedy entered the White House. They would be bearing their first blossoms soon. Whether caring for his orchids or developing a double agent or working out strategies for retribution, Mother was a patient man.

Moving on, he busied himself culling retrograde hybrids. As he pulled the condemned plants, he amused himself by repeating over and over again to himself:

"And this is the director"—yank—"and this is the secretary"—yank—"and this is the director" . . .

Mother's taste in orchids had evolved over the years. In the beginning, his favorites had been the gaudier cattleyas, but he had ended up preferring the lady slippers, which were more understated and harder to grow. The flower's "slipper" was a large, protruding pouch which looked ugly to some, but not to Mother. It was an acquired taste. He wanted his plot to be like the lady slipper—complex elements reduced to simple lines.

Once he was satisfied with every detail of his plan, Mother began to feel better. He was more relaxed and sleep came more easily. Mother was an orderly man who liked to know what was coming. He knew to the week when his orchids would bloom. And now he knew, as certainly as he knew which cattleyas would flower at Easter, that he would have his revenge.

When the bell chimed, Mother put down his book, unfolded his tall, thin body from his miniature antique chair, and slouched toward the front of the house. Opening the door, he stopped frowning. All the wrinkles in his face—and there were more now—turned around.

Mother had called Paul and asked him to come over. In the living room, the old man sat back down in his boy's seat and picked up his book once again. It was a volume of Pound's poetry.

"I like Ezra better than ever now," Mother said. "They thought he was crazy, too."

"Why do you think he frightened people so?" asked Paul.

"Because he hated Communists more than he hated Fascists."

"Yes."

"Do you remember these lines?" Mother said, turning the pages and beginning to read, his voice barely betraying the self-pity:

> *For three years, out of key with his time*
> *He strove to resuscitate the dead art . . .*
> *Wrong from the start—*

Mother paused and looked up.

"That's *Hugh Selwyn Mauberley,* isn't it?" Paul said.

"Right. I've been reading it over and over, and I've come up with a theory about the title. You see, I think Pound was indulging in a French pun. I believe he was saying: *'Ou se loigne Mauberley?'* You understand?"

"I think so. You think Pound was asking, 'Where is Mauberley going?' Right?"

"Yes, of course. Pound knew his country and his age had rejected him, but he didn't know where he could go. Does that make any sense?"

"Certainly. You ought to write a monograph."

"No, no," Mother said. "Tell me, would you mind helping me with some gardening?"

"Let's go."

"I've got more time to spend in my greenhouses now. My flowers are finally getting the attention they deserve."

Mother put on a long black coat and a black homburg against the winter cold. Looking like a crooked stovepipe, he led the way out into the backyard. Mother headed for Dark Side, the cooler and darker of his two hothouses. Shaped like a Quonset hut and covered with green plastic, this greenhouse really was green. Entering it was like stepping into a giant emerald balloon. The light streaming through the plastic gave everything a greenish hue, as if undersea.

Inside, among the orchids, Mother removed his green overcoat but not his green homburg. It perched atop his head like a mossy lump of coal.

"I thought we might do some transplanting," Mother said. "Would you get some pots?"

"Sure," said Paul, who knew the drill. He went to a cache of empty pots and returned with a stack of them.

"No, these slippers aren't ready for sevens. Put them in sixes."

Paul returned the pots and came back with a stack of smaller ones. They potted in silence for a few minutes.

"I'd like you to help me with something else," Mother said.

"Of course."

Mother picked up a green towel and wiped the green dirt off his green hands. Then he reached into his pocket and withdrew a green envelope which he handed to the green young man. Paul started to say something, but Mother put a green finger to green lips.

Paul opened the envelope and took out a green sheet of paper. He read a short, typewritten message which asked if he would be willing to become an accomplice in an unspecified "extralegal operation" which Mother planned. The note stressed that Paul's exposure would be slight, but that if found out he would face criminal prosecution. Paul read the request several times to give himself time to think.

Mother had always issued orders and Paul had always taken them. It had never occurred to him that he could ever refuse the head of KUDESK anything. But now Mother was unemployed. The actual chain of command was broken, but the symmetry of their relationship remained. Paul still felt he could not refuse Mother anything. Not even this. Yet he knew that until he agreed he would enjoy a certain leverage. And Mother had always taught Paul to exploit every advantage, so he indulged his indelible curiosity.

"Before I answer your question," Paul said haltingly, "would you answer a few questions of mine?"

"Perhaps."

"Ever since you left, everybody at Langley's been talking about your feud with O'Hara, but nobody's sure what's really behind it. What is?"

Paul separated several plants and inserted them in number six pots. He was letting the silence work for him. Mother knew he was being Mothered, his own tricks used against him, but he did not mind. He took pride in Paul's technique.

"I've always blamed my father," Mother said, his eyes on a clump of orchids he was prying from a pot. "I also blamed Wild Bill Donovan."

"Why?" Paul asked, remembering too late Mother's rule about letting people tell their own stories in their own way until they ran down.

"Shortly after O'Hara arrived in Rome, my father got a letter from General Donovan asking a favor for old time's sake. Wild Bill wanted my father to look after 'his boy.' Remember, O'Hara'd worked briefly for his law firm after the war. Anyway, Donovan wanted my father to hold O'Hara's hand and help him get started. And, for old time's sake, my father did. He and O'Hara got pretty thick. I thought my dad was a little too generous—even introducing O'Hara to *my* former agents. And I was irritated. I'd made it a point of pride to reject the help my father was always trying to press on me. And there was O'Hara lapping it up. *Aw, hell!*"

Mother had accidentally dropped a pot, which broke when it hit the ground. Paul started to pick up the pieces.

"No. I clean up my own mistakes."

The old man knelt down, almost as if the greenhouse were a church, and began collecting the green pieces of crockery. He worked silently. Paul was afraid the accident had ended the story prematurely.

"Was your father really a lot of help to him?"

"Well, he certainly tried to be," Mother said, rising to his feet. "Take the business about an opening to the left. What did my father do? Wrote me a letter saying O'Hara was right. I'm sure O'Hara put him up to it. O'Hara thought he could manipulate me through my father. Thought I'd do what Daddy said. Of course he couldn't have been more wrong. The worst way in the world to try to get me to do something was to have my father tell me to do it. If O'Hara'd been smart, he'd've had my father write and tell me I was right. That might've changed my mind. But, of course, he wasn't smart."

Mother paused to plan his sentences, almost as if he were preparing to commit his story to paper rather than to the air.

Paul remained dumb and waited.

"Several years after the fight over the opening to the left, I returned to Italy. My father, who was living all alone after the death of my mother, asked me to come to dinner. I accepted. Then he asked if I'd mind if he invited O'Hara, too. He wanted us reconciled. He wanted to be the peacemaker. I hated the idea, but I said it was all right."

The story broke off again. Mother seemed totally absorbed in his orchids. Paul let the silence work.

"There were too many bottles of Verdicchio," Mother resumed. "We were all nervous, so we all drank too much. A lot too much. Glasses were overturned and a few broke. The table was a shambles. I looked down at one point and noticed I'd collected all the silverware and lined up the pieces in neat parallel lines. Make what you will of that."

Silence.

"At any rate, in the glow of the wine, O'Hara and I were becoming friendlier and friendlier. It was as though we were brothers who had quarreled and now we were making up. Really, we were on the verge of weeping on one another's shoulders. And my father was beside himself with pride at having pulled it off."

A long silence.

"In our intoxication, we both seemed to feel a need to purge the past through confession. We were two inebriated Catholic boys trying to do right. I apologized for going over O'Hara's head to Allen Dulles. He apologized for appealing to my father for help."

Another long silence.

"And then suddenly he was telling me in a very frank, honest, friendly way that the whole fight would never have happened if I hadn't hated my father so much. Then he said hate wasn't really it: the problem was that I felt so unworthy of my father that I hated him as a defense. He said that was why I couldn't stand it when he and my father got along so well. It was as though O'Hara were the good son and I were the bad son. He said all this in a very helpful tone, as though once I understood the problem, I'd be able to lick it."

Silence.

"Before I knew what I was doing, I slapped O'Hara across the face as hard as I could."

Mother took two pots and slammed them together as if they were the heads of his two worst enemies. Paul cringed, but Mother just chuckled. This time he did not clean up the mess. He left the pieces of his anger lying all about him.

"My father threw me out of the house. The house I grew up in. I never saw the old man again. He died a couple of years later . . . I think we need more sixes. Would you mind?"

Since Paul did not know what to say, he was happy to have a job to do. He loaded up his arms and returned to Mother.

"I'm not sure we'll need that many. My story's over. Any questions?"

Paul knew Mother would be disappointed in him if he asked an easy question.

"Why'd you get so mad?"

"That is *the* question, isn't it?" Mother said. "I've asked myself many times. Obviously I was angry, in part at least, because O'Hara was right. We *were* locked in some kind of sibling rivalry. But that raises more questions than it answers, doesn't it?"

"What questions?"

"Well, for instance, why were we both acting like schoolboys? I'm not sure I know the answer, but I have my suspicions. I think it goes back to what we've talked about before: people in our business don't grow up. Especially my generation. We were college boys when we joined the OSS, and it seemed like a fraternity. We weren't so much fighting the enemy as hazing him. Playing pranks on him. Like collecting all that pornography to drop on Hitler. Then that collegiate tone carried over from the OSS into the CIA. You must've seen it: Langley's New Haven all over again right down to Nathan Hale."

"I noticed him. So I haven't graduated yet. I'm still stuck in fraternity land."

"Secret society'd be closer, like Skull and Bones."

"There are a lot of Bones men around, aren't there?"

"Oh, Langley's a regular haunted house. It's as though we began as boyish pranksters and we're still boyish pranksters. How else do you explain my trying to win an Italian election with a movie?"

Mother chuckled softly; then Paul did, too.

"Or our operation to make Castro's beard fall out?" Mother continued. "Or our plan to plug all the toilets at the International Communist Youth Festival, to show that communism doesn't work?"

"No kidding?"

"No kidding."

"You once told me," Paul said, "that the best book ever written about the agency is *Huckleberry Finn*. Is that what you meant? That we're all like Tom and Huck?"

"Sure," Mother said, smiling broadly for the first time in weeks. "Especially those last chapters—the ones most English teachers like least and I like best. Remember, they try to rescue Jim from the plantation. Dig a tunnel. Bake a pie with a rope in it. Write all those 'nonamous' letters. And they make poor Jim keep a diary, in code, in his own blood." He stopped smiling as he added, "They went to all that trouble and almost all of it was totally useless. Just like so many of our own operations . . . Sorry, I shouldn't keep saying 'our,' but it's hard to break the habit."

"I liked the end of the book, too. Especially the very end where Huck runs away because he's afraid Aunt Polly's going to make him wear shoes and go to church."

"Well, er, yes," Mother said, but it was obvious that something bothered him. Then he added: "Huck didn't go to church, but that didn't mean he wasn't religious. Because he was. So was Tom. That's another way Twain's boys are like our boys—oh, I'm sorry, another 'our.' Anyway, since intelligence officers never grow up, they never lose their child's faith. I mean faith in the agency."

"I sometimes think of the company as a kind of church."

"Not just *a* church, but *the* Church. Langley's a Vatican on the Potomac. We—I mean *they*—I mean the agency recruits its boys early and then keeps them cloistered. And that's a good way to keep them faithful. Of course, faith can lead to religious wars."

"Like the Cold War."

"Yes," Mother winced. "Or like my feud with O'Hara. That's a religious war, too, a boys' religious war. We each think the other's a heretic. Once he got to be director, it was only a matter of time before I'd be excommunicated."

He paused to crush a bug between his thumbnails.

"Have you lost your faith now? I mean in the company."

"Not really," Mother said. "I haven't changed. I'll never change. That's one of the troubles with my code name. In some ways, Mother's no more grown up than the Fathers of the Church."

"You've been doing a lot of thinking about the agency."

"Yes, but I've known most of this all along. What's

always puzzled me is that understanding something doesn't necessarily change it. I used to believe that motto about the truth making you free, but I don't anymore. Because I know I'm a fossilized undergraduate, but knowing doesn't change me. Not even now that I'm retired. I've still got one last prank to play. Will you help me?"

Paul nodded his consent.

"Are you sure?"

"Yes," Paul said in a very low voice.

Mother handed Paul another green envelope. This time the message was longer, three green pages. Paul read that, for security reasons, he was not to know what the operation concerned, just what his role was to be in it. Reading over his instructions, Paul realized that he would finally be getting a chance to use some of the tradecraft he had learned at the Farm. He was to buy a 7 ½-inch chauffeur's cap, acquire a few locksmith's tools, map a Capitol Hill garage used by senators, and procure a pistol from a company stockpile. But his most important job was to pay another man who would actually mount the operation. Since Mother was not a particularly wealthy man, he planned to use the company's money to underwrite his game. So he needed the help of someone still installed at Langley. Using a code supplied by Mother, Paul would withdraw twenty thousand dollars from a secret KUDESK contingency account, ostensibly to bribe an official in the Polish embassy. The good thing about a bribe was that no receipt was required.

"Oh, no," moaned Mother, "this is terrible."

"What?" Paul asked, still in a daze.

"There's dry rot on this pseudobulb."

Leaving the Dark Side greenhouse with its murky green light was like coming up from underwater.

29

Preparations

PAUL, WHO WAS SUPPOSED to fly to Florida for a clandestine rendezvous, gave the meet-site a lot of thought. He wanted a crowded public place where strangers might naturally be thrown together. Since he had never visited the state, Paul's musing was limited to famous places. He considered Miami Beach, the Everglades National Park, Disney World . . . then he remembered baseball spring training.

Calling from a pay phone into which he fed a dozen quarters, Paul arranged to meet his contact in front of the Mets' St. Petersburg clubhouse on Sunday at 10 A.M. The young spook was delighted with his choice. It appealed to his sense of humor, for a meeting at a ball park would be in the finest KUBARK tradition, as Mother had described that tradition to him. After all, a professional ballplayer and a professional spy had a lot in common. They were both adults playing a boy's game. Besides, Paul had wanted to go down to Florida for spring training ever since he was a boy.

He booked the flight to St. Petersburg under a pseudonym, Roger Bell, and paid for it in cash. When he got off the plane Saturday evening, seventy degrees caressed him. He checked into the Hilton Hotel under a second pseudonym, Walter Miles, and spent the evening in his room watching television because he wanted to stay out of sight.

The next morning, Paul walked over to the ball park. Joining the crowd in front of the clubhouse, he felt a momentary twinge: he wished he had brought his first baseman's mitt. His left hand felt nude.

Then he heard a click, like a gun misfiring. The sound gave him a bad scare, not because he really thought it was a gun, but because he knew it was a camera. Suddenly he was no longer so proud of the meet-site he had chosen. It had not occurred to him that so many of the fans would be snapping pictures of their favorite ballplayers. Not wanting his rendezvous recorded, Paul retreated several yards from the players and the photographic crossfire.

Paul recognized his contact by the red golf cap and pigskin golf gloves the man had promised to wear. The cap sat atop long flowing tresses. Mother's boy, carrying a brown paper bag that was supposed to look like his lunch, walked up to the golfer.

"What was Tom Seaver's earned run average last year?" Paul asked.

"Three point five six," said Gloves.

That was not the right answer, but it was the correct one. Paul and his contact had agreed on that figure during their telephone conversation.

"Let's go watch batting practice."

"Okay," said Gloves.

They walked over behind the chain-link backstop and climbed up in the bleachers. Now all the cameras were pointed at the field, safely away from them. Paul's "lunch" sat between them.

"Have you seen the new roster?" asked Paul, handing over several mimeographed pages.

The top sheet, which bore the Mets' insignia, was crowded with columns of players' names and numbers. The second page also contained columns which looked like a continuation of the roster. But it wasn't.

Rather than players' names, the vertical rows of type were made up of nouns, verbs, and prepositions which formed sentences. Gloves sat reading instructions that told him how to begin but not how to end the operation. The roster said that orders for the final moves to be carried out on the final day would be communicated by telephone. Gloves was told where and when to wait for the call. From time to time he looked up from his reading to see a home run.

"Any questions?"

Paul himself had plenty. What was this all about? What prank was Mother playing? What was the old man's game? He was tormented by unrequited curiosity.

"Just one," Gloves said.

But before he could ask it he was interrupted by a pop foul. The ball arched up over the backstop and dropped toward the conspirators like a grenade. Paul was terrified because suddenly everyone was looking in his direction. Was he found out? He tried to wish the dreaded ball away, but when he found he could not, he reached up and caught it. Then abruptly his whole attitude toward the ball changed: he didn't want to give it up.

"Hey, ball! ball!" shouted a coach.

Paul started to give the man an argument, but all those eyes panicked him. He wound up and threw a blooper to no one in particular.

"Nice catch," said Gloves.

"What's your question?" Paul asked, getting back to business.

"Did you bring the money?"

"Yes," Paul said, nodding at his lunch.

"Good. Let me read this again."

One of the instructions was to memorize all the instructions and to return the Mets' roster to Paul. Gloves labored over the pages like a fan trying to commit to memory every player's name, number, and lifetime batting average.

"Thanks," said Gloves at last, handing back Paul's roster.

"Anytime."

As Mother's boy got up and left the bleachers, he forgot his lunch.

Gloves clutched the brown paper bag.

Paul sadly strolled out of the ball park. He knew it was not good tradecraft to hang around a meet-site longer than necessary. Besides, he needed to get indoors before he acquired a sunburn that would look suspicious back at Langley. Still, he deeply regretted leaving the baseball behind him.

Paul flew back to winter and Mother. Landing at National Airport on Sunday evening, he went home and unpacked. Then he took a taxi over to Mother's house. In the cab, he had time to dwell on how much he missed Frances and her Datsun.

Mother invited Paul in and asked him if he would like a drink. The young man asked for a Scotch on the rocks and followed the older man into the kitchen.

Opening a cabinet door, Mother took out two glasses and set them on the countertop. Then he walked to the refrigerator, which had an automatic icemaker. Mother picked up one cube of ice, carried it across the kitchen, and dropped it into one of the glasses. Then he returned to the refrigerator. He picked up a second ice cube and carried it across the kitchen to the waiting glasses. Then he returned to the icemaker. He picked up a third cube and made his way back across the kitchen floor. Mother reminded Paul of a hard-working ant moving a mountain one grain of sand at a time. When the two glasses were filled with ice cubes, Mother drowned them in Scotch.

They returned to the living room. Mother sat in the antique child's chair. Paul took a seat on the couch facing a recently hung photograph of David Ben-Gurion. The retired KUDESK chief had had time to do a little redecorating. Paul had seen defectors undergo the same sort of transformation: Mother had become a housewife.

"Cheers," said the former boss.

"Cheers," said the former subordinate.

After the first sip, Mother set down the drink and picked up a legal pad.

On it he wrote: *How did it go?*

Paul took the pad and wrote: *Fine.*

Mother wrote: *You gave him the money and the instructions?*

Paul wrote: *Yes.*

Mother wrote: *Well done. You'll be director yet.*

Legal pads cannot be bugged. Mother carried the sheet with the writing on it, as well as the next few pages which might have absorbed the imprint of the words, over to the fireplace. He held the flame of his gold lighter to them.

Then they talked about poetry for half an hour. Mother abused Frost while Paul defended him.

"Like another drink?" Mother asked.

"Okay."

They returned to the kitchen. Mother carried the ice to the glasses one cube at a time. He was a patient ant who could move mountains.

That night, Paul had trouble going to sleep. He was tired but excited. The young intelligence officer was beginning to feel like a spy.

At 3:30 A.M., Paul got up. He thought he might read, but a tour of his paperbacks failed to produce a book he wanted to spend the night with. Then he had another idea. He went to the telephone and dialed zero. He told the operator he would like to place a call to West Germany. A female voice said she would give him an overseas operator.

"Hello, I'd like to call the American embassy in Bonn, West Germany," Paul told the overseas operator. "I'm sorry, I don't have the number."

He stayed on the line while the operator got the number from German information. He was asked if he wished to place the call person-to-person. He thought the matter over carefully and announced he would speak to anyone at the embassy. The phone rang a long time before a male voice with a German accent answered.

"Frances Fisher, please," Paul said.

As a favorite of the director's, she had gotten a foreign assignment years ahead of schedule. Paul listened to her extension ring a dozen times. There was no answer.

Returning to bed, Paul wished he had called person-to-person. Half an hour later he got up again. He went back to the phone, but by now he had lost his faith in station-to-station.

Once more an overseas operator dialed the number of the embassy in Bonn. When a German-accented voice answered, the operator asked for Frances Fisher. Paul listened again to her phone ringing five thousand miles away. Since he was calling person-to-person this time, of course, she answered right away.

"Hello, Frances, you're late."

"Hello, Paul?"

"Yes."

"How'd you know I was late?"

"I've got my spies."

"Very funny."

"I called earlier."

"Oh."

"How are you?"

Paul asked the conventional question, hoping for something other than the conventional answer. He wanted to hear a hint of loneliness in Frances's voice. He was not anxious to be told that she was fine.

"Fine," Frances said. "This is the most fun I've ever had in my life. How're you?"

"Oh, not too bad," Paul said, his voice sounding melancholy, at least to him. "You *really* like it?"

By putting the question less conventionally, he hoped to coax from Frances an admission of homesickness for loved ones left so far behind. He did not want to hear that life in Bonn was wonderful.

"It's *wunderbar*. You should try it. Get out of Washington. Get out into the field."

"I'd love to, but no one's offered me a foreign post. I'm not the head man's favorite, like some I know."

He was careful to say "head man" rather than "director" in case someone might be listening in; he did not want to blow Frances's cover.

"You're jealous," Frances said. "I used to be jealous of you and now you're jealous of me. I love it."

"Isn't Bonn a little small compared to Washington?"

Paul was still determined to elicit some tinge of regret from Frances. He did not want to hear that she liked Bonn better than home.

"I've lived in Washington all my life. To me it's a very small town. Bonn seems bigger because it's full of strangers. Right now I like Bonn better."

"You're right. Washington's not much fun anymore."

It was his way of telling her he missed her.

"See, you should make them send you somewhere," said Frances, not taking the hint.

Paul wanted Frances's sympathy, but he did not want her to keep reminding him that she had gotten ahead of him. He almost told her that he *had* been sent somewhere, that he was working on something important, that he had been down to spring training. But he didn't tell her. He couldn't.

"Maybe someday," Paul said. "By the way, how's your German?"

"Es geht," Frances said proudly.

Finally Paul decided to ask the question bluntly: "How's your social life?"

If she was ever to tell him that she missed him, now would be the time. If she was ever to confess any loneliness, it would be at this moment. If this call were to be something other than a mistake, Frances would have to make it so with her answer to this question. Paul did not want to hear that her social life was good.

"Good—ever since I met Orville Brinkley."

"Orville," Paul said, trying to make his tone derisive. "Does he have a brother named Wilbur?"

"No," Frances said coldly.

"Is he in the air force?"

"Orville's a lawyer. He runs Coudert Brothers' Bonn office."

"A real grown-up."

"That's right," Frances snapped. "He keeps asking me when I'm going to grow up and get a real job."

On operation eve, Paul met his Florida friend in the monkey house of Washington's National Zoo. The contact looked different, for he had cut his long hair in accordance with instructions. While they watched orangoutans flirting, Paul handed the other man a bag of peanuts. The Floridian grasped the bag in black calfskin winter gloves. Mixed in the peanuts was a key to a locker.

"You should drop by Union Station," Paul suggested.

In the locker at the depot, Gloves would find a chauffeur's cap, locksmith's tools, a pistol, and a map of Capitol Hill showing subways, underground passageways, and subterranean parking lots.

The contact tossed a half-dozen peanuts to the orangoutans; then he shelled and ate another half-dozen without removing his gloves.

Paul, who was on his lunch hour, reluctantly returned to Langley. He found the Toy Factory much less fun now that Mother no longer inhabited it. Not only did he miss Mother, but his assignments had suffered. Being Mother's boy was no longer a help but a hindrance.

Back at his desk, Paul put on earphones and turned to his typewriter. He now spent his days transcribing tape recordings of bugged conversations. It was drudgery. The talk on the tapes was always boring. Occasionally a company husband and wife would have a fight, or a company parent would spank a child. But nothing more dramatic ever happened. No national security secrets were ever discussed. No plans were ever laid to overthrow the government. The only secret Paul unraveled was that spies actually live dull domestic lives.

And not only were the tapes dull, but the mechanics of tapes transcription were even duller. Paul had to sit for hours running the reels forward, then backward, then forward, then backward, going over the same words time and time again to be sure he heard them correctly. He was on a transistorized treadmill.

That evening, Mother drove out to the Seven Corners shopping center and parked near a phone booth. He checked his watch. At exactly 10 P.M. he went to the pay telephone and dialed a number which rang another pay phone.

Sitting in the last booth in the phone bank of the Madison Hotel, Gloves reached up and lifted the receiver. Mother gave him his final instructions.

His errand completed, Mother returned to his Arlington home. He read Pound's *Cantos* to make him sleepy and went to bed shortly after midnight. It did not surprise him to discover that he could not sleep.

Lying on his back, Mother thought of his grandfather, who had also been troubled by insomnia. Letting his memory wander back to his early childhood, Mother recalled his granddad regularly getting up in the middle of the night and leaving the house. Once the grandson had followed. His grandfather had gone out to the stable, climbed into the seat of a carriage, and sung until morning. He had never sung the same song twice.

Mother got up, but he did not sing. He began circling the telephone. It was 2:30 A.M. and he wanted to reach out to someone. He sat down in the child's chair beside the phone, then got up again. There was someone with whom he had wanted to talk for years. He had played out the conversation in his imagination many times. In his mind, he had heard the sound of shock and fear in the other man's voice. It had become one of his favorite fantasies, ranking not far below the great revenge tableau which dominated his musings.

Sitting down in the juvenile rocker again, Mother picked up the telephone receiver and asked for an international operator. Then he placed his call.

"I would like to call Moscow," Mother said slowly and distinctly. "The number is two two one, zero seven, six two."

"Person-to-person or station-to-station," asked the operator.

"Person-to-person," he said. "I would like to speak to Mr. Kim Philby, please. That's K-I-M as in mother. New word, P-H-I-L-B-Y."

Mother held on for five minutes while the operator worked at putting the call through. He was surprisingly calm until he heard the phone ringing in Moscow Center, the headquarters of the KGB; then his heart began to beat out a May Day signal.

The KGB operator answered. The American overseas operator asked for Kim Philby.

"He is not here now," the KGB operator said in heavily accented English.

"He isn't in," the American operator repeated the news. "Would you like to leave word?"

"Yes," Mother said breathlessly. "Tell him . . . Let me see, tell him Mother almost got him. I had a plan. And it would've worked. Tell him O'Hara saved him—"

"You can't leave a message like that," the American operator interrupted. "All you can do is leave your name and number."

"Oh, hell!"

Mother slammed down the phone so hard he almost tipped over the little rocker.

30

Vengeance Is Mine

THE TELEPHONE RANG in the Madison Hotel. The assassin answered it. The hotel operator informed him that it was 7 A.M. He thanked her, pulled himself wearily from the bed, and turned on the *CBS Morning News*. Lesley Stahl was doing a stand-up in front of the Capitol. She said that the secretary of state and the director of the Central Intelligence Agency were both scheduled to testify before congressional committees that morning. The secretary was to be questioned by the Senate Foreign Relations Committee, the director by the Senate committee which had been impaneled to investigate the CIA. While Hughes Rudd reported on a further downturning of more economic indicators, the assassin showered. While Roger Mudd was interviewing a Democrat who wanted to be President, there was a knock at the door. The eggs Benedict had arrived. The killer always liked to eat a good breakfast before going to work.

Dressed in a conservative blue suit, his short hair neatly combed, he descended to the hotel garage, where his rented Dodge Dart awaited him. Pulling out onto Sixteenth Street, he did not notice the rented Pinto which moved away from the curb. Heading downtown, the killer turned on WTOP all-news radio. He heard once again that the secretary and the director would be testifying on the Hill. He groaned at the thought of all the TV cameramen, soundmen, still photographers, and reporters who would be staking out the Old Senate Office Building that morning. And he winced at a vision of dozens of Secret Service agents running around wearing hearing aids.

When he reached Seventh and F streets, N.W., he parked his Dart outside the Hecht Company building. Leaving the car unlocked, he hailed a cab. The Pinto pulled into a parking lot and then pulled out again. The taxi dropped the assassin at the Capitol on the Senate side, where he entered, nodding to the policeman at the door, who nodded back. The policeman checked briefcases and packages for weapons, but he did not check people, so the .44-caliber magnum revolver, carried in the hired killer's belt, went unnoticed.

He took the elevator down to the basement, where he boarded the Capitol Hill subway for the short ride to the Old Senate Office Building. Then he made his way to an unmarked door which he knew led to the senators' underground parking garage. Inside the garage, he pulled a blue chauffeur's cap out of his pocket and put it on his head.

He walked over to a black Fleetwood limousine, which belonged to one of the nation's most powerful senators. The assassin happened to know that the senator was out of town. This was not the first time he had seen this car. Several days earlier, armed with a locksmith's tool, he had visited the garage in order to make keys that would unlock and start the senator's limousine. He pulled on a pair of brown leather driving gloves, opened the door, crawled in behind the wheel, turned on the ignition, and drove the black car up out of the garage into the daylight.

The man in the blue chauffeur's cap stopped the

limousine on Delaware Avenue near the main entrance to the Old Senate Office Building. He kept the motor idling. There was a policeman wearing an orange vest directing traffic about twenty-five feet away, but he paid no attention to the throbbing black car. Through some perversion in the laws of protective coloration, a huge black limousine in front of a white government building is invisible.

It was 9:15 A.M. The man in the blue cap watched the white steps and waited. There were television crews camped on the steps and on the sidewalk. They waited and watched, too. It occurred to the killer that he and the TV crews were really in the same business: waiting. The actual time they spent practicing their crafts was infinitesimal compared with the time they spent loitering.

The man in the cap noticed a man in a business suit killing time in the park opposite the Old Senate Office Building. The wire leading from his ear made him look like a robot—he was definitely Secret Service. If a Secret Service agent were lucky, the assassin thought, he would spend his entire career waiting for some dreaded event which would never happen.

The counterfeit chauffeur turned on the car radio and kept punching buttons until he found WTOP. The State Department had just announced that the secretary of state would once again visit the Middle East. He planned to leave in two days, after he completed his testimony before the congressional Committee on Intelligence, which wanted to go a few rounds with him after it finished with the Director of the Central Intelligence Agency.

The killer reached out and turned off the radio. He eased the .44 magnum out of his belt. He touched a button and the glass on the passenger side sank out of sight. He saw his target approaching.

A block away, Paul Fitzsimmons sat at the top of the Capitol steps as if they were marble bleachers. He carried a pair of binoculars which he occasionally raised to his eyes. Cursed with a child's curiosity, Paul had not been able to resist staking out and then following the man who loved gloves. He had to know what Mother's secret operation was.

While Paul waited for something to happen, he passed the time the way he often passed it lately: thinking of Frances. Paul wondered how high she would rise in KUBARK. Perhaps higher than any other woman ever had. It was not altogether impossible to imagine her rising all the way to the top. After all, she was literally an heir to the company. The agency had always been elitist, drawing its leaders from its own aristocracy, the corps of former OSS officers. Now, as these OSS warriors died off, they might well pass the baton to a son or daughter of an OSS Brahmin.

Paul wondered if this second generation would be any different from the first. Or would the sons and daughters be just like the founding fathers and Mother of the agency? The parents had in many ways remained children, but did that mean the parents' offspring would? Was it possible for children to give birth to adults? Paul thought that Frances might be good for the agency, for how could a woman be as boyish as the men, like her father, who had so long set the tone at Langley.

Paul felt an undeniable tingle of jealousy. While Frances was rising, he seemed to be stagnating. Although his alliance with Mother was no longer an advantage, he, too, hoped to advance once the current troubles subsided into the past. Frances had gotten ahead of him, but he was not unhappy. Actually, he had never felt more like a "spy" in his life.

Paul had practiced his Farm tradecraft in this morning's chase and, much to his surprise, it had worked. And at last he had realized what had, in a sense, been a life's ambition: he had crept inside a big secret. Which was where he had always wanted to be.

He had joined the agency because it had seemed romantic to see behind the curtain. Curtains always made him curious. And yet the company was so compartmentalized that he had only been allowed a peep.

He had never been allowed inside the most important secrets. But now he felt the way that he had imagined an intelligence officer should feel. He enjoyed a strange excitement because he was finally inside the clock, knowing which cog was going to turn next, feeling the mainspring unwind, anticipating the alarm bell.

Paul had once been desperately curious to know God's secret. He had hoped to enter His mind. When he failed, he left the seminary. Then he had tried earnestly to get inside poetry. It had seemed to him that the great poets were in on a great secret, but try as he would, he could never see more than a tiny glimpse of what they knew. He had even tried to write poetry as a way of attempting to understand how poets thought, but he was always left on the outside trying to peek in through curtained windows, his curiosity unsatisfied. He had wanted to enter the poet's mind, but he had failed, and eventually he had gone off in search of easier secrets, state secrets.

Paul lifted the binoculars to his eyes once again, but this time he did not lower them. First he saw the gun. Then he saw a face he recognized. He was suddenly terribly frightened.

A man came up the sidewalk and began to ascend the marble steps.

The assassin raised the revolver. He steadied the hand which held the gun on the edge of the open car window. He remembered shooting rabbits the same way when he was a kid. He would drive very slowly along country roads, scanning the brush for cottontails. When he spotted one, he would stop and aim a rifle or a pistol out the car window. Rabbits would run from a man on foot, but they had no reason to fear a man in a car. They would just sit there while he knocked them over. Men, especially men who worked in government, were the same way about limousines. They did not expect assassins to arrive in long black Cadillac Fleetwoods.

The chauffeur sighted down the barrel of the .44 magnum at the back of a long black coat. He squeezed the trigger. When the man pitched forward, his black homburg fell off and started rolling down the white steps.

The television cameramen, who had waited so long for something to photograph, dropped their equipment and ran. The chauffeur fired five more 240-grain slugs into the hunched, twisted back. Then he calmly drove the black car down the avenue toward Union Station. The television crews picked up their cameras and stared through their viewfinders at a tall, crooked black corpse sprawled on the marble steps.

Paul was falling. At the sound of the first shot he had started running as fast as he could, unaware that he was at the top of a long flight of steps. He sprinted halfway down the deadly marble Niagara before he lost his balance. He did not feel his tooth break; he did not feel and hear the bone in his left arm snap. Paul stopped rolling a few steps from the bottom and lay there, a crumpled denim rag.

Then Paul wanted to pass out, but he couldn't. He could not even shut his eyes. He had fallen in such a way that, even where he lay, he could see another body lying on another flight of federal steps. Nothing had ever hurt that much, nothing in his life.

Two strangers helped Paul to his feet, one lifting him by his good arm, the other by the broken one, this good samaritan act filling his entire body with unbearable pain. When his head cleared slightly, Paul limped off in search of a taxi, glancing back over his shoulder from time to time at the body. Furious, frightened, unbelievably sad, and in agony, Paul was spitting blood and crying. He had not been on the inside of the clock, after all. Once again his hopes had been betrayed. Once more he could feel himself losing his faith. He already knew he would soon be leaving another seminary.

At about the time that the chauffeur parked the senator's limousine in front of Hecht's, an ambulance pulled up in front of the Old Senate Office Building. While they loaded the body onto a stretcher, the killer, leaving his hat and gun on the front seat of the

Fleetwood, got out and walked into the department store. While the ambulance was speeding toward George Washington University Hospital, the killer left Hecht's, dropped his gloves in a trash bin, got into the rented Dart, and drove away.

At the hospital, where the bullet-riddled man was pronounced dead on arrival, the police went through his clothing and found in the breast pocket of his suit coat a folded two-page typed transcript of a recorded telephone conversation. The typescript contained the following exchange:

THE SECRETARY OF STATE: Kimball wants revenge. He's been in touch with that Senate committee that's investigating your agency. He told them he could destroy you.
THE CIA DIRECTOR: He's got to be stopped.
THE SECRETARY: Will you take care of it?
THE DIRECTOR: I will.

The conversation had never taken place. Mother had faked the transcript, but that would be hard to prove. The media played up the possibility of a conspiracy. In a sense, the story had been leaked by a dead man.

The senator whose limousine had been stolen could be counted on to pursue the targets of that leak vigorously. The appropriation of his car would not only make him mad, but it would also make him anxious to shift suspicion to others before it settled on him or his office. He would trail the putative killers into the highest reaches of government.

Mother, who had plotted so many murders which looked like suicides, had at last plotted a suicide which looked like a murder.

At the requiem mass, in accordance with a provision in Mother's will, the only flowers allowed were white orchids.

ABOUT THE AUTHOR

Born in Spur, Texas, AARON LATHAM graduated from Amherst College, and received a Ph.D. from Princeton University. Successively a reporter for the *Washington Post*, an editor of *Esquire*, and a senior editor of *New York* magazine, his perceptive writing about the manipulation of power in Washington, D.C. and more far-flung places has been published in many journals in the U.S. and abroad, including the *New York Times Sunday Magazine*, *Harper's*, *The Village Voice*, *Paris Match*, *Le Nouvel Observateur*, *France Soir*, the *Glasgow Herald*, and the *South China Morning Post* (Hong Kong). He is the author of *Crazy Sundays: F. Scott Fitzgerald in Hollywood*.

First FIREFOX!
Then FIREFOX DOWN!
Now
LION'S RUN!
by Craig Thomas

Craig Thomas, bestselling author of FIREFOX, and most recently FIREFOX DOWN!, has a riveting new story to tell. This time it's espionage at the highest levels of British Intelligence: a KGB mole has been brought to light. Headlines proclaim as traitor a man whose integrity is beyond question—the Director-General of British Intelligence, Sir Kenneth Aubrey himself!

In LION'S RUN Craig Thomas has created a masterpiece of suspense, a thrilling novel of intrigue, friendship, and betrayal!

Look for LION'S RUN, as well as other Craig Thomas titles wherever Bantam Books are sold.

LION'S RUN

a Bantam Hardcover
On-sale December 1985.